LANDFALL

LANDFALL

A NOVEL

Tony Gibbs

WILLIAM MORROW AND COMPANY, INC.
New York

It is the policy of William Morrow and Company, Inc., and its imprints and affiliates, recognizing the importance of preserving what has been written, to print the books we publish on acid-free paper, and we exert our best efforts to that end.

Library of Congress Cataloging-in-Publication Data

Gibbs, Tony.
    Landfall : a novel / Tony Gibbs.
      p. cm.
    ISBN 0-688-11102-5 :
    I. Title.
PS3557.I155L36 1992
813'.54—dc20
                                       92-28132
                                           CIP

Printed in the United States of America

First Edition

1 2 3 4 5 6 7 8 9 10
BOOK DESIGN BY PAUL CHEVANNES

For the usual suspects, with love

Alert readers will quickly remark that the island of St. Philip is located in more or less the same place as the British dependent territory of Montserrat. The two places are, however, entirely different, and the one does not in any way stand for the other.

PROLOGUE: CHAPEL OF ABRAHAM AND THE SACRED BLOOD, SUNDAY MORNING

The congregation drew a deep, collective breath, and those who knew the words launched a capella into the hymn's final verse:

Thro' many sorrows, toils, and snares
I have already come . . .

The rest, not to be left out, simply opened their throats and roared out the tune.

To the Reverend Dr. Harkness, who was not musical, the result was a generalized barnyard clamor streaked with high-pitched squeals. But it was certainly heartfelt, and at moments like this he could sense an almost physical bond with the gleaming faces ranked before him. They were simple folk, like his mother's people so far away. He would be sorry to leave them.

Sorry, at any rate, to leave most of them. In the congregation's front row, the massive figure of Mrs. Darley shifted impatiently from foot to foot. Her broad, damp brow wrinkled with the pleasurable effort of numbering the sins of her neighbors. She would remember every peccadillo, though. She always did.

'Tis grace has brought me safe thus far . . .

In Mrs. Darley's case, Harkness reflected, grace had nothing to do with it. For a moment he almost regretted having included public

7

testimony as a regular part of the weekly service—but no, he corrected himself: As a way of making the natives put themselves under his control, it was inspired, the cleverest move he had made in his six months on the island.

and grace will bring me home.

Mrs. Darley's lips were moving, but not with the words of the hymn. Harkness wondered who—besides her hapless spouse—would be the victims today.

At the back of the chapel a lean dark-suited figure materialized in the doorway. Even without his glasses Harkness recognized the tense, almost quivering figure of his acolyte Monasir, the man the Philipians had nicknamed Mista Mongoose, as much because of his chittering, dancing rages as for his narrow, pointed face and fierce red-rimmed eyes. Illiterate the islanders might be, and often credulous, but they could be keenly perceptive, too, as if in compensation.

The singing trailed off, and Mrs. Darley's beefy arm was waving frantically for attention. Harkness ignored her. With a gesture more regal than ecclesiastical he summoned Monasir forward. Heads turned as the wiry man stepped quickly down the aisle, but no one, Harkness noted, cared to stare directly at him.

"Yes, my son?" To the natives Harkness always employed the plums-in-syrup voice he remembered from his long-ago tutor at All Souls. And he always spoke in English, even to his own men, and insisted on their using the same language. It brought the acolyte up short, as Harkness had intended. He could see the mental struggle in the younger man's face, as he ransacked the language he had not quite mastered for an innocuous phrase that would still carry his meaning.

"They have come," he offered at last, and hesitated.

It took Harkness a long moment to comprehend. "The two?" he asked finally. "The man and the woman?"

Monasir looked puzzled, then shook his head. "No, no, the others. The four we were warned of."

So. The threat *had* materialized, after all; the enemy was in the field. Harkness felt the sharp, exhilarating thrill of engagement, but he knew his round, sweat-streaked face reflected nothing but near-sighted benevolence. The congregation was listening as with a single ear, and the blank faces told him the dialogue was going safely over their heads. "Where have the four come?" Harkness asked, and, before

Monasir could blurt a too-revealing answer, prompted, "To the place foretold?"

The acolyte's brows knitted as he wrestled with the unfamiliar word. "I think so, yes." He paused again. "Where they were supposed to come," he added.

"Excellent." So his mission, almost derailed, was again in hand—or soon would be.

Monasir swallowed, wet his lips. "Our friends want to know—" he began.

Harkness cut him off. "They have been instructed. The four are to be welcomed, exactly as it was planned."

A muscle jumped in the young man's cheek, but he nodded.

"And when the two appear," Harkness continued, "the woman is not to be"—he caught himself at the last instant—"not to be troubled." He waited until understanding erased uncertainty on Monasir's narrow face. "Go and tell our friends," said Harkness. "Now."

As Monasir hastened back up the aisle, Harkness lifted his gaze, surveyed the small building as if to fix every detail in memory. The place had a simple dignity he always found restful: wood-beamed ceiling supported by plain white plaster walls, with here and there a carved and gilded plaque memorializing a dead benefactor; tall, unglazed windows, their frames picked out in light blue (and yellow, where the blue paint had run out); outside, rustling greenery that was almost iridescent in the Caribbean sun.

Yes, Harkness thought, he had been at peace on this island, or as close to peace as his need for vengeance would allow. In many ways this was the home he had never had. An Eden of sorts—with himself, the fatherly Dr. Harkness, its own particular serpent. His eyes lit on Mrs. Darley, whose face now reflected a fearful surmise, as if she somehow guessed the truth—though of course, it was impossible: that the Reverend Dr. Harkness had just condemned five people to execution.

And those executions were only a prelude. A curtain raiser. Once the five were disposed of, the way would be clear for a far, far greater . . . Harkness pulled his roiling thoughts back from the brink before his expression could betray him.

But he could not help thinking that if Mrs. Darley—if any of them—knew what he intended, their horror would be uncontrollable. Horror was exactly his aim. Horror, magnified by the knowledge of helplessness. And for his audience not just the humble peasants of this island backwater but the whole arrogant Western world.

SUNDAY

Patrick: Philipsburg, Saint Martin, Netherlands Antilles, early afternoon

A shower had pattered down Voorstraat minutes before, but already the noonday Caribbean sun was fiercely bright again, and except for its streaming gutters the narrow street was nearly dry. Two big cruise ships had anchored off Groot Baai earlier in the morning, and their passengers, ferried ashore by launch, were surging in and out of the duty-free arcades, rhapsodizing over Korean cameras with Japanese labels, mystery liqueurs based on cheap rum and chemical flavorings, and swatches of mildew-spotted lace that smelled of fish glue.

Patrick O'Mara, who had learned about duty-free the hard way, ignored the shops and their bannered promises of fairy gold as he picked his way easily through the chattering crowd. His thoughts were on the two damp paper sacks he was clutching to his chest—or, more precisely, on the likelihood of cockroach eggs in the bags' glued seams.

That was what the tropics were really all about, he thought: bugs. Every island was alive with the damn things, and if you lived on a boat, the battle to keep them ashore never stopped. It was one of the first things Patrick had learned in his still-new life as cook and mate aboard the charter yacht *Glory*, and the lesson had stung.

Last winter, over in Antigua, he'd innocently brought aboard a cardboard carton full of fruit. Fruit and, it soon developed, something more lively. At first there were only hints, glimpsed from the corner of his eye: a brown shape darting behind the row of spice containers in the gallery; a plantain with an oval brown spot that was gone the next time he looked. Muttering under his breath, Patrick scrubbed and swatted and sprayed and nearly convinced himself he'd wiped out the little bastards. And then one night Gillian Verdean, *Glory*'s owner and Patrick's boss, crept into the galley for a midnight snack.

She snapped on the overhead light, and the verbal explosion nearly blew the skylights off the deckhouse. Not that Gillian was afraid of roaches or of anything else that crawled, hopped, or walked. But vermin aboard *Glory* was something she took as a very personal insult. Luckily there was a three-day gap before the next charter began. Just enough time for Patrick to haul every rag and stick and pot up on deck and scrub them and then bug-bomb the whole interior, cabin by cabin, while enduring an acid running commentary from Gillian and occasional half-suppressed chuckles from *Glory*'s skipper, Jeremy Barr, to whom bugs were a fact of tropical life, certainly nothing to get excited about.

Inside a few weeks Patrick's Roach Blitzkrieg was stitched into the patchwork of anecdote the crew of *Glory* swapped with other charter skippers and cooks, outside the hearing of their customers, in noisy saloons from the BVI—the British Virgin Islands—down to the Grenadines. Patrick didn't even mind being the butt of the story; it certified him as one of the Caribbean charter fleet's regulars. He was surprised how important that was to him, being part of something again. And by being aboard *Glory*, the mahogany swan among Tupperware ducklings, Patrick automatically picked up the status of respected insider. It was a feeling that reminded him a little of his Army days, when he'd come back from El Salvador and found himself the only three-striper his age on the base who'd actually been shot at.

So why was his life suddenly going sour around the edges? Nothing had changed. He had a job that challenged him, but not too much; a revolving collection of admiring women, none bad-looking and a few knockouts; the friendship of two people he deeply admired; and day after golden day of lazy cruising, among the most beautiful islands in the world. But something was missing, and it was gnawing at his soul.

On the sidewalk just ahead of him a pair of shabby men walking side by side glanced at each other, then separated to flank an elderly tourist they were overtaking. The glance, quick and covert, caught Patrick's attention, and a half second later he realized he was watching a bump-and-grab pickpocket team moving in on a victim.

He had opened his mouth to shout a warning when a hail from across the street—"Hey, over there! *Glory!*"—froze the thieves in mid-grab and Patrick in mid-stride.

It was the genuine, effortless bark of command, a tone familiar to Patrick from a dozen parade grounds in as many Army posts, over six long years of service. Without thinking, he caught his balance with a quick half step and spun toward the voice.

The far sidewalk was mobbed, but to Patrick's informed eye one man stood out. He was balancing on the balls of his feet in an un-mistakable parade-ground stance—chest out/shoulders back/belly in—accentuated by the Hawaiian shirt in primary colors stretched taut across the barrel torso and worn outside his trousers (suntans with a knife-edge crease). The effect was to make his legs look shorter than they were, and though he seemed at first glance almost as broad as he was tall, he was no more than an inch or so under middle height. His square face, slashed by a wide grin, was tanned dark, but newly sun-burned scalp showed bright pink through the close-cropped, thinning black hair. His forearms were as thick as Popeye's, with faded tattoos just discernible in the coarse, curly underbrush.

"You want me, sir?" Patrick shouted, the "sir" an automatic acknowledgment of what his instinct had recognized. Put in words, the instantaneous appraisal might have run: *Stands like a Marine, but the pants are Army issue . . . twenty-year man, with that haircut . . . Officer, but the tattoos say up through the ranks, not West Point . . . a field soldier, for sure—Airborne, maybe Green Beret.*

"Affirmative," the man called back. "If that shirt you're wearing means what it says."

Shirt? Oh, right: One of Gillian's many would-be money-makers—crew T-shirts with a silk-screen silhouette of *Glory* under full sail across the back, the yacht's name in block letters under the picture. Twenty-five bucks a pop to the customers unless they were favorite clients. Barr hated them, of course, but he wore one; Barr had mel-lowed a lot in the months since he and Gillian had finally got together.

"*Glory*, right," Patrick called back. "That's me." His words were drowned by a volley of car horns, from traffic blocked behind a stalled van.

The man across the street shrugged incomprehension and shook his head, then took a step off the curb to cross. The slender dark-haired woman at his side reached out and grasped his arm. As he turned to her, the stalled van roared into life.

It was, to Patrick, like watching a movie in slow motion. From where he stood on the far curb he had both the stocky stranger and the van—a plain white Toyota, no lettering on its side—in full view. It leaped forward, dodged around a cab at the curb, and suddenly veered toward the stocky man, who was saying something emphatic to the woman holding his arm.

Patrick's yell was drowned as the van shifted into second, but the hollow, metallic thud of fender against flesh was louder still, followed a millisecond later by the pop and tinkle of a breaking headlight. The van rocked, steadied, and picked up speed, but Patrick's eyes saw only its victim, sprawled on the sidewalk with his companion half lying on her side next to him. Three long strides, and Patrick was across the street, still clutching the two bags.

The stocky man was on his back, a broad streak of dirt and grease slantwise across his aloha shirt. Setting down his groceries, Patrick dropped to one knee by his side, feeling the stab of broken glass through his khakis. Tiny, glittering fragments sprinkled the sidewalk and the man, whose face was nicked in a dozen places. But there was no pulsing gush of blood, no spreading scarlet pool under the motionless body.

The woman beside him was sitting up now. She was gasping for breath, and her eyes, wide with alarm, were fixed on her companion.

"You okay?" Patrick asked her. She tried to answer, settled for a nod. Even with her mouth gaping she was beautiful. Face like a queen of Egypt, Patrick thought—proud, high-nosed, full-lipped, and milk chocolate skin with the faintest reddish tinge to it, glowing as if it were lit from inside.

The man on the ground stirred, opened his eyes cautiously, as if testing the light. "Well, shit," he whispered.

"How's your side feel?" said Patrick.

"How d'you think it feels?"

Patrick considered the ruined shirt, the quick, shallow breathing. "Broken rib?"

The man pursed his lips, drew in a slow, deep breath, and let it out. "Maybe. I don't think so."

"Oh, *Jake*." The woman seemed to have gotten her breath back. She glared around and upward at the silent crowd that surrounded them, watching with interest. "What are you waiting for?" she snapped. "Some of you call an ambulance!"

"Calm down, Isabel," her companion said. Patrick had the sudden feeling that he said it a lot. "Just a couple more dings in the old chassis. I'll be all right in a minute."

She turned to Patrick, as if to a referee. "It's the same if that truck cut him in two pieces: 'I'll be all right in a minute.' Huh." Her dramatic shrug encompassed all the stupidity of mankind.

Spanish, Patrick thought. *That's her first language.* To the man called Jake he said, "I'll get a doctor. And the cops."

"No!" The command snapped like a whip, and the man looked startled by his own vehemence. "Doctor's not required," he said, grinning up at Patrick. "And there's no point getting the local gendarmes into the act."

Well, that was fair enough, Patrick thought. The St. Martin cops would screw around for the rest of the afternoon, but they'd never catch the guy in the van; they never caught anybody. "Whatever you say," he agreed. A thought struck him. "Say, how come—"

"How come I yelled at you?" The man extended his powerful arm, and Patrick took his hand—as big as Patrick's own and as calloused, though in different places. "I'm your customer," the man continued. Patrick braced himself, gave a heave that pulled the man to his feet. "Jesus, that smarts . . . Your customer, passenger, whatever you call it: Jake Adler. And this cute little lady"—he was looking past Patrick—"must be *Glory*'s famous female captain."

Gillian

She saw the knot of spectators from half a block down the street. A minute before, some jackass driving a white van with a crushed headlight had almost flattened her toes as he squealed around the corner, and the manila folder with *Glory*'s registration document and port clearance had been knocked right out of her hand. Luckily the clearance paper landed on dry pavement, and the now-sodden document she fished from the gutter was only one of half a dozen photocopies *Glory* carried. Still, it was another annoying moment in an already irritating day. Instead of crossing the street to avoid the little crowd, Gillian deliberately pushed her way through.

A pair of unmistakable broad shoulders in a too-familiar T-shirt loomed ahead. (Barr had been right. The damn thing did look tacky. So why hadn't he insisted? Love, of course. She felt a tiny, warm detonation just under her rib cage. *He loves me*, she thought, and felt it again.)

A small boy clutching a very large paper sack backed into her, bared his teeth in what could have been a snarl or a grin, and scuttled away.

Gillian was reaching up to tap Patrick's shoulder when she realized the blood-spattered man beyond him was addressing her.

"I beg your pardon?" she said.

"I said, 'You must be *Glory*'s famous lady captain.' Am I right?"

Technically incorrect, she thought, *but I sure do like the sound.* His grin was infectious, and she returned it with interest, her hand going out to meet his. "Owner, actually. Gillian Verdean. And you're . . ."

"Jake Adler. I've chartered your boat, remember? Oh, this"—he lurched painfully to one side—"is my friend Isabel Machado."

"How do you do," Gillian replied automatically, taking in the haughty face that clashed with the peasant outfit—off-the-shoulder blouse and a ruffled skirt that emphasized her tiny waist and was a little too tight across the hips. *Not his wife*, her mind was saying. *Not anybody's wife. And so what?* But what had happened to Jake Adler's face? And his clothes? She constructed a smile. "Did you have an accident, Jake? You look a little—"

"I look like a hundred and ninety pounds of hamburger." Adler seemed delighted by the idea. "Isabel and I were just walking around town, and I recognized Patrick, here—his shirt, that is—from across the street."

"And then this asshole in a van ran Mr. Adler down," Patrick put in. "Damn near killed him."

"Really?" Gillian said. That accounted for Adler's appearance. And for the muscle that kept twitching in Isabel's cheek. But there was something funny about Patrick, the way he was standing—hands at his sides, thumbs along the seams of his perfectly pressed khakis. Not quite at attention, but the next thing to it. Now, that was interesting. After a year of chartering, Gillian had come to realize that you could learn more about your charterers in the first five minutes than in the subsequent week. She also recognized (since she had few illusions about herself) that when it came to people, her careful observations were no match for Patrick's instincts. It was like perfect pitch: You either had it or you didn't, and when it came to people, Patrick O'Mara was a human tuning fork.

Now Isabel (what was her name? Machado) was saying something about Jake Adler's injuries, that maybe he didn't need a doctor, but she wanted to check him over. Her tone was proprietary but not exactly romantic, more like a nurse than a lover . . . Gillian found herself glancing at Patrick, saw the flicker of alertness in his blue eyes.

"Isabel's had nurse training," Jake explained, beaming down at her.

"But I'm okay. Honest." He shifted his weight cautiously. "Well, maybe not perfect," he added.

"Isabel's right," said Patrick. "You at least ought to get off your feet."

"Tell you what,' Jake replied. "We'll split the difference. Let's go back to my hotel and we'll all sit down. And have a drink on me."

"You can see *Glory* from here," Gillian said, pointing across the harbor. "The green ketch, this side of the fake schooner."

"Fake schooner?" said Jake, leaning forward out of the shade and squinting in the laserlike sunlight.

Patrick, who had been fumbling through the sack of groceries between his feet, looked up, "The big white thing with the four tiny masts," he put in. "She's a cruise ship. The sails are just for show." Even after three Heinekens, *Glory*'s cook was still smoldering visibly. Half a sweaty—and expensive—morning's shopping stolen from under his nose, in front of a dozen witnesses, none of whom had seen a thing or said a word.

"To her left," Gillian said, "about a quarter mile farther into the harbor, that's *Glory*."

"I see," said Adler slowly.

But Gillian wondered if he really did. Groot Baai was packed with yachts of all sizes, and *Glory*'s low dark green hull was partly masked by a faded top-heavy–looking sloop—an ex-bareboat, from her battered appearance.

Jake himself was looking considerably less battered, now that he'd changed into a fresh shirt and Isabel had sponged the blood spatters from his nicked face and forearms. The four of them were sitting around a table on the outdoor dining porch of a small, old-fashioned hotel right on Philipsburg's narrow beach. Gillian had been mildly surprised at Jake's choice: The Pasanggrahan was the kind of understated place favored by sophisticated travelers. The flowered shirt would have looked more at home in one of the big air-conditioned tourist traps outside town.

"I don't know where the others are," Isabel was saying to Patrick. "They were supposed to be here sooner than us." She sounded puzzled and upset, and Jake patted her hand. The gesture was presumably intended to soothe, but it seemed patronizing to Gillian—and maybe to Isabel, who pulled her long, slender hand from under his big, bearlike paw.

"It'll be okay, hon," Jake said. "You know ol' Mookie. He'll be late for his own funeral, but he'll get there before they fill up the hole."

"Mookie?" said Patrick, looking surprised.

"Not the ballplayer," Jake said quickly. "An old buddy of ours, flying down from Atlanta."

"I used to know a guy named—" Patrick began, but Jake cut him off.

"Say, I've got an idea. How about Isabel and I move onto *Glory* this afternoon instead of tomorrow morning? Would that be a problem?"

"No sweat," said Patrick before he caught Gillian's stony glare. "That is, the boat's not quite—"

"Noon tomorrow is when we'd planned to welcome your party on board," she said, forcing a smile.

"Understood. That's when the charter begins," Jake replied, "but I'm—"

"I don't want to be rigid about contracts and stuff," Gillian interrupted. "We just don't like our guests to see *Glory* without her makeup on."

"I was going to say I didn't mind paying for an extra day," Jake said. Was that the ghost of a grin?

"Well, in that case I guess we don't mind taking your money," Gillian said, not missing a beat. "Just so you realize—"

"And I've never been much on white-glove inspections." Definitely a grin.

"We're at your service." *Come on, Gillian*, she told herself, *make a little nice for the customer*. "Look, if you check out of the hotel right now, you can probably talk your way out of paying for tonight. I'll get the drink tab."

"Oh, we already checked out," said Isabel, who had been following their exchanges like a spectator watching volleys at a tennis match.

Jake shrugged, an expression of exaggerated innocence lighting his pleasantly ugly face. To her own surprise, Gillian laughed aloud. "Then we might as well get going." She flagged the waitress.

"Cinnamon," snarled Patrick, who had resumed his inspection of the paper sack.

"Say again?" said Jake.

"The little bastard in the street stole the bag with my cinnamon," Patrick explained. "Can't cook without cinnamon."

"We'll make a stop at Sang's on the way to the dinghy dock," Gillian said as the waitress approached, waving a slip of paper. "Here, give me the check."

"This is a note for Mr. Adler," said the waitress. "Somebody left it at the desk while you were out."

"A note?" Jake echoed. He ripped open the small, smudged envelope and unfolded the single sheet inside. Gillian, who had been taught it was rude to watch people read their mail, looked discreetly out to the harbor. "Now that's damn strange," Jake said, to no one in particular.

Surprise in his voice and, she thought, a trace of concern. For some reason his words seemed to light a spark of apprehension in Isabel Machado's eyes.

Barr: Groot Baai

Sitting cross-legged on *Glory*'s foredeck, Jeremy Barr regarded the jib sheet's end with disfavor. The goddamned thing looked more like an amputated stump than a proper back splice, he decided—which was what happened when you used braided line for the sheets just because the customers said it was easier on their soft landlubbers' hands. Grasping the wire lifeline (plastic-covered, another concession to *Glory*'s charterers), he pulled himself upright, laid the splice on the teak deck, and rolled it back and forth under his bare foot, waiting for his irritation to subside.

He was, he knew, being childish and silly. Gillian had it right. *Glory* was in business to please her customers, not her crew, especially not that member of her crew who (in Gillian's words) thought that if you closed your eyes and wished real hard, it would be 1950 again.

Her eyes really did flash when she got mad, Barr recalled; with her wide cheekbones and pointed chin, she reminded him of a furious kitten. And then her anger would be gone, and her quick grin would light up the cabin. What was it Patrick said she looked like when she grinned? A smart-ass Peter Pan, that was it.

There were times Patrick could surprise you, especially if you let yourself think that six feet of solid muscle with a movie star's face on the top precluded a brain inside the head. And these days, Barr reflected, something uncomfortable was stirring inside that brain, though Patrick might not be aware of it himself.

Barr picked up the spliced end of the jib sheet. Well, maybe it wasn't all that terrible-looking once the lumps in the splice were rolled out. He began to coil the half-inch line with automatic skill, his big, scarred hands forming each loop exactly the same size as the one before, while his fingertips imparted just enough twist to keep the line from kinking. All the while his eyes scanned the crowded waters of the harbor.

The place was even more crowded than last year, just like the rest of the Caribbean. Only the start of October—still hurricane season— and already the anchorages were filling up. By January Groot Baai would be as big a mess as Newport before the Bermuda Race. Farther south was no better. In Antigua, English Harbour was a floating traffic jam, and in Bequia's Admiralty Bay the bareboat skippers would be yelling at cross-purposes in four different languages.

And the cruise ships were making it worse. Right now there were four riding to anchor at the bay's entrance, their shore boats buzzing back and forth to the ferry dock. Two were big pastel wedding cakes out of Port Everglades, and the third was a real old-timer—Liberian flag at her stern, with white paint slapped over the rust stains on her high sides, and a five-degree starboard list. Probably Italian officers and an Indonesian crew, with Greek owners screwing a few more years' service out of her.

But at least she was recognizably a ship, unlike the monstrosity beside her that Barr had nicknamed the White Abortion—lower hull like a car ferry, below three superfluous decks and the superstructure off a cargo liner, the whole topped by four reedlike masts that were supposed to make her into a sailing vessel.

"Grotesque," called a high, clear voice, exactly echoing Barr's own thought.

The runabout, which had come silently up from astern, lay right alongside, rolling gently in the oily swell. "Hello, Deedee," said Barr.

"Or maybe 'hideous,' " said the woman at the helm. "You're looking well, Jeremy."

Barr wanted to return the compliment, but the words stuck in his throat. He had known Deedee Etheridge forever, from the time she was a skinny teenager crewing Lightnings in Long Island Sound and he was a skinny teenager driving the yacht club launch. The years of tropic sun and salt water that had bleached Barr's hair to straw and tanned his skin to leather had done much the same thing to Deedee, and while his thin, angular face was essentially unchanged by time, her naturally round features seemed to have thickened and blurred. The muscles that competitive sailing had given her were softening, and the skin over them was beginning to slip. She was still a handsome woman, Barr thought, but now it was force of character more than physical appearance that drew one's attention.

Considering the size and nature of the sailing world, it wasn't surprising that their paths had crossed and recrossed over two decades and several oceans. When both of them were in their twenties, Deedee's pursuit of an Olympic sailing medal took her into some of the same distant harbors to which Barr was delivering yachts. Later the charter-broking firm owned by Deedee's father had represented Barr's own *Windhover*. Besides the normal run of customers, Etheridge & Co. had come up with a few who were looking for a captain willing to run unadvertised nautical errands, often of a technically illegal nature. Barr's attitude toward authority—alternating between contempt and indifference—suited his employers, as did his lack of curiosity about them. (He assumed, without really caring, that they were either intelligence bureaucrats or smugglers.) Working *Windhover* into reef-studded coves on moonless nights amused him and was just the talent his anonymous paymasters seemed to value. The arrangement had gone on for several years, until Barr's marriage; he hadn't run into Deedee since shortly after *Windhover*'s loss on Anegada Reef—the wreck in which his wife had died.

"You could ask me aboard," she said. Her voice was still light, but he could see she had noted his silence.

"Sure. Of course. Just let me put over a couple of fenders." He pulled two fat cylinders from a deck locker and clove-hitched their lanyards to the rail. Balancing easily, Deedee tossed him the bow line. By the time he made the runabout fast, she'd hoisted herself up over the lifelines. She was wearing white slacks and an open-necked navy blouse and a sun visor with "ETHERIDGE CHARTERS" in blue lettering; her figure was holding up, he saw, though the freckled skin at her cleavage was showing wrinkles that hadn't been there the last time he'd seen her—it must be three years ago now.

"Welcome aboard," she said. "Or is that your line?"

"Consider it said," he replied. "How about a drink?"

"These days it goes right to my hips." She paused. "But what the hell."

He led the way down *Glory*'s nearly vertical companion ladder, not bothering to offer her a hand (which would have been insulting). At the foot of the ladder she paused for a quick, appraising look around—through the open door aft into the largest of the three guest cabins, to starboard at the waist-high chart table with its shelves full of Sailing Directions and Light Lists, and forward into the big main cabin, the center of the yacht's accommodation.

"I was aboard during the charter boat show," she said. "You've got a fabulous vessel, Jeremy. As elegant as *Endeavour* or *Shamrock* and miles ahead of anything else."

"Gillian's got a fabulous vessel," he corrected her. "I just work here." He followed her into the main cabin, a low, square chamber twenty feet on a side, gleaming with varnished mahogany. The big skylight overhead was open to catch the breeze, but an awning over it cut the sunlight to a bearable level.

Deedee subsided on one upholstered settee. "Gillian's the owner, you're the skipper, and that muscle-bound young stud's the cook and deckhand—is that how it works? It's not quite clear from your brochure."

"We keep the job titles a little blurred," Barr said. Deedee was clearly waiting for him to explain, but he had no intention of doing so. While Patrick O'Mara was indeed *Glory*'s cook—and one of the best in the charter fleet—he was also the yacht's professional captain of record, by virtue of the Coast Guard certificate he possessed. His slightly rough-edged sexiness melted the mostly middle-aged female customers, while their spouses were being charmed by Gillian's elfin looks and brisk competence (she handled *Glory*'s bookings, her finances, and any dealings with the shore). Barr, who stayed out of the way as much as possible, actually sailed *Glory* and dealt with the navigation when there was any. He had let his own hundred-ton master's license lapse after the wreck of *Windhover* and had not applied to reinstate it, despite Gillian's urgings; his reasons were unclear even to him.

"Well," said Deedee, after a long moment, "you must have rum in here someplace."

"How about a dark and stormy, for auld lang syne?"

"That'll do fine, but easy on the stormy, please."

Barr stepped through the narrow passage into the yacht's galley. After pulling two ceramic mugs from the padded rack over the sinks, he filled them with cubes from the icemaker, Patrick's newest toy. "So what brings you here?" he called over his shoulder. "If you're looking for a listing, that's Gillian's department." He poured three wide fingers of Black Seal rum into each mug, squeezed in a lime section, and topped it up with ginger beer.

"Here you go," he said. "Put hair on your teeth."

She took a long swallow, her eyes never leaving his, then cradled the mug in her two hands. "Actually it was you I came to see." She paused. "Friends of yours in the charter fleet say you're in love."

"Do they?" Barr could feel himself bristle, but he realized her question was meant to put him off-balance. He managed a neutral shrug. "Maybe they're right."

She had not, he saw, expected that answer—but he knew she wouldn't let one misfire stop her. "I can still remember the other time," she said, watching him from under her lashes. "When you fell head over heels for Anne."

Anne. Even after five years, the sound of her name could derail his train of thought. She's dead, he reminded himself. Anne is dead. But he took a deliberate breath before he answered. "That was infatuation. As you pointed out, several times." And might have added: *I knew you were right, even then. Not that it made any difference.*

"Are you going to marry this one, too?" Deedee must have sensed, from his total lack of expression, that she had gone too far: "Not that it's any of my business."

"It's not, is it?" he said.

Despite the dimmed light in the cabin, Barr could see her stiffen. "Not any more," she agreed. "Back then it was different. I had a job to do, even if I didn't like it."

"Just following orders."

"That's right," she replied quickly, then reddened as she picked up his real meaning. "You knew who I worked for," she said, "You must have known. And you were on the same payroll."

The automatic denial was on his lips, but it got no further. He *had* known—just hadn't admitted it, even to himself.

Deedee was taking his tight-lipped silence as assent. "In our business," she said, leaning just a little on *our*, "security is everything, and Anne was a security risk. A classic security risk, even if she wasn't actually running the dope she was smoking. She made you vulnerable, so . . ."

Barr cut her off with a gesture. "So you dropped me. I'm not complaining. But why are you here now?"

She took another long swallow of her drink. "There's an old friend who'd like to talk to you."

"A shy old friend, since he's using you as go-between," Barr observed. "What does he want to talk about?"

"That's not for me to say. But he's willing to pay for the privilege."

She seemed to be waiting for him to ask, "How much?" In negotiations like these, Barr knew, the first person to name a price lost the game. Not that he cared because he wasn't playing. "Not interested," he said.

She seemed unsurprised. "Don't you even want to know who's asking?"

"What makes you so sure you know who's *really* asking?" He saw the shot had gone home. When you dealt with someone in Deedee's position, an appeal to paranoia could hardly fail.

"I mean, the individual," she replied.

"Not especially," he said. "Look, if that's all you've got on your mind . . ." He got up as he spoke and raised his glass to drain it.

"Wait a minute," she said, rising. "This is important, Jeremy."

"To you, maybe." He set the glass down on the varnished mahogany table, then quickly retrieved it and wiped the wet ring off the wood with a paper napkin.

"To more people than me. A lot more people." Her voice, he noted, was actually vibrating with sincerity. "This comes right from Washington, Jeremy. They need you." She was, he now remembered, one of those people who edged closer as they got more earnest. He took a half step backward.

He could feel annoyance deepening to anger. "Washington's not exactly a magic word with me, Deedee. You ought to know that."

Her voice was suddenly as hostile as his own. "It's still because of Anne, isn't it?"

"Maybe. Yes."

Deedee slammed her fist against the bulkhead. "*Damn* it, Jeremy, she wasn't worth two cents alive, and she's certainly not worth it dead. She was a druggie. She slept with any man she met, and at least one wo—"

The slap cracked like a pistol shot in the confined space. Barr looked at his tingling hand with genuine surprise, then at Deedee, who was sprawled back across the settee. He couldn't trust himself to speak, not least because she was absolutely right.

For a full minute the silence between them was complete. Barr could hear the faint squeak of the runabout rubbing against the fenders, the even fainter whir as *Glory's* automatic bilge pump kicked in. "I think you'd better go," he said, his voice hoarse in his ears.

Deedee got up slowly, her left hand pressed to her cheek. "My daddy always said a man should never hit a woman without a good reason," she said. "You had a good reason. I shouldn't have said that."

"Forget it."

"Don't be stupid, Jeremy." She took a deep breath. "Okay, let's try it another way. You owe me a favor, a big one; I'm collecting."

"A favor?" What was she talking about?

"You remember when *Windhover* was wrecked." It wasn't a question, of course. How could he forget the worst night of his life, when his own charter boat was destroyed, his wife drowned, his life laid in ruins?

Windhover had been making a night run across the Anegada Passage, with Anne and the charterers—friends of hers—on watch. Barr had gone below, as much to escape the three of them as to rest, and had knocked himself out with rum, something he was doing often in those days. Instinct brought him on deck, with the breakers on the reef clear ahead, but the sight of Anne and her friends in a naked tangle had frozen his reactions.

The rest of it was pure nightmare, and not one he was going to share with Deedee. "I don't remember a hell of a lot," he said. "The coral cut me up pretty badly. I lost some blood."

"According to the doctor, you had about a shot glass left in you," she said. "Do you remember them finding you?"

A boatload of skin divers, all jabbering at once. He could still feel Anne's naked, cold, bloodless body in his arms. "Yes."

"They took you to the little clinic in Road Town. Remember that?"

"No. I remember waking up in San Juan, in some military hospital." Wrapped like a mummy, fighting to get free.

"How do you think you got there?"

"You?"

"*Moi.*"

"Then I do owe you one."

"Not to mention the lawsuit," she said. He felt his neck go hot. *Windhover's* charterers, high-rolling friends of Anne's from Chicago, had wasted no time finding a lawyer. But the suit—malfeasance, barratry, consorting with Martians, and fifty-six other trumped-up charges—had somehow evaporated. Barr, stunned and apathetic, had barely noticed.

"You did that?"

"I just suggested the BVI cops check your customer's pockets for cocaine traces. After that it was no problem."

Cocaine? Barr had no idea whether Anne and her friends had been drunk, drugged, or merely sated that night. And he never would know for sure. What he did know now was that he really owed Deedee Etheridge a favor.

"When and where do I meet this guy?" he asked.

Gillian

Perched on the bow of *Glory*'s inflatable tender, Gillian held the grab ropes with both hands as the little boat bounced across larger boats' wakes, toward where the yacht rode at anchor. The outboard motor's high-pitched snarl reduced conversation to shrieks, and Jake and Isabel, balancing their luggage in the middle of the tender, had quickly given up trying to talk with Patrick, who was seated in the stern, steering.

She could see Barr on the foredeck with his back to them, staring down at something on *Glory*'s far side. From a hundred yards away the lean, deeply tanned figure wearing only an old pair of swimming trunks looked almost like a boy. Gillian wondered for perhaps the hundredth time how it was possible to love one person so much. It didn't make any sense on the surface. Barr was ten years older than she, totally helpless anywhere except on a boat. His body looked like bundled wire tightly wrapped in old leather, his face was all sharp angles, and nothing short of varnish would make his hair lie flat.

He'd entered Gillian's life three years ago, when *Glory* belonged to her dying great-uncle Dennis, and Barr was his paid skipper—a silent presence who seemed at first like an extension of the wonderful old yacht that Gillian had loved from the moment she'd taken the wheel.

After a while Gillian began to appreciate just how skilled a sailor Barr really was, and found herself torn between admiration of his talent and irritation at the way he ignored her. She assumed, from his manner, that he saw her only as the boss's bossy niece; her perverse reaction was to behave exactly like a spoiled brat (just thinking about it now made her cringe), while Barr withdrew even further into himself. Only the near-loss of *Glory* and both their lives had bridged the gap, brought them together—as friends. By then, she already wanted more.

Once he lowered his guard, he was tactful and kind and generous, but that alone wasn't what made her heart turn over. His unworldliness sometimes made her feel he needed protecting, and then suddenly he'd reveal a streak of resilient toughness beyond anything she'd encountered. Best of all, he seemed to have nothing he needed to prove, to women or to other men. So why, she'd asked herself, couldn't he love her?

She hadn't known about Anne back then—hadn't known much of anything about Barr's past, except that he'd sailed and lost a charter yacht of his own in the Caribbean. But Gillian wasn't a person who would tolerate ignorance, especially in herself. From Barr's acquaintances in the charter fleet she pieced together the outlines of his story, including his totally unexpected, miserably unsuccessful marriage. The fleet's gossip about Anne was unforgiving: a blond airhead, a slut, a pothead, pure trouble. The consensus was that she'd probably married Barr while she was stoned. Except for Barr, no one mourned her.

The stories about Barr himself were all strangely impersonal. Sailing with him, one delivery skipper remarked, was like having the Flying Dutchman aboard. No one could handle an unfamiliar boat as well, especially in heavy weather, but he hardly ever went ashore, even after the roughest passage. And when he did, he preferred to drink alone.

When Barr had been running his own boat, *Windhover*, she made port or departed after sunset as often as in the daylight, behavior that seemed bizarre among a chain of reef-strewn islands where charts were seldom up-to-date and buoyage was distinguished by its absence. *Windhover* was seldom on view in Marigot Bay or English Harbour or the other anchorages favored by the fleet, though alert skippers might catch an occasional glimpse of her tall, varnished mast through the palms, tucked into tiny coves that most of them would chance entering only by dinghy.

Gillian was prepared to believe the worst when it came to Anne, but Barr's behavior she put down to simple reclusiveness; when at last he came to her bed, she was prepared to make allowances for shyness, clumsiness, inexperience. She loved him enough to ignore all that; she was eager to teach him how to love a woman.

How wrong you could be.

Their first, delirious night was the way she long ago dreamed sex might happen before experience lowered her expectations. Gillian's fiercely independent life had included a fair number of men, some of them accomplished (at least to hear them tell it). Not one of them came close to Barr. Considerate she had expected; imaginative surprised her. What took her breath away—literally, and more than once—was the way he knew exactly what she wanted and exactly how to supply it.

Only afterward did she begin to wonder when he had learned those skills. More important, who'd taught him, and was she still around? Six months after their first encounter she was hopelessly in love and consumed by something more urgent than curiosity.

From behind *Glory* a runabout pulled away, gathering speed. A nondescript fiber glass skiff, faded by the sun, with a woman at the helm, a blonde. Gillian had seen her before, and not all that long ago; someone in the charter world, someone bossy and well known, but the name remained glued to the tip of her tongue.

Patrick brought the inflatable to a perfect stop inches from *Glory*'s gleaming hull. Barr took the line Gillian passed him and made it fast without a word. He seemed barely aware of her or the others; she saw right away that he was, in Patrick's words, "inside himself." When Barr got like that, he was unreachable, even by her.

"Captain Barr, this is our charterer, Jake Adler," she said, when they all were in *Glory*'s cockpit. "And his friend Isabel Machado." Handshakes; Jake was staring intently into Barr's closed face, but Isabel's eyes had gone back to Patrick, who was looking slightly embarrassed. Gillian felt a stab of apprehension. If Isabel was going to make a wide-open play for *Glory*'s cook, the coming week could be painful.

"I bet you thought we were coming on board tomorrow," Jake was saying to Barr.

"Tomorrow?"

"Barr doesn't concern himself with earthly things," Gillian explained. "He just drives my boat."

"I see," said Jake. From his expression she could tell he hadn't missed the faint stress she'd put on "my." "Then we might as well get on our way now."

"The rest of Jake's party has gone ahead to St.-Bart's," Gillian said. "They're going to meet us there."

"Oh, really?" Barr's tone was marginal uninterest, but his left eyebrow cocked up, and that meant real surprise.

"They left a note in my hotel," Jake said. "Apparently they were here in St. Martin, missed us, and decided to fly across for the day."

Isabel tore her gaze from Patrick. "We didn't come down here together, you see. Jake and I flew from New York, and the others from Georgia."

"Whatever," said Barr. "But there's not much sense in sailing over to Gustavia this late in the day. Customs'll be closed by the time we get there."

Of course, thought Gillian. *I should've remembered that.*

"Does it make a difference?" Jake asked.

"On a Dutch island it probably wouldn't," said Gillian. "But St.-Bart's is French. They take their paper work seriously. We could anchor off, but we can't go ashore till *Glory* clears customs."

"It's only a couple hours' sail," said Barr. "If we head out right after breakfast, we'll be there by the time the harbor office opens."

"I see," Jake replied. The news seemed less than welcome, but after a moment he shrugged. "Well, I guess it doesn't matter. Can you recommend someplace Isabel and I can get dinner? Someplace not too expensive?"

"You forget, you're paying for an extra night aboard, and that includes meals," Gillian said. And to Patrick: "How about satay? We've got beef, and there's a big container of your peanut sauce in the fridge."

Patrick gave her a startled look, which she ignored. The leftover beef had been a subject of discussion earlier in the day, Patrick warning that it was already a little high, and Gillian pointing out that it also represented close to forty dollars from *Glory*'s food budget. On balance she was prepared to gamble that Patrick's fiery peanut butter, garlic, and jalapeño sauce would disguise it.

"Maybe raita—cukes and sour cream—as a side dish," Patrick offered. "Lots of cold beer to wash it down."

"Sounds fine to me," said Adler, his good humor obviously restored. "And I might have one of those beers right now, while Isabel and I settle in."

Ten minutes later Gillian came up on deck, to find Barr had changed into rumpled khakis and a faded red polo shirt that hung on his wiry frame like a tent. The shirt had been left behind by a charterer from Southern California, and Barr had razored off half the stitching over the breast pocket, so that what was left read only "YACHT CLUB."

"I put Jake and Isabel in the forward cabin." She met his raised eyebrow with a deadpan face. "Figured we might as well have one more night in the double, while we can get it."

"Oh, was that it?" he said; the unexpected conspiratorial smile made her heart break stride. "I thought maybe you wanted to locate Isabel conveniently near Patrick."

"You noticed? I hope Jake isn't the jealous type."

"Tell you the truth, I thought he was paying more attention to Patrick than to her," Barr said.

"My God, d'you mean—"

"No, not that way. You want my guess, he's an old soldier, and he found out Patrick's a young one. I bet Jake just wants somebody to talk army with."

That might be it, she thought. For a man who never seemed to be paying attention, Barr could come up with some surprising observations. "Well, I guess we'll . . . say, what're you doing, Barr?"

"Hanging my shoes around my neck."

"You're going ashore?"

"I've got an errand," he replied.

"It wouldn't be with that blonde who was out here before?"

"Blonde?" He must have seen from her face that denial wasn't going to work. "Oh, Deedee Etheridge. No, she wanted us to list *Glory* with her." As he talked, Barr unhitched the inflatable's bowline and slipped over the side like an eel. His last words floated up over the gunwale. "I said she'd have to see you about it."

"Then what—" But her question drowned in the roar of the outboard. He turned once to wave at her, but she kept her arms folded, her fingers biting into her biceps. *It's her,* she was thinking. *It's that Deedee, and there's not a damn thing I can do about it.*

Barr: Philipsburg, 5:30 P.M.

The restaurant's owner—French, by his accent—picked Barr off as he stepped through the door, blinking in the sudden twilight. "This way, m'sieu. Your friend is already waiting."

The man at the corner table was backlit by the late-afternoon panorama of Groot Baai outside, but the long-nosed, round-shouldered silhouette would have been unmistakable even if Barr hadn't been expecting it. "Mr. Tarleton. What a surprise," he said.

Stuart Tarleton got to his feet in sections, like some long-legged marsh bird rising from its nest. Beaming, he extended a bony hand, which felt dry and fragile in Barr's grasp. "Thank you for coming, Captain." His voice went with his appearance, Barr thought: creaking and high-pitched and British to the echo (though he had once, while very drunk, confided to Barr that he'd been born and raised in San Francisco). He motioned Barr to the other chair and sank back with a sigh into his own. "Sorry to be so importunate, but time is pressing. I really had to talk to you right away."

Barr shook an unfiltered Camel free from the pack and lit it, watching Tarleton through the smoke. He hadn't changed much in three years—the colorless hair brushed straight back over his long skull was a little thinner, and a few more liver spots speckled the backs of his dry, wrinkled hands—and the faded, bloodshot eyes still had the same gleam of private amusement. Back then Tarleton's sartorial trademark had been a rumpled seersucker suit; its pockets had bulged with the scribbled notes that established his identity as an expatriate scholar, a student of West Indian language and custom, with two fat, obscure books to his credit.

In time, of course, too many people came to guess his real function.

Now he was relegated—so Barr had heard—to first-contact work, evaluating the potential usefulness of troublemakers and dissidents and the more convincing lunatics. And with his new function went a new outfit, a tan cotton bush jacket, as rumpled as his suit had been, and an open-collar shirt that revealed his stringy throat.

A waiter appeared at Barr's side and set down a tall, frosted glass. The deep amber color and the smell of ginger and rum told him what it was. "How thoughtful," Barr said. "You remembered."

"It's in your file, old boy," Tarleton replied. "People come and go, but files are forever. Cheers." He raised his own glass—white wine, Barr noticed; in former days it would've been scotch, no ice. Barr lifted his own glass in salute, deliberately set it back down without drinking.

"Why'd you want to see me?" he asked.

Tarleton produced a withered smile. "You're about to be keeping bad company. Certain people are concerned."

Barr dragged his chair close up to the table. "Look," he said, "that way of talking drives me up the wall. Why don't you just tell me what's on your mind, straight out?"

Tarleton pursed his thin lips as if considering the suggestion. "It's not easy after all those years of circumlocution. But I'll try." He stared down into his wineglass for inspiration, then fixed Barr with his slightly rheumy gaze. "How much do you know about your charterer Colonel Adler?"

"Colonel?" said Barr, not trying to pretend surprise.

"Light colonel, actually. Lieutenant Colonel Jacob Joshua Adler, U.S. Army. Silver Star, two Bronze Stars, Infantry, Airborne, et cetera, et cetera."

"I don't know as much as you do, obviously." Barr sluiced down half his drink. Ginger ale instead of ginger beer, but they'd done their best to duplicate the dark and stormy that had always been Barr's drink of choice. "So he's a foot soldier. Does that mean he's not allowed to play boats?"

"Well, a two-week charter in your yacht is close to a half year's salary for a lieutenant colonel," Tarleton replied. "And I doubt the bill's being split six ways. Miss Machado—his mistress, by the way—is a Cuban refugee. Doesn't have two dimes to rub together, and the other four members of the party are noncommissioned officers, with large families back in Fort Benning."

"Is that so?" But it probably was. In their previous association Tarleton had often—had nearly always—held back information, but you could rely on the accuracy of what he chose to tell.

"Didn't the composition of Adler's group strike you as odd?" Tarleton asked. "Five men and one woman?"

"Gillian said something," he admitted. All of *Glory's* previous charter parties had been composed of families or couples; it was the kind of thing she noticed. "So who's paying the freight?"

"The money is coming through a group Colonel Adler belongs to, the Ethan Allen Society. Ever heard of it?"

"Any relation to John Birch?" Barr asked.

"Theoretically none," Tarleton said. "But I see you've taken the point. The Ethan Allens got started right after Vietnam, as a patriotic support group of and for regular Army people. Gradually, of course, they lost that . . . fine edge of dedication." The older man made a noise somewhere between a snort and a chuckle. "Now it's just a camorra made up of Army losers—the ones who got left out of Desert Storm and the macho dolts for whom too much is never enough. Plus a few hungry field grade officers like Adler, who need one more jump to be sure of their star." Barr wondered if Tarleton's grimace was for losers or the hungry or both. "Of course, to create a properly explosive mixture, you have to add funding."

"As in money," said Barr.

"Yes. In fact, your terminology is more accurate than mine." Tarleton smiled at such a peculiar notion, before he explained. " '*Funding*' is government, and Washington's not in the giving vein these days, now that the bill for Iraq is on the table. '*Money*,' on the other hand, is cash—unaccountable, untraceable, always welcome, thoroughly delightful."

"But it does come from somewhere," Barr put in.

Tarleton shrugged. "Bible pounders, drug runners, the spiritual heirs of United Fruit—or even the odd Beltway commando. Remember, this administration's very partial to military solutions."

Barr stubbed out his cigarette and decided against lighting another. Unfiltered American cigarettes were almost impossible to find in the islands, and only three cartons remained of the six Barr had bought back in the Virgins. "Military solutions? What do they do, these Ethan Allens—start wars?'

"Since you ask, yes."

Tarleton's prim answer caught Barr with his drink half swallowed. When he had blown his nose and wiped his eyes, he managed a hoarse laugh. "Give me a break, Tarleton. A handful of has-beens don't just go out and start a war."

"You think not? That's how Fidel did it. And besides, if push comes to shoot, the Ethan Allens can probably put a hundred trained men in the field, with some pretty sophisticated weapons."

Barr shook his head reluctantly. "Well, I guess it's just possible. A hundred men would be an army down here. But who—"

"Last year," Tarleton interrupted, "the freighter full of arms that got picked off in Antigua? Surely you remember the stories. They were in all the papers."

"I thought those guns were on the way to Colombia."

"That was the official version," Tarleton agreed. "In fact, they were *from* Colombia, and word has it they were bound for St. Kitts."

The rest of the equation wasn't far to seek. "Anguilla again?" Barr asked.

Tarleton nodded. "When Anguilla seceded from St. Kitts, it made the Bassetcrre government look like buffoons—"

"What did they expect?" Barr put in. "They *were* buffoons. Sorry, go ahead."

"As I was saying, it was embarrassing enough that they walked out of St. Kitts's so-called federation, but now Anguilla's coining money—brand-new hotels popping up like—like . . ."

"Pimples," said Barr.

"If you say so. Point is, Anguilla's rich, and there are people in St. Kitts daft enough to try to invade them again."

"That's not U.S. turf, though," Barr objected. "The Brits guarantee Anguilla's independence, same as they do for Belize. If your Ethan Allens tried anything there, they'd get their heads blown off by the Brigade of Guards. Even a light colonel must know that much."

But arguing with Tarleton, as Barr now recalled, was like trying to herd mosquitoes. He just came at you from a different direction. "How about the Bahamas then? The government's in bed with the Medellíns. Everybody knows it. But Washington can't do anything overt since the silly queen knighted the Bahamian prime minister."

Tarleton certainly had a point there. "Well, at least we're not talking Cuba these days," Barr said, thinking aloud. "A handful of *yanquis* with guns would be a godsend to them. I suppose Haiti's a possibility, though."

"The man who can solve Haiti hasn't been born yet," said Tarleton. "But that doesn't mean some fool won't take a swing at it." He glanced meaningfully at Barr's empty glass. "Another?"

Gillian thought he drank too much; she never said so, but he could often feel her not saying it. She was probably right, but she wasn't herc. "Straight rum this time."

When the waiter had taken the order, Tarleton continued. "In fact, that's the problem. One can list half a dozen potential playgrounds, but we don't know which one the Ethan Allens are considering."

"And you think that's why Adler's down here?" Barr asked. "He must be quite a guy, to start a revolution with four guys and his girl friend."

"He is quite a guy," said Tarleton, ignoring Barr's tone. "You've heard the expression 'loose cannon'? Jake Adler is the Delta Force version, a loose missile. But my people think this exercise is preliminary—a scouting expedition. That's why he's chartered you."

"Because *Glory*'s in his target area?"

"The boat's incidental," Tarleton said. "Jeremy Barr is what he wants, your expertise."

Barr spluttered an objection, but Tarleton rode over it. "False modesty. Colonel Adler helped compile the after-action data on the Grenada invasion. He must have read your report on the landing areas."

"I didn't think anyone had read it," Barr said, hearing the edge of bitterness in his voice.

"Very few did," Tarleton agreed. "Before the invasion, anyway. It was sat on by the highest buttocks. Too many uncomfortable truths. Afterward, of course, you became the Caribbean Cassandra—among the few who recognized what a botch it was, the ones who weren't blinded by the shower of medals."

Odd how angry the memory could still make him, after all this time. He lit another Camel and took a long, deep drag before he could trust himself to speak coolly. "Well, Jake Adler's friends can't be planning to hit Grenada again."

"No," Tarleton said. "In fact, my people are completely baffled. The Windwards and Leewards don't exactly figure in grand strategy. A fact reflected in the intelligence budget," he added, then went on. "But the rumors are too strong for Washington to ignore. Someone's looking for trouble, and we plan to head them off."

"I like that 'we,' " said Barr.

"Oh, relax, Captain." The waiter set down the drinks, and Tarleton waved him away. "All I need to know is where Colonel Adler's going. We'll take it from there."

"Well, *Glory*'s sailing to Gustavia tomorrow morning. The rest of Adler's group flew there from St. Martin today."

"Yes," said Tarleton. "Didn't that seem odd to you? I mean, why pay to fly across, plus a hotel and meals, when you've already got a ride arranged?"

Tarleton or his unspecified "we" were certainly on Adler's heels so far, Barr reflected. After twenty years in the Caribbean Tarleton probably owned the islands' airport counters and hotel desks, but a yacht still had the ability to vanish from the board, at least for a day or so.

"And after Gustavia?" Tarleton asked.

"I don't know," Barr admitted. "Gillian must've sent Adler the usual cruise questionnaire, but I guess he didn't specify an itinerary." And in answer to Tarleton's unspoken question: "Lots of people don't. They let us pick it or decide when they get here."

"Well, old boy," said Tarleton, reverting to what Barr thought of as his colonial voice, "his itinerary is what we need. And try to remember any leading questions he asks you. As I say, it's quite vital."

Maybe to you, Barr thought.

His reluctance must have shown in his expression because Tarleton leaned forward, lowering his voice. "There'd be something in it for you, of course."

"What?"

"How would you like to have your master's ticket back?"

Barr's license, in all its archaically engraved glory, had occupied a framed place of honor on *Windhover's* main cabin bulkhead. At the worst of times he had taken strength just from knowing it was there, the affirmation that he'd been found competent by men he respected to command vessels up to one hundred tons in displacement on any waters in the world.

Technically the license had simply lapsed, during the bleak gray hiatus after *Windhover's* loss. Reapplying should be simple enough, but there would, inescapably, be questions about *Windhover*, questions he had asked himself, over and over, in the hours before dawn, questions he still couldn't—or wouldn't—answer.

Barr felt the older man weighing him. "And afterward," Tarleton said, "who knows? It could be the restoration of a beautiful arrangement. As I said, you're very well thought of in Washington these days."

That settled it. "No," said Barr.

"I'm sorry you feel that way," Tarleton said. "But I'm afraid we just can't accept your decision."

"You'll just have to. That ticket was the only string you had on me."

"On you, perhaps. But what about Mr. O'Mara's license? Didn't he certify to a vast number of hours at sea, in order to qualify for it?"

Tarleton shook his head in mock sorrow. "I've been told Mr. O'Mara was nowhere near the sea during much of that time. Africa, wasn't it?"

It was. At the end of his second hitch in the Army Patrick had been talked into signing up with a mercenary force in Chad and had spent a harrowing year in the desert before deserting. Officially, however, he had never left the United States, and five old friends of Barr's had sworn in writing that Patrick had spent the whole time making ocean passages under their supervision. In *Glory's* deliberately noncommittal brochures, Patrick was only the yacht's cook and mate, but in the eyes of government he was her licensed captain, too.

"Everybody fakes those applications," said Barr, but he could feel the ground slipping from beneath his feet.

"No doubt," Tarleton replied. "But the Coast Guard doesn't like to admit it. And if you were going to tell me that *Glory* doesn't need a licensed skipper to charter outside American waters, I'd remind you that the Coast Guard has a very long arm in these lawless, drug-infested times. As a U.S.-flag vessel, *Glory* can be boarded and searched anywhere, as many times as necessary. You know how it is with drug searches, how destructive they can be."

Barr did indeed. An enthusiastic boarding team could make a shambles of a cabin, looking for secret compartments; a bunch of teen-age Coasties who'd been encouraged to release their inhibitions could reduce *Glory's* interior to kindling.

"Besides," Tarleton was saying, "word would get around among the charter agents . . ." It was checkmate, as Tarleton could clearly see, and he let his words trail off.

"All right," said Barr.

"—and it *is* only for a day or so. Now, why don't we have a spot of dinner while we run over the contact procedures?"

Gillian

Lying rigid in the big berth she shared with Barr when *Glory* was between charter parties, Gillian ordered herself not to fall asleep until he came back aboard. From the main cabin came the rise and fall of voices—Patrick's smooth baritone alternating with Jake's abrupt tenor—as the two men refought Patrick's final campaign as a mercenary in Africa, two years before.

Until tonight Patrick's short, aborted career as a soldier of fortune had been a subject sealed under impenetrable layers of scar tissue, proof against Gillian's most pointed probes. (Barr, of course, never showed any curiosity about his shipmate's past at all; Barr seldom seemed curious about anything, yet maddeningly, people often seemed eager to tell him the inmost thoughts Gillian could seldom pry out of them.)

But Jake had opened Patrick's floodgates. First he let drop that he was a professional soldier—a colonel, no less—on vacation. Gillian could see Patrick was impressed, but no more surprised than she herself was. The minute Jake announced he was a military man, everything about him—manner, speech, dress—fell into place. Gillian, who was on her third rum and Coke, said exactly that, and Jake flashed his infectious grin.

"People spot me all the time," he admitted. "I used to think it was just the haircut"—he flattened the thinning bristles on top of his skull with one meaty palm, then let them spring up again—"but after a while I figured it was the whole construct." He turned to Patrick, who was watching him almost hungrily. "Could say the same of you, I think."

To Gillian's astonishment, Patrick went scarlet under his tan. He opened his mouth to speak, but Jake held up his hand. "Let me guess. You're—you *were* Army, too." Patrick nodded. "Infantry? Of course." He glanced at Gillian, his eyes sparkling. "Now, this is the tough one, Eighty-second or First Cav." She could scarcely believe her eyes. Patrick, Mr. Smooth himself, was squirming like a schoolboy with what could only be abashed delight.

"Staff Sergeant, A Company, Second Battalion, Three-twenty-fifth Infantry," he blurted, all in one breath. Gillian could almost hear the words "reporting for duty, sir," hanging in the air.

"Three twenty-fifth. Of course," Jake said. "Did you know old Matt Schofield? Or was he before your time?"

"Well, I *saw* him a lot," Patrick replied. "But I was just an E-six in a line company. I didn't have conversations with colonels. Not"—he grinned—"till tonight, anyway."

"But you didn't stay in," said Jake quickly. "How come, if you don't mind my asking?" And to Gillian: "Always burns my ass—pardon my French—when we can't hold guys like this."

Patrick's color, which had faded to near normal, heightened again. He shrugged and launched on a long, complicated explanation that meant nothing to Gillian but seemed to fascinate Jake. "Don't blame you," he said at one point, and, "Might've done the same myself," a couple of minutes later. He swallowed the last of his beer in a long gulp and reached for another bottle. The plastic ice bucket was empty, and Gillian excused herself to refill it from *Glory*'s galley. While she was groping head down in the vast top-loading fridge, she heard Jake's whoop of surprise from the main cabin.

"*Hals?* You fought with *der alte Kämpfer* in Africa? Well, I'll be goddamned." By the time she returned with a half dozen nearly frozen squat green bottles jammed in the melting ice, Patrick had dived headfirst into a sea of reminiscence. For an hour, or maybe two, Gillian heard about a segment of his life nearly unknown to her, a segment whose smallest details seemed seared into his memory.

Old Hals she had encountered—an ancient German leader of mercenaries who'd been fighting other countries' battles since just after World War II, with a private army of stateless black Africans led by an international assortment of whites. Hals needed young, professional soldiers, having just been hired by dissidents who hoped to overthrow the government of Chad; in fact, Hals and the dissidents themselves were being financed by Chad's neighbor, the Libyan dictator Qaddafi. It soon developed that they were opposed by not just the feeble Chadian Army but also Egyptian regulars and French paratroops, whose unexplained presence seemed quite reasonable to Jake.

The war, as Patrick told it, sounded to her pointless beyond belief. If Chad was half as arid and useless as he made it sound, no rational person would have lifted a finger—never mind fought to the death—either to seize or to defend it. And after a while the brutal sameness of the events became unbearably depressing to listen to: meaningless battles against faceless enemies; a seesaw struggle that finally tilted against Hals's outnumbered legion; an endless fighting retreat across the dusty vastness of a country Gillian had barely heard of.

Clearly, though, it was important to Patrick that he tell his story—all the more so, perhaps, for having suppressed it for so long. The words poured out of him in an uncontrolled torrent, with Jake at first nodding silent support, then supplying a chorus of technical observations.

Isabel seemed used to being ignored; she sat motionless and without expression, only her eyes moving from man to man. Gillian, unwilling to be frozen out, conducted her own rearguard action to stay in the conversation, but soon saw it was futile; the two men were communicating at some primal level she couldn't match, like two women dissecting a man who had once been loved by each of them. When

Patrick and Jake began to refight the last battle, foot by agonizing foot, with empty beer bottles (by now an impressive number of them) to represent the opposing forces, she slipped from behind the table without a word. Neither man noticed her go, though Isabel, surprisingly, gave her a slow, deliberate wink.

Half asleep, Gillian brushed her teeth, then brushed them again in a futile effort to scrub off the garlic-jalapeño-crushed peanut residue that was eating through her tooth enamel. Patrick's satay sauce, Jake had observed, was even fiercer than the version he'd eaten while stationed in Bangkok.

She peeled off her clothes, stacked them conveniently next to the berth, and climbed into *Glory*'s only double, three feet above the deck. It felt huge and cold and empty without Barr's naked body beside hers. Not that he was anyone's idea of a pillow—mostly sinew and muscle, with sharp bones in the most inconvenient places. Still, Gillian had learned to coil her own slender form around his, so that they slept as a single shape. And awoke mutually aroused.

Damn Barr. She knew she ought to have more faith in him, but there was so much about his past she didn't know. Events she hadn't shared, old friends she'd never met . . .

The murmurs from the main cabin were soothing her right out of consciousness. Her eyelids seemed weighted with lead, and she amended her earlier resolution: Five quick minutes of nap, and she would be alert when he returned.

The muffled thump of wood against wood, seemingly inches from her head, brought Gillian up from a deep slumber, out of a dream that evaporated as she woke, leaving behind only a sharp feeling of loss. Her first conscious thought was a question: Why was Barr in a wooden dinghy instead of *Glory*'s inflatable? Then, a demisecond later, she reminded herself that Barr, who could lay *Glory* exactly two inches off a pier when he was too drunk to stand, was not the man to scrape any small boat against the yacht's side.

Even while the thought was forming, she was tugging her jeans up over her hips. She pulled a sweat shirt over her head, aware, as she did so, of the deep silence belowdecks. Where was Patrick sleeping? she wondered. Had he heard the noise, too?

As Gillian slipped barefoot out of the cabin, she heard a scrabbling, like someone hauling himself up over *Glory*'s gunwale, through the lifelines. Passing the chart table, she remembered she was unarmed. *Glory*'s sole formal weapon, an ancient Army M-1 rifle, was carefully hidden under a water tank in the bilge—and it was broken down into its three main components and wrapped in plastic anyway. No help there.

The Very pistol. Of course. She pulled open one of the drawers beneath the chart table and groped for the clumsy old flare gun before she remembered that Patrick had been working on it, machining a stainless steel tube that would fit inside the regular barrel and enable the pistol to fire 10-gauge shotgun shells as well as 20-mm flares. The last time she'd seen the gun its barrel was clamped in a vise up in the fo'c'sle.

The feel of a cold metal tread under her bare soles brought her back, and she realized she was possessed by fury at the idea of someone—anyone—invading her boat. Weaponless, she darted up the steep ladder to the cockpit. She paused in the hatchway, conscious of a big, shadowy figure crouched over the steering wheel at the cockpit's after end, his back to her.

The sight galvanized her. She snatched from its retaining clip one of the heavy bronze winch handles, swung it high, and brought it down on the man's shoulder. The ugly *whack* of three pounds of metal meeting bare flesh was echoed by an explosive grunt of agony. An instant later Gillian's arms were pinned from behind, and she was lifted off her feet in a grasp as unyielding as wire cable—but cable with the rank, acrid odor of unwashed human. Her anger mixed now with terror, she kicked back with both heels, but struck only unyielding muscle sheathed in coarse cloth. She opened her mouth to yell, and as suddenly as he had seized her, the unseen figure let her go, and she fell to the deck with a thump that turned her cry to a gasp.

As she lay breathless across the teak deck, her captor stepped over her to his comrade, who was curled up and moaning with pain on the cockpit floorboards. Urgent, half-heard words, and the moaning figure was dragged to his feet, clutching at his shoulder. In the moonlight Gillian saw his left arm hanging, awkwardly helpless.

Now she heard what had distracted her attacker—the nasal burr of an outboard motor, approaching fast. "Barr!" she called And as the two attackers stumbled over *Glory*'s rail and half fell into their own boat: "Barr! Hurry up!"

"I don't get it," she said a few minutes later. "What was that guy doing?"

"Beats me," said Barr, who was crouched on his heels behind the binnacle, examining the steering wheel column in the light of a small flash.

Jake, who had appeared on deck just as Barr had come over the side, bent and picked up a heavy, rusty metal tool from the cockpit grating. "What's this thing?" he asked. "Looks like oversize wire cutters."

Patrick, standing in the companionway, waited for Barr to reply, then said, "That's pretty close. They're for cutting through stays and shrouds if a mast goes down."

Jake was wearing only a pair of abbreviated boxer shorts, and the matted black hair on his barrel chest and thick, bowed legs made him look more apelike than ever. "How about if somebody wanted to make a mast fall down?" He flexed the tool's long handles, producing a harsh scraping sound from the blades.

Barr didn't even look up from the binnacle, but Patrick's eyes widened. "Sure," he said. "Like three snips on one side—two lower shrouds and the upper—and the mizzen'd go right over the side." He turned to Barr. "D'you think—"

"No." Barr straightened up. From five feet away Gillian could smell the rum on his breath, yet his speech was clear and precise. "You couldn't cut a sausage with those things," he said. "Dull as a butter knife, not to mention too small for our mizzen shrouds in the first place."

"Then what're they for?" Patrick demanded, clearly annoyed by Barr's dismissive tone.

"As I said, beats me." Barr got awkwardly to his feet, stuffed the flashlight in his hip pocket, missing on the first attempt. Gillian wondered if he was as sober as he sounded. "Nothing broken or stolen, as far as I can tell. I'm going to bed."

By the time Gillian shepherded Jake and Patrick back to their cabins (Isabel had seemingly slept through everything) and double-checked the galley (Patrick, as usual, had left it clean enough to perform surgery on the countertop), Barr was in bed, a sheet pulled up to his chest, staring at the tongue and groove ash planking of the overhead.

She closed the cabin door behind her, glanced at the open ports, and said, "So what's going on?"

He regarded her for a second or two before replying. "What do you mean, 'what's going on'?" He could, when he wanted, hide behind a smooth, bulletproof obtuseness; it was a manner that drove her crazy, and she took a firm grip on her emotions before speaking.

"I mean this whole charter. First"—she held up a finger—"that so-called accident with Jake—"

"You saw it?" he interrupted.

"Well, no. But Patrick's sure the van deliberately tried to run Jake over."

Barr sat up, and the sheet slid down below his navel, to where the skin, untouched by sun, was nearly as white as milk. Gillian's eyes automatically followed the sheet. Had he been with her? Had she marked him? Her stomach knotted, but it required a real effort to wrench her gaze away.

"I thought you said the same van almost ran you down, too," Barr said. "Was that on purpose?"

"Of course not," she snapped. "But that was different. He was trying to get away."

"Oh, sure." His tone was absolutely, hatefully neutral. And he was right, which was worse.

"Then what about just now?" she demanded. "What were you looking for in the binnacle?"

She saw, with satisfaction, that she had put him off balance. He hesitated, and she knew he was weighing his answer. "I wanted to see if they'd opened the access plate in the steering pedestal," he said slowly. "Those cutters wouldn't have done anything to the shrouds, but—"

"They could've snipped the steering cable," she supplied. "And?"

He shrugged. "Maybe. One screw in the inspection plate was half-way backed out. How long did he have before you got on deck?"

"Just about long enough," she replied. "Considering he was working in the dark, on a strange boat." She sat on the edge of the big berth, her face inches from his. "You didn't answer my first question. What's going on?"

She knew he was forcing his eyes to meet hers. "I don't know. Honestly."

Part honestly, she decided. *He knows more than he's telling me.* She expected something like his answer, had braced herself for it, but the hurt was far sharper than she was ready for. To hide her face, she pulled the sweat shirt up over her head and turned away from him to toss it onto the built-in bureau. In the mirror she could see he was watching her; his face, unguarded for a moment, was concerned. Well, let him worry.

She slid off the berth, and wriggled out of her jeans. She folded them and the sweat shirt, laid both on the deck beside the berth. His eyes were on her naked body as she turned to face him. Half formed in the back of her mind was the need to punish him, to withhold herself; fighting it was the need to prove she was still desirable—more desirable than whoever or whatever was distracting him.

"Come here," she said at last.

MONDAY

Barr: Groot Baai, 0800

Sometimes when he was afloat—and often when he was at *Glory*'s helm—Barr's consciousness focused down tightly, acutely sensitive to nothing but the forces affecting the boat, blocking out all distractions. So now, balanced lightly behind *Glory*'s inlaid mahogany steering wheel, he was aware of the engine's vibration (a little uneven) coming up through his feet; the rattle of the chain anchor rode, felt and heard, as *Glory*'s electric windlass dragged the links over the bow roller; the pressure of water on the rudder, transmitted up through the steering linkage to the wheel and thence to his fingertips; the building morning breeze, ruffling and snapping the luffing sails.

But had anyone asked, he couldn't have said what day it was, or when he had eaten last, or what he was wearing. Once one of *Glory*'s charterers, a Manhattan psychiatrist, had spent a futile half hour attempting a clinical explanation, only to be interrupted by her lover, a professional musician: "Christ, babe, it's so obvious. He grooves with the boat." It was a talent that Patrick nearly understood and that Gillian recognized and envied.

Patrick, with Gillian on the foredeck, was feeding the incoming chain down into the anchor locker. He looked over his shoulder to the helm, raised his right hand, and Barr took the engine out of gear.

44

Glory coasted slowly ahead, losing speed as momentum alone pulled her twenty-seven tons toward the still-buried anchor.

"How long d'you think it'll take to sail to St.-Bart's?"

Barr started. He had completely forgotten the two people standing behind him in the cockpit. Jake looked terrible in the unforgiving light—looked, in fact, like what he was, a middle-aged man who had barely survived a marathon drinking contest. Barr could sympathize with his physical state, but he had no time for it just now. At Jake's side, Isabel was silent and unmoving, giving off an almost visible aura that was part disapproval, part condescension; in Jake's place, Barr thought, he might just have put her over his knee.

"Couple of hours." Barr heard, a second too late, the annoyance in his own voice; Gillian lectured him often—and with reason—on the need for being minimally polite to the charterers. Making an effort he hoped didn't show, he added, "It'll be good sailing, a close reach, once we're clear of the harbor."

The windlass slowed and labored, then raced as the anchor broke out of the mud and sand. *Glory* was still inching ahead, and Gillian was watching him, her hands on the staysail boom, ready to push it out to starboard and, by backwinding the sail, drive *Glory*'s bow off to port.

Her intent, expectant look told Barr that she thought the vital moment was passing. She cocked an eyebrow for emphasis, but Barr shook his head. She was too eager; she was always too eager. Patrick flung up his left arm to indicate the anchor was clear of the water. Barr nodded, and Gillian threw her hundred-odd pounds against the staysail boom, forcing the sail out to windward. As she did so, Barr eased the helm over; he felt *Glory*'s bow begin to swing through the eye of the wind.

A rattle and thump told him the big plow anchor had seated itself in its roller chock on the bowsprit. As Barr saw Patrick stoop to secure the chain, he switched off the engine.

Releasing the staysail boom, Gillian came bounding back along the side deck and hurtled into the cockpit. She flipped three turns of the staysail sheet around a winch, grasped the line in both hands, and braced her foot against the edge of the cockpit footwell. She was wearing a one-piece bathing suit, and the cutaway back showed every tensed muscle beneath the smoothly tanned skin. "Not yet," said Barr quietly as the bow continued to swing. And when he knew the timing was exactly right: "Now—but *easy*."

Patrick was back in the cockpit, ready with the mainsheet. Moments later *Glory* had slid off onto a reach and began picking up speed in the unobtrusive way that made Barr love her above all other boats he had ever sailed. She slipped past an anchored sloop, no more than an arm's length distant, just as the bleary-eyed skipper stuck his head out the companionway; at his awed "Holy *shit!*" Patrick grinned delightedly. In the year and a half he'd been aboard—the year and a half he'd been sailing—Patrick had come a long way, Barr reflected; the mate's big hands had the helmsman's touch, and he seemed to sense when *Glory* could find her way through the seas and when he had to lead her.

"If we don't tack in about ten seconds," said Gillian calmly, "we're going to be in the Pasanggrahan's dining room."

"Jibing," Barr snapped. He spun the wheel, and the big ketch swung through a tight arc. Patrick and Gillian played out the sheets, and *Glory* steadied up, her bow aimed at the harbor entrance. Yesterday's cruise ships had vanished in the night, and today's crop had not yet appeared. "Want to drive?" he said to Gillian.

As a rule there was no one readier; this morning, though, she shook her head. "You take her, Patrick." Something too even in her voice drew Barr's attention. She was upset, and now that he came to think about it, he realized she'd been upset when she'd rolled out of their berth two hours before.

Patrick stepped to the helm; his sidelong glance, Barr to Gillian and back, said that he'd noted Gillian's tone. As the mate's hands grasped the wheel, Barr released it, saying, "This heading till we clear the point." Patrick liked clear, unequivocal orders, and Barr made a point of obliging him.

Was Gillian still angry about his going ashore last night? He'd thought all was forgiven in the heat of their passion . . . her passion, anyway; he hadn't been completely present, though he thought she hadn't noticed. Wrong again, apparently. Automatically he eased the mizzen sheet six inches.

"Have you sailed down here before, Jake?" Gillian asked. Standing on the cockpit seat, one hand on the mizzen shrouds, she smiled down at their charterer—and, in some way he couldn't define, excluded Barr.

"Never even been here before," Jake said.

Could it have been Deedee? *No*, Barr told himself. That was too silly even to consider. "When we're abreast of the big pier," he said to Patrick, "you can head up to about one twenty-five. Take Île Fourche just to port."

*   *   *

Gaunt, brown, and bare, Île Fourche was sliding past; its rocky spine blocked the boisterous easterly trade wind, and *Glory* had slowed to a genteel lope. "Now that," said Jake, "is my idea of a desert island."

"Something is alive there," said Isabel—the first words she'd spoken in over two hours. Her cheeks still had an unpleasant greenish tinge beneath the normal milk chocolate, but she had won, this time, the clenched-jaw battle with seasickness that began the moment *Glory* lifted to the first trade wind sea.

"Goats," Gillian said. "They eat the cactus. God knows what they drink." A mile ahead of *Glory* rose the abrupt green hills of St.-Bart's, with Gustavia's faded red roofs clustering around the narrow, crowded harbor. She turned to Barr, who was scanning the harbor mouth through binoculars. "What's the plan?"

If she wanted to be cool, he would match it. "The usual," he said. "Round up off Gros Ilets and get the sails down; then motor in and tie up stern-to while you clear us through the port office. Maybe your friends," he said to Jake, "will spot us coming in."

"Maybe," said Jake. "Say, did I hear you right about clearing through some office? Is that really necessary?"

Barr shrugged, but before he could respond, Patrick spoke up. "It's so they can sock us for the port fee. No big deal—Gillian takes care of it."

"It's only a few minutes," Gillian said. "You guys can get a beer in the meantime. Just leave me your passports."

"Passports? What for?" Jake seemed genuinely annoyed.

"They like to fondle them," said Patrick. "It keeps them happy."

"And in our business," said Gillian, "keeping port captains happy is a high priority."

"No sweat," said Jake, but his tone sounded forced to Barr. "Just a goddamn waste of time—and who's going to know, anyway?"

"In Gustavia?" Patrick said. "They know. Take my word for it."

"They check the harbor every day," Gillian explained. "Besides, we need a clearance paper from St.-Bart's to present when we enter the next port."

"Jesus," said Jake, "red tape comes to paradise."

"Well, you know what they call red tape," Gillian said. "Next to cooking, the great French art form."

Off the pair of steep, bare rocks called the Gros Ilets the ancient cruise liner rode at anchor, a cluster of launches at her gangway. *Glory* slid past her narrow stern, where welded-on metal letters that spelled *Trumpington* were clearly visible beneath several layers of white paint and her present name, *Euphoric*, in flaming purple.

"Wasn't she in Philipsburg yesterday?" Patrick asked.

Barr, draped over the main boom with his mouth full of sail ties, nodded. Up close, the old ship spoke to an educated eye of decades of neglect quickly camouflaged by a minimum of paint and putty, though not even a complete overhaul could do much to revive a vessel so out of phase with modern design. Barr wondered how her owners—Greeks for sure, despite the misleading *Monrovia* on her stern—managed to keep her cabins filled.

The outer roadstead, off the point that was topped by the ruins of Fort Oscar, was already speckled with anchored yachts, which meant that the inner harbor would be jammed. As *Glory* motored past the buoys marking the fairway entrance, Patrick stared hard at the uncompromising row of immense yachts lined up hull to hull, sterns to the stone pier, anchor chains stretching out into the narrow channel. He looked sideways at Barr, cleared his throat twice, and finally asked, "You want me to handle the anchor?"

"Yes," said Gillian quickly. Patrick stepped aside, one hand still on the wheel. Gillian looked at Barr, her jaw set, and he knew this was not the moment to tease her.

"I've got the wheel," he said. The breeze was gusting erratically over the low saddle of land between Fort Gustave and the village of Corossol, taking *Glory* mostly on the port quarter. But once she was fully into the slot of the harbor, he saw, the hill behind Fort Gustave would probably bend the wind direction to dead aft—broadside on, when the yacht positioned herself to back into the pier. To make the maneuver more interesting, *Glory*'s stern tended to pull to port with the engine running astern, and as it swung, the high bow would fall away to starboard, away from the wind. A sudden gust, or a sudden lull, or a slight lapse in timing, and *Glory* would find herself lying across half a dozen anchor chains, an object of derision for the whole harbor.

Clearly, Gillian had already worked out the possibilities. "You find us a slot, and I'll run a stern line to the pier with the dinghy," she said.

It was the sane, safe, sensible maneuver, and Barr discarded it without a second thought. "Patrick, get the anchor ready. Don't snub it till I tell you. Gillian, you've got the stern line. For God's sake, toss it to somebody who looks reliable."

"What do you want Isabel and me to do?" Jake asked.

Barr indicated a deck box. "Grab a couple of fenders and stand by on the port side—in case I screw this up."

"If you screw this up, it'll take more than fenders," Gillian muttered, but Barr thought he saw a glint of reluctant admiration in her brown eyes. Aloud, she asked, "Tuck the dinghy under the starboard quarter?"

"Please," Barr replied. And then he saw it, a gap between two grossly fat power yachts just wide enough for *Glory*'s slender beam. On the larger of the two, up forward, a pair of uniformed crew stood gaping down. As they realized what Barr intended, their faces went blank with astonishment.

"Here we go," he said to no one in particular, putting the wheel hard over and, as he did so, slamming the engine into full reverse. *Glory* swung sharply to starboard, still moving ahead, but slowing as the reversing propeller began to bite. He was already spinning the wheel in the other direction when he called, "Patrick, now."

As *Glory*'s forward motion stopped and she began to slide astern, the anchor went over, so smoothly Barr felt only the vibration of the chain. Up on the big power yacht's bow, the two crewmen had been joined by a bearded officer in whites. All three of them were waving frantically, shouting, "*Non! Non! Non!*" down at *Glory*.

The ketch was moving straight astern, aimed precisely for the narrow opening between the two high hulls, but angled downwind. Just as it seemed certain that *Glory*'s transom would grind itself to matchwood against the steel hull on her port side, her stern began to swing away, dragged by the propeller's torque.

Barr spared a quick glance to where Gillian stood poised on the starboard quarter, holding the stern line coiled to throw. She saw his look and sang out, her clear voice cutting through the noises of the port, "You without the hat, take a line, please?"

Barr jammed the gear lever into forward and gunned the engine. "Now," he said to Gillian. As *Glory* lay for an instand dead in the water, the line sailed in an arc toward the pier, where a grizzled, deeply tanned man in shorts and undershirt fielded it with assurance and dropped a hitch over the nearest bollard. Barr took the engine out of gear. "Tie it off," he said to Gillian, and nodded to Patrick, who triggered the electric windlass that would bed the seventy-five pound plow anchor securely into the harbor bottom.

Only then did he spare a look upward to where the three uniformed sailors stood in a frozen, gaping row. The officer recovered first. Rolling his eyes to heaven, he gave a majestic shrug, turned on his heel, and stalked away.

Two bewildered American skippers were ahead of Gillian in the small, cluttered fort office. The table was awash with clearance papers, registration forms, crew passports; the two sets of documents were hopelessly mingled, and the young French port official, cool and crisp in his white uniform, was making the most of the delightful opportunity to bait the pair. As Gillian opened the door to enter, the American voices had already begun to rise.

Barr took Jake's arm. "This may be a little longer than usual. Where were you going to meet your friends?"

Jake fumbled in his shirt pocket and produced the note. "Is there a bar or something called the Select around here?"

"Le Select," Patrick put in. "Big yachties' hangout. Right around the corner."

"Great. I'll buy us all a drink." He grinned at Isabel, who regarded him coldly. "You, too, *chiquita*."

Patrick looked at Barr, who said, "Go on ahead. I'll bring Gillian."

He watched the three of them walk arm in arm along the pier, Isabel between the two men. She was looking up at Patrick, Barr saw. Or away from Jake. When they rounded the corner, he sauntered over toward the pierhead, drawn by the sight of a smart-looking little sloop moored in the public anchorage. Before he had taken three steps, however, a high-sided ship's motor lifeboat, painted bright orange, coughed asthmatically up to the stone pier. Its stern carried the roughly stenciled name *Euphoric*, and its complement was clearly some of the liner's passengers—loudly conversational older women, for the most part, wearing slacks and determined shoes, festooned with cameras and canvas shopping bags. The men who accompanied them seemed built on a smaller scale, Barr thought—or maybe they had just shrunk over time.

A hand fell on his elbow. He turned; it was Gillian, looking puzzled and, he thought, worried. "Where'd the others go?" she asked.

"Jake's meeting the rest of his party at Le Select. D'you want to walk over?"

She wrinkled her nose in distaste. "Loud rock music and the smell of stale beer at ten in the morning? No, thanks. Besides"—she lowered her voice—"we need to talk. Alone."

"You're right," he said, the decision making itself. Then, as he saw her expression: "What's up?"

"It's Jake." Her eyes panned across the chattering crowd on the pier before she continued. "Look, when I was in the port office just now, I handed over everybody's passport, same as usual. You know how it goes. They just check to make sure the name's the same as the one on the crew list?"

Barr nodded, wondering what was coming next.

"Well, the guy behind the desk opens up Jake's, and he reads every single page—every single damn rubber stamp—and then says to me, 'Do you know M'sieur Adler well?' " She paused for Barr's response and, getting none, demanded: "I mean, what the hell? Since when do they ask questions like that in Gustavia?"

Since somebody tipped them off about the too-well-known Colonel Adler, Barr thought, but he said only, "Was that what you said to the port cop?"

A momentary grin lit her face. "Something like that. He really caught me off guard. Anyway, he went all huffy-puffy: 'Nothing personal, mam'zelle. Always a good idea to know who ze crew is. The captain, he is responsible for everyone aboard.' " She shook her head, as if to clear it. "He was warning me, though. I'm sure of it."

"He wouldn't specify."

"No. The more I pressed, the more he waffled." Her face hardened. "But you know something about this, Barr. And I think it's time you told me what it is."

"What what is?" Jake's voice, from just behind them, was totally unexpected. Barr and Gillian spun around together. Jake's grin was as wide as ever, but Barr saw what might have been suspicion in his deep-set eyes.

"We were just having a little spat," Barr said, and felt Gillian stiffen. "No referee required." He paused. "Something wrong?"

"No," Jake said quickly. "At least I don't think so."

Behind him, Patrick said, "Jake's friends weren't at the Select, but they left him another note."

"They are sight-seeing," Isabel put in. She was standing next to Patrick, her arm through his. "We are to meet them at six."

"Is that a problem?" Gillian asked Jake.

"No, no. Inconsiderate, though—I apologize." Barr, with more than an inkling of what might be running through Jake's mind, was impressed at how well he concealed his emotions.

"It is just like Mookie," said Isabel. "He is never where people expect him."

"Well," said Gillian, "it's understandable. St.-Bart's is a beguiling island. In fact"—as if the thought had just occurred to her—"why don't we just let it beguile you?"

"What?" said Isabel, looking puzzled.

"Why don't you and Isabel and Patrick rent a car, and he'll show you the sights?" Gillian explained. "After all, it's your vacation, too."

"That's right," Jake said, looking hard at Isabel. "It's our vacation. But the three of you will be our guests."

Patrick: Anse des Flamandes, 5:00 P.M.

Isabel, who had been lying silently on her back on the sand, sat up in a single, liquid motion. "One thing I am curious to know," she said to Patrick, propped on his side next to her.

He dragged his attention from the woman standing thirty yards away, hip-deep in the azure water. She was binding her long blond hair (bleached, and not all that well) in a loose knot, and her movements made her full, bare breasts move invitingly. Patrick groped for Isabel's words. "What was that?" he asked, rolling over on his belly.

The other three had deposited Patrick and Isabel—abandoned them, almost—on the nearly empty beach some three hours earlier, but he hadn't minded. Barr and Gillian were on edge with each other, and the last place Patrick wanted to be was between them. There was something wrong with Jake and Isabel, too, though he didn't know them well enough to guess what it might be. And Patrick himself felt borderline terrible. He hadn't drunk so much in years, and the beer had combined with the satay to produce a kind of dull smolder just under his rib cage.

Isabel, on the other hand, seemed untouched, though, of course, she'd drunk hardly anything. Even so, she hadn't smiled much since the two of them had been alone, and when she tried—in response to Patrick's efforts—it hadn't looked real. But now, all of a sudden, that exotic face of hers looked as if it had the shadow of a grin. "You like her tits," she said. It wasn't a question.

"Well, yes," he said. "Yes, I do."

"They are pretty great," she allowed, almost deadpan but not, he thought, absolutely. "Voom-voom-voom every time she moves."

"True," he said. "Definitely triple voom."

"Triple voom now," she said. "But they are not for the long lift."

"Say again?"

Her eyes widened. "That's not right, 'the long lift'?"

"I hope not," he replied. She was playing with him, he decided. And he was enjoying it. A second after he spoke, he made the translation: "The long *haul?*"

Her face cleared like a sunrise. "*Sí,* that's what it was: *long haul.*" And under her breath: "Goddamn idioms."

"I see what you mean," said Patrick reluctantly. "Ten years from now—"

"Five."

"Well . . ."

"Down to her belly," Isabel said. "Unless she has the operation. You know—" Her long thumbs made a quick, incisive gesture below her own high breasts. She was wearing a plain black tank suit that covered but scarcely concealed. The breadth of her shoulders made her breasts look smaller than they really were, and her hips seemed wider, because her waist was so tiny. It was anything but an ideal figure, and the way she carried herself told the world she didn't give a damn.

By God, she's making a pass at me. He had no doubts, even with his perceptions blurred by last night's beer. The opening moves were too familiar to miss, and so was the dumb-stud role she'd apparently picked for him. Patrick often found himself playing the same part in the vacation fantasies of *Glory's* female customers, and he'd been able to laugh about it for quite a while. Lately, though, he'd found being Mr. Beefcake less and less funny. Still, it was easier to go along; all he had to do was flex his muscles and be agreeable, and he could do that with half his mind on something else.

She was watching him, waiting for his reaction, but he couldn't retrieve what she'd said. Not that it mattered. The music was what you followed, not the words. He gave her his best not-too-bright grin.

"I embarrass you?" she asked. He was almost sure he saw the corners of her mouth twitch.

Well, you sure are trying, he thought. He asked, "What was it you wanted to know before we got sidetracked on tits?" he asked.

"Oh, that." She seemed to be groping, but he had his doubts. "Yes, I wanted to ask why you became a cook on a sailboat. It is a big change from being a soldier." And not a change for the better, her tone was saying.

"I spent a lot of time on boats when I was a kid—a small boy," he began.

"I know '*kid,*' " she said quickly.

"Of course. Your English is very good."

"My English is—what's the word?—from a school book. I learned myself, in Cuba."

"Cuba?"

She shook him off. "Later we talk about me. So you were a lot on boats when you were a kid, but you went in the Army, not the Navy."

This wasn't following the usual script at all. It sounded as if she really wanted to know. But what surprised him more was his own impulse to spill the whole story. Instead, he said, "I guess I didn't think of it at the time." That was a lie. In the depth of panic he'd figured that the Navy or the Coast Guard was just where they'd look for him: Joanie's father the cop, and his buddies

Isabel was looking at him hard, as if she was unexpectedly seeing him as a real person. "Not a good memory," she said. "It's better if you don't stir it up." The challenge was plain in her voice, all the same. Challenge and maybe just a shade of the triple-proof contempt that some women could use like a scalpel. Or was he imagining that part?

"You're right," he said, not sure if he meant she was right it was a bad memory—true enough—or right about not stirring it up. Too late to worry about that, anyway. He suddenly realized that he hadn't talked seriously with anybody, not even Barr or Gillian, in a long, long time. He'd almost forgotten how, but the way he felt, the need must've been building inside him, till now it was ready to explode.

"Then how you got in the Army is not something you are proud of," she said slowly.

"That's for sure," he heard himself say, with a laugh that came out all wrong. He could feel himself being weighed, appraised. This was not the hot-blooded bimbo he'd arranged his head for; he wasn't at all sure he liked the new Isabel, but something about her was drawing him on. Correction: something about the way she seemed to be taking him seriously was almost irresistible.

He was still searching for words when she tired of the silence. "Okay," she said, and lay back on the sand.

"Anyway, it was a long time ago," he said, unwilling to break off but unable to take the plunge into confession.

"No matter," she said, and managed to convey in the one word that she was still listening but wasn't going to make it easier.

Christ, I can't let this fade away. "I was running away," he blurted out.

"Lots of men are," she said, sounding unimpressed. But she had risen on one elbow and was watching him. "Running away, running toward—it's the same thing."

"No, this was for real," he insisted. "I was on the run."

"Police?"

"Not exactly," he said. "I mean, I didn't hold up a bank or anything. It's hard to explain." But he wanted to, desperately.

"I won't tell Jake"—she pronounced it 'Jek'—"if that is what worries you."

It hadn't even occurred to him. "No, it's mostly because I acted like such a gutless shit."

She leaned forward until her face was no more than a foot from his. He felt as if he might fall right into her eyes and drown there. "Look," she said, "nothing you have done is half as bad as the thing I live with."

"That's ridiculous," he said.

"How can you say? You don't know me at all."

She was right, of course, but he knew in that instant there was no one on earth he wanted to know more. "Can you tell me, then?" he said.

"If you don't tell Jake."

For only a moment he thought she was joking. "Of course not."

She took a deep breath, looking past him, and then began. "Like I said, I'm a *cubana*." She hadn't exactly, but he nodded. "I am what we call a child of the revolution. Without Fidel, I would be burning charcoal in Oriente, with six kids hanging on me."

It was a story Patrick had heard before. "I know," he said gently.

"No, you don'," she replied, annoyance slurring the word. "My generation owes him everything. Everything. Because of him, we could fight you *yanquis* to a stop."

She waited, her eyes blazing, for him to contradict her.

"And you did," he said.

"We had no choice. Win or die. Or worse. I have heard Americans—Jake's friends—talk about Havana in 'the good old days.' You know what they would make me if those good old days came back? A whore. Spreading my legs for gamblers, for the U.S. Navy, for yachtsmen from Miami. Maybe for you, Patrick O'Mara."

"No," he said, with absolute certainty. "Not you."

"Sí." Her expression softened just slightly. "I see you do understand, a little."

In Patrick's platoon at Fort Bragg there had been two Cuban NCOs, older than he was, but a stripe below him. He'd learned a lot from them, including what Isabel was going to say next. "After a while," Patrick said before she could speak, "it started to come apart. The revolution."

She closed her mouth slowly. Nodded. "We wanted to make paradise, and we thought socialism would do it. Why not? We could already see what capitalism led to." She pursed her lips. "It's a very bad system, capitalism. But—"

"The others are all worse?"

She managed a faint imitation of her glorious smile. "Something like that. Do I sound like a schoolteacher?"

"Maybe a little."

"That's what I was, when I met Ernesto. He was older, also a teacher, and from a very fine family. Not oppressors, but the government took everything from them anyway. They were too old to run, but they wanted their son to live in freedom. They also thought"—a tight smile—"that if he went to the States, he would get away from me."

"Away from you?"

"Because I was a *campesina*. And a Negro. My mother's parents were from Haiti—very dark." She shrugged it off. "Ernesto didn't care. I think my color excited him."

Patrick realized with surprise that he hadn't noticed Isabel's skin all day. No, that was wrong. He'd never stopped noticing, but not in terms of race. Right now, as the afternoon sun gleamed off the smooth, oiled surface, his first thought was that she'd taste like nutmeg. Not her mouth, though; he hadn't decided what her mouth would taste like.

". . . Decided to escape," she was saying. "We had no boat, of course, and we could never have got a *permiso*."

"Because of Ernesto's parents, you mean."

"*Sí.* So we did what others have done. We built a raft, from car wheels."

Inner tubes, she meant. Cross the Gulf Stream hanging on to six old inner tubes lashed together or riding a couple of homemade crates. It was pure crazy, but Patrick had seen the photographs—of survivors' rafts. Nobody knew how many didn't make it. "What happened?" he asked.

"At first it was easier than we thought. Ernesto paid the captain of a fishing boat to take us into . . . what do you call it?"

"The Gulf Stream?"

"I think so. The current would carry us north, into the Strait of Florida, where someone would find us."

Someone would find us. A raft like the one Isabel was talking about might be seen a quarter of a mile away. At the most, in broad daylight, and by someone with good binoculars who was looking for it. Even then the chances were that a lookout would take it for some piece of floating junk.

"I know what you are thinking," she said. "We had no other chance. None at all." She was sitting hunched up in a sort of knot, her chin on her raised knees, and her arms locked around her legs.

"It's okay," he said. He could see the ending now; only the details were missing. "You don't have to tell me the rest."

"Yes, I do," she said, looking right through him. "The fishing boat captain betrayed us. He cut us loose only two miles from the shore. We drifted for three days, in sight of land, and then the storm came."

"It tore the raft apart," Patrick said.

"Partly. And some of our water was lost. After that we just drifted and drifted. Ernesto made me stay on the raft, and he floated next to it, holding on. He gave me water, until . . ." She shook her head, unable to continue.

Patrick put his arm around her, but it was like embracing a trapped animal. "What was it?" he asked. "Sharks?"

"No," she whispered, barely loud enough to be heard over the baby surf a few yards away. "No, it was the thirst. He gave the water to me and kept none for himself. So he died."

"He was very brave," said Patrick. *Understatement of the year.* "But what did you do that was wrong?"

"I took it. Don't you see? I knew he was giving it all to me, and I let him."

"But—"

"Never mind," she said, her voice level again. "It's done, and I live with it." She turned to face him, an expression that could only be amazement spreading across her tear-stained face.

"What is it?" he asked.

"I never told that to anybody before," she said, shaking her head.

"Not even Jake?"

"Especially not him," she said absently. "I can't believe I said those things to a man"—she forced a watery smile—"to a man I only met."

"Happens all the time," Patrick said. "On a cruising boat, you're . . . it's kind of like being outside the real world. Life speeds up. You find yourself saying things you'd never say ashore. To people you only just met."

"But we *are* ashore," she said. "Or does this strangeness include beaches, too?"

He grinned at her. "Absolutely," he said. "As long as you get to them from a boat, beaches come under the rule."

"What about you?" She sounded, just for the moment, about twelve years old. "Does the same thing happen to you?"

He replied, "All the time," though he knew that wasn't what she was really asking. This was not a moment that would vanish painlessly, but he owed her a piece of himself.

Patrick gave her shoulder a squeeze and felt her body respond— just barely and just for a moment. "You think you did something bad to one person," he said. "I know I did something bad to two . . . And one was my own kid."

She said nothing, but he could feel her waiting. And then it was all pouring out, just like last night, only cold sober: about how he'd got Joanie pregnant their last year in high school, and she was going to keep the baby—and didn't care if he married her or not. "I didn't want to get hitched, didn't want to be tied down—for sure, not by a kid. I lost my head," he said. "Ran like a rabbit. Her father was a cop; so were her uncles. I just knew they'd kill me if they found out."

"So you hid yourself in the Army."

"Not the first, probably not the last," he said. "Took awhile before I found out nobody back home even cared."

"That you had bugged out?"

It was a piece of slang he hadn't heard since Salvador, and he turned to her. She was smiling up at him, her eyes warm. "What's so funny?" he demanded.

"You. Do you wan' me to tell you what you did next?" Every once in a while she would drop a *t* at the end of a word, and for some reason he didn't understand, it made him melt inside.

She turned, inside the curve of his arm, and tapped his bare chest with her forefinger. Her hands were delicate and long-fingered, the nails cut short. "I tell you anyway," she said. "After the baby came— a girl, right?"

"How did you know?"

"Never mind. After your little girl was born, you sent her mother money whenever you could."

He gaped down at her, tried to speak, but she laid her finger across his lips. "Shut up," she said. "I bet the mother wouldn't take it at first, but now she does." He nodded, spellbound. "An' she made you promise something—what? That you would stay away from them?"

"She wanted to make a life for them," he said. "And she found a guy—"

"Of course she did," said Isabel.

"A nice guy," Patrick said.

"A wimp," she replied, though it came out "weemp."

It was exactly what Patrick had thought, remembering the man in question, a class behind him and Joanie in Bay Shore High, but he shook his head. "No, he really is a nice guy. And he loves Tracy, the baby."

"Sure," said Isabel. He was suddenly very aware of the smell of her hair, a heavy, musky perfume. And of her breasts, with just a layer of fabric between them and his chest. "She picked a man she could count on, one she could manage." She grinned up at him. "I would have done the same myself in her place."

"What do you mean?"

She drew away a couple of inches, looking up into his face with a half-smile. He could see, through the black nylon, that her nipples were hard. "She had one thing she wanted, don' you see? Your baby."

"But—"

Again she silenced him with her finger, but this time she left it against his lips. "She saw she couldn't hold you, so she got herself another man." Isabel paused. "She is beautiful, of course. She would have no trouble getting a man."

Her body was just barely not touching Patrick's. He felt as if he might explode. He bent his face down to hers, felt her full lips open to meet his. After a long, long minute Isabel pulled slowly back, lips still parted. "She didn't want you around," she said, a little breathless. "Remind her of what she settled for."

He felt as if he'd been slugged with a two-by-four: chest tight, breath coming short and fast. But he heard, in the distance, the throaty roar of a Mini Moke's unmuffled engine. "What is it?" Isabel said.

"They're back. The others." Damn it to hell.

"We talk more later," she said. "And"—picking the thought out of his mind—"I know what you're thinking. Don't worry about Jake."

Patrick rose, his mind spinning, and saw over Isabel's shoulder three men coming across the sand at them. Young, dark-skinned, but not, he thought, West Indian. His first thought was they were thieves, but their set, closed faces told him they were looking for more than a tourist wallet.

"Run," he said to Isabel as he stepped past her. She looked a question, and he snapped, "Don't ask. Get going."

Instead of separating, the three were still bunched, and there seemed to be some hesitation about who was in charge. Baggy trousers and long-sleeved shirts. And city shoes—but no sign of any weapons. Patrick, a veteran of half a hundred beer hall fistfights, and other brawls a lot more serious, knew without thinking about it that he'd be lost if he let the three sort themselves out. His 180 pounds of bone and muscle were moving at a full run when he hit them.

The leader—by default, since the other two had pushed him forward—received Patrick's right shoulder directly in his sternum. Lifted off his feet, he took one of the other two down with him. The third man, who had stepped to the side, produced the kind of long-bladed filleting knife Patrick disliked most. He held it half extended in front of him, serrated edge upward in the approved style, but Patrick sensed no real street-fighting experience behind his stance.

The force of Patrick's charge had carried him to his knees. As he came up, he hurled two handfuls of beach sand directly in the knife wielder's face. The sand fell short, but the man flinched, and Patrick was on him. Down they went, but Patrick's opponent, forty pounds lighter, rolled free, still holding the knife, and scrambled to his feet.

From the corner of his eye, Patrick saw the man he had hit with his shoulder writhing feebly on the ground, out of the fight. The second man was up, though, and the tide had turned. Patrick feinted toward the knife wielder and spun to meet the second man's charge. The man skidded to a halt and, before he had his balance, attempted a karate kick. Patrick grabbed the airborne foot in both hands and lifted it above his head.

As he did so, he heard the crunch of sand at his back. Before he could turn, he felt flame etch its way down his shoulder blade, and his cry of triumph turned abruptly into a grunt of pain. Patrick released the foot he was holding; off-balance, its owner fell backward, and Patrick pounced on him, driving him into the soft sand, both hands around his throat and one knee rammed hard into his groin.

Behind him he heard a barrage of incandescent Spanish, knew it was Isabel, though rage had pushed her voice up half an octave. Patrick rolled off the agonized man beneath him and saw the knife wielder, utter confusion written plain on his face, backing away from the weaponless Isabel, who was stalking him like a tiger, spitting curses as she came.

Now the man saw Patrick, breathing hard and moving more slowly, but with death in his eyes. "*¡Mierda!*" said the man with the knife.

He hurled it at Patrick's head, turned on his heel, and ran, followed by his limping, gasping, doubled-over companions.

Patrick managed one lurching step in pursuit, but Isabel, still spitting Spanish curses, had him by the shoulder. He could feel something hot and wet running down his bare skin, and he was only too glad to let her hold him back.

Gillian: Gustavia, 6:30P.M.

Over Patrick's loud objections, Isabel and Gillian put him facedown on his berth in Glory's narrow, triangular fo'c'sle. With the aid of a sponge and a bowl—Patrick's favorite stainless steel salad bowl—full of warm, soapy water, Isabel detached the blood-crusted shirt that adhered to his back. Gillian was at first slightly annoyed to find herself demoted to scrub nurse—patching the cuts and scrapes and stings picked up by Glory's complement was one of the dozen jobs she'd acquired by default and come to take pride in—but she was quick to recognize in Isabel a level of skill she herself didn't approach, and she watched with a student's appreciation as the other woman gently moistened the fabric just enough to loosen the dried blood, then deftly lifted it away from Patrick's skin.

Behind Gillian, blocking the fo'c'sle doorway and cutting off most of the air circulation, Jake stood fuming, impatience and irritation coming off him like steam. Above, his head and shoulders framed in the open foredeck hatch, Barr watched quietly.

"You got a pair of scissors, shears, something like that?" Isabel asked. "I cut this shirt away, so he doesn't have to roll over."

"No!" Patrick said, his voice slightly muffled by the pillow.

Isabel seemed surprised by his alarmed tone, and Gillian murmured, "It's just that we don't have all that many shirts. Can't you push it up out of the way?"

"Oh, I suppose," said Isabel, sounding annoyed. She eased the bloodstained cloth away from the wound, now barely seeping. It was not nearly as bad as Gillian had feared—three short, individual gashes in a diagonal track down Patrick's right shoulder blade.

"You see," said Isabel, her long, slender forefinger tracing the line, "that *puta*, he strikes downward, so his knife bounce its way down Patrick's scapular—"

"Scapula," said Jake.

"—without doing hardly any real damage. If he stroke"—her brows knitted, and she looked at Gillian—"strook? What's the word?"

"Struck," said Gillian.

"Okay. If he struck from below, the way he should have, he get Patrick right here in the kidneys. Kill him."

"Thanks a lot," Patrick mumbled.

"These probably ought to be stitched up," Isabel went on. "Jake, I got a sewing kit from the hotel in my—"

"Not on your life," Patrick roared, pushing himself up from the mattress with both hands.

"Down, boy. Down." Isabel pressed him back. "You get blood all over your sheet. It's okay. I tape it closed." She half turned to Gillian. "Why don't the rest of you get out of here? Go have a drink or something. I can finish up."

Gillian had opened her mouth to object when she felt Jake's hand on her elbow. "She's right. We're just using up the air." As Gillian let herself be led away, she caught a glimpse of Barr's angular face in the hatchway, looking down on Isabel and her patient with an oddly speculative expression.

In the galley Gillian rinsed out the bowl (trying to recall whether *Glory*'s dinner menu was to include salad). Jake stood with his back to the fo'c'sle doorway, his broad torso nearly filling it, but not so completely that Gillian couldn't see Isabel bend over her patient and kiss his ear with a warmth never taught in first-aid courses.

"What's the matter?" said Jake. "You look like you saw a ghost."

"Nothing," Gillian said firmly, and dropped the salad bowl on the deck. "Shit, now I have to wash it again."

"Don't worry about the damn bowl," Jake said, scooping it up and setting it in the galley sink. "You feel like a little walk?"

"A walk? Where to?"

"That bar. I was supposed to meet my friends there"—he glanced at his watch—"a goddamn hour ago. The way Mookie's been fading on me, I don't want him and the troops wandering off someplace to eat."

Eat. *Dinner!* Who was going to cook dinner with Patrick down? Dinner for six charterers in one of the stratospheric restaurants around Gustavia harbor could scarcely run to less then five hundred dollars. Probably a lot more, if Jake's buddies drank the way he did. Distracted, Gillian found herself being led aft. "What do you need me for?" she asked.

"Only in case there's some kind of mix-up," Jake said. "I don't speak French, not even a word."

It was probably the least she could do, Gillian reflected. And if it kept Jake from seeing his lady friend with her tongue in Patrick's ear, that might be just as well, too. "I'd be delighted," she said.

The tropical evening had draped itself over Gustavia like a hot, damp, clinging sheet. The hideous orange launch from the old cruise ship was wheezing out of the harbor with the last load of chattering passengers, the accents of Long Island and New Jersey cutting through the engine noise like saw blades. *Le tout* Gustavia was in the streets, Gillian saw, circulating slowly from bar to bar before settling in for the evening.

Even from around the corner, the amplified music coming out of Le Select was deafening. The little bar was jammed to the doors with yachties, would-be yachties, and pseudoyachties, all talking at once in half a dozen languages. "The Tower of Babel gone to sea," Gillian yelled.

"Got it," he roared back, his eyes scanning the gaily dressed crowd. "D'you see them?"

"No." He put his heavy shoulder down, forcing his way toward the bar. Some of the customers, especially the younger ones, seemed disposed to block his way, but then they would glance at his face and step from his path. Gillian, towed in his wake by one arm, wondered what it was about the small, nondescript, smoke-filled, shatteringly noisy place that drew so many sailors and decided it could only be the presence of other sailors.

At the bar Jake produced an untidy fistful of the francs he had acquired earlier in the day and waved them at the bartender, who slid over. He ordered a rum and Coke and a glass of the house white wine. When the drinks came, Gillian neatly intercepted the rum and Coke, but Jake didn't even notice. Counting out bill after bill as he spoke, he quickly had the bartender's complete attention.

The massed clacking around them drowned out Jake's question, but Gillian saw the bartender register exaggerated surprise.

Gillian pressed nearer, in time to hear the man say, "They left an hour ago, m'sieur. At least—maybe longer."

"And the man they went with—he had a message from me?" Jake demanded.

The bartender shrugged. "He said from *le colonel*. Is that you, m'sieur?"

Ignoring the question, Jake consulted the balled-up currency in his hand and extracted a hundred-franc note. "Where did this messenger say he would take them?"

"I didn't listen, m'sieur," the bartender said. "I'm not paid to eavesdrop."

Jake apparently heard the same subtext Gillian did. "But somebody mentioned a place, right?"

"Perhaps it was when they were leaving . . ." The bartender, supplicated by a young woman with a moray eel tattooed on her bicep, built a complicated drink that seemed to involve half the bottles at his command, but he never took his eyes off the hundred-franc note, now joined in Jake's hand by its twin.

As he wielded the cocktail shaker, the bartender rolled his eyes to signify deep thought. With a snarl Jake produced a third bill and added it to the first two. "That's my limit," he said. "And I'm in a hurry."

The bartender poured his masterpiece, took the eel woman's money, and made change before coming back to Jake. He leaned across the bar and said, "Île Fourche."

"What?" Jake demanded. "What did you say?"

"That's where the messenger said *le colonel* was waiting: Île Fourche."

"Jake can help with the stern lines," Barr said. "Can you get the anchor up?"

"Of course," Gillian snapped. "It's only pushing a button, for God's sake."

"It's only pushing a button as long as everything works right," he replied, pressing the starter. *Glory's* diesel, still warm, kicked in immediately. Barr turned to Jake, who was poised with the dockline in his hands. "Set?"

Before Jake could reply, Patrick exploded out of the companionway. In the light from the pier his face looked pasty white, but so, Gillian saw, did everyone else's. "What's going on?" he said. "How come we're leaving?"

"Jake can tell you as soon as we're clear," Gillian said. She turned to Barr. "I'll get up to the bow."

"Right."

She darted forward along the side deck, where the high steel hull of the nearest power yacht was close enough to reach out and touch. On *Glory's* foredeck it was almost completely black, but Gillian knew exactly where the power switch for the anchor windlass was. She flipped back its protective cover and tapped the button lightly. Under her feet the electric motor gave a low growl, and the anchor chain, nearly taut, clattered softly as two links came in over the roller.

She felt footsteps behind her. "What's the matter? Don't you trust me?" she said, not looking back.

"Sure I do," said Patrick, but he stayed where he was, just over her shoulder. "If the chain starts to twist, coming in—"he began.

"I'll make sure the twist doesn't go down into the chain locker," she assured him. "You just take it easy, okay? It's not every day you get stabbed in the back. Make the most of it."

"With two beautiful women to wait on me hand and foot?" he said, sounding a little more like himself.

"And one of them can't keep her hands off you," Gillian said.

"Well," Patrick began, but from aft Barr's command—"Go!"—cut him off. She leaned on the windlass switch, and the anchor chain began to rattle in.

"What about the sails?" she asked, when *Glory's* anchor was lashed down and the yacht was pointing down the channel toward the harbor mouth.

"Barr said he's going to motor out to Île Fourche," Patrick said. "We'll anchor there for the night, once we pick up Jake's friends." He paused for a beat. "Say, what—"

"Damned if I know," Gillian replied, staring intently back at the cockpit. Silhouetted against the glitter of harbor lights, Barr was clearly visible at the helm, and he was alone. "Damned if I know," Gillian repeated, "but I plan to find out. Can you stand lookout up here?"

"Sure." With scarcely a trace of effort Patrick got to his feet. "Where you going?"

"To eavesdrop on our guests," she whispered, pointing to the tall, shiny ventilator that took air down to the forward guest cabin. It was a standing joke in the charter fleet that you could have any kind of privacy you liked on a boat as long as you were stone deaf; landlubbers never seemed to realize just how sound carried through thin bulkheads or, in this case, up metal pipes that seemed almost designed for listening. Barr seemed to have perfected some kind of selective hearing, but both Patrick and Gillian had often found themselves listening willy-nilly to their customers.

Jake's halfhearted attempt at a whisper came through the tube clearly. "I said, I feel like some kind of goddamn puppet, like somebody offstage is jerking me around."

Isabel's murmured question was too low for Gillian, holding her breath now, to make out, but she didn't have to.

"The way we're being led on, what else?" Jake said. "The note back in Philipsburg—in Mookie's handwriting, I'm sure of it—well, it was the kind of thing that peanut brain might do. But this morning the message somebody left with the bartender in that dive by the harbor, that felt like a stall to me."

Another murmur from Isabel.

"What else could I do?" Jake's voice was tight with tension and suppressed anger. "Call the man a liar?" Not waiting for a response, he went on. "So this afternoon you and Patrick get jumped, and by the time we're untangled from cops and medics and assorted shitheads, it's an hour past the time we were supposed to rendezvous with Mookie." Jake's angry voice was picking up volume with every vibrating word. "I told you, when I went back to that Select place, they told me Mookie and the others had been and gone. Somebody took them to meet me on Île Fourche—Île Fourche, for chrissake! You saw it when we sailed in here. A desert island. Who told them we were there? How the hell would they get there?"

Isabel began to speak, and Gillian jammed her head against the horn-shaped opening of the ventilator, her hand flat against her other ear. She could hear Isabel plainly now: ". . . about those three who jumped Patrick and me?"

A pause, and Jake spoke, his tone plainly dubious. "You think they were just local thugs, over from St. Martin?"

"Sí. I hear one of them speaking papiamento."

"I didn't know you spoke that gobbledygook."

"I don't. But I know it when I hear it."

Gillian could believe her. Papiamento, a weird Portuguese-Dutch-African blend, was like no other language heard in the West Indies. Blacks from the Dutch island of Curaçao spoke it, mostly among themselves, and it was jobless oil field workers from Curaçao—and Aruba and Bonaire—who were responsible for much of the crime wave that had swept St. Martin in the last couple of years.

But Isabel hadn't said anything about papiamento to the police. Nor had Patrick, who would have recognized it, too. And three assaults in twenty-four hours—if you counted the van running Jake down—was ridiculous. As was robbery at knife point in hoity-toity, upscale St.-Bart's. No question, Gillian thought, she would have to force an explanation from Barr, the explanation he'd seemed on the point of making earlier in the day, before Jake had swept them away.

With Barr in the forefront of her mind, she jumped at hearing his name come up through the ventilator. "As soon as Captain Barr gets us over to this Île Fourche it will clear up," Isabel said. "Once we find Mookie and the troops, we get back on the track."

Patrick was watching her as she took her ear from the vent. She shook her head at him, moved quickly to the open foredeck hatch, and dropped through into the fo'c'sle. As Isabel and Jake came out of the guest cabin, Gillian was standing in the galley, running water into the kettle. "Figured I'd help Patrick out," she said. "Get a head start on dinner, for when your friends come aboard."

Jake eyed her with suspicion, then turned and went aft. Isabel waited till he had vanished, then asked, "So what are we having for dinner? Can I help?"

"No, thanks." Gillian put the kettle on the stove, fired up a burner beneath it.

"You don't have to worry about me and Patrick," said Isabel from behind her.

"Worry? About what?" Gillian asked, stiffening.

Isabel's smile was sardonic. "Lovers and that," she said, and added, "It happens a lot, I bet."

Denial was pointless. "I just don't want any trouble with Jake," Gillian managed.

"No problem," said Isabel. "Jake and I burned out long ago."

"Oh. That's—" She pulled herself up with "nice" on the tip of her tongue, but Isabel wasn't paying attention.

"Yes," she said. "Just like you and Barr."

Patrick: Île Fourche, 8:30 P.M.

As he walked aft along *Glory's* side deck, Patrick flexed his right arm, trying to gauge the still-burning sensation down his back. He was reasonably sure the long muscles over his shoulder blade hadn't been nicked, but as he came abreast of the main shrouds, he reached up, grabbed a lower, and pulled down on it with all the force he could manage.

From the cockpit, where she was standing with Barr, Isabel, and Jake, Gillian called out, "Stop that, you big dope! You'll just mess up another shirt, and one a day is all I wash."

He felt—or thought he did—a warm dampness under the thick bandage Isabel had taped over the cuts. But the pain wasn't nearly as

sharp as it might have been. He swung into the cockpit, careful not
to favor his injured side. "One boat in the harbor," he said to Barr.
"Nobody I can see on the shore, but there's something moving up the
hill."

"Goats," said Gillian, who was holding *Glory*'s big 7 x 50 night
glasses. "Something on four legs anyway."

"Mookie's going to wish he was a goat by the time I get through
with him," Jake muttered.

"We must be nearly invisible, with just the running lights," Gillian
said. "I'll hit the spreader spots. That should bring them running."
She bent over the binnacle and tripped the switch. *Glory*'s foredeck
was bathed in white glare from a pair of floodlights mounted on the
main spreaders, forty feet above the deck. Patrick glanced at his companions, whose faces, harshly lit from above, looked as if they'd been
carved from pale stone, with black pools for eye sockets. They all
looked older than they were, and Isabel seemed suddenly to have aged
ten years. What was she? he wondered. Her body was no more than
thirty—he'd put money on that—but she seemed a lot older somehow.
Maybe growing up in Cuba did that to you, though she didn't have
the beat-up, dried-out look most women in the tropics seemed to get
once they passed twenty-five.

Barr, who was steering blind in the glare from the spreader lights,
headed up into the wind, its cool gusts streaked with warmth from Île
Fourche's still-hot ground.

"I'm not going to anchor," he said. "Patrick, you feel up to taking
the dinghy in?"

Patrick's "Sure" was seconded by Jake's "I'll come, too."

With six in the inflatable, plus four people's gear, it was going to
be a tight squeeze, but when Patrick caught Barr's eye, the skipper
only arched his left eyebrow and pursed his thin lips, an expression
that Patrick had learned meant "Yes, it's dumb, but do it."

Glory was dead in the water, her idling engine blanketed by the
noises of wind and wave. But no sound came from people on the
shore. "Hit the horn," said Gillian.

"Hold your ears, folks," Patrick replied, pressing the button. *Glory*'s
air horn, mounted on top of the mizzen spreader, unleashed a screech
Barr had once compared with a pig in labor. The awful noise bounced
back at them off Île Fourche's rocky slopes.

"I can't see a damn thing with those lights," Jake complained, and
Gillian, without a word, switched them off. The sudden darkness was

thick as velvet to their blinded eyes. After a couple of minutes Patrick could just make out the ghostly white hull of the anchored boat.

"You don't suppose they're on that sloop?" he said.

"Well, they're certainly not on the shore," said Gillian. "Not unless they've passed out behind a rock someplace."

"There's a light in the sloop's cabin," Patrick said.

"An oil lamp, it looks like," Barr added. He was staring fixedly at the anchored boat, some hundred yards away. After a moment he shook his head slightly.

"Well, let's go check it out," said Jake. "You coming, Patrick?"

Patrick decided, when the dinghy was fifty yards or so away, that something was wrong about the anchored boat's silhouette. He throttled back, trying to figure what it was that looked strange enough to attract his half-trained eye. Barr had seen it; Patrick was sure of that. So why hadn't he said something?

Patrick brought the dinghy slowly alongside, his nerves twanging like guitar strings. *A typical charter bareboat*, he told himself. *Maybe a little small, a little old. Badly furled sail. No anchor light. But that light in the cabin . . .*

"That's funny," said Jake, over the outboard's subdued low-throttle chatter. "The windows are open."

No. The main cabin ports weren't made to open at all, and the glass in them was just gone. Patrick tied the dinghy off to the sloop's stern cleat and pulled himself aboard, feeling the bandage on his shoulder tear loose. Without his exactly knowing why, his hand went to the rigging knife in its leather sheath on his hip.

"What's wrong?" said Jake, sprawling his way awkwardly over the transom. "Smell that?"

"Smoke," Patrick said, but it wasn't what he meant.

"Cordite," Jake corrected, his voice tight.

"Anybody aboard?" Patrick called. He didn't expect an answer, but the knife was ready, just in case. He could see a faint gleam of light between two warped hatch slides in the companionway. Taking a step forward, he pushed the main hatch open. "Jesus Christ," he said softly. "Oh, God."

The four men were sitting two and two on the settees at opposite sides of the cabin. Between them was a blackened, gaping hole in the wood floorboards, down to the raw fiber glass that covered the keel. Charred splinters of the table that had filled the space were driven into the bulkheads, the overhead, the bloodied faces of the four men. But

it was the blast that had killed them—ripped open the bellies of the
two farther aft and neatly disemboweled the other pair. In the closeness
of the cabin, Patrick could smell blood and excrement and diesel oil
under the familiar, sharp odor of explosive.

Beside him, Jake was tugging at the jammed hatch slides, cursing
under his breath. Patrick pushed him aside, braced himself, and kicked
the boards out of the twisted track that held them. He went down the
companionway ladder a careful step at a time; one of its risers had
been torn off by the blast.

In the flickering light of a bulkhead-mounted oil lamp, he saw that
the biggest of the four men was black, the other three white. All four
were young and muscular, and all were wearing khaki slacks and
Hawaiian shirts, like Jake's. He turned to Jake, and saw the answer to
his question in the older man's iron face. "Your friends," Patrick said
softly.

Jake nodded. He stepped past Patrick, pulled the nearest man gently
away from the seat.

"It's no good," Patrick said.

"I know," Jake replied, his hand in the dead man's hip pocket.
"Wallet's gone," he added. "Check those two, would you?"

It was years since he'd had to do this kind of thing. He took a deep
breath and bent over the nearest man, then straightened up quickly.
"Hey, we shouldn't be doing this. The cops—"

"Fuck the cops," said Jake, not unkindly.

Patrick closed the knife and stuck it back in its sheath. He patted
the hip of the corpse nearest to him. A blond, like himself, with a
lantern jaw and wide, accusing blue eyes. No wallet, no passport. He
stepped carefully over the man's mangled legs, sprawled obscenely
apart. There'd been a time, not so long ago, when he'd been able to
stare down a sight like this and not even feel it. No, that was a lie,
not feel it until he fell asleep and woke up yelling.

The other man, he saw, had no midsection left, not in any real
sense. His head was thrown backward so that it rested on the settee
back, staring upward at the torn and blackened cabin roof. The boat
rolled slightly, and the dead man fell forward. Without thinking,
Patrick caught him under the thick, powerful arms. The right bicep
was tattooed, in neat dark blue type, "Death Before Dishonor." The
letters formed a circle, with a skull at the center.

Patrick felt the breath lock in his throat. Still holding the burly torso,
he turned to Jake, who was watching him silently. Jake nodded yes.

The dead man's head had fallen forward, so that all Patrick could see was crew-cut brown hair. And one cauliflowered ear.

I gave him that, Patrick thought. *In a crummy Salvador bar called La Encantada: A straight right and a taped roll of quarters in my fist for the weight.* Gently he eased the corpse back on the settee, tipped up its head. "It's him," he heard himself whisper. "It's Mookie."

"It was," Jake said. He straightened up. "All their wallets are gone. Luggage, too."

Jake's icy tone cut through the fog in Patrick's brain. "Robbed?" he said slowly.

"Don't be stupid," Jake said. "How would you sink this boat?"

"Sink it? Why?"

Jake grabbed him by the shoulders. "Don't worry why, Sergeant. Just tell me. Now."

Patrick straightened, trying to form some kind of thought that didn't have a dead man named Mookie in it. "Head compartment. Just pull the toilet hoses off the seacocks."

"Can you do it, O'Mara?"

Patrick's "Yessir" was automatic, ingrained by seven years of service in two very different armies. Shock had stunned him, but trained obedience cut through the blur of shock, pointed a path of action that required no thought. And right now coherent thought was beyond him.

"Then go to it, Sergeant."

"Sir." It was better not to look down as you stepped over a leg that wasn't attached to anything, move forward to the compact toilet-cum-shower. Dropping to his knees, he opened the locker beneath the sink, located the intake seacock and the larger exhaust hose. With quick, sure movements he snapped open his knife and used the blade as a screwdriver to back off the doubled clamps that held each hose tightly over its seacock. Two hard tugs, and the hoses came free.

"Done?" It was Jake. The colonel. Standing in the doorway.

"Just turn the handles, sir, and she'll flood. Take about an hour, maybe a little more."

"Do it, Sergeant."

The water—surprisingly cold—burst from the opened seacock in a solid stream, hitting Patrick in the chest with enough force to knock him backward. And to snap him out of the shock that gripped him. "Sir," he said to Jake, "we can't do this."

Jake grabbed Patrick's arm and hauled him to his feet. The water was already over the head compartment shower pan, but there was plenty of time to save the yacht. "Son, I can't explain, but it's absolutely vital that we sink this boat and get the hell out of here." Jake's deep eyes fixed Patrick's. "You've simply got to trust me, soldier to soldier. I'm on an official assignment—top secret—and I need your help. Desperately."

As Jake spoke, he was walking Patrick back into the main cabin. Three of the dead men stared at Patrick; Mookie's head had fallen forward again, for which Patrick thanked the God in whom he only rarely believed.

"Time to go, Sergeant," Jake was saying. "I'll explain it all to you when we're back on *Glory*. Right now we've got to get clear of here."

"Yes, sir," Patrick replied. It was the easiest thing to say. It always had been.

Barr: 9:00 P.M.

"They're coming back," said Gillian, focusing the binoculars. "Just the two of them."

"Yes," Barr said. He could hear that Patrick had the outboard opened up all the way, and the premonition of trouble he had felt since *Glory* entered the little harbor was now overwhelming.

"Gillian, take the helm, please. Keep her as she is."

She had learned early on that when Barr said "please," he meant "Do it now and argue later." As she stepped behind the wheel, he tore off the sail ties holding the mizzen and threw his weight on the halyard.

"Isabel," he said, hauling hand over hand as he spoke, "would you . . . give Jake and Patrick . . . a hand . . . getting back aboard."

She gave him a long, appraising stare but moved over to stand by the lifeline gate. Patrick brought the dinghy alongside with a roar, reversing the engine at the last moment. Barr cleated off the mizzen halyard and started forward.

As Jake scrambled clumsily through the lifelines, he yelled, "We've got to get out of here!"

"That's what we're doing," Barr snapped. "Jake, get the mainsail ties off, please. Toss them in the cockpit. Isabel, would you help him?"

Patrick was crawling up over the gunwale, the dinghy painter between his teeth. He moved like an old man, and Barr dropped to one knee beside him. "What happened?"

Patrick turned his head slowly, spit out the light line. In the faint light from the binnacle he looked like death itself. "It was Mookie," he whispered. "He was . . ." He shook his head, unable to continue.

Barr picked up the dinghy painter. Automatically he glanced down into the inflatable to make sure the outboard was safely tilted out of the water, then cleated off the line. He turned to Gillian, who was watching him intently. "I'm going to raise the main. Soon as it's up, start heading out. Nice wide turn to port."

Her eyes told him she was bursting with curiosity, but she said only, "Wide turn to port, aye. Back to St.-Bart's?"

"Christ, no!" said Jake, stumbling into the cockpit. "Anyplace but there."

So it had been a trap after all, Barr thought. And a bloody one, to judge by Patrick. Gillian was looking to him for orders, her face an obedient blank. He wanted to comfort her somehow, but instead he said, "Head off for a reach. About one-fifty should do it."

"One-fifty it is."

"When you're on course, you might kill the engine."

"Right," she said.

He raised the main, trimmed it and the mizzen, stealing looks at Patrick as he did so. The mate was sitting on the deck, one arm through the lifelines, staring back at the dim shape of the anchored boat behind them. Barr followed his gaze, turned to Jake. "That sloop's sinking."

Jake regarded him coolly. "I sure hope so."

"You've got a lot of explaining to do," Gillian said, "I don't know that we ought to go anyplace until you do it." Barr recognized the rising tide of stubbornness in her tone, wondered if Jake did, too.

Their passenger drew in a deep breath, and for a moment Barr thought he might make the mistake of putting on some sort of parade ground performance, but his voice, when he spoke, was mild. "Gillian, I really think it'd be a wise idea to get the hell out of here. Now."

Barr's mind was racing. If Jake had been set up at Île Fourche, the St.-Bart's cops would probably be appearing in the anchorage at any moment. Discovery meant that Jake's crazy scheme would go up in smoke, and Tarleton would still be on *Glory*'s back. Worse, the gendarmes might impound *Glory* or tangle her in some French bureaucratic snarl. "Patrick," Barr called, "set the big jib."

Barr had to repeat his order before Patrick pulled himself slowly to his feet. "Barr," said Gillian, "are you sure Patrick—"

"He's better off with something to keep him busy," said Jake, voicing Barr's own thought.

"What did you do to him back there?" Gillian demanded.

"It's a complicated story," Jake replied. Suddenly he sounded to Barr near exhaustion.

"Then you'd better get started telling it," said Gillian. "As soon as Patrick has the jib set."

"And that's the whole situation," said Jake. "Everything." He sat back in the cockpit and regarded his audience with what might have been expectation. *Maybe he thinks he's snowed us,* Barr thought. In the binnacle's reddish glow Gillian had a wide-eyed, innocent stare that took five years off her age; only someone who knew her the way Barr did would realize that she was simply shaking down her impressions—"packing the disk," in her words—and had not yet come to any conclusion at all. Patrick was clearly stunned, his mouth half open, though it was probably due more to shock and exhaustion than Jake's narrative. And Barr himself, standing behind *Glory's* wheel with the compass light hitting his bony jaw from below, probably looked only like an aging sailor up past his bedtime—close enough to the truth.

Barr had to admit that Jake's performance was masterly, though, especially in view of what he himself already knew. The story was essentially similar to what Tarleton had told Barr back in the Philipsburg restaurant, twenty-four hours—it felt like twenty-four months—ago. Only the players' motives had been changed, Barr reflected. And that made all the difference.

To replace the mob of wackos and grifters with whom Tarleton had staffed the Ethan Allen Society, Jake trotted out an organized, thoughtful, concerned group of mostly senior active-duty officers from all the military services, assisted by a handful of dedicated, volunteer freedom lovers like Isabel Machado (who, standing just behind Jake, preserved an absolute poker face through the whole recitation).

In the Gospel According to Jake, the Ethan Allens, far from looking for trouble to cash in on, existed only to check out the concerns of the administration ("our own elected representatives, after all") in certain specialized areas where regular intelligence was somehow inadequate.

"I'm not running down the CIA, mind you," said Jake firmly. "A fine, able body of men—and"—looking quickly at Gillian—"women, of course. But . . ." Jake managed to load the three-letter word with a whole world of mal-, non-, and misfeasance, then let it hang accusingly undefined.

"Okay," said Gillian. "Say we take it as read that you're the good guys. Why are you down here? Or, to put it bluntly, who in D.C. gives a damn what happens in the Leeward Islands?"

"Oh, Washington gives a damn," Jake admonished her. "Washington is deeply concerned. Problem is that we're working on rumor in this case. That's why my—my team was sent." He sketched a twisted smile. "Seems as if rumor was correct this time."

"About that rumor . . ." said Gillian, whose hostility seemed to have backed off perhaps half a notch.

"It might be dangerous for you to know too much."

"It already is dangerous," Gillian corrected him. "May as well be hanged for a sheep as a ram."

Jake stared hard at her for a second, turned to Isabel. "What do you think?"

The light in the cockpit was minimal, but to Barr Isabel's expression looked like icy loathing. "Tell them," she said.

"Well, all right." The rumors that had reached Washington, Jake said (and how Washington? Barr wondered), spoke of an invasion or a coup—maybe one following the other—on the island nation of St. Philip, south of St.-Bart's, north and west of Antigua.

"St. Philip?" Gillian burst out. "Who'd even want St. Philip? And for what?"

"I don't know," said Jake. "But that's—"

"I mean," she went on, ignoring him, "St. Philip's dead broke. They don't grow anything. Since Hurricane Hugo they haven't even got a usable pier, much less a harbor. Nobody goes there. Invade it? You could buy the whole place for a handful of peanuts and still have the shells for change."

"As I was saying," Jake replied smoothly, "the whys are secondary. My primary assignment is to find out what's happening and who's behind it. By then I'd bet you'll have all the why you need."

"St. Philip, for God's sake," Gillian said. "It's hard to believe."

Without shifting gears, Jake suddenly became all soldier. "Gillian, there's four brave men back at Île Fourche who'd believe it if they were still alive."

Not the right way to talk to her, Barr thought, feeling her bristle from three feet away.

"That may be," she replied evenly, and then canceled any concession her words might have suggested. "And it may not. All I can be reasonably sure of is that you've put my boat—and my crew—in a hell of a questionable spot. Running away might have been a big mistake. What if they can connect us to . . ." Her words trailed off.

"Nobody saw us," said Jake. "There's no proof."

"Just the same—" Gillian began.

"French cops," Barr put in. "French *colonial* cops. Running's a risk, but trying to play footsie with the Code Napoléon would be a lot riskier."

"Okay," said Gillian reluctantly. "But damn it," she burst out at Jake, "why didn't your bosses in Washington use one of those billion-dollar spy satellites? Fly over a Blackbird, or whatever they're using these days? Your operation seems pretty primitive to me."

"Sometimes primitive is what's called for," said Jake. "Intergalactic hardware's all very well in its place. Wonderful stuff. Reads a license plate from twenty miles up. But when it comes to a heavily forested, unbuilt place like St. Philip, the eye in the sky can't see the forest for the leaves." He hesitated. "We found that in Grenada, didn't we, Captain Barr?"

"If you say so, Jake," Barr replied. "I wouldn't know about that." But Jake obviously did—so Tarleton's information was proving out again. And now that Barr knew what the Ethan Allen's target was, the next job was to get Jake and Isabel off *Glory*, let them get themselves killed someplace else.

"Seems to me," Gillian was saying, "that what you ought to do is send for the Marines. I mean, you've got real proof something's going on. Now you need some muscle."

"I wish we could," said Jake, the voice of sweet reason. "Nobody wishes it more. But we can't just call in a strike, much as it might be justified. The Caribbean's a tricky place, politically speaking. The British have a big stake in it; so do the French. And, in this case, the Dutch."

"St. Philip sent the Dutch home," Gillian said. "Ten years ago. It's an independent nation now."

Her facts were right enough, Barr thought, but in practical terms she was dead wrong. The colonial past—or European qualms about the colonial past—threw a long shadow over the new island nations. Some of the Philipians still held Dutch citizenship; and there were Dutchmen back in the Netherlands who owned property on the island.

"Who governs St. Philip isn't the point," Jake said. "The U.S. can't just waltz in and throw its weight around again. We got away with it in Grenada, but we had those American students we could rescue. In St. Philip we don't have that overt excuse. That's why we have to run an undercover recon like this one."

"Undercover?" Gillian's laugh had no amusement in it. "Your operation's about as secret as the location of Yankee Stadium. Is there anybody left in the Caribbean who doesn't know what you're here for?"

"Or," Barr put in, "that you're on our boat."

"That's right," said Gillian. "Jake, you may be on the side of the angels, but I haven't heard any reason for me to risk *Glory* and my crew—"

"Four dead American soldiers is no reason?" snapped Isabel. "I thought I saw big American flag on this boat today. Maybe I was wrong."

"Mookie," said a voice Barr barely recognized as Patrick's. "You knew we were buddies, didn't you—*Colonel* Adler?"

"That wasn't why I included him," said Jake quietly. "You're right. I knew you two served together once. But I didn't bring him to put the arm on you."

"How'm I supposed to believe that?" Bitterness and anguish rasped Patrick's tone.

"It is true," said Isabel. "Mookie volunteered for the mission before Jake told him you were on this boat."

"I don't know . . ." Patrick sounded uncertain.

"Sure, he wanted to see 'my ol' buddy from Salvador' "—Isabel's rendering of a piney woods accent was bizarre but somehow convincing—"so what's wrong with that? He was a soldier, and this was his job. You being here, that was extra."

"So why didn't you tell me before that he was in on this?"

"He said not to. Wanted to make a surprise." Isabel's hand was on Patrick's shoulder, gently kneading the muscles. " 'Wait till that peckerwood bastard sees me, his eyes pop right outa his head.' That's what he said."

Barr saw that her imitation of the dead Mookie had tipped the balance. "Okay," Patrick said. "What do you want from us anyway?"

"Patrick . . ." Barr heard the warning note in Gillian's voice, but Jake was on top of the question.

"Take us to St. Philip. Land us at the port—William Town, isn't it?"

"Port, capital, and only town," said Barr.

"Our source will make contact with me there," Jake continued. "He'll see *Glory* coming in—"

"He and everybody else," Gillian muttered.

"—and he'll make his approach when he decides it's safe."

So Jake doesn't know who his contact is, Barr thought. *Beyond the fact that it's somebody unofficial. He's jumping into this blind. Well, he's got balls to spare—or ambition, if Tarleton's got him figured right.*

"And then what?" Gillian demanded.

"Then what?" Jake's teeth gleamed in the light from the binnacle. "Then you sail away, and Isabel and I carry the ball."

"You mean you'll finish the mission?" said Patrick. "Just the two of you?"

"Unless you've got a recon platoon in your pocket," Jake said. His square-jawed face split in a manic grin, and Barr for the first time had a hint of just how dangerous a man he might be.

Clearly Jake's attitude struck a chord in Patrick. The mate, on his feet now, said, "Gillian, I think—"

"No." Her voice was utterly resolute—though, Barr guessed, a couple of notes higher than she intended. "Patrick, I'm sorry about your friend, but sailing *Glory* into William Town is the craziest thing I've— What're you doing, Barr?"

"Switching off the running lights," he said, reaching past her. "Hear the engine out there?"

"Cops?" Gillian asked, on tiptoe behind the big wheel. "Where are they?"

"I don't hear—" Jake began, then corrected himself. "Now I do. Christ, Barr, you've got some ears."

Impatiently Barr motioned them into silence. A *four-cylinder diesel,* he thought, old and noisy and familiar-sounding. (*Why familiar?* He shelved the question for the moment.) The moon would not be up for another hour at least, and the mystery boat was showing no lights; still, he was sure it was approaching Île Fourche from Gustavia, aiming for the wide-open harbor's southern end.

"Head up," he said to Gillian as he began sheeting in the mainsail. "Patrick, sock in the jib sheet, as quietly as you can."

Against the faint glow of the stars, Barr saw Gillian's head cocked, listening. "They're slowing down," she said.

They must be going alongside the sinking sloop, Barr decided. They probably hadn't noticed *Glory* ghosting out of the anchorage, but they would in a minute. "Head up a little more," he said to Gillian. His eyes strained to make out Île Fourche's western point.

"Isn't there a reef off that end?" Gillian asked. "How close can we go?"

"Not close enough," Barr replied. Any small power craft drew less water than *Glory's* nine and a half feet. There was no chance of scraping off a pursuer on the underwater ridge off Île Fourche's southern tip. But they might just be able to double around the point and hide behind the island. . . .

From the anchorage behind, thumps and thuds and angry, raised voices. A spotlight, waving wildly, lit the anchored sloop's side. A moment later an unmuffled gasoline engine kicked in, the echoes clattering off the bare hillside.

"Back on the reach," Barr said to Gillian, easing the mainsheet as he spoke. "Patrick, switch the engine on; they'll never hear us over the racket they're making."

"And the way they're using that spotlight," said Jake, "they'll be night-blind for the next half hour."

"What the hell are they up to?" Patrick asked.

"Saving the evidence, I expect," said Barr.

"That noise is a pump then?" Jake put in.

"Gasoline-driven," Barr agreed. "They were in plenty of time to keep the boat from sinking, but it'll take them awhile to get her empty. We're off the hook."

"For the moment," said Gillian. She had clearly made up her mind, and when she went on, he knew what her decision was. "Barr, what's the course for Statia?"

"You're steering it," he said. "Be there before dawn if the wind holds."

He knew she was smiling at him, and the knowledge warmed him amazingly. Never again, he told himself, would he let a shadow of doubt come between them. Once this was over, once he'd made the necessary phone call to Tarleton, he would put all the past behind him, and they could start fresh.

"What's Statia?" asked Jake.

"Short for Sint Eustatius," Gillian answered. "A Dutch island, about twenty-five miles ahead. It's where you're getting off, Jake."

"Somehow, I thought it might be," he said.

"There's an overseas phone center," Gillian went on, sounding just a shade apologetic. "Daily flights to St. Martin. It's not like you were being marooned."

"I appreciate that."

Gillian apparently heard the edge in his voice that Barr had missed. "Look, I'm sorry, but invasions just aren't our thing."

"Understood," said Jake.

"I don' understand," Isabel said angrily. "What about you, Patrick? You agree with this—this . . ." Barr sensed she was groping for a word insulting enough to galvanize Patrick, but Jake headed her off.

"Isabel, *Glory* is Gillian's boat. She's the owner. When it's a question of *Glory's* safety, she has the only vote."

Patrick raised his head. The shock was wearing off, and he had not missed Jake's unspoken message. "Maybe," he began, "when we get to Statia—"

"I think you'd better get your head down, soldier," Jake said. "You've had a bad jolt."

Patrick's head, in silhouette against a sky dusted with stars, was turned toward Jake. Barr wondered what the mate was thinking. "You're right," said Patrick slowly. "I'm going to hit it." He took a step toward the companionway, and Barr saw he was once again moving with something like his customary muscular grace.

"It's—" Gillian tilted her watch, but Jake cut in.

"Twenty-one forty-five."

"Quarter of ten," said Gillian. "Barr and I have the watch till midnight."

Patrick: 11:00 P.M.

Glory was swinging along with the quartering sea, heeled over to starboard just enough so that Patrick lay cradled in the V formed by his berth and the yacht's side. Her motion, even up in the triangular fo'c'sle where he lay, was a sort of easy lope; that and the sounds transmitting themselves through the yacht's fabric—rhythmic creaks of wood, many-toned chords of breeze in the standing rigging—would normally have toppled him headlong into a dreamless sleep. Instead he writhed and twisted in his narrow bunk, trying to escape the image of a cabin with four dead men in it.

Once he drifted off, but the corpses pursued him; only now they were in *Glory's* main cabin, all in dress greens, sitting around her big table. Patrick was standing in the doorway to the galley, holding a serving tray piled high with sausages. The four men turned to him, watching him with their flat, dead eyes, and then Mookie said, "Those belong to us." Patrick looked down at the tray, knowing what he was going to see there.

He sat up with a start that nearly pitched him to the deck. His body was soaked in sweat, his heart hammering. One hand was clutching the bunk board in a death grip. He forced himself to take half a dozen deep, slow breaths, then turned on the light over the berth.

Across from him, on the high side, Barr's empty berth was bare, the thin mattress rolled up at the head. Barr's tight-packed row of paperbacks, most of them with spines reinforced by silver tape, occupied the entire shelf above his bunk. Over the shelf an enlarged color photo of *Glory* under sail, taken by a grateful client, was the only decoration on the flat white paint of the bulkheads.

What's happened to me? Patrick asked himself. *I saw worse in Salvador. A hundred times worse in Chad, and day after day. Didn't fold up then—why now? Plain surprise, that was what blindsided me. In combat you were always halfway nerved up for the worst. No matter what happened, you weren't taken completely off guard because you never let your guard down. I must really be losing it, especially when you think how many warnings there were, before Jake and I ever got on that damn boat. . . .*

He pulled the Walkman from the string hammock above his head, clamped on the headphones, and hit the switch. Liam Clancy's softly rough-edged voice filled his ears. The song was one Patrick had been teaching himself to play, transposing down a half octave. It was a standard Irish ballad, all betrayal and bloody death; he'd never really noticed the words before.

He yanked off the headphones, cursing under his breath, and rolled out of the bunk. Pulled off the T-shirt he'd been wearing and felt a twinge as the taped bandage across his shoulder blade pulled taut. The shirt was soaked with sweat, but not, thank God, with blood. He balled it up and stuffed it in his laundry bag and took a fresh sweat shirt from the drawer under his berth.

Tugging on his pants, he felt the lump of his watch in his hip pocket and pulled it out. Less than an hour till he relieved Barr and Gillian, and he'd never been more awake in his life. Once up in the fresh air, though, sleep could sneak up on you; a good thing the midnight watch was only two hours.

What he needed was a drink. Not coffee or tea—either one, and his eyes would be out on stalks. And for sure not booze; after sailing with Barr, Patrick had no illusions about his own capacity for hard stuff. Cocoa with just a shot, that was it. Suddenly he could nearly taste it, thick and hot and sweet, and the molasses undertone of rum that lingered on your taste buds.

He stepped barefoot into the galley. Automatically he glanced aft, past the forward guest cabin's closed door, through the main cabin, toward the companionway. From above faint, watery light picked out the treads of the ladder. He needed no light to find the burner knob and turn it to ON. The automatic spark igniter clicked a couple of times, and the flame leaped up. The kettle was already three quarters filled with warm water, and all he had to do was slide it into place on the burner. He pulled down his personal mug, the one the Antiguan potter had made to order, with "Patrick" lettered on the side. Measured out the powdered cocoa—the real thing, from Holland—he'd picked up in St. Martin.

He set his feet flat on the linoleum and braced his buttocks against the after bulkhead to wait for the water to boil.

The voice—it had to be Jake's—was not so much heard as felt through the quarter-inch mahogany tongue and groove that separated the galley from the forward guest cabin. After a moment it stopped, to be replaced by Isabel's. She had a deep voice for a woman, and she knew how to use it like a caress, but now it was a rasp he'd not heard before, harsh and urgent.

Wedged in the dish drain by the sink was a tumbler, one of *Glory's* only good set. Without allowing himself time to think about what he was doing, Patrick picked it up and set its open end against the thin wood, pressing his ear to the base. Though he'd heard about the trick from other charter crews, he was startled when Isabel's voice cried out—seemingly in his ear—"Then make them!"

Jake's voice, deeper and more blurred, was harder to understand, though the tone was easy to read. He was kidding her along. "Make them how?" he asked, and, before she could answer, added, "Mookie was going to bring the weapons, remember?"

"They got knives in the kitchen," she said. "You're supposed to be Green Beret, Delta Force, all that shit—you think of something."

"Let's say we could force them to sail us down to St. Philip, never mind how," Jake went on. "After we went ashore, they could just tip off the authorities. Besides"—his voice rose, riding right over her angry objections— "besides, I don't want so-called compadres who're just looking for a chance to frag me from behind. I had enough of that in Nam to last me a lifetime."

Isabel's snarl—pure frustration—masked the rattle of the doorknob. Patrick barely had time to pull the glass away from the bulkhead before, she was standing in the galley doorway, the light from the cabin behind her. "You think I wouldn' do it?" she challenged, on tiptoe with barely controlled emotion, fists clenched at her sides, chin thrust out. She was wearing only an oversize man's T-shirt that said "Fort Benning— Home of the Brave" on the front. Every time her chest heaved, her small, high breasts were outlined against the cheap cotton fabric.

For a moment she reminded Patrick of Gillian in just such a stubborn rage. "I don't blame you for . . ." he began, but she was having none of it.

"*Vayase!*" And to Jake, who had appeared behind her, grinning, "You, too!"

Gillian, in jeans and a foul-weather jacket gleaming with spray, clattered down the companionway ladder and strode aft. If she'd heard Isabel, she gave no sign of it. "Half an hour," she said to Patrick, and, eyeing him narrowly, added, "If you're feeling up to standing the watch. Barr and I can—"

"I'm fine," he said quickly. "The water's just about boiling if you guys want cocoa."

"Thanks," she replied. "Just leave the kettle. We'll make some when we come off."

"I want to sleep upstairs," Isabel said. "On the deck."

Gillian's eyes went from Isabel to Jake and back again, but her expression gave nothing away. "No problem," she said after a moment. "Patrick can set up a mattress for you in the cockpit."

"Not there," said Isabel. "Someplace up in the front. I want to be alone."

It wasn't a totally unusual request. Other charterers had asked to bed down on deck, singly or together, for romance or privacy or just the feel of the salt breeze on their faces and the swaying view of the heavens. "How about right abaft the mainmast?" Patrick suggested.

Isabel regarded him with suspicion, and Gillian said, "I suppose so. But rig a net or something to leeward. I don't want anybody sliding through the lifelines."

Barr stepped up on the cockpit seat and took a long, slow look around *Glory*'s decks. "Well, the ship is yours," he said to Patrick, standing at the wheel, and then added, "You're sure your shoulder's all right?"

"It's fine," Patrick replied. Gillian had already asked him the same question, two minutes before.

"Then I'll leave you to it." He dropped out of sight down the companionway.

Taking a deep breath, Patrick concentrated on the feel of the boat. Barr had left *Glory* perfectly trimmed, of course, with just enough weather helm so the wheel had a slight tug under his hands. An unusual haze had dimmed the stars, and the moon had gone behind a cloud bank. The only light in view was on the stern of a fast-moving freighter that had overtaken *Glory* ten minutes before.

Isabel was up forward; Patrick couldn't see her in the shadows at the base of the mainmast, but he was as aware of her presence as if she'd been standing beside him. The smell of her perfume, light and astringent, had been on her blanket and pillow when he carried them forward. Just a trace of it was still on his fingertips.

The cool easterly had enough bite in it to keep him awake—and to make him glad of the old army field jacket over his bare chest. *Glory* held her course with only the slightest pressure of one hand on the wheel. Patrick almost felt himself an extension of the yacht, or maybe it was the other way around. And the sea all around was a part of him, too, so that his soul stretched over the rim of the world, running free. That feeling was the gift sailing could give you, without warning and never on demand. It was what he'd needed to pull his spirit up from the depths.

He moved down to the leeward lifeline in order to see under the foot of the big jib. He could still make out the freighter's stern light, several miles to leeward now. But that didn't mean that it and *Glory* were out here alone. Native boats almost never carried lights, and law enforcement vessels and smugglers, in their endless hide-and-seek, kept theirs off, too.

Something moved, up by the mainmast. He saw the shapeless silhouette of Isabel feeling her way aft along the side deck, wrapped in her blanket. She stepped awkwardly over the cockpit coaming, lost her balance, and caromed off the binnacle and into Patrick. He caught her easily in the crook of his arm and realized that she was naked under the blanket.

"You okay?" he asked.

"*Sí.*" She hadn't moved away from him, and her flank pressed against his hip. "I wanted to apologize for the way I was yelling at you before."

The images of bloody death had vanished. Here at the helm Patrick was alive and in control. His body was responding to the feel of her against him, even though warning bells were going off in his head. "Okay."

"You don't believe me," she said, and, to his surprise, laughed softly. "I don't mind."

He looked down at her. In profile, lit by *Glory*'s stern light, her face looked more Egyptian than ever. And more desirable. "I figure you and Jake have told us a good many lies," he said.

"Oh, not so very many," she replied, smiling up at him. A smooth, bare arm emerged from the blanket and snaked around his waist, under the field jacket. "Mostly we just didn't tell you everything."

Patrick was acutely conscious of her thumb, hooked casually over his belt. "Did Jake pick *Glory* because of me?" he asked. "Because I was in the crew?"

"No. Because of the captain, Barr." She laughed again, and he wondered if she could see his expression. "Jake said Barr knows the islands better than anybody. When Mookie recognize your name, it was only extra for us."

Mookie. Hearing her say it made Patrick realize how he'd been suppressing the sound of it. But he made himself push on, sure he was hearing the truth at last. "Well, you're right about Barr," he said. "But why him? Any skipper could sail you into William Bay."

Silence, and he had the feeling she was deciding whether to tell him the rest of it. "I suppose," she said at last. "You could do it, right?"

"Anybody could do it who could read a chart," he said. "So why did Jake pick Barr?"

He thought she wasn't going to answer. "It was part of Jake's plan," she said finally, her voice dropping nearly to a whisper, so he had to bend his head to hear her. "He wanted to land Mookie and his team first, in a deserted *bahia*—a little bay, I forget the name—in the north of St. Philip. Jake said Barr was the only one who could find it in the dark."

Jake had sure picked the right man for that job, Patrick thought. In the first couple of months after he'd joined *Glory*'s crew, Patrick had watched Barr shoehorn the big yacht into unmarked coves stuffed with rocks, day or night, never a glance at the chart. For a while the mate figured Barr got away with it by some kind of fantastic luck. Slowly it dawned on him that he was seeing the product of ten years' experience poking around places nobody else had the nerve to go into.

And luck had little to do with it. Once anchored in a harbor, Barr would spend hours—first with *Glory*'s beautiful old Plath sextant, then with the dinghy and a sounding line—surveying the place and sketching the results on sheets of plain paper. Each tiny, nameless cove, each just-submerged reef, each mark for the channel was drawn and labeled with a precision that amazed Patrick, especially when he considered Barr's usual chicken track handwriting.

"Mookie was your friend, right?" Isabel demanded, breaking the silence.

He stiffened, then realized it was a question, not an accusation. "That's right," he said warily. "We were in Salvador together as advisers—I don't remember the Spanish word."

"*Consejeros*," she said, nodding.

"Yeah. There were a bunch of us, sent down from the States to shape up the government troops. Only we had to do it in the field, with the other side shooting at us. It got pretty crazy sometimes."

"But you liked that, being adviser."

"Hell, no," he said automatically. Then: "Well, it had its moments, as they say. The thing that could freak you out was that us Americans weren't supposed to do any fighting, no matter what." He shook his head at the recollection. "I mean, here's incoming splattering your guys right and left, and they're really spooked, and you know—you just *know*—you could turn the fight around yourself. But you've gotta try and tell a bunch of little s—" He caught himself, he thought just in time, and segued without a pause. "Little half-trained, underfed guys what to do. And tell them in goddamn *Spanish*."

The old anger had fanned up to rage in moments, but not enough so that he missed the deadpan mockery when she replied, "Spanish is easier for us spics, however."

"Sorry."

"*De nada*. But you two were advisers together, you and Mookie?"

"For a while," he said. Why did she keep bringing Mookie into it? "I finally flipped. Picked up an M-sixteen and started spraying the shrubbery. So they chewed me out and sent me home." *Where I got officially chewed out and unofficially pissed on till I did something really stupid—signing up with old man Hals's private army.*

Isabel's hand moved up from his waist. Her long fingers were kneading his back, just below the bandage. "Mookie said that about you," she remarked. " 'The mick'—he called you that, did you know?— 'the mick was just too quick on the draw.' "

Mookie's words, all right. If he'd said it once, he'd said it fifty times, and Patrick could still hear his voice, that Carolina drawl that sounded like it was coming from up in his nose somewhere.

"But I guess you changed since then," she was saying. "Not too quick on the draw anymore."

She didn't sound as if she were putting the needle in. And she was right. He wasn't the hard charger he'd been. "You think I'm a coward," he said; it came out more than half a question.

"I did before," she said evenly. "Now I'm not sure. But it is hard for someone like me to understand the way you *yanquis* think."

"Lately it's hard for me to understand, too," he said.

A ghostly oblong appeared in the compainway hatch. It was Barr's angular face. "All secure up there?" he asked.

"No problems," Patrick replied. "But you're awake early, unless my watch has stopped."

"Gillian and I can't sleep. Feel like being relieved?"

He was on the point of saying no when Isabel's nails raked down his bare back. "Uh, fine with me," he managed. "If you're sure . . ."

"I go back to bed," said Isabel, removing her arm, slowly, from under his jacket. "Sleep well, Patrick."

Exactly fifteen minutes after Patrick turned off the reading light over his fo'c'sle berth, he heard the soft tap-tap-tap on the foredeck hatch above him. He'd allowed for a ten-minute wait, and even though he never doubted she'd come, the extra time had set him on fire. He made himself run through the good reasons for ignoring her signal, starting with the certainty that she was trying to wind him around her finger and ending with the argument from plain common sense about unknown women (an argument that Gillian had given up making).

He sat up, undogged the hatch, and raised it silently. Without a word she slid over the hatch's raised lip, headfirst into his arms. Along the way her blanket came free. Against his bare body, her skin was cool where the night air had licked it, hot where the blanket had covered it. In the near-absolute blackness of the fo'c'sle her open lips searched hungrily across his chest, up to his mouth, her tongue probing urgently.

With his free arm he reached up and lowered the hatch, then let her pull him down onto the mattress. Her hands searched him, and his slid over the incredible smoothness of her skin.

"What are you doing?" she said a minute or so later.

"I want to see you."

"All right, but hurry." His groping hand found the reading lamp and snapped it on. She blinked in the sudden glare, and he tilted the gooseneck to direct the light against the varnished ash strips of the overhead. She lay on her side, with her back against the white-painted bulkhead, one arm resting on the shelf above the berth. Her skin, which had looked only slightly darker than his own out in the sunlight, seemed to glow now with the reddish tints of mahogany.

Her mouth was slightly open, her breath coming fast. Her huge eyes surveyed his body with slow deliberation, and then she reached out and took hold of him.

He had never been so aroused, and he knew somehow that it was the same for her. Always before he had been able to distance himself from himself, channel the flood of passion, and direct it, even while enjoying it to the full. Now all considerations of pacing, of technique were swept away by a desire so absolute he could only surrender unconditionally. He was at the center of a prolonged, almost unendurable barrage of the senses. Yet in the middle of the storm were instants of incredible clarity that he knew would stay with him as long as he lived:

Her lips at his ear, her barely voiced Spanish coming far too fast to translate, and suddenly, in English, "Help me, help me, help me."

She astride him, her body gleaming, desperate concentration on her queen's face, the long-awaited mutual explosion, and afterward the air of catlike satisfaction that transformed her.

His own breathless voice, muffled by her damp hair: "You *do* taste like nutmeg."

And her gasping reply: "Keep tasting me."

And at last, as he rolled back—soaked, drained, sated—the intensity of her eyes as she whispered, "I am what you needed."

TUESDAY

Gillian: Oranje Baai, Sint Eustatius; 8:00 A.M.

Just after dawn the trade wind swung into the northeast, so that by full light a marked surge had crept down the island's leeward side. Anchored two hundred yards off the ruins of Oranjestad's Old Town, *Glory* received the swells on her port beam and began to roll slowly from side to side. In the double berth aft, Gillian lay with Barr's arm around her. They had come below at five, after setting the anchor in the predawn blackness, and had fallen into each other's arms with a silent, almost desperate hunger. But sleep for her had been a succession of dozes, and each time she surfaced, Barr was awake, staring up at the overhead.

"*Glory*'s really starting to roll now," Gillian said quietly.

"So she is."

"Maybe we ought to run a stern anchor off the quarter, head her into the seas."

"Why bother?"

"Well, the motion's a little hard on people who aren't used to it," she offered, turning so she could look up into his face. An oval patch of sunlight, moving with the yacht's motion, swept back and forth across his angular features and made him blink.

"Speed the parting guests," he said. "Another hour of this, and they'll be glad to get ashore, no matter what shore it is."

"That's easy for you to say," she retorted. "You don't have to clean the heads after they chuck their cookies."

"If it means seeing the last of Colonel Jake and his Latin femme fatale, I'll be delighted to clean the heads for a week."

"You're on," she said quickly. And then: "D'you think we're home free?"

"Hard to be sure," Barr said, so fast she knew his thoughts had been paralleling hers. "Nobody saw us at Île Fourche; I'm pretty sure of that." He pursed his lips in thought. "Depends mostly on that bartender in Gustavia. If he remembers Jake. And if he goes to the cops at all. Even then there's no proof we actually went out to the sloop."

"Could be worse," Gillian said, wishing she believed it.

"Could be a lot worse," Barr said firmly, squeezing her shoulder. "And once those two up forward are off *Glory* for good, we should be in the clear."

"Isabel's still up in the fo'c'sle?" Gillian asked.

"Haven't heard her leave," he replied. She felt his chest heave in a soundless chuckle. "I make it thirty-two hours, introduction to seduction: a new record."

"Which one of them gets the trophy?" she said. "Isabel was the one doing the hunting." *But why?* she wondered. Somehow it didn't figure.

"Speaking of our passengers, there's something I've got to tell—" Barr began. From somewhere up forward came the loud slam of a door, followed by the sound of retching. "Oh, shit," he said.

"Remember what you promised about cleaning the head," she replied.

Breakfast was a silent meal. Jake was glowering like a banked fire, and Gillian wondered just how much he'd heard from the fo'c'sle during the predawn watch—or if it even mattered to him after what he'd seen last night. If Isabel felt either grief or guilt, it didn't show. Most of her color had returned, but when Patrick brought in the serving dish heaped with pancakes, she turned a startling olive green and fled to the cockpit. Barr seemed lost in a private contemplation. He barely touched the food, got up twice to tap the big brass barometer without result, and finally grabbed his mug of coffee and vanished up the companionway.

And since Patrick seemed disinclined to join them at all, that left Gillian facing Jake alone. "Pancakes all right?" she asked, breaking a five-minute silence.

"Fine," he said. "Just great." But he had eaten only two, she saw, and barely touched the bacon.

"Nice day," she said, scarcely believing she could have said anything so inane.

He glanced up through the open skylight. "Looks like it."

"Listen," she said, "I'm sorry about your friends—"

"Not your fault."

"Sorry about the way things turned out."

"Like I said, not your fault."

She couldn't let it lie unresolved. "The thing is, we've gotten in trouble before when we—"

"Got involved?" Jake suggested. She had the feeling he might be needling her and was all the more determined to explain.

"When we messed with things we weren't equipped to handle," she said.

He was smiling at her, but it was a nice smile, fatherly and understanding. "You don't seem to believe me, Gillian. I'm not blaming you, any of you. Really. This was my defeat; I take full responsibility."

He meant it, she was sure. So why didn't she feel more relieved?

He glanced over his shoulder at the galley, where Patrick could be heard cleaning up the remains of breakfast. Jake bent toward her, lowering his voice. "I don't mind about that either," he said. "Isabel and I had something going once. Mostly she was grateful to me for getting her out of South Florida. Lately, though . . ." He shrugged.

Male confessions—even the threat of them—always made Gillian uneasy. "There really is good phone service from Statia," she said quickly. "Winair can get back to St. Martin in half an hour, and if you can't get a flight today, you're welcome to stay over till tomorrow." She swallowed hard and continued, avoiding his eye. "I can't return your money now, but I'll send back your deposit in a couple of weeks— less the two days you've been aboard, of course."

"Fair enough," he said, with what she thought was the shadow of a smile.

"I'd better change my clothes if we're going ashore," she said, getting up. She saw him eyeing her green tank suit and explained: "The smaller the island, the less the officials have to do and the more self-important they get. A place as small and out-of-the-way as this, you've got to dress like a goddamn nun just to get through immigration." She was on the point of adding that Jake might want to tell that to Isabel, then decided against it.

In the aft cabin she pulled on what she thought of as her *Little*

Women outfit: pleated white blouse and loose tan culottes, nothing remotely suggestive yet at the same time distinctly feminine, suitable for climbing a rusty, barnacled ladder, if that was necessary (and it had been), yet formal enough to make the most two-bit bureaucrat feel he was being taken seriously by a mere woman.

Gillian had tried several ensembles before she'd settled on a rig she could stand, and she was convinced it helped grease *Glory*'s way through the official gauntlet, though Barr claimed it was the personality she put on with the clothes: "Uriah Heep in a split skirt," as he put it.

Nearly colorless lipstick—but no other makeup—and an old-fashioned straw boater with a red and blue ribbon completed her outfit, except for the Top-Siders she wore once ashore. As she adjusted the tilt of the hat, she heard Jake's heavy tread on the companion ladder. Jake said something inaudible, but Barr's reply made it clear: "Don't worry about luggage. Once we get your plans squared away, we'll bring your gear ashore."

On deck Gillian found herself squinting in the dazzling early-morning sun that had just cleared the island's central hills. To the south a few cloud streamers clung to the peak of the Quill, the somnolent volcano that was Sint Eustatius's primary landmark, and fifteen miles to the northwest Saba's cone had an even thicker mantling. The rest of the sky was clear to the horizon, a perfect morning.

Sint Eustatius—which old Caribbean hands invariably shortened to Statia—was one of the area's more forgotten islands, and *Glory* had not visited it before. The open roadstead contained only an ancient tug, three other yachts (anchored perilously close to the rocky shore), and a small power cruiser. During Statia's trading heyday in the eighteenth century, Barr had told her, this exposed arc of so-called bay had held as many as two hundred merchantmen at once. Along the beach had stretched the Lower Town of Oranjestad—a shelf of land on which stone warehouses stood in solid ranks, represented now by a few isolated structures and the rubble of a hundred more, loose stones washed smooth in the low surf.

A hundred feet above the Lower Town, topping a sheer cliff, she could see the unimpressive ramparts of Fort Oranje, whose battery of smoothbore cannon had once protected the anchorage from the sanctioned piracy of England's admirals. Behind the restored fort was the maze of narrow streets that was present-day Oranjestad, a typical West

Indian backwater town, according to Barr: shabby all-purpose stores, eating places, and homes, leavened by a scattering of small souvenir shops operated by and for off-islanders. It was a place the twentieth century hadn't really disfigured and (not surprisingly) was one of Barr's favorites among the islands.

"Shore party all set?" asked Gillian, forcing an extra briskness into her voice. Isabel, she noticed, looked drawn and defiant, if not as pale as she'd been at breakfast. She was wearing one of *Glory's* beach towels as a sort of sarong. Though it covered her adequately, it was an invitation to trouble. Gillian knew she should take the woman aside and explain but found she simply lacked the energy to do it.

Everyone seemed to be avoiding everyone else's eye, and finally Barr said, "Isabel wants to get a little more sun, so she's going to stay aboard. I'll run you and Jake to shore." Barr's eyes were locked on to hers, as if to prevent either of them from having to look at the unmentioned fifth member of the company, staring fixedly off into space, or at Jake, whose attention seemed riveted by something in the middle distance.

Screw it, Gillian thought. *Or, more accurately, let 'em screw each other blind.* "Who's got the passports?" she asked, and Barr held up a waterproof plastic envelope. "Then let's go."

She and Jake settled themselves in the fore part of the rubber dinghy as Barr busied himself with the outboard. On *Glory's* deck above them Patrick held the painter's end, while looking back over his shoulder into the cockpit. Gillian wondered idly if Isabel had shucked the towel already and if she cared that she could be seen from the fort on the cliff.

"You clear in at the police station, in the Upper Town," Barr said. "The telephone office is right across the street. Private booth and everything," he added to Jake.

"Things must've changed since you were here in *Windhover*," Gillian said, smiling.

He looked annoyed. "What do you mean?"

"I checked the cruising guide: Boats clear in with the port captain, in the little house at the end of the big wharf. Saves a hike up to town."

His smile seemed stiff and unnatural. "You're sure?"

"Remember what you always tell me?" She laughed. "I'm the only woman you know who reads the directions."

He shrugged. "I'll drop you off at the smaller pier. It's got a ladder. I'll pick you up there."

"Right," she said, and he pulled the starter cord.

In practice—in West Indian practice—regulations never worked the way they were supposed to. "Police got to stamp your passports," said the large, vaguely hostile figure behind the port office desk as he fingered *Glory*'s clearance from St.-Bart's. He pushed aside the five passports and the crew list.

"That's no problem," Gillian said. "Where are the police, please?"

"Up to the airport. They's a plane coming in. But they be here later."

She was unsure if the big man's seeming hostility was real or if he was just enjoying himself. But then she was never sure what lay behind the masks of stony indifference that West Indian officials all seemed to wear. "When do you suppose they might turn up?" she asked, keeping her voice even.

The big man shrugged. "After a while. Pretty soon."

Gillian's heart sank. In her experience of the islands, "after a while" meant either "I don't know" or "I don't care," and sometimes both. "Pretty soon," by contrast, had a single, invariable meaning: "any time between five minutes from now and Judgment Day."

"Look," she said, "the gentleman with me has got to get to an overseas telephone right away. It's an emergency."

"I don't know about that," the big man mused. Then he seemed to come to some inner decision. "You could go up the town—to police station. Somebody there clear you in right away."

"Great," she said, grasping at the shreds of self-control. "And the overseas phone is right across from the police station?"

He thought about it for a moment. "That's right."

"How do we find it, please?" she asked, her fists clenching involuntarily.

"Cab take you." The man behind the counter seemed to have lost interest in them, rooting among an untidy stack of papers.

She looked out the door. In the unpaved parking area outside, the only visible vehicle was a small truck with two flat tires, simmering in the coruscating sun. "There doesn't seem to be any cab," she said, between gritted teeth.

The port official bestowed a condescending smile. "He on the way," he said. "He my cousin."

Barr

He anchored the inflatable off the pier, with a line run to one of the big iron cleats on the crumbling wharf. After pulling himself in, he scrambled up the shaky ladder. The inevitable small boy was sitting a few yards away, watching him. "You want to make a dollar?" Barr asked.

The boy nodded but kept his distance.

"I'm going down to the Golden Era." He indicated the nondescript two-story building a hundred yards down the road. "If a lady comes by, asking for me, tell her you don't know where I went, but I said I'd be back in a few minutes. Okay?"

The boy considered a moment, then shook his head. "Two dollars," he said.

"Done," said Barr, producing two bills. "Now, remember . . ."

He heard the soft grate of rubber on sand and, looking up, saw a dusty sedan coming slowly down the paved road toward him. It drew up alongside, and Gillian leaned out the window. "You were right after all," she said. "If we want customs to clear us in any time in the foreseeable future, we've got to go up to the police station."

She was seething, he could see. Concealing his own relief, he shrugged sympathetically. "Welcome to the islands," he said. It was a ritual they'd devised for defusing infuriating situations, and she picked up on it, forcing a smile.

"How many does that make?" she asked.

"Eight hundred and seventy-three," he said. "This year."

"Things are getting better," she replied. This time her smile was genuine, warmed by affection. "What are you up to?" she asked.

He felt guilt wash over him. "Thought I'd get a beer," he said. His glance went to the boy, who had drifted close enough to hear every word. "I'd just hired this young man to watch the dinghy."

The boy stirred as if to speak, and Barr glared him to silence. "Oh," said Gillian, looking from Barr to the boy and back again. "Well, I guess we'd best get rolling."

The boy watched the dusty sedan vanish down the road. "That be another dollar," he said.

The Golden Era was a dormitorylike establishment that catered mostly to scuba divers; in the evenings its dining-room bar was often noisy with construction workers from the oil storage tank farm that was spreading, like a vast, metallic blight, along the island's western shore. At midmorning this early in the season, the place was deserted. Barr went into the office, which might have been lifted from a cheap motel almost anywhere in the United States. There was a telephone on the desk, but no one in sight, and he was toying with the idea of attempting a call to the number Tarleton had given him, back on St. Martin, when he heard the door behind him open.

"I think we can save you the money," said Tarleton. In the doorway behind him stood Deedee Etheridge.

"Never mind how we found you," Tarleton was saying five minutes later. "The point is, your passenger has managed to set the entire Leewards ablaze."

They had adjourned, at Tarleton's suggestion, to one of the upstairs rooms. With the air conditioner roaring full blast, the tiny chamber was already icy. Tarleton sprawled across the swaybacked double bed; even though it hadn't been slept in, it managed to seem rumpled— though not as rumpled as Tarleton himself, who had shaved only sketchily and looked as if he'd slept in his bush jacket. Deedee, her blond hair tucked up under a broad-brimmed hat, was wearing slacks and a short-sleeved shirt. She stood with her back to the closed door, and Barr straddled the only chair. Behind him a curtain was drawn across a sliding door that opened onto a minuscule porch.

"That's right," Deedee put in. "St.-Bart's is crawling with police— flown in from Guadeloupe. They're even supposed to be sending to Paris for a forensics team from the Sûreté."

Barr hitched his chair halfway around and pulled the curtain open a few inches. A few yards away was the back wall of the inn next door to the Golden Era. By craning his neck, he could see a slice of Oranje Baai and *Glory* riding placidly at anchor. No one was visible on her decks. He swung back to face Tarleton. "How *did* you find us?"

"I know the way your mind works," he said. "That puts me one jump—one small jump—ahead of the authorities."

Barr considered Tarleton's answer for a moment and then said, "Well, Jake didn't kill those men. They were his friends. His team, he called them."

"I daresay he did," Tarleton sniffed.

Without moving from her post by the door, Deedee spoke again. "Adler was seen in Le Select, asking about them," she said. "Twice. The description is perfect." She paused. "He was with a female, but it doesn't sound like the Machado woman."

Perfect, Barr thought, his heart sinking. *As soon as the cops get around to checking the Pasanggrahan, they'll have us all ID'd.* "I don't plan to toddle quietly off to the slammer, you know," he said to Tarleton.

The older man seemed unperturbed. "Front-page revelation, is that it? CIA cell unveiled as captain tells all?" He shook his head. "I'm underwhelmed, Jeremy."

The threat Barr had kept up his sleeve didn't seem so threatening when it lay on the dusty carpet between them, but the game had to be played out. "I hope your employers will understand," Barr said. "I know where Adler's target is," he added.

"Where?" Deedee demanded, but Tarleton ignored her. His yellowed, slightly bloodshot old eyes contemplated Barr for a full, silent minute.

"So that's your deal?" he said at last. "The name of Colonel Adler's target in return for . . .?" He raised his bushy eyebrows quizzically.

"A cleanup, or whatever you call it," Barr said. "I don't know how you square the St.-Bart's police, but I'll bet you can do it."

Tarleton nodded. " 'Sanitize' is the term," he said. "Just thank God no one involved is a French citizen."

"Then it's a deal?" Barr said.

"No," said Tarleton cheerfully, "not yet."

Barr hadn't let his spirits rise, so he was surprised when they fell. "What now?" he said.

There were hurrying footsteps in the corridor and a quick double knock. Deedee looked at Tarleton, who nodded, and she opened the door a crack. The old man could see who stood in the hallway, but Barr could not. From outside a Caribbean voice said, "Comin' now."

"I think," said Tarleton, with a sharp look at Deedee, "it would be best if you did the honors, my dear."

Deedee looked nervous, even apprehensive, Barr thought. As she slipped out, closing the door behind her, Tarleton never took his eyes from Barr.

"Here is what I am empowered to offer you," Tarleton said when Deedee's footsteps had faded. "First, you tell me the name of the Ethan Allen's target and whatever else Colonel Adler has let slip." He waited, and Barr nodded to get him going again. "Next, you will take Colonel Adler, plus whatever backup group he may be able to raise, to that target—"

"But why?" Barr interrupted.

"And cooperate with him until I pull you out."

Barr shook his head. "Not on your life," he said. "That guy's crazy. We'd all get killed."

"We wouldn't let it go that far," Tarleton said soothingly. "We'll guarantee it."

"Tell that to Jake's four friends back at Île Fourche," Barr snapped. "You know, I'm beginning to think he's on to something."

"So do we," said Tarleton. "Don't you see? My superiors take the good colonel's information very seriously now. We just don't think he and his troop of March Hares can handle what they want to bite off."

"Well, I don't know . . ." Barr said, vamping while he tried to evaluate what Tarleton had told him. And, what was probably more important, the things the older man had left unsaid.

"I'm sure I needn't bring up the matter of your licenses," Tarleton said.

"This thing is way past licenses," Barr said impatiently. "In fact, it's not something I can decide alone."

"You refer to *Glory*'s owner, the peppery Miss Verdean?" Tarleton's wrinkles effectively hid whatever expression he might have had. In the light of the room's single lamp he looked like an ancient tortoise.

"Yes," said Barr, more firmly than he had expected to.

"Fine," Tarleton replied, lumbering to his feet. "Then you can ask her yourself. Now."

Two pairs of footsteps in the corridor. Barr jumped up as the door burst open and Gillian strode in on the half volley, suspicion shadowing her face. Behind her, clearly shaken, stood Deedee Etheridge. "What is this, Barr?" Gillian said, her voice not quite steady. "What're you up to?"

Whatever Barr might have said, given a minute or two for preparation, was blown from his mind by the accusation in her brown eyes. "It's not what it looks like," he managed to say, feeling his face go hot.

"Not with him here," she agreed. "Who the hell are you?" she said to Tarleton.

"My name's Tarleton," he replied. "I'm not Captain Barr's pimp, if that's what you're thinking."

Gillian's smile showed all her white teeth, but it never reached her eyes. "I guess not," she said. She regarded Tarleton narrowly. "You aren't a cop, but I bet this has something to do with Jake Adler."

"Very perceptive," said Tarleton. "Where is the colonel now?"

"Still on the phone, I guess," she replied. "Now, suppose—"

Tarleton held up his hand, and Gillian fell silent.

"I was going to let Captain Barr tell you," Tarleton said, "but he still looks a bit taken aback."

"I'll hear your version then," she said, and threw Barr a single, contemptuous glare. "And yours later. Maybe."

"As you wish. Would you care to sit, Miss Verdean? No?" Tarleton settled back against the headboard of the bed. "Captain Barr and I— and Miss Etheridge—go back a long way. . . ."

It was the truth, only slightly veiled by omission, unadorned by flowery double-talk. Barr watched as Gillian, at first coiled like a spring, slowly began to relax. She never looked at Barr, and only once or twice at Deedce, but focused on Tarleton the unblinking concentration that was one of the things he loved in her. With the knowledge that grew out of three years' almost daily association, Barr found he could almost track her thoughts from the infinitesimal lift of an eyebrow, the widening of her eyes, the twitch of her lip.

The older man briefly sketched in Barr's years of service for an unnamed government agency, performing unspecified tasks for equally unspecified rewards. He dealt even more quickly with Barr's fall from grace after his marriage, emphasizing the reluctance with which Tarleton's superiors had let him go.

"Now my people need Captain Barr again," Tarleton said.

"Just like that," said Gillian. It was the first time she had spoken in five minutes.

"Just like that," Tarleton agreed. "It's the way they are. How much has Colonel Adler told you?"

She responded with a crisp summary of Jake Adler's self-described mission. "How much of it's true . . ." She paused, waiting.

Tarleton gave her an avuncular smile. "All of it perhaps. Or none. Or something in between, which is the usual state of affairs. That is the first question my superiors want answered."

She believed Tarleton, Barr was certain of it. And why not?

"So you put the arm on Barr," she said.

"And, by extension, on you," Tarleton said. "I think you should know we had to pressure Captain Barr to agree."

"I'm glad to hear it." Her voice was sub-zero, her eyes colder than Barr had thought brown eyes could get. "What did he agree to?"

The accent on "he" was more than Barr could bear. "I said I'd find out Jake's target, and that was all."

Gillian picked it up, as Barr had known she would. "He hasn't told you, has he?" she said to Tarleton. The tight smile was back. "Why not? No, don't tell me—you want something else."

Tarleton spread his hands in a graceful gesture of surrender. "Miss
Verdean—" he began, but she cut him off.

"Tell me now exactly what we have to do. Don't bother with the
threats; I can supply those myself."

"I didn't have any choice," Barr said.

"It doesn't matter," Gillian said. The two of them were walking
back along the road, toward the pier where the dinghy was tied up.
Tarleton's watchers said that Jake was on his way back from the telephone exchange. Only half an hour had passed from the time Barr
had entered the office of the Golden Era, but he felt a decade older.

"It does matter," he replied. "I see that now." She paced steadily
down the paved road, looking straight ahead, her back as straight as
Glory's mast. He took her by the bicep, felt her stiffen. But she halted
and turned to face him. "I was wrong," he said. "What can I do?"
He wanted desperately to tell her he loved her, but something in her
eyes held him back.

"I don't know," she said. She shook her head as if to clear it. "I
thought we were really partners—"

"We are."

"Then the word means something different to you than it does to
me," she said.

He was saved from what he knew was another useless protestation
by the sound of a car. It was the taxi, with a subdued Jake Adler sitting
beside the driver. If he noticed the tension between Barr and Gillian,
he gave no sign of it.

"What's—" Gillian began, just as Jake said, "Look—" Weak smile
met weak smile, and Gillian said, "You first."

"I'm having trouble getting through to the people I need to talk to,"
Jake said. "The girl in the exchange said some lines were down someplace."

"Welcome to the islands," said Barr automatically. "They say to try
again later?"

"Tomorrow morning," Jake said. "So if you meant what you said
about Isabel and me staying over . . ."

"As a matter of fact—" Barr began, but Gillian was ahead of him.

"As a matter of fact, Jake, things have hit the fan," she said. "It's
not safe for you to fly back to St. Martin."

Jake looked quickly around him, but they were alone on the pier.
"How—"

"Word travels fast down here," she said quickly. She had half turned so as not to risk meeting Barr's eye. "The thing is, the French police are looking for you, and they seem to have a line on me, too. There's no going back, not for any of us." She took his arm and began to lead him toward the dinghy. "Barr and I talked it over, and we agreed— didn't we, Barr?"

"Absolutely," he said, sure only that he was going to regret whatever he was supposed to have agreed to.

"The only way to clear ourselves," she continued, talking up at Jake earnestly, "is get behind your mission. And hope like hell you know what you're doing."

"Well," said Jake slowly, "how about that?" He seemed, Barr thought, less than overjoyed.

"What're you doing?" Gillian whispered an hour later. Jake and Isabel were below, restowing their gear, and Patrick was in the galley, making lunch.

"Putting two and two together," Barr replied, without lifting his head from the seat locker he was burrowing into. He straightened up and surveyed the cockpit. His eye fell on the mahogany box which had the bronze ventilator from the aft cabin mounted on it. "A little small," he said. "But these days . . ."

"Small for what?" Gillian demanded suspiciously. She had changed back into her swimsuit and was perched like a water nymph on the edge of the companion hatch, her tanned legs dangling.

"Wait," said Barr. The top of the vent box was designed to swing open, to allow for cleaning the interior. "Ah," he murmured. "Have a look."

The black metal container was no larger than a pack of cigarettes. Sealed in a clear plastic Ziploc bag, it had been wedged between the edge of the box and the metal ventilation tube that led down into the cabin below.

Gillian reached for it, but Barr caught her wrist. "Leave it."

"What is it?" she asked. "A tape recorder?"

"Nope." Barr lowered the lid gently. "A transmitter."

She rocked back on her heels, working it through. "So someone could track us," she said after a moment. "Tarleton?"

Barr nodded. "He may know how my mind works, but he doesn't mind having an electronic watchdog." It was funny, he thought, how easily the old habits of thought returned. Tarleton wanted *Glory* on a short leash. Why?

"Those clowns who came aboard in Groot Baai," Gillian said. "They were Tarleton's, right?" Her brain was still several steps behind his, but she would start seeing the wider implications soon enough.

"Yes." Barr was wondering if Tarleton had someone watching from ashore, maybe with binoculars. If so, the old man would soon know his little toy had been found. What would he do about it?

"But you're not going to smash it?"

"No," he replied. "We might want to use it for something."

She looked doubtful and disappointed in about equal parts. He had to fight down the impulse to embrace her. "Well, I guess you know more about this kind of thing than I do," she said.

"I'd better," he said. "Look, in Tarleton's business, nothing is ever what it seems to be, and that goes twice for the people involved. Anytime there seems to be one absolutely clear course of action, you know that's the one thing you shouldn't do."

"I couldn't live like that," she said simply.

"You get used to it," he said. He was on the point of adding that deviousness could even be fun, but he stopped himself.

"That's what I'm afraid of," she said. "I was worried because I knew so little about you. Now I don't even know if I know that." She paused, clearly dissatisfied with her words. "If you get what I mean."

She was trying to grin, but he knew better than to take her expression literally. "I—we just have to get through this craziness," he said. "Then we can go back to reality."

"Just so you know which is which," she said.

Ten minutes later, when he was alone in the cockpit, Barr extracted the metal container from the ventilator box. He stuffed it, Ziploc bag and all, into a wide-topped plastic jug a quarter full of powdered teak cleanser. He screwed the jug's top back on as tightly as he could, then put a double layer of waterproof tape over the joint. With a quick glance down the companionway he leaned over *Glory*'s side and gently dropped the jug into the water, where it bobbed gently up and down.

He watched as it drifted slowly away from the anchored boat, riding the wavelets that were pushed by the gathering breeze. "Bon voyage," he whispered.

The second rule of dealing with the Tarletons of the world was never miss a chance to screw them up.

Patrick, 6:30 P.M.

"This is one hell of a crazy time to fall in love," Patrick muttered. He was addressing the meat loaf he was molding, but the voice that responded came from behind him.

"Why?" asked Gillian. "Or do I mean, 'Why not?' " She was leaning against the doorjamb, her arms clasped around herself as if against the cold. But she could hardly be cold, in jeans and a sweat shirt.

Patrick turned back to the meat loaf, gave it a couple of unnecessary pats, and shoved the pan into the oven. "It's crazy because of all this," he said. "The dead guys back there at Île Fourche, Colonel Adler's screwball mission . . ." He let his voice trail off.

"That's not what's bothering you," Gillian said.

"You're right." He lifted the lid of the ice chest, fished a beer from its nest of cracked ice, and held it out to Gillian. She shook her head, and he twisted the cap off and took a long swallow.

"You're right," he repeated. "It's her. Isabel. She's got me on the ropes for sure, but . . ." He groped for the words that were just over the horizon. "I mean, it feels like she's what I've been looking for all my life, only . . ."

"You don't know who it is you've found," said Gillian.

"That's it," he said quickly, and then saw she hadn't been speaking to him at all. He wanted to put his arms around her, to comfort her— could feel her wanting it, too—but not so very long ago he had pursued her desperately and unsuccessfully, and though they had come through it as friends, they weren't completely easy with each other yet.

"It's different with Barr," Patrick protested. "He just got sucked back in."

"He didn't tell me. Anything." Her voice was quietly bitter.

Well, he didn't tell me either, Patrick thought. But he said, "Barr thought he could fix things himself."

"You don't understand," she said angrily. Then: "I think I will have a beer."

"Sure," Patrick said. "And maybe we better see what the others are up to."

Barr had the chart spread out on the main cabin table. It was one of the oldest in *Glory*'s inventory, the thick paper yellowing at the edges, and the fat peanut shape of St. Philip rendered in shades of brown. The printing looked as if it had been lettered by hand a long time ago. "Based on a Royal Navy survey of 1846," read the legend.

It said a lot about St. Philip's place in the world that for a century and a half no nation had found the island important enough to do a new survey of it.

Isabel was standing behind Jake, peering around his shoulder at the chart. She glanced up, caught Patrick watching her, and flashed him a private smile. He felt his face go scarlet and forced his attention back to the tabletop. Because he knew what to look for, Patrick could distinguish Barr's own updatings among the spider web of data on the chart: faint pencil lines that marked bearings and sextant angles, corrected soundings in the tiny printing that was so unlike Barr's normal writing.

Patrick let his gaze idle over the page, trying to make the data flow over him, form a mental picture of the place itself. He'd never seen St. Philip up close, only as a couple of distant lumps on the horizon. The spatter of elevations rose to twenty-nine hundred feet at the wider, northern end, where a single big peak dominated the landscape. A dead volcano, more than likely, like Statia's Quill, five miles from where *Glory* rolled gently at anchor. Probably the same steep bright green sides and a hollow top, too.

St. Philip's big peak was named Mauvis; from it a sort of saddle, or maybe a low ridge, swooped down and then back up, running southeast along the island's windward side to where the island widened once again, around a cluster of smaller peaks called the Jumbies. The slopes on the leeward side of the central ridge looked fairly gentle, probably the closest to farmland that the island offered.

Villages were spotted here and there—Oldroad, Vorstrait, Liberta—but Patrick had already learned how mapmakers hated blanks on their page and were likely to give a label to any collection of shacks, no matter how small. William Town, on an exposed bay halfway down the leeward side, was the only place big enough to earn the cross-hatching that represented streets.

The leeward coast was smooth, with beaches here and there, but the windward side, which Barr and Adler were examining, looked steep-sided, ragged, and torn. That was what happened when a few million years' worth of waves, pushed by the trade winds, bashed up against a rocky shoreline. Lots of dead-end coves and exposed rocks, lots of places where a boat could tear her bottom out.

"Here's the best place," said Barr. His big, scarred finger was indicating what looked to Patrick like the deadliest area along the windward coast, a stretch of low cliff fronted by a jumble of islets, and scattered among them, like raisins in a fruitcake, the crosses and asterisks that represented rocks, dozens of them, some a few feet above the surface, some lying in wait beneath the wind-driven waves, and most just awash—a classic sailors' nightmare.

Adler had another objection. "There's a village there, a little ways behind the cliff."

"Maria's Hope," Barr said. "It's an old coconut plantation, abandoned for years. Nobody lives in it, not even squatters—place is supposed to be haunted."

Isabel, still half hidden behind Adler, crossed herself, threw Patrick a quick, shamefaced smile across the table.

"Wait a minute," Patrick said. "I thought we were going to sail right into William Town and drop Colonel Adler there."

"We are," said Barr. "What we're looking for is someplace, a different place, to put Isabel ashore."

"She'll be my backup," Adler explained. "In case anything happens to me."

Isabel chimed in, "It is like the first plan; only we're fewer."

"It's crazy," Patrick snapped. "I mean," he continued, after a long minute of silence, with all of them watching him, "what can she do from up there? You're just stranding her, that's all."

"It's not like that," said Jake. By now Patrick had learned to recognize what he thought of as the colonel's hearty, sure-you-can-take-that-hill voice and distrust it. "She'll have a radio, and so will I," Adler continued. "Hand-held VHFs. One of them's Glory's, in fact."

Barr must have seen the objection Patrick was about to make. "Once Isabel climbs up on that ridge, she'll have a clear line of sight to William Town. Jake'll be able to pick her up, and even if he can't, Glory can be the relay."

It might work, Patrick had to admit: Glory's VHF antenna was at the mainmast head, eighty-five feet above the water. As long as Isabel wasn't behind Mount Mauvis, she'd have no trouble reaching Glory. And she should be able to get Jake, too, though with radios, especially portables, you never could be sure.

"I still don't see what Isabel's supposed to be doing," Gillian said. "If all you want is for her—"

Barr and Jake interrupted her together, but Adler's voice was the stronger: "Isabel's vital, from a tactical point of view. Just take my word for it." For just a moment Adler's self-confidence seemed to slip, and Patrick thought he saw something like desperation behind it.

"Begging the colonel's pardon." Patrick was astonished to hear himself slip into the old army way of addressing a superior, and even Adler's eyes widened slightly.

"Yes?"

"If I get the idea of this," Patrick said, "you and Isabel were going to go ashore at William Town—according to your first plan, that is—like a couple of tourists, and somebody was going to make contact with you."

"That's right," Adler said, watching Patrick intently. "But Mookie's team would've been back up the coast. If things went off the rails, they might be able to pull me out. Even if they couldn't, we'd have a better chance of knowing what happened."

"Understood," said Patrick, restraining his impatience. "But it seems to me like all the original bets are off. The bad guys know who you are, they know you're coming, they know you're on this boat. The minute *Glory* comes into William Bay, it's like—like hiring a skywriter to advertise you're here."

"You've got a point, Patrick," said Jake. "And"—talking the way he would to a bright but not too bright child—"I *have* taken all that into account. The problem is, I haven't any fallback procedure for the meeting. We have to assume that my contacts are natives, and they'll be able either to get past whoever's watching me or to steer clear."

"Sir, why not just bag it?" Patrick asked. "It wasn't much of a plan to begin with, and now it's been, like they say, overtaken by events."

"Run away," said Adler. It wasn't a question.

"Live to fight another day," Patrick replied.

"No," said Adler, shaking his head slowly. "No. No. No. It's now or never. Don't you see? If they weren't scared I'd find something, they wouldn't have been so violent. Whatever they're up to, it must be pretty far advanced."

Now or never. That was it, of course, Patrick realized. *I should've seen it. Light colonel in an army that's shrinking every day; this is his one chance for a star.* He looked into Adler's eyes and knew, beyond any doubt, that he was right.

"Okay," said Patrick. "But when you put Isabel ashore, I'm going with her."

Gillian: Off St. Kitts, 9:30 P.M.

A mile or so to leeward the shore swept by. At this distance the heavy crash of surf was completely drowned by the wind in *Glory's* rigging, and the breaking seas themselves were invisible. But Gillian could feel them just the same, could sense the hostility of those reefs and rocks and of the wind and sea that kept trying to force the yacht down on them.

"You're steering too high." It was the fourth or maybe fifth time Barr had told her that, and she could hear his annoyance.

"Sorry." She made herself turn the wheel to starboard, watched as the red-tinted numbers on the compass card danced back to the course he had given her. She had watched him lay it out on the chart, knew it cleared all the shoals with room to spare, but up here in the whistling night the knowledge somehow wasn't as reassuring as it had been in the cabin.

"After you've sailed down here awhile," Barr observed, "you get gun-shy about a lee shore. I do, anyway."

She doubted that; he was just trying to gift-wrap the reprimand, and she wasn't in the mood for diplomacy.

A few minutes later he pointed to a tiny glitter of lights off the bow. "Sadler's Village." He stretched, yawned. "I'm going to get my head down for a while. The second town you see, give me a shout."

Now, that's more like a real show of confidence, she thought as he edged past her to go below. But the town's name kicked up the recollection of Barr's remark when he'd gone over the course with her and Patrick earlier: "After Sadler's you've got ten fathoms practically into the surf for the next five miles or so. A baby could steer it."

Besides, Barr at sea slept like a cat. If she let *Glory* slide too close to the shore, he'd feel the shock of the breakers on the reefs, transmitted through the hull, before she either heard or saw them. How to build up your crew's self-confidence without actually taking risks. Or was she being unfair?

She glanced down at the binnacle, saw that *Glory* had crept five degrees away from the course, and wrenched the wheel to starboard.

By midnight, with Nevis well astern and open water all around, the wind had dropped. She was relieved at the helm by a tense, monosyllabic Patrick, Isabel a silent shadow at his side. As Gillian slipped below to make the hourly log entry, she saw light under the door of the forward guest cabin and wondered what was going through Jake Adler's mind as he lay alone in his berth.

The log, a schoolchild's cardboard-covered notebook, lay open on the chart table. The previous entry was in Barr's typically minimalist style: "2305. Nevis airport abeam 2 mi. Wind ENE 15. Bar. 30.12." Patrick, as might be expected, imitated Barr, even to the handwriting, but Gillian's part of the ship's record was more expansive, studded with useful telephone numbers, fragments of shopping lists, the names of restaurants to seek out or avoid, amusing anecdotes, even (to Barr's unconcealed disgust) snapshots of *Glory*'s guests.

For the past two days, however, she'd been able to think of nothing about this voyage that she wanted to see in cold print. She would probably have left the pages blank, except that to Barr such a thing was unthinkable. Now she wrote: "0010. Nevis bears 175 M., approx. 5 miles. Wind E 10–12." Setting down the ball-point, she stretched to tiptoe height, reached out and tapped the brass barometer three times with her fingernail. With each tap the needle dropped a hair. She wrote "Bar. 30.10" and replaced the log.

Glory would be off St. Philip a little after three, Barr had said. The sensible thing was to get some sleep or at least rest. But she knew rest would be impossible when her insides were knotted with apprehension. What she wanted was to turn the clock back three days. No, what she really wanted, more than anything else in the world, was to erase the lot of them from memory: Jake Adler, who she knew was up to more than he was saying; and Isabel, who had Patrick turned inside out with what he thought was love; and that old spider Tarleton; and Deedee Etheridge, too, with her knowing smile and her fat thighs.

"Hey, Gillian, you awake?" It was Patrick's voice, and he sounded not scared but definitely uneasy. Gillian had her foot on the companion ladder before she realized her fists were still clenched so tightly that her nails had put deep grooves in her palms.

She emerged into the cockpit, blinking like an owl in the sudden glare from *Glory* spreader lights. Patrick, at the wheel, and Isabel beside him were staring back over the stern. Outside the narrow cone of white that lit *Glory*'s decks and the water rushing by alongside, the night was black and almost palpable. "What's going on?" she said.

Patrick bent forward and flicked a switch, and the spreader lights died. After a few seconds the blackness seemed to thin, and the moon appeared halfway up from the horizon. "Behind us," he said.

The lights were faint at first, almost too faint to see: green on the left and red on the right and two whites in an almost vertical line between. "That's a big one," Gillian said. "How far off?"

"No more'n a mile, now—and coming right up our ass," Patrick said. "I've changed course three times since I saw her, but she keeps matching us."

"Coast Guard, you think?" asked Gillian. But as soon as the words were out of her mouth, she remembered that Coast Guard cutters, like their prey, didn't show running lights when on the prowl.

"Probably some dimwit freighter with a sense of humor," said Patrick.

Gillian could tell he didn't believe it, and neither did she. "Let's see if he's got somebody awake on the VHF," she said, and dived back down the companionway. She flipped on the set and pulled the microphone toward her. "Big ship, big ship, big ship," she said, pitching her voice louder and a little higher than usual. "This is—"

A big, scarred hand plucked the mike from her grasp. It was Barr, stark naked, his hair sticking up on one side of his head like straw. "No names, tiger," he said. "You never know who's listening."

You, for one, she thought, not trying to stem the flood of relief that warmed her. "Got it," she said, and took the microphone from his hand. "This is the sailing yacht dead ahead of you. I say again, this is the sailing yacht under your stupid bow. Do you see us?"

She released the mike's push-to-talk button, and the cabin was flooded with the sound of voices—at least two, talking at once and loudly in a language she couldn't understand. Baffled, she looked to Barr. "What the hell?"

For a moment he seemed as much at a loss as she. Then comprehension widened his eyes. "Son of a bitch is jamming you," he said, and leaped for the companion ladder.

"Hey!" she called over the babel of voices from the radio. "What about pants?" But he was already on deck, and there was nothing to do but follow.

Her eyes went first to Isabel, but the other woman seemed transfixed by the lights behind them—so close, now, that the two whites were screened by the huge, shadowy bow, and only the enormous red and green were visible.

Patrick seemed barely to notice as Barr took the wheel from him, but he obediently took the jib sheet in both hands in response to Barr's tight "Ready about."

Gillian scrambled past the bewildered Isabel, grasped the mainsheet. "Ready," she said.

"Tack." Barr spun the wheel, and *Glory* turned on her heel as nimbly as any twelve meter. Gillian was still horsing in the mainsheet, hand over hand, as a ghostly white steel cliff loomed over them, but going in the opposite direction now. A single lighted porthole swept by, a dozen feet above their heads, and Gillian had an instant's glimpse of an elderly woman's angry profile. At the same moment the ship's bow wave, a breaker that looked ten feet high, struck *Glory* on the quarter and exploded over the gunwale. Gillian, with less than a second to react, still managed to wrap the mainsheet around both wrists. As the wall of water tore her off her feet, she saw Barr, clutching the wheel, disappear beneath it.

For a moment she thought her arms would simply be torn from their sockets. Then she thought she had gone over the side and was being dragged in *Glory*'s wake. And then she was stretched on the bridge deck planking, choking and spluttering, looking down at Patrick, cocooned in jib sheet and clearly dazed, wedged halfway through the lifelines.

"Gillian!" It was Barr's voice, cracking with urgency. There was no earthly way she could find the energy to roll over, but she did.

His hair, she noticed with mild surprise, was plastered flat against his skull. He was wrenching the steering wheel hard over again, in the opposite direction. *Glory* had staggered under the ship's bow wave but had never fully lost way. Gillian could feel the yacht, her cockpit still half full of seawater, responding. Her bow was swinging to starboard, her stern turning toward the ship—a cruise liner, Gillian noted groggily, and somehow familiar—that had just passed.

Of course, she thought, as she struggled to free her hands from the mainsheet. The ship's stern wave, larger and more dangerous than the bow wave, hadn't yet reached *Glory*, and Barr planned to take it on the yacht's stern. But he'd tacked too sharply, and *Glory* was coming around too far, presenting her lee side to the foaming, cresting wave.

The jib, without Patrick handling the sheet, had backed as *Glory* came about. The ketch lay over, exposing her vulnerable cockpit again to the breaker.

"Close the hatch!" Gillian had forgotten the amount of lung power Barr could put behind a command when he had to, or the amount of authority. Jake Adler's blood-steaked face, framed in the companionway, looked stunned, but the hatch slammed shut.

Glory fell off into the trough, and the cruise ship's stern wave, thundering like a train on a trestle, bore down. Suddenly she realized what was wrong with *Glory*'s cockpit. "Where's Isabel?" she cried to Barr.

He didn't answer, didn't even seem to hear, his eyes fixed on the breaking sea looming over them. As Gillian nerved herself for the shock, she saw what Barr was watching: Isabel Machado, her face a mask of terror, was flailing helplessly in the breaker's crest. She must have been sluiced out of *Glory's* cockpit by the liner's bow wave.

For the second time *Glory* was swept by solid water, and Gillian heard the agonized rending of wood. *The mizzen's gone*, she thought, and the resultant surge of adrenaline brought her out of the wave fighting mad, but with a strangely slow-motion clarity of perception. In one clear sweep she took it all in: The cruise liner's narrow, old-fashioned stern, with its single white light, was moving steadily away to the south; Patrick, holding in his right hand the knife with which he'd sawed his way half free from the jib sheet, clutched a choking, gasping Isabel with his left; the mizzen boom—not, thank God, the mast—had snapped cleanly in the middle and hung from its sail like a bird's broken wing; Barr, ashen-faced, still naked as a jaybird except—weirdly—for a scarlet mitten on his left hand, clung to the wheel.

Not a mitten, she realized. His hand was streaming blood.

What do I do? But before the question had fully formed in her mind, she was tearing the mainsheet from her bruised wrists, calling out as she did so, "Jake, up here on the double!"

He must have been waiting for it, so quickly did his solid body appear in the hatchway. He looked quickly at Barr, then addressed Gillian. "There's about fifty gallons of water sloshing around down there, and some broken glass, but nothing too serious. I hope."

She felt a flood of gratitude for his obvious competence and threw him a fierce grin that was matched by his own. "We'll make it," she said, stepping carefully to the wheel. "I'll take the helm if you'll sort out the wounded."

"Roger, Skipper." He pulled the T-shirt over his head and began to tear it into strips. "Bandage," he explained to Gillian. "You want to pass him over here?"

"Keep her on a reach." Barr's voice was barely audible, and he had begun to shiver. "Get the mizzen off. We'll see if . . ." His voice faded out. Separated from the wheel, he folded down onto a cockpit seat, where he sat huddled while Jake, with a gentleness that amazed Gillian, began to wrap his damaged hand in strips of white cloth that turned first pink and then red.

"Patrick, get up off your ass—if you can stand," Gillian heard herself say.

The mate shook himself, looked down at the knife in his hand and Isabel clasped in his arm. "Sure," he said. He returned the knife to its sheath on his hip and placed Isabel gently on the seat across from Barr. Aside from a bruise on one cheekbone, she seemed to Gillian unharmed and almost indecently beautiful, her eyes wide and glazed, her full lips slightly parted, and her clothes pasted to her body.

"I'm going to head up into the wind," Gillian said to Patrick, thinking it through carefully as she spoke. "Get the mizzen off the track and the front end of the boom off the gooseneck. Just bundle the whole mess up, and put it out of the way below—in the guest cabin across from the chart table."

"Right," said Patrick. He got to his feet awkwardly, and Gillian guessed he must be bruised all along his left side, where he'd landed on the genoa track. But he was up, and that was what counted.

"I'll get Barr below where I can see what I'm doing," said Jake. "You, too, *querida*—you're the nurse." On the lip of the companionway, watching as Barr inched his way down the ladder toward Isabel, he asked, "What happened, anyway? I missed everything but the cleanup."

Gillian's laugh almost got away from her, and she bit it off—but, she saw, not so quickly that Jake didn't notice how close to the edge she was. "That ship"—inclining her head toward the fast-disappearing white light—"almost ran us down. Barr saved our bacon." She gave him a carefully rationed smile. "That's the compressed version. Barr can tell you the details."

"I see," said Jake. "Then I'd better get started on him."

As Jake's head vanished down the companionway, Patrick, on his knees on the afterdeck, looked up from the sail he was carefully stripping off the broken boom. "Did Barr do what I think he did when Isabel went over?" he asked slowly.

"Believe it," Gillian snapped. The high was wearing off fast, and she was afraid she might burst into tears.

"You're telling me," Patrick continued, shaking his head, "that Barr used a sixty-five-foot yacht like a fucking fielder's mitt to scoop a woman out of the water on the fly?"

"What choice did he have?" Gillian replied. "You and I were swaddled in Dacron spaghetti, and Jake was down below. Barr was the only one who saw Isabel go. He knew where she was, and he knew he had to do it alone."

"Jesus, whoever heard of anything like it?" Patrick said. "Spin the boat on a dime, and lay her exactly where she had to be for Isabel to get washed back on board."

"And just in time for you to grab hold of Isabel as she whizzed by," Gillian said. "It wasn't entirely a single-handed rescue."

"Close enough," he said. He rose, holding the two pieces of the boom. "I'll take these below, then bring down the sail." He paused, balancing easily on the bridge deck. "One thing I don't get. How come those goddamn Greeks didn't come back and finish us off?"

"What're you talking about?" she said. "They were probably as scared as we were, once they saw what their little joke did. And what do you mean, Greeks?"

"Didn't you see her name? It was that old barge, the . . . *Euphoric.* We saw her back in Gustavia. Anyway," he continued, starting down the ladder, "it was no joke. They were trying to sink us. Maybe Barr or the colonel's got some idea why."

She made a noncommittal noise to speed him on his way. Right now, she wanted to be alone—but not to think. She knew the near collision was no accident, had known since she saw the high, narrow bow bearing down on them. But somehow the thought was just one too many to handle. She felt the gulping sobs rising in her throat, barely managed to hold them in until Patrick was out of hearing.

Half an hour later it was Jake who came up on deck, carrying a heavy sweat shirt and wreathed in an odor that was pure heaven. "Put this on," he said, ignoring her sniffles. "I'll aim the boat while you do."

As her head emerged, he continued. "Barr's all right—well, a couple of broken fingers, but Isabel did a nice splinting job. Now, you're going below and get some hot food into you and a couple hours' sleep."

Food. She was, without warning, ravenous beyond belief, ravenous, moreover, for the one particular dish she was sure she smelled on Jake's clothes—Patrick's special linguine with pesto, *pesto alla cojones,* he called it. The spiritual essence of garlic, plus an even dozen other ingredients he refused to reveal. "Why all this solicitude?" she said, or mostly said, because she was salivating so hard the words came out sloppy.

"You need your rest," said Jake benevolently. "We've got a busy night ahead of us, especially with the regular skipper out of action."

She was halfway down the companionway ladder, and it was indeed Patrick's pesto that was wafting back from the galley, when she decoded Jake's last statement.

"Oh, no, I'm not," she muttered under her breath. "I'm not taking *Glory* in there, not in a million years."

WEDNESDAY

Patrick: Spaniards Bay, St. Philip, 3:30 A.M.

"Tack again," said Barr, from his position in the companionway.

Gillian's voice, weary and tense, responded, "Ready about," and Patrick and Jake, standing by the sheets, echoed, "Ready."

"Hard alee." Patrick felt *Glory* swing into her turn. As he had twenty times already, he cast off one jib sheet, scrambled past Jake, across the cockpit, and snatched up the other. Thanks to three months of handling heavy lines, his hands were thickly padded with callouses; he could barely feel the difference between the old jib sheet and the new one, still stiff from the reel, that replaced the line he'd had to cut. He could imagine how Jake's palms must be burning, but there had been no complaint from the older man.

Nor from Isabel, who had been crouched in *Glory*'s leaping dinghy for the past hour and more, towed back and forth across the narrow entrance to the bay on St. Philip's raw windward coast. Patrick straightened up and threw a quick glance astern. With the moon riding behind a scrim of light cloud, the gray rubber dinghy was nothing more than a pale white wake, and Isabel—wearing Gillian's foul-weather gear—a yellow heap in its center.

"In about five minutes"—Barr sounded calm, almost detached—"we're going to have a hole in that stratus. We'll take her in then."

Five minutes: another tack or maybe two. Patrick stretched mightily, shaking the muscle kinks from his arms. He flexed his legs, feeling

114

the play of muscles. *All right*, he thought. *Almost time to move.* His gut still felt hollow, and his mouth had the old, familiar copper taste in the corners, but it'd be okay as soon as he went over the side.

"You sure you don't want the engine on?" Gillian murmured to Barr, leaning across the binnacle toward him. There was no light in the cockpit, no light in the boat at all, except for the faint spaceship green glow of the depth sounder dial inside the companionway.

"Better not," Barr replied. "*Glory* handles a lot better under sail, and I don't like the idea of that prop spinning away down there, grabbing at lines that go over the side."

He was missing the point of her question, Patrick thought. What she wanted was reassurance. "You're doing great, Gillian," he said. "You don't need the engine—you'll have *Glory* in and out of that cove like . . . like shit through a goose. Won't she, Barr?"

Barr looked startled and even, Patrick thought, slightly amused. "Of course she will," he said. "Why not?"

"Here comes that hole in the clouds," Jake said.

Even before the moon's rim poked clear, the light increased dramatically and as smoothly as a rheostat. The jumbles of rock to leeward began to take on weirdly jagged shapes: a slouching giant, a castle with towers. The mouth of the bay was wider than Patrick had thought, with a broken-back islet in the middle surrounded by seething foam. "Head up," said Barr. "Ease the sheets."

Glory swung her bow closer to the wind, the main and jib slatting hard. The yacht was still making headway—and leeway, too, sliding almost diagonally into the northernmost corner of the bay. Suddenly the shore was bathed in sharp moonlight, and Patrick felt the breath go out of his chest as if he'd been struck. The low cliff beetled over the water, and breakers exploded like shellfire beneath the overhangs. *We're going to land a rubber boat on* that? he thought, his heart sinking.

"Stand by to jibe." Barr had raised his voice, and it cut through the crash and splutter of the breaking seas. He was out of the companionway like a cat, standing behind Gillian, his bandaged hand held stiffly out to the side. "Steady," he said, drawing the word out. "Steady . . . Now!"

Perfect, Patrick thought, casting off the jib sheet and letting it run like fire through his palms. *Perfect.* He dropped the line, bounded across the cockpit, grabbed the other sheet.

"Just a little," Barr called, and Patrick nodded. He took in enough line to keep some air in the sail, but not enough to make it draw fully.

"Trim the mainsheet. *Trim* it, Jake." But all those tacks and then a jibe had left Jake numb. Kinked line was jammed in the block, Patrick saw, and Jake was pulling hard at the wrong part of the sheet; in a couple of seconds the whole thing would be a tangle that would take twenty minutes to unsnarl.

"D'you want—" Patrick began. He wasn't quick enough. Barr was at Jake's side, grabbing the line in his good hand and giving what looked to Patrick like a single, hard tug with an odd twitch in it. Jake nearly went over backward as the kink came free. Before he could regain his balance, Barr had horsed in another ten feet or so, using his hand to pull and his teeth to hold.

"Barr! You all right?" Gillian called as Jake took hold again, breathing hard.

"The man with the iron jaw," Barr said, laughing. "Now, head up, Gillian, and you two strap in those sails. Flat as they'll go."

Patrick could feel *Glory* hesitating. Just a hair too much and she'd be in irons, stalled out in the eye of the wind, ready to sag helplessly down on the rocks and sure destruction. But Gillian was playing the yacht as well as Barr could have done, heading up and falling off, while Patrick and Jake scrambled down into the dinghy. Isabel had the outboard going, and Patrick gave her arm a quick squeeze as he grabbed for the steering handle. "Cast off!" he shouted.

From down at water level *Glory* seemed endless, as big as *Euphoric*, and as potentially deadly. With relief, Patrick watched her head fall away from the wind, saw her begin to pick up speed. He sat frozen for a moment, bouncing up and down in the unsteady dinghy, with the water splashing around his ankles. It looked as if *Glory* were headed straight for a pillar of rock at the south end of the bay, but there was no time to worry about that. A second set of clouds, moving across the path of the first, was already beginning to dim the moonlight.

He scanned the corner of the bay. In the Airborne he'd been no better or worse at map reading than any of the other junior NCOs, but that year in the desert with old man Hals had sharpened his eye for hidden detail, and then sailing with Barr had put a fine edge on his skill. He had no trouble finding the patch of inky blackness where Barr said there was a tiny beach, shadowed behind the huge hunch-backed boulder the natives called Lebron.

No time to waste. Patrick twisted the throttle at the end of the steering handle, and the dinghy lurched ahead, sending a wavelet of icy bilge water surging back into his crotch. As the little boat rounded the rock, the light from the sky faded out. A second's glimpse into the shadows was all Patrick had: a swatch of smooth, wet baseball-size rocks about fifty feet square—Barr's so-called beach.

But the water behind the boulder was nearly flat and, when Patrick jumped over the side, exactly waist-deep, as Barr had promised. Jake held the waterproof flashlight and Patrick steadied the dinghy while Isabel climbed awkwardly over the gunwale. Jake passed her the heavy bundle, double-wrapped in an old sail cover; the smell of bilge and canvas cut right through the iodine-laden sea air. She balanced it carefully on her head and stumbled toward shore.

"Watch your step!" Patrick called. "The rocks are"—under she went, with barely a splash, everything but the canvas-covered package immersed—"loose," he finished, as her spluttering face broke the surface.

At last she was on land, shaking herself like a dog. Jake had been scooping water from the dinghy with the bailer. Now, as he settled himself in the little boat's midsection, he held out the flash. "Good luck," he said.

"And to you, sir," Patrick replied, taking the light.

Jake grabbed the back of Patrick's neck—with his fingertips; his palms must have been on fire—and pulled his head forward. Patrick, ready for anything from a curse to an embrace, heard the older man's penetrating whisper clearly: "Watch your back, Sergeant."

"Sir?"

"You heard me." He took the handle gingerly. "Shove me off."

Stumbling, Patrick swung the dinghy around. "Barr'll have the running lights on," he said. "Remember to come up on the starboard side—the green light. Look for the plastic float on the end of the dinghy rode. Just pull yourself—"

"I was at the briefing, too," said Jake. "*Hasta la vista.*" He pushed the gear lever, and the boat squirmed out of Patrick's grasp. He stood in the waist-deep water till it was out of sight, till the engine's high snarl was absorbed in the dull booming of the surf.

Behind the tiny rock beach a path switchbacked its way up the slope to the abandoned plantation whose blind-eyed windows overlooked the sea. Barr had told Patrick where the track began, warned him that it might be overgrown in stretches. In the light of the waterproof flash, Patrick saw that goats or mules had been this way not too long before, and people—one drinker, at least, of Jamaican Red Stripe beer and someone else who preferred Night Train by the pint. That bottle had come a long way to end up propped against a Turk's-head cactus in the middle of the Caribbean.

He paused to let Isabel catch up and looked out over the endless expanse of sea. It was still a good hour before sunrise, but already the eastern horizon was etched clearly, a hard, straight line below the sheet of gray cloud. Patrick scanned across the line, but nothing broke it. *Glory* was probably doubling the northern end of St. Philip by now, to glide down the coast and drop anchor off William Town. She should be there by eight, Barr had figured, but Patrick wanted to be tucked safely out of sight long before then.

He shifted the improvised pack to a more comfortable position on his stinging shoulder and extended his arm to Isabel, whose new deck shoes were slipping on the dry, crumbling ground. Bare feet would have the best traction here, but only if they were West Indian feet, used to going shoeless most of the time. Patrick's Top-Siders were already filled with grit and amazingly sharp little stones, which he was determined to ignore until he attained the top of the hill.

Isabel reached for his outstretched hand and missed. Wobbling off-balance, she grabbed at what looked like a fat tree trunk and gasped in pain.

"You okay?" he called softly.

"*Cacto!*" she snapped.

"Hold still." Patrick held her trembling hand in his, inspected her palm under the flashlight beam. "There's a couple of spines still in there," he told her. "I'll get 'em out as soon as we're sitting down. Otherwise they infect."

"Fucking stupid island," she said. Just then it seemed to him an understatement.

Patrick's tongue traced the heel of her hand, slowly and delicately, until it located the tiny protrusion. His teeth pressed down on either side of the broken spine, closed firmly on it, like the jaws of a trap. He drew his head back with infinite care, feeling the spine drag its way out of her flesh.

He turned his head, spit. "There. Now let's slosh a little of that booze on the hole." He felt her tense for the sting of the alcohol, but she never flinched. "Here, have a slug," he said. "You've earned it."

"*Gracias,*" she said, and took a healthy swallow. She shuddered and passed the plastic bottle back to him. "You finish. You earned it, too."

Raw rum, at slightly less than body heat, seared its way down his throat. Barr's sovereign remedy for everything. He set the empty bottle down and looked around the room they sat in. Like every abandoned building in the islands, this one had lost not only every stick of furniture but also its door and window frames. Would've had the plumbing and wiring ripped out, too, if there'd been any plumbing or wiring in the first place. The roof was gone—courtesy of Hurricane Hugo, probably—and dawn was just beginning to probe the corners, where the wind had piled surprisingly neat heaps of dead leaves and light brush.

They were high enough on one of the ridges of Mauvis so the portable VHF should have no trouble reaching William Town. At 0800, when *Glory* should be entering William Bay, Barr would give a call on the yacht's radio, ostensibly to the port authorities. Instead of speaking, Patrick would key the transmit button three times. The clicks would come up nice and sharp on *Glory*'s VHF. He glanced at his watch; another hour at least.

He went to one of the room's two windows, standing back from the opening in case there might be anyone outside. From the ridge St. Philip's forested slopes swept away toward the leeward side. Beyond the overgrown courtyard a packed dirt road wandered down the hill and lost itself in the trees a few hundred yards away. *A bad place to defend*, he found himself thinking. *Too much cover, too close.*

Not that he had anything to defend it with, in any case. Jake had flatly vetoed bringing *Glory*'s ancient M-1 rifle, the only weapon aboard. And he was probably right. If—when—something went wrong, guns and dope were the two things that made the islands' cops go crazy.

A hand plucked at Patrick's shirt. "Why don't you change?" Isabel asked. "We brought dry."

She had a point. Soaked by seawater to just below the rib cage, Patrick had been soaked again, top to bottom, by sweat. His T-shirt and khakis were half dry now, stiff and sticky. She was probably right, even if they had no extra freshwater to wash off the salt. He pulled the shirt off over his head, and as he turned saw her standing naked in the thin gray light.

It was bad from the start. Not sweet stolen love, the way it'd been the day before in Statia Harbor, or straight, molten-rock sex, like the first time. This was more like fighting for your life, against someone who was drowning and dragging you down with her. At the end of it Patrick lay gasping on his back in the gritty dirt; Isabel, silent as she had been throughout, was mounted on him, her head down, her rigidly extended arms braced on his shoulders. As she forced him toward a climax that he knew wasn't hers, tears fell on his chest like warm rain.

By then he might as well have been hit over the head with a brick.

He was aware of her rolling off him, falling heavily against him, but he was like a man underwater, moving his limbs slowly and heavily. He knew when she eased herself away from his side, when she got to her feet and, after a minute, slipped out the door.

Even then it seemed impossible to get up. Only when he heard her voice outside, low and urgent, did the sound knife him into full consciousness. Instinct rolled him over, brought him silently to his hands and knees. Framed by the ripped-out-doorway, Isabel stood alone, some fifty yards away, the portable VHF set held to her ear. The sun, shielded by clouds, still lit her sweat- and dirt-streaked back, revealed the darkening bruise along her hip that marked where she'd struck something falling overboard.

She put down the set, picked up a dry shirt, and pulled it on. The whole time her eyes were fixed on the southwest horizon; even when she bent to lift a pair of jeans from the ground, she never looked away. She wriggled her way into the pants, quickly wrapped a square of cloth around her hair. She picked up the portable radio and stood for a moment, apparently lost in thought, as she toggled a switch on and off several times. Then, without a backward look, she strode barefoot down the path and out of sight.

Why am I not surprised? Patrick asked himself as he struggled into his own clothes. She'd been saying good-bye with her body, he saw that plainly now. But for some reason he was just as certain it wasn't the good-bye of betrayal. Or not betrayal of him, anyway.

Nothing was gone but the radio, though that was bad enough. Without it he might as well be on the moon, as far as Adler was concerned, and his assignment was up the spout. "Stay put and listen," was what Adler had said. Stay put *or* listen was more like it, and Patrick wasn't about to stay put.

He started down the dirt road, moving fast. It was a much better surface than the path up the windward slope, and now that it was full light he could stretch out his stride. What about the other thing Adler said? "Watch your back." Had the old man expected Isabel to pull something like this?

Trees hung completely over the road, and the underbrush was thick and wet and bright green. This was the island's rainy side, a downpour every day here, or even more often. Yet the road was basically clear, except for light growth between two bare ruts. Somebody used it, and used it regularly.

From up ahead he heard the crash of a body smashing through bushes, followed by Isabel's angry "*¡Mierda!*" She was gone by the time he rounded a bend, but it was easy to see what had happened: a root ankle-high across one rut, the cuplike mark where one knee had gone into the soft ground, a stalk with elephant-eared leaves snapped off where she'd grabbed at it.

The road down the hill burst suddenly out of the trees and, a few yards into the open, met another, wider dirt thoroughfare that wound off down the island. Isabel had pulled up just inside the shelter of the trees and was sitting on a thatch of dead palm leaves, massaging her ankle and staring intently down the road. The portable radio lay on the ground beside her, its antenna bent double.

She looked up as Patrick appeared, and the blood drained from her dirty face. "Go away!" she said, and though he had not heard fear in her voice before, he recognized it.

"Why?" he demanded. He couldn't wait for an answer and didn't expect one. "How come you ran out? What—"

She was on her feet, looking scared and angry both. "No! No! Go away quick."

"Fuck that," he said. His voice sounded flat and ugly to him, and she recoiled as if he'd hit her. Picking up the radio, he said, "Why're you running away, Isabel? Whose side are you on?"

"I have no choice," she said. "You have to believe." Another woman, he thought, would have been crying now, but Isabel had pulled herself together. She was dry-eyed, back straight, proud as Satan.

"I can't believe you," he began, but she was pressing the palm of her hand on his chest to shut him up. A second later he heard it, too: the roaring of a vehicle—a light truck, it sounded like—double-clutch-ing its way over dirt.

"Hide," she said. "If they find you, I cannot save you. Not from these." The bruise on her cheek was bigger than he'd realized. He found himself trusting her, but he took the portable radio with him as he faded silently back into a chest-high stand of brush.

The truck, when it appeared, was at once strange and familiar. Square and chunky, with an open back, it had been painted a shimmering black; another soldier of Patrick's age might not have recognized it at all, never mind repainted and stripped of canvas, but in the African desert there were still Korean War-vintage U.S. Army three-quarter-ton utility trucks serving out their last days, and Kampfgruppe Hals had owned no fewer than five of them.

The two young men who got out weren't anyone's idea of soldiers, though both were carrying assault rifles. Old Yugoslav weapons, Patrick thought, heavy but reliable, and chambered for the same rounds as the AK-47. They were dressed like West Indians—dirty T-shirts, baggy pants, unlaced hightop athletic shoes with no socks. But their mustached faces were narrow and clay-colored, topped with long, straight black hair. *East Indians maybe,* Patrick thought.

"Where is the man?" one of them demanded. "Take us to him." His accented English was clear enough, but it had no trace of Caribbean lilt.

"Never mind about him," said Isabel. "I must see the leader right away. I have information."

"Soon," said the one who had spoken. His stained and spotted T-shirt had what looked like a college seal on the chest. "First the man."

"I told you. Forget him." Bruised and dirty as she was, she had the manner of a command. Patrick had the sense that she was used to ordering people around but that these men frightened her.

"We must bring him to the leader," the second man said. "We have been ordered." His English sounded near perfect, but much slower, as if he were constructing the speech in his head before he said it.

"Then you are too late," Isabel replied. "I have already killed him. With his own knife."

The two of them regarded her silently. She certainly looked as if she might've been in a fight, Patrick thought, but saying that about the knife was a mistake. With a knife—unless you were an expert—there was always blood, all over everyone.

The man with the college T-shirt said something, very fast, in a language that sounded familiar. Not Creole, Patrick decided, certainly not any Spanish he'd ever heard. But he had heard it before, somewhere.

Now the second man's eyes were following where the first pointed. To something on the ground. Patrick didn't have to be able to see his own footprints to know what they were looking at, the word "boat shoe" stuck out of the second man's rapid-fire response. And even while Patrick was feeling the bottom of his stomach fall out, his memory was raking over the sounds. Where in hell had he heard that jabbering before? With only a moment more to think, he could make his memory tell him.

But there was no moment. Without a word the first man grabbed Isabel. Before she could struggle, he had her arm hammerlocked up behind her back. The second man chambered a round in his assault rifle and placed the muzzle, with loving care, against her heaving breast.

"You come out, man," he said, and paused.

Once again Patrick felt he was assembling the words of his next sentence; when it came, it left no room for maneuver: "You come with your hands up, or I shoot her breasts off."

Barr: Off St. Philip, 7:30 P.M.

The tension of *Glory*'s predawn approach to shore had ebbed, leaving Gillian stretched limply across the forward end of the cockpit. Jake, on the other hand, seemed to have wound himself up to a high pitch and stuck there, so that Barr, who had been steering one-handed for the past three hours, finally put him at the helm to give him something to do. The yacht was barely ghosting along in the wind shadow from Mauvis peak, and while the breeze would pick up again in a mile or so, there wasn't much that could happen to *Glory* on a beam reach a good two miles from shore. Barr was suddenly overtaken by hunger, and he remembered that he'd been too taut last night, and his broken fingers too sore, to think about eating.

What little of *Glory*'s cooking Patrick didn't handle was picked up by Gillian, and as a result Barr, who had largely rebuilt the yacht's galley with his own hands, was a virtual stranger to its lockers. Not that it made a great deal of difference. His deep disinterest in food remained as untouched by Patrick's superb cuisine as by Gillian's amateur imitations of it. On his rare forays into the galley, Barr worked from the assumption that anything wrapped, canned, or refrigerated was edible, and since it all ended up in your stomach anyway, why quibble about the way items were combined on the way down?

Barr's *specialité du chef* was ketchup and peanut butter sandwiches, but something as complicated as that required two sets of functional fingers to construct. He settled instead for the peanut butter alone, fished from the jar with his knife and licked off its point, followed by an already opened tin of smoked oysters and two nearly frozen Mars bars, the whole washed down with an emergency rum and Coke— about a third of the can of soda poured off and replaced with dark rum. He debated bringing the drink up on deck and decided against it. Gillian disapproved of drinking at breakfast, and anyway Barr wanted—needed—the privacy to sort out his thoughts.

Gillian seemed to think that they were nearly home free, that once they dumped Jake Adler on the wharf at William Town, they could just sail away—after picking Patrick up, of course. (No mention of Isabel.) Gillian's ability to ignore unpleasant truths was one of her strongest attributes. She had, after all, been able to ignore the economics of the charter business for a year and a half; at least she never talked to Barr about the state of *Glory's* finances, itself an ominous sign.

Propping himself against the galley counter, Barr gently swirled the can of liquid while he considered a new and unnerving possibility that had popped into his head between bites of oyster: What if it was Tarleton who'd arranged the deaths of Jake Adler's men? If it was, then he was probably also herding Jake and Isabel—and *Glory* and her crew—off some as yet invisible cliff.

In the old days—only five years ago—Barr would have assumed the worst about Tarleton the moment he showed himself. Or even sooner, when Barr felt the first offstage tweak of that duplicitous hand. Now he found himself shuttling between paranoia and trust—or was it naïveté?

One thing he was reasonably sure of: Tarleton did still represent some element of the sprawling American intelligence establishment. If the old man had lost that connection, the word would've flared from one end of the Caribbean to the other, as it did every time the CIA replaced one of its station chiefs. So if Tarleton was acting for the government, what did official Washington want from the Caribbean these days? Well, that was easy enough to pinpoint: no explosions, no scandals, and, above all, no expense.

Then maybe Tarleton's story was the truth. It did have the classic keep-the-cash-and-take-the-credit-too touch of Beltway bureaucracy: *Let loose-cannon Jake rumble about the Caribbean on his own dime, looking for bad smells. If he finds nothing, great—we all can return to the serious business of bilking the taxpayers. If, on the other hand, there really is a threat and Adler uncovers it, we can bring in whoever's necessary to handle the situation properly (read: steal the headlines).*

And therein, Barr thought, lay the problem. This caper might be Jake Adler's last chance for his star. He'd hold on to it like a mongoose with a chicken, and there was only one way to break a mongoose's hold. Kill it.

Gloomily Barr drained off the rest of his drink and tossed the can in the bin below the sink. Feeling a thousand years old, he hauled himself up the ladder into the watery sunlight. Jake, his attention locked on the compass, barely nodded; despite the gray of fatigue, he looked ready, even eager, for a fight. Gillian still lay stretched across the bridge deck; her eyes opened as she felt his step on the rungs. Like the colors on a dying dolphin, expressions chased each other across her face: recognition, love, suspicions, apprehension. Then, as she saw how he was reading her, she reddened. "Hello, Barr," she said. "Where the hell are we?"

"About halfway down the lee side. Bwapen Point is just ahead."

"Bwapen," Jake repeated, glancing quickly up at the high spur of land on their port bow. "That an African name?"

"Creole," Barr replied. "From the French *bois* and *pain*. 'Bread-fruit,' to you. It's the site of an old plantation."

"I thought St. Philip was a Dutch island," Jake replied. "Before independence, I mean."

"Before independence, it was," Barr agreed. "But before the Dutch, it was British. They and the French took turns conquering it from each other for a couple of centuries, after the French threw out the Spanish, who discovered it in the first place. The Spanish were the ones who named it—San Felipe—when they took it from the Caribs, who'd taken it from the Arawaks."

"Sounds like a popular little place," Jake said. "Everybody fighting over it like that."

"Back then they fought over all the islands all the time," Barr said. "St. Philip was never one of the real prizes—not enough good land and no protected harbor." He pulled a crumpled pack of cigarettes from his hip pocket and ducked into the shelter of the companionway to light it.

"Speaking of land," said Gillian, "what happened there?"

Barr flicked the match over the side, his eyes following her gesture. St. Philip's central ridge was high here, and its upper slopes were the familiar thick, shiny deep green of rain forest. But the flatter areas along the leeward shore were swathed with stark, lifeless brown. "That's the old MacIntyre plantation," he said. "Citrus, mostly limes. As big once as the Rose estate on Dominica."

"But what happened, Barr?" Gillian demanded. "I mean, that's hundreds of acres of dead stuff."

"Hurricane Hugo, I expect," Barr replied. "It trashed all the islands down here."

"Most of these trees are still standing," said Gillian, who had picked up *Glory*'s cockpit binoculars.

"Salt water killed them," Barr said. "Roots flooded, leaves drowned by windblown spray. They're as dead as if somebody'd put an ax to them."

Gillian was sitting upright now, her attention gripped by whatever she was seeing through the field glasses. "I guess Hugo blew off those roofs, too," she said. "Looks like a factory or something."

"It was a canning plant, for the lime juice," Barr said. "Been like that for years." Even without the binoculars he was able now to make out the tumbledown wreck of the old plantation pier, the cluster of tiny fishermen's shacks at its head end, the brightly painted boats drawn up on the sand.

When he thought of St. Philip—and it wasn't often—he thought of those tiny, lopsided fishing boats, framed with bent tree limbs and planked with old furniture or whatever flotsam came ashore, and not caulked at all. They always carried crews of three, he recalled: one man to row, one to steer, and one to bail. The bailer had the hardest job. The boats went no farther out to sea than the nearest reef, but many of them never came home. Renowned for their skill even by the expert mariners of Saba or Bequia, the Philipian fishermen were also stubborn, narrow-minded, hagridden by superstition; they were the bravest men Barr had ever met.

"What do they do now, with the trees all dead?" Gillian asked. She was still panning the binoculars across the gently sloping hills.

"Same thing they did with them alive—nothing," said Barr. "People down here call agriculture slave work. They won't touch it, beyond scraping a half acre of dirt for themselves. The MacIntyres used to bring a shipload of Dominicans in for the harvest, but the economics of that don't work anymore."

"Well, if they don't grow things, how do they make a living?" Jake demanded. "The damn island's got to have some kind of economy."

Barr laughed. "Why?" He flipped the cigarette butt off to leeward. "Jake, you're looking at a place that's an hour from San Juan and hardly in the twentieth century at all."

"Well, what about tourism?" said Jake. "There's tourists, right?" He sounded angry, as if the Philipians' poverty were some kind of personal insult.

"A few," said Barr. "One hotel, gets a trickle of skin divers in season, and a couple of guesthouses. A few of the less elegant windjammers make day stops, but the regular cruise ships don't come in at all. William Bay's got a surge that'll roll your fillings out. There's a few small coves, but even the yachties give the place a pass, ever since a couple of the locals got drunk and boarded a boat waving cutlasses. Cutlasses," he added to Jake, "are what they call machetes down here."

"But there is an airstrip," Jake said.

"Prince Bernhard International Airport," Barr agreed. "The building's two feet shorter than the sign on top of it. It's on the far side of the central ridge. LIAT flies in once a week, and Winair comes in every two days."

"Subsistence agriculture," Jake said, nodding. He seemed to like the sound, and repeated it, drawing out the syllables: "Sub-sis-tence."

"And a little subsistence fishing," Barr added.

"And a lot of little checks from overseas, I bet," said Gillian, setting down the binoculars.

Jake raised his eyebrows, and she answered his unspoken question. "It's the same story all over the Caribbean," she said. "The young people go up north, get a job parking cars or taking care of other people's kids, live sixteen to a room, send money home."

That wasn't all of it, of course, Barr reflected. The small islands got poorer and poorer, the people left behind more and more bitter, and what passed for government more and more fragile and corrupt. People from the States could not understand how hard and narrow life could be on a place like St. Philip; all they saw was another tropical paradise, where you could pick your lunch off a tree.

"Sure looks peaceful," said Jake. "Too damn peaceful." Gillian looked at him sharply, and he flashed her a grin. "Just a joke." *He's really looking forward to this,* Barr thought.

An errant puff of wind rippled the flat water ahead of *Glory*. A moment later her sails filled, and she picked up speed. Jake glanced at his watch, which he had twisted to the inside of his wrist.

"We're running a little slow," Barr said. "But William Bay's just beyond Castle Point there."

"We'd better make that radio call now," Jake said. "It's just coming up on oh-eight-hundred."

Barr shrugged, but Gillian got to her feet. "I'll do it. Who're we supposed to be calling, Barr? The port captain?"

"That's as good as anybody," he replied. "If they answer—which I doubt—say we'll be anchoring in half an hour."

"Be sure to listen for those three clicks," Jake said as she slipped by Barr, down the companionway. It seemed to him she made a small, unnecessary effort to avoid brushing against him. A moment later he heard her radio voice, each word carefully and crisply articulated. She was better on the VHF than Barr, who hated all electronic devices, and the ship-to-shore especially.

He turned to Jake. "How do you want to handle it when we get in?"

Jake seemed to consider the question, but Barr was sure he'd worked it all out in his mind. "You'll have to go ashore to clear customs, right?"

"Probably." Barr couldn't remember if St. Philip's customs officers even had a launch. He thought they didn't.

"I'll come with you, if that's acceptable."

"Customs people don't care, as long as you don't wander off till we're cleared," Barr replied.

"I meant, acceptable to you. It might be dangerous having me along." Jake's voice was matter-of-fact, but of course it was his business they were talking about.

"I doubt we're going to be met on the pier by a firing squad," Barr said, trying to keep his voice light.

"That's my reading, too," Jake agreed. "Whoever's running this will probably want to have a look at me, out in the open, before he does anything."

Let the trapped mouse scamper a little before you step on him? Somehow it didn't jibe with what had been happening so far. The hidden enemy seemed much more interested in fast, bloody solutions, and no fooling around.

"You forget," Jake said, exactly as if he'd been reading Barr's thoughts, "they'll want to know who my contact is."

Assuming they haven't already bagged him, Barr thought. "But you don't know who it is either," he said.

"I don't," Jake agreed. "None of us does. But he's clearly a pro."

"Really?"

"Absolutely," said Jake, so firmly that Barr wondered if he was trying to convince himself. "He found us, for one thing. The Ethan Allens aren't exactly in the yellow pages. Yet we haven't been able to identify him—and believe me, we've tried." He saw the expression Barr was unable to conceal and quickly added, "Discreetly, of course."

"Of course," Barr echoed. "Just how is your Scarlet Pimpernel going to make contact, if you don't mind my asking?"

"Classic tradecraft," Jake replied. "He assumes I'll be spotted right off—"

Like a snowman in a coal bin, Barr thought.

"—so we're using a decoy drop technique. I'll make a round of all the tourist sights: the two churches, the old fort, the museum. Sit in the chairs, feel around underneath them. I'll hire a guide, or maybe two. Talk to everybody I meet. Give away small coins to any panhandler who asks. By the time I get halfway through town, I should've pulled every watcher they've got."

It made sense, in a suicidal sort of way. "I still don't see how your man makes contact, though."

"Oh, that." Jake looked far too pleased with himself, and Barr felt his suspicions rise. "The actual instructions for a meeting will be delivered here, while I'm ashore."

"Here?" Barr was incredulous. "To *Glory*?"

"Of course. You'll have the usual crowd of people around the boat, trying to sell you fruit and souvenirs, right?"

"And your contact will be one of them?"

"Affirmative."

Parlor sleight of hand, Barr thought, but it might just work. The last time Barr had sailed into William Bay, aboard his own *Windhover*, four years ago, she had instantly been besieged by a dozen skiffs at least, not to mention as many swimmers, carrying their pathetic wares between their teeth. Other charter skippers had told tales of having to threaten desperate boarders with winch handles and boathooks to keep them off the decks.

"Well?" Jake demanded. "What do you think?"

"No answer from shore," said Gillian's voice, from the companionway at Barr's back. He wondered how long she'd been listening.

Jake craned his neck to look past Barr. "And Patrick's signal?" he asked. "The three key clicks?"

Barr saw the answer in her eyes, even before she shook her head no.

"You're sure?" Jake persisted. "You know what—"

"Yes," she snapped. But it was more than annoyance, Barr saw.

Jake clearly saw it, too. "What's eating you, Gillian?"

"When your mystery friend on St. Philip was setting all this up," she asked, "did he tell you to split your force in two?"

Jake's air of cautious indulgence was suddenly replaced by surprised respect. "No, that was my idea. I wanted an ace in the hole."

"But that's not why you wanted to put Isabel ashore, is it?" she said. She was watching Jake like a small hawk about to pounce.

"I wondered when you'd guess about her," said Jake.

Gillian

"When did I guess about Isabel? Just now," Gillian replied. Jake was nodding and smirking, like a grade-school teacher encouraging a dull pupil. "And how long," she asked, "have *you* known about her?"

"I don't *know* anything." Jake's shrug was so stagy she knew he was toying with her. "But the possibility was always there."

"What possibility was always there?" It was almost all Gillian could do to keep her voice level when what she wanted was to shake him till he rattled. Barr's carefully blank expression could have meant anything, and Gillian wondered if the notion of Isabel as traitor had occurred to him.

Jake was clearly eager to explain. "Well, she was from Cuba, wasn't she? Half of South Florida is Cuban these days, and it stands to reason a lot of them are Castro plants." He smiled condescendingly. "She was just too good to be true, Our Lady of the Inner Tubes."

"So Castro is invading St. Philip then?" Barr asked innocently.

Maybe too innocently. Jake's face, already red from yesterday's sunburn, reddened by a shade. "You think because I'm a soldier, I'm a paranoid dimwit?" he said. "Of course, Castro's not invading anybody anymore, but he's still playing footsie with every terrorist left in the world."

"But you think Isabel set up your friends, back at Île Fourche," Barr said, ignoring Jake's hostility.

"If I was sure"— Jake's voice was harsh—"I'd have killed her myself."

"Then—" Barr began, but Jake had only paused to organize his argument.

"Look, you must've noticed how the opposition—never mind who they are, for a minute—how they've stayed one step ahead of us? How they know where we are before we get there?"

Gillian, suddenly remembering Tarleton's hidden locating transmitter, darted a look at Barr. His own eyes never left Jake's, but she had the strongest sense of his willing her to keep silent. "You think she may be feeding information to whoever it is," Barr offered.

"If she was, I've taken her out of the loop," Jake replied.

"But why in hell did you let Patrick go with her?" Gillian exploded. "What were you thinking of—your stupid mission?"

"Right!" Jake's eyes blazed. "My stupid mission. It's already cost four of the best men who ever served under me. And you know what?"

His forefinger, like a gun barrel, poked straight at Gillian's face. She saw it coming just in time and nerved herself not to flinch. "If it succeeds, it'll be worth their lives. And mine, too."

She knew, beyond any doubt, that he meant what he said. Unthinkable as it might be to her, he was ready to die if he thought it was necessary. "Why?" she said.

He looked hard at her, apparently trying to decide if her question was serious. "Why?" he repeated. "How about because I'm a forty-five-year-old light colonel who was left out of Desert Storm, and this is the only way I can get a star to retire on."

It was, she saw, an accusation he'd used on himself—and one he half believed. "Not good enough. Try again," she said.

Surprise widened his eyes, but his faintly mocking smile was still there. "Grunts like me don't have reasons worth trotting out in public. I'm a trained soldier, and all my training tells me now's the time to march to the sound of the guns."

That, she decided, was an honest answer, as far as it went. And one that Patrick would've understood. The thought of him brought a rush of concern that tightened her stomach muscles. "Why haven't we heard from Patrick?"

"I don't know," Jake admitted. "I did try to warn him, but . . ." He stretched his pleasantly ugly face into an almost convincing grin. "Look, I could be dead wrong. He and Isabel are probably shacked up in that old plantation house, screwing their brains out."

"And even if Isabel is a double-crosser," Barr put in, "Patrick's big and strong and no fool—" He caught Gillian's look of scorn, and corrected himself: "Well, big and strong, anyway. He can take care of himself. It's probably something wrong with that portable VHF. I never trust those hand-helds."

But what was the difference? she asked herself. The fact was that they were in Jake's mission up to their necks, with no retreat. "Up ahead there," she said, "that must be William Town."

Before *Glory* had cleared the bluff that marked the northern end of William Bay, the shore boats were already making for them, pulling so desperately that one of them snapped an oar and spun in a half circle, nearly ramming another just astern. Gillian glanced at Jake, whose jaw had dropped, and at Barr, whose eyes were like pale blue ice. He hated being hassled by shore boats, she knew, hated it with a passion, which was strange when you considered how well he got along with West Indians generally.

"Christ!" said Jake. "Are they attacking us?" For the first time since he'd come aboard, he looked apprehensive.

"No," Barr said through clenched teeth. "They're just racing for the Yankee dollar. Listen."

The noise of shouting had been audible for several minutes, but only now, with the boats a couple of hundred yards away, could Gillian make out words: "Hey, Cap'n—I anchor you boat!" "Throw me line, Cap'n! I tie you up!" "I pilot! I pilot!"

"What do we do?" Jake asked, then added, dropping his voice: "One of them might be my contact."

"Well, I'm not going to let more than one of them aboard," Barr said. He looked to Gillian. "You pick."

There was little time for choice. Two boats were neck and neck, the rest in a clump thirty yards behind them. "Green boat!" she called. "You there!"

The bowman of the boat in question, one of the two leaders, waved his bailer at her; his rower seemed to redouble the stroke, and the steersman glanced nervously over his shoulder.

She tried again. "Green boat, are you a pilot?" To Jake, she murmured, "Don't let anybody over the rail. Whack 'em on the knuckles if you have to."

"Pilot, sure!" the bowman called back. "Guide, watch your boat, anything you want. Twenty dollar U.S."

"Twenty dollars EC," she retorted automatically. It was a standard Caribbean bargaining ploy, based on the Eastern Caribbean dollar's exchange rate of forty cents U.S., but Gillian wasn't bargaining.

The bowman strained up to grab *Glory's* gunwale. He was a short man, square-built, with thick, powerful arms and a handsome, sullen young face. "Fifteen dollar U.S.," he said. "Show you place to anchor." His West Indian accent was heavier than she'd expected, his tone hostile and aggressive.

Behind her she heard the solid clunk of a pulling boat hitting *Glory's* hull. Jake's snarled "Off the boat, man" blended with the unseen boatman's "I give you better price."

The green boat's bowman was still clutching the gunwale, balancing on the balls of his feet and somehow holding his heavy, clumsy little vessel away from *Glory's* side. His bloodshot eyes were fierce, his whole attitude demanding, and Gillian was surprised and angry to find herself afraid. She wanted Barr's reassurance and was damned if she would let him know it. "Twenty EC," she said to the bowman. "Take it or leave it."

He scanned her face, as if trying to read her determination. "Gimme line," he said, after a long moment.

With the green boat towing precariously off *Glory*'s starboard quarter and the bowman, whose name was Hubert, standing beside Barr at the helm, the other shore boats turned reluctantly away. "They'll be back," said Barr.

"Oh, yes," Hubert agreed. Now that he was aboard, he seemed uninterested in piloting but fascinated by the limited view down the companionway hatch. "They just go get things to sell—carvings, coral, plantain," he said, scorn dripping from the words. "You buy from me. Mo' betta deal."

Glory's depth-sounder was the old-fashioned style, with a circular, flashing dial. It was mounted on a hinged arm, so it could be swung out into the helmsman's view. Right now, Gillian saw, the flashing light indicated a depth of forty feet, nearly shallow enough to anchor.

"What's the bottom like, Hubert?" said Barr. "Hard sand, mud, or what?"

"Good ground, Captain," said Hubert. "All through here hard sand. Hol' like death once the anchor bite."

Gillian craned her neck to look past Hubert to the depth-sounder. Its flashes were sharp and narrow, indicating a hard, flat surface below *Glory*'s keel. Barr caught Gillian's look, but aside from a slightly raised eyebrow his face never changed. Hubert, she thought, had just passed the first test.

"Where do we go ashore?" Jake was asking. "That dock doesn't look too sturdy."

The only pier, built of huge, rough-trimmed balks of timber, thrust nearly a hundred feet out into the bay. In two places its supports had fallen, and Gillian could see that much of its surface planking was gone. Her eye took in the rest of William Town's straggling waterfront. Its builders had given it an impressive stone quay that ran the full quarter mile of its frontage, but most of the cemented boulders had long since subsided into heaps and drifts of loose stones, with here and there gobbets of the original cement locking a few of them together.

William Town's important structures lined the bay, or their remains did. Most were wood, the once-colorful paint almost entirely weathered to bleached gray; they were two stories, with a shop below and living quarters on the second floor, surrounded by a narrow porch to which bits and pieces of fancy scrollwork trim still clung. The ground-floor windows were empty or curtained off, except for those of two establishments—a general store calling itself Lady Queen's Emporium, and next door, a rumshop of grim aspect, whose sign announced "Manhatan Nightclub."

A few other structures were of plastered stone, with the plaster fallen away in patches. The largest of them, at the head end of the derelict pier, had lost its roof, the glass from its windows, and most of its interior partitions. Yet even as a shell it was the most impressive building on the waterfront, and the reason was carved into the stone over the ground-floor windows: MACINTYRE LIME & PRODUCE LTD.

In the overgrown lot next to it was a formless heap of planking, topped with rusted sheets of corrugated metal, that might once have been a warehouse. On the adjoining corner a single-story stone building with heavy metal shutters seemed to be the police headquarters, to judge by the three khaki-uniformed loafers gaping out the windows and the flagpole on top; beside it was a similar building that was probably the post office, front wall papered with frayed announcements. Behind the quayside buildings, the town—village, really—straggled back from the water: patched and mostly paintless houses, a few more shops, a couple of churches, the whole thing giving off an aura of penniless despair that even Jake seemed to feel. "God help the people who live here," he murmured to Gillian.

"He don't be helping much lately," said Hubert. The bitterness in his voice was startling, Gillian thought—the rawness of a fresh wound.

Behind the buildings were fields, gone mostly to weed, that rose to a low ridge. Gillian made out, half concealed in the thick growth of bush and tree, a low cut-stone parapet that must be the remains of Fort George, the old colonial bastion whose battery had protected the harbor. According to the chart's large-scale inset of William Town, the fort's storehouses and magazines, probably roofless now, still lay behind the walls.

"Well," said Barr, "we seem to have the anchorage to ourselves." It was true. Not another vessel was riding in William Bay, though two big, rusty mooring buoys lay, side by side, a hundred yards or so off a narrow stretch of beach. The Philipians' own boats were being pulled up onto another patch of sandy shore, from which the remains of the old seawall had been cleared away.

"We could tie up to one of those floats," Jake said, but Hubert shook his head emphatically.

"They for the freighter," he said.

Barr amplified: "A front loader—like a World War Two landing barge. She ties off her stern to those buoys and runs up on the beach and drops the ramp to unload. When she's through, she just winches off." To Hubert, Barr said, "The *Doris B.* still call here?"

"That's right, Cap'n. Once every month, sometimes twice."

Barr grunted. "When's she due next?"

"Maybe soon," Hubert replied. "Cap'n Vreelan' come when he feel like."

"You know him, this Captain Vreelan?" Jake asked.

"Vreeland. We've met," Barr said. "Comes from Curaçao. Half Dutch, half East Indian, and all prick."

The remark was utterly unlike Barr, but the sentiment seemed to strike a chord in Hubert, who smiled for the first time, revealing white, irregular teeth. "You anchor over there," he said, pointing to the far side of the crumbling pier. "That the best place."

Barr: William Bay, 10:00 A.M.

"You sure you don' got more money?" Hubert asked again.

Barr, who had never gotten used to the West Indian habit of re-negotiating every agreement, simply shook his head. Hubert already had his promised twenty dollars EC, plus a handful of Netherlands Antilles guilders Jake had produced to shut him up. As Barr had known it would, Jake's largess had exactly the reverse effect from the one desired; what annoyed Barr even more was that Jake—still ashore with Gillian—wasn't even around to live with his mistake.

Except for Hubert's green skiff riding astern and a dugout tied up alongside, the other shore boats had been and gone. One by one the skippers had been invited aboard to display their wares. Barr had listened, bargained ineptly, bought (with a pocketful of EC dollars from Gillian's emergency hoard) as little as possible. And waited in vain for anything that might have been a contact routine.

At the end of an hour's time *Glory*'s cockpit was filled with withered fruit, pathetic trinkets—and goddamned Hubert, who had departed only to slide undetected back over the gunwale, bearing a crudely carved pine crucifix for which he demanded and got ten American dollars.

Hubert, Barr had decided, was the archetype of the two-bit Caribbean hustler, with spiritual relatives in every port from Charlotte Amalie to Spanish Town. He eyed the bottle wedged between Barr's bare feet. "Any mo' rum?" he asked.

"It's empty," Barr said. "You drank it." He had the two sections of the mizzen boom laid end to end on the side deck and was ostensibly splinting them together with extra battens from the mainsail. In fact, he was trying to eavesdrop on the two men in the dugout canoe tied alongside. The St. Philip version of West Indian Creole was no harder to understand than most—far easier than St. Lucia's patois, Barr had always thought—but his ear had not yet retuned itself to the rhythms that were the key to comprehension.

The men in the dugout, who wanted to sell Barr a stalk of stunted plantains, were arguing lethargically. The question seemed to be whether they had to split what they got for the fruit with a third man, who bore the unlikely name Mr. Mongoose and whose connection with the enterprise was unclear.

"I buy you rum," announced the enterprising Hubert. "Good stuff-Barbancourt from Haiti. Ten dollars U.S."

God alone knew what would be in the bottle, but it was probably the only way to get Hubert off *Glory* without physically pitching him over the side, and one look at his massive, low-slung frame put that idea on the shelf. "Okay," said Barr. "You've got a deal: ten U.S. for a liter of Barbancourt."

Hubert blinked twice. "You want two bottles?" he said.

"No. Just one." Barr got to his feet, uncleated the line that held Hubert's pulling boat off *Glory*'s stern, and hauled it in. "Climb down."

Hubert lowered himself gingerly into the little boat. His two crew members huddled aft to make room for him. "Give me money, man," he called up to Barr.

"I haven't got anymore," Barr said. "The big man will pay you. Tell him Captain Barr said so." Hubert started to object, but Barr rode him down. "That way you don't have to row all the way out here again."

Hubert's frown suddenly vanished. "What's his name, the big man?"

"Adler," said Barr. "Rich Jake Adler."

The two men from the dugout were easier to have around. Barr bought their plantains for half again the going rate and suggested a drink to seal the bargain. The senior member of the pair, whose name was Joop, quickly accepted. Barr unlocked the companionway, which he had secured along with the forehatch and all the opening portholes, and brought on deck a bucket filled with cold bottles of beer.

At first Joop and his cousin Cecil were silent and withdrawn, but two greenies apiece opened them up. Times were indeed bad, they agreed. No jobs and practically no tourists. *Glory* was the first charter boat in a month, and Hurricane Hugo had made the town pier too shaky for even the smallest cruise vessels or interisland freighters. Now only the *Doris B.* serviced St. Philip, and Captain Vreeland was taking advantage of his monopoly by screwing the islanders left and right.

"'Specially ol' reverend," said Cecil. "That Vreelan', he ripped the reverend good las' time."

"Never did," Joop replied. He flipped the cap off a greeny with his thumbnail and sluiced half the contents down his throat. "Never," he repeated.

"Did so," Cecil insisted. "Those hugeous cases? I seen ol' reverend givin' that Vreelan' thousands of dollars for bringin' them."

Barr, whose attention had been wandering, darted a surreptitious glance at Cecil. The younger man—he looked to be about fifty, but the absence of front teeth probably accounted for twenty years of it— was stubbornly shaking his head under a barrage of ridicule from Joop.

"'Twas so," Cecil insisted. "I seen inside the bag, man. It was full of money. Full to the *top*."

"How you know what was under?" Joop demanded scornfully. "Coulda been anything."

Indeed, it could, Barr thought. "Who's the reverend?" he asked.

The two men looked at each other. "He the chaplain," said Joop cautiously. "Down to the castle."

Barr lit a cigarette while he considered. The "castle" was Highland House, of course—the old MacIntyre estate down the coast, a Leeward Islands landmark for nearly a century. Much of it was in ruins, and half the rest had been converted to a distillery and then abandoned, but when Barr had been on St. Philip five years before, the last MacIntyre was still living in one wing. Visitors from the outside world hadn't been welcome at Highland House—as they had not been welcome in Barr's memory—but William Town gossip had said the old man was attended by a handful of servants even older than he, including a coal black bagpiper. Rumor said nothing about a chaplain, though, and Barr was sure that so unusual a retainer would never have escaped comment. The unnamed reverend must be a new addition.

Joop and Cecil were watching Barr's cigarette with intent, and he reluctantly passed the pack around. "I didn't know the castle had a chapel," said Barr, tossing the matchbook to Cecil.

"Not at the castle," Cecil allowed. He lit up, inhaled, regarded the cigarette with appreciation. "This *smooth*, man."

"The reverend preach at old St. George's," Joop explained. "On'y they call it Chapel of Abraham an' the Sacred Blood now."

St. George's, Barr recalled, was the island's Anglican church; he could see its steeple from where he sat. Like so many other established churches in the islands, it had been losing worshipers for years, had probably gone under in the face of encroaching evangelicals. They were all over the Caribbean these days: earnest, syrup-voiced radio preachers, from Southern California and the Midwest. Presumably the reverend was one of them and had somehow wormed his way into old MacIntyre's bosom. "This reverend," Barr said, keeping his tone careless, "he's an American?"

Once again Joop and Cecil traded glances. "Not American," said Joop. Clearly he had no intention of amplifying, and Barr was afraid that any further questions about the reverend might turn the limping conversation off entirely.

"How's the old man these days?" he asked. Joop and Cecil regarded him with bewilderment, and he suddenly recalled the Scottish title the old man insisted on. "The MacIntyre, I mean."

"He all right," Joop allowed, and shut up like a trap. Now that was interesting, Barr decided. In years past the islanders seemed to spend half their time speculating about the last survivor of the clan that had ruled St. Philip, economically and politically, for almost two hundred years; now he, too, seemed to have become off limits for comment.

"Your friends comin' back," Cecil put in.

So they were. *Glory's* inflatable had appeared from behind the ruined pier, trailed by two or three of the shore boats, which turned back as it became apparent that Gillian and Jake would not stop. "We go now," said Joop. He seemed unable to take his eyes off the hunched figure of Jake. The Philipians knew more than they were saying, Barr decided, but something was holding them back.

"Take down the quarantine flag," Gillian snapped as she swung herself aboard. Barr had held a hand out to help her, and she thrust a wad of coarse cloth into it. "Run this up to the spreader." He shook it out—the familiar Dutch tricolor, across which an amateur hand had stitched a diagonal black stripe.

"The new Philipian flag?" said Barr. "I've never seen it before."

"Well, take a good goddamned look," said Gillian. "It cost us fifty bucks, U.S."

"The clown at customs wanted to soak us another fifty," said Jake. "For not flying it when we sailed in. Gillian talked him out of that, though."

There was nothing to say, nothing that was going to soothe Gillian anyway. The racket was an old one, and every skipper was stung by it sooner or later. *Glory* already carried most of the West Indian national ensigns in her flag bag, and some of them had cost her dearly. Barr pulled down the yellow quarantine flag and ran the replacement up to the starboard spreader, where the rising offshore breeze caught it. "How much to clear in?" he asked, and saw too late that it was the wrong question.

"Forty for the boat," said Gillian, dropping to the seat and pulling the last beer from the bucket. "Plus twenty because it's a holiday . . ."

"Queen Beatrix's birthday," said Jake, shaking his head. "So much for independence."

"—plus another twenty for a cruising permit. Eighty dollars. At least it's only EC money." She surveyed the cockpit's contents with distaste. "How much did you have to shell out for this junk?"

Barr had no idea, but he wasn't about to admit it. "Forty," he said. "U.S., that is."

"Make it sixty," Jake corrected him. He held out what looked like a cylinder of filthy newspaper. "The rum you ordered from Hubert." He looked narrowly at Barr, the train of thought plain on his face. "He ripped me off, right?"

Barr found he didn't trust himself to answer, but he managed a nod as he opened the paper. The bottle bore the elaborate Barbancourt label, much scuffed; the contents had an ominous appearance that evoked old crankcases. He decided not to open it.

"Welcome to the islands," Gillian said with a crooked smile. She picked something from the litter at her feet. Barr saw it was a doll, not unskillfully carved from a single piece of some hard, fine-grained wood. The unknown maker had clothed it in scraps of colored fabric that might have been meant to look like a carnival costume. Gillian turned it over and over in her hands, examining it, and when she looked up, Barr was startled to see her eyes were bright. "Guys like those customs bandits make you forget how poor these people are. This doll isn't new," she continued, a little unsteadily. "I bet somebody made this for his kid, but we turned up, and it was the only thing he had that he could sell."

Jake was clearly considering a facet of Gillian he hadn't yet seen. "For every Hubert," he said, "there's half a dozen people just trying to scratch out a living. And on this island I don't see how they do it."

Gillian was on her feet, still holding the doll. "I'll get a box from below to put this stuff in for now. We'll keep it in the dinghy." She saw Jake's question in his face. "Cockroaches," she said. Her voice was businesslike again. "Spiders. Maybe the odd scorpion. The locals have to live with 'em. We don't."

She was out of earshot when Jake turned to Barr. "Any nibbles?" he asked.

"Not even a hint. You're sure your man was coming to the boat?"

"Positive." Jake pursed his lips. "Maybe he was scared off. A watcher . . ."

"Nobody was here the whole time, not even Hubert."

"Could they've been double-teaming you?"

"Possible, but I don't think so," Barr replied. A cardboard box appeared in the companionway, and he took it, revealing Gillian's intent face. "Spooks down here tend to look like spooks, because everybody knows who they are anyway," he said.

"Damn." Jake watched as Gillian began to stack Barr's purchases in the carton, food at one end, trinkets at the other. Without warning his hand shot out and grasped her wrist. "Let me see that," he said.

It was Hubert's ten-dollar crucifix. Not a bad piece of work, Barr had to admit, but hardly worth Jake's rapt attention.

Gillian's eye caught Barr's, and he shrugged. Jake held the crucifix at an angle, so the back caught the sunlight. "Look there, under the paint. Can you read it?"

A second coat would have obscured the stenciled printing, but as it was, the words on the crosspiece were just readable: "CAL .30 BALL AMMU." "Now that," said Jake cheerfully, "is a damn funny thing to write on a cross."

"Cheap symbolism," Barr observed. Beside him he heard Gillian gasp; he looked to her, then followed her eye. As he did, he heard Jake's unbelieving "Son of a *bitch*."

In two decades of seafaring Barr had encountered most of the Western Hemisphere's small craft and had sailed a good many of them. But he had never seen anything remotely like the vessel that was gliding silently into William Bay, coming straight at *Glory*. Forty feet long and narrow for its length, it was painted a gleaming black, picked out with gilded carving at the bow. A cloth canopy—red and white stripes, with a fringe—fluttered over the open cockpit, and above it towered a brass stack, polished so it gleamed like gold, belching black smoke. The Philipian flag snapped at the stern, and a pennant Barr didn't recognize fluttered at the bow.

"What is it?" Gillian asked; it didn't seem odd that she was whispering.

"A steam launch," Barr heard himself say. "Seventy years old if she's a day."

"They're going to run into us," said Jake.

About fifty yards away the launch swung into a smooth, sweeping curve. Barr could see a man at the wheel amidships, amazingly tall and thin, brown skin looking nearly black against a high-necked white uniform. Two other crewmen, in khaki, stood ready at bow and stern with coiled lines. "Fenders," said Barr, gauging the turn with his eye. "Port side."

Jake was still gaping, but Gillian had anticipated Barr's order. She tossed him a fat cylinder, dropped a second over the side and lashed it in place with one deft gesture. As she stood waiting for a line—straight as a mast, the breeze whipping her short brown hair—Barr felt his love for her well up unexpectedly, and stronger than he would have thought possible.

He was dimly aware, as if seeing it through a fog, of the launch's skipper bringing his craft to a perfectly timed stop no more than a foot from *Glory's* side. The bowman handed Barr the line, and the feel of damp manila rope—when had he handled real manila last?—seemed to dispel the haze. Now that she was so close, he could see that the old steam launch was not nearly as perfect as she had appeared at a distance. Paint could not completely hide the gouges and scars in her planking, and the funnel's high polish only emphasized the dents in it. Behind the sharp tang of kerosene was a sour smell that Barr recognized, after a moment, as that of mildewed canvas from the canopy.

The skipper had stepped to the launch's stern. He was, Barr guessed, easily six and a half feet tall, with a narrow, hawklike face and bulbous dark eyes with yellowed whites. Up close his uniform—it looked to Barr like a set of ancient navy officer's whites—was stained and patched, the sleeves ending well above his thin, bony wrists. He was younger than any Philipian Barr had met except for Hubert, mid-twenties at the most.

"Miss Verdean?" Not a West Indian, Barr thought. But what was that accent? Gillian, still holding the stern line the deckhand had passed her, nodded. "I have this for you." He held out a large, square envelope.

Awkwardly she accepted it with her free hand and looked around for assistance. Jake, eyeing the skipper as if he were a dangerous animal, stepped to her side and took the line. She ripped open the envelope and extracted a single folded sheet. From almost forty feet away Barr could see only that the message was short and handwritten. "What's it say?" he asked.

It was Jake, looking over her shoulder, who responded. " 'Tammas Ban MacIntyre,' " he read, " 'The MacIntyre of that Ilk'—that's really what it says, 'Ilk'—is pleased to invite Miss Gillian Verdean and her guests to take dinner with him today at Highland House.' "

"What do you think, Barr?" said Gillian.

Before he could answer, Jake said to the launch's skipper, "We'll be there with bells on."

The tall man eyed Jake silently. After a moment or two Gillian said, "Please tell The MacIntyre that Miss Verdean accepts his invitation with pleasure."

"Of course, it's probably a trap," said Jake five minutes later. "And of course, I'm going. Unless I'm missing something, it's the only game in town."

"What do you know about The MacIntyre?" Gillian asked Barr. "Isn't it possible he's Jake's contact?"

Barr hesitated, assembling his thoughts, and Jake said: "Go ahead."

Repressing annoyance, Barr said, "I really don't know that much about MacIntyre. He must be about seventy—though to hear the Philipians tell it, he's been around forever, like Mount Mauvis. Born here, educated in Scotland, like his father and grandfather before him. He's spent his adult life watching the family empire crumble. And he's the last of the line, unless he's got a little bastard tucked away someplace."

"You didn't answer the second part of my question," Gillian said.

"Is he Jake's contact?" Barr repeated. "How the hell should I know?" He shrugged. "For what it's worth, he just might be."

"How do you figure that?" asked Jake.

"Well, this island is up against the wall economically," Barr began, feeling his way. "You don't need a survey to tell you that. The MacIntyre may be broke—almost certainly is—but he still owns just about all the best land on St. Philip. And he's standing in the way of progress. Maybe somebody's seen that, made some moves to chuck him off the throne, so he sent a bleat for help to your people."

"Because we look like the kind of guys who'd prop up a throne?" said Jake. "Thanks a lot. But I think you may be right. It's worth the trip to find out."

"We'd better get cleaned and primped then," Gillian said. "That captain with the evil eyes'll be back in an hour."

"What do you mean, 'we'?" said Jake.

"You think I'm going to leave one of my crew marooned ashore?" Gillian demanded. "But someone's got to stay with *Glory*, and Barr's the only one of us who could get her out of the harbor alone. So I'm elected."

"You're out of your mind," Jake said, his voice harsh. "This is my line of work, and I don't need some stubborn young woman getting underfoot."

The muscle jumped along Gillian's jaw, but her voice, when she spoke, was icily calm. "You're forgetting one thing, Colonel: *I* was invited. I'm going." She turned to Barr. "And you're staying with the boat."

"Absolutely," Barr replied. "I wouldn't walk into that old spider's parlor for anything."

Patrick: 2:00 P.M.

The road twisted like a corkscrew, and every time the three-quarter-ton skidded its way around a curve Patrick slid from one side to the other, across the steel floorboards. It was even worse when the old vehicle hit one of the canyon-deep potholes that gullied the surface; he'd feel himself airborne for an instant as the truck fell away under him, then hit with a crash that drove the air from his lungs.

The two men had worked him over before they'd dumped him in the truck—partly for the fun of it and partly, Patrick thought, to see what Isabel's reaction would be. She'd watched the whole thing stone-faced, without turning a hair. Only once, when the two men were momentarily distracted by a wild goat crashing its way through the brush, did she allow Patrick's eyes to meet hers.

Their intensity was like a high-voltage jolt through his chest. He almost cried out then, but she looked away quickly. When the beating started again, he pulled his arms in close to his sides and tucked his head down as well as he could and tried to be thankful that the men were using bare fists and sneaker-shod feet, and not assault guns.

In the end, though, it was the gun that knocked him cold. Isabel was in the front seat with the driver, and Patrick shared the back with the second man, who was too busy bracing himself with hands and feet to do more than give Patrick the occasional kick as he slid helplessly back and forth.

South, Patrick kept reminding himself. They were heading almost directly south. It might be useful to know later—and at least it was better than thinking about what probably lay at the end of the ride. The road under them was sometimes smooth enough to be asphalt, alternating with stretches of pure washboard that must be ridged hard sand and then a deeply pitted surface that felt like washed-out paving.

Once the truck bucked and splashed its way across a shallow stream, dropping down into low-low gear to fight its way up the far bank and back onto paved surface. From the speed at which the branches overhead went by, Patrick figured they must be averaging no more than ten miles an hour.

Then, on a relatively unrutted stretch, the truck slowed to a near halt, and the driver snapped something over his shoulder. Patrick's guard bent forward and laid his assault gun on the floor, one hand resting on the trigger guard. "Do not move," he said, but his eager eyes dared Patrick to try something.

What was happening? What were they up to? Lying on his back, Patrick could see only sky—no clouds, but a gathering, hazy overcast. Over the asthmatic whine of the truck engine, he heard a sudden chatter of voices, a quick blare of reggae that faded behind them. They must, he realized, be passing through a village. And whoever these men were, they didn't want the villagers to see him.

A small jolt made the guard grab for a handhold. With a desperate wriggle Patrick got his legs under him and thrust with all his force. He shot straight up, head and chest clearing the sides of the truck. It was a village—a small, desperately shabby cluster of wooden shacks, with flattened tin cans for roofing patches. People in the doorways, dressed in rags, staring at the truck. Their eyes widened as Patrick appeared like a jack-in-the-box.

"Help!" he yelled just as his guard grabbed for him and the truck swerved sharply. Patrick crashed back to the floor, felt the truck hit something soft, heard an anguished squawk. Rolling over, he saw the guard raise the assault gun, bring it down.

His head felt as if it were splitting—no, it *had* split, just above his right eye. The floor under him was as hard and cold as metal but, he decided blurrily, it was something else. Stone, smooth and thick with dust. He was lying on his side, more or less; his wrists and ankles were still tied.

The light was faint, but he could make out a wall that looked like drywall masonry, a few feet in front of his face. Slowly, jaw set against the stabbing agony in his skull, he rolled over onto his back. The ceiling was wood, supported by heavy beams, and—he turned his head—the opposite wall had a door in it. Solid wood that looked almost as heavy as the ceiling; no handle, but a small window toward the top, a square window just big enough to put an arm through, if it hadn't been blocked by crossed bars.

Outside the window was where the light was coming from. Open flame, Patrick decided, from the way it was flickering. He wanted only to close his eyes and wait for the stabbing ache to go away, but he forced himself to examine the room more closely. No windows, except for the one in the door, and no furniture at all. Too big—about twenty feet square—to make sense as a cell.

He rolled painfully onto his side, raising his head a few inches. The floor was filthy as hell, a thick, grainy dust in which he could see footprints from the door to where he lay and the twin skid marks of his own heels. Over by the wall opposite the door, though, the dust wasn't nearly as deep, and it was marked in a way suggesting that stacks of things with square bottoms—crates, maybe—had sat there for a long time.

The dust was in his nose, and he sneezed. Outside in the hall a man said something, and another man laughed. A shadow filled the small window. Patrick made himself lie still and relaxed, his eyes narrowed to slits.

Then he heard the clatter and squeal of unoiled metal—the door lock, he guessed—and the door swung open, the hinges squeaking. The door was wide enough for only one man, and he was holding something that didn't seem to be a weapon. Patrick had the sense that another, shorter man was standing just behind him.

A beam of light wavered toward Patrick. He closed his eyes and concentrated on controlling his breathing. The light was playing across his face—he could see the brightness through his eyelids—and then it flicked away. The man in the door said something over his shoulder, and again Patrick knew it was a language he'd heard before, though not one he actually knew.

"Speak English, Monasir," said a second voice. "I shouldn't have to tell you that." The tone was abrupt, the accent British and educated, so surprising that Patrick's eyes opened involuntarily.

The flash in the first man's hand was directed at the floor, about halfway to the door. Neither man was more than a silhouette—the one with the light slender and tense, the other short and round.

"I think that he will soon wake," said the man called Monasir, speaking slowly and carefully. "Will you wish to question him?"

"To what end?" the short man asked, clearly surprised. "Oh, I understand." He sounded weary and disapproving, as if Monasir had let him down in some way. "No, my friend, I take no pleasure in pain for its own sake."

What the hell's he talking about? Patrick asked himself, but there was something in the short man's voice that made the hairs on his spine bristle. The door slammed shut, and the lock squealed, but Patrick made himself lie still for five minutes—counting off the seconds—before he turned his head for a look. The observation window was clear. Rolling back over onto his side, he tried to bring his ankles up to where his fingers could get at the lashing, but his muscles were too stiff to hold the position long enough.

The wrists then. He had been tied with scraps of twine that his captors had found loose in the truck. String, practically, but strong enough for this job. There was nothing in his pockets to cut with, and the room was bare.

Or was it? One way to find out—and nothing else to do, anyway. He rolled over onto his belly, began to worm his way across the smooth stone. The center of the floor was completely bare, but around the edges the dust and grit of years had heaped itself up in little windrows.

Halfway around the second wall he found the nail. It was almost completely buried in sandy dust, and only a pair of eyes six inches from the floor could have caught its gleam. A good-size nail, slightly bent and its end blunted, which accounted for its having been discarded. The bend, about halfway along the nail's shaft, made it just possible for Patrick to grasp it with his fingertips, while probing the knot that secured his crossed wrists.

The trouble was, he decided half an hour later, that the damn string his captors had used was so shapeless the knot almost had to be picked apart strand by strand. And the strain on his fingers tied them up in cramps after five minutes' work.

Concentrated work it was, too, so that he nearly missed the distant sounds of shod feet. He dropped the nail on the cell floor, rolled over and scooped it into his mouth with his tongue, and rolled back, very conscious of the nail pressed diagonally against the inside of his cheek, the tip stabbing into his gum. And then all thought of it was driven from his mind by a high-pitched Spanish curse—Isabel's voice, he thought, but so hoarse and exhausted he could not be sure.

They're going to put her in with me. He felt his heart leap in his chest. With her to help, he could be untied in a few more minutes, and after that . . .

But the footsteps—several sets, one scuffing the ground—went right past his cell door, with a quick shadowing of the light outside. He heard the sound, through the stone wall, of a heavy door opening and a thump, as of a body hitting the ground.

Maybe she's hurt, he thought. *They must've been working her over. But who the hell is she to them?*

"No!" It was Isabel's voice for sure, furious but scared. "Get your hands off!"

For a couple of minutes he tried to convince himself that he wasn't hearing what he knew he was hearing. Not that there was all that much to hear: men's voices, laughing at first and then, after a yelp of pain from one of them, angry and breathless; Isabel's defiant curses tailing off into gasps of pain; grunting male effort, and the slap of flesh against flesh, and moans that didn't sound like her at all.

Patrick's teeth were gritted so hard his jaw ached. Over and over he told himself that any sound from him would only make it worse for her. Finally the noises tapered off. A man, breathing hard, said something and was answered with an uncertain laugh. A minute later the door crashed shut, and feet echoed down the corridor.

From the next cell, not a sound. Now, with the energy of desperation Patrick worked at the knotted twine around his wrists, totally heedless of the agony in his fingers. It seemed like forever before the twine gave way, and then another eternity while his numb and bloody fingers clawed at the line around his ankles. But finally it was done, and he crawled to the wall of his cell and tapped on the stone with the bent nail. The sound echoed off the walls, surprisingly loud. But could Isabel hear it on the other side of the wall?

No answer. He called softly, then more loudly, but there was still not a sound from the other side. So they had killed her after they were through. He slumped down, exhausted and despairing.

Gillian: William Bay, 5:45 P.M.

She had promised herself not to look back as The MacIntyre's steam launch cut easily through the harbor. From the corner of her eye she had a blurry image of *Glory* riding easily at anchor, Barr standing silently at the mizzen shrouds. They had talked it over, she and Barr and Jake, had convinced themselves—for the moment anyway—that what they were doing was the best course of action: she and Jake to beard The MacIntyre in his lair; Barr to mount guard aboard *Glory*, keeping radio watch in case Patrick got his VHF working.

If, as Jake now seemed to believe, The MacIntyre turned out to be his contact, then Gillian had privately decided she would demand the old man's help to find Patrick. (And once they had Patrick back, *Glory* would be on her way, no matter what Barr's former boss threatened them with.) If, on the other hand, The MacIntyre turned out to be a false lead, they'd be no worse off than they already were.

If Gillian and Jake weren't back by midnight, Barr had instructions to up anchor and go—head for Antigua, only thirty miles away, where there was a U.S. Air Force base and, more important, a friend of a friend of Jake's who might be able to stir up some government muscle.

Having *Glory* run for it had, of course, been Jake's idea; Gillian found herself going along with it in part because she couldn't think of a better plan and mostly because she hadn't thought for a moment that Barr would agree to sail off without her. When he did, she was thunderstruck, then furious.

How could he? And in such a goddamn matter-of-fact way, almost as if he wanted to be rid of her. Even Jake had looked a little startled. Not, she told herself firmly, that she thought for a moment he did want to be rid of her. It was just his obtuse way, part of the never-apologize, never-explain mentality he'd grown up with. You might be able to bet your life on Jeremy Barr—and Gillian had—but you'd look to him in vain for any kind of overt moral support. Sailors, especially deep-sea sailors, were like that. Once you had the boat snugged down to face the storm, there was no more to be said. Perfectly sensible.

Still, he could have said more than "good luck," though of course The MacIntyre's launch captain was standing right there with his ears flapping.

All in all she was angry enough, and jumpy enough, to bite off the first head that presented itself—exactly the most dangerous frame of mind to be in. *Calm down, Gillian,* she told herself. *This is one situation where blowing your cool won't get you anyplace.* And having so resolved, she decided to allow herself one look back at Barr, but he was nowhere to be seen.

Jake was talking a mile a minute, had been almost since The MacIntyre's launch pulled away from *Glory*'s side. It was some incomprehensible military babble, all about fields of fire and landing obstacles. What it seemed to boil down to was that St. Philip would be a very difficult place to assault, with even a handful of resolute defenders. Well, it didn't take a military genius to see that. The shore, south of William Bay, was all steep cliff, fifty feet straight up at the least, with nothing in the wind- and wave-smoothed rock that looked like even a handhold. And to make attack even more impossible, just offshore a line of sawtooth reef lay in wait below the surface, with the light sea creaming over it.

She tried to recall the chart they'd studied a few minutes before leaving *Glory*. The fringing reef ran all along this part of the leeward side, and the shore was all steep cliff, inaccessible except where a succession of MacIntyres had built Highland House.

According to Barr, the fortunes of the place had paralleled those of the MacIntyre family. The first of the clan, who had left Scotland in 1715, two steps ahead of the executioner, had begun Highland House as a pirate's eyrie, a fortified refuge. His descendants had prospered and legitimized themselves, during the high tide of the plantocracy in the 1800s, and the grim old fort had blossomed into a typical West Indian great house; but drink and the devil had cut back the MacIntyre family tree throughout the nineteenth century, and as it withered so did its home—rooms closed off and then whole wings abandoned. In the 1920s there had been a brief revival of the family prosperity, when Highland House became a rum distillery and warehouse, but Depression and the repeal of Prohibition in far-off America killed that enterprise for good. Now Highland House was said to be nearly in ruins, though photographs of it still appeared in some guidebooks, and the last MacIntyre was an ancient recluse flitting through its deserted grandeur.

The tower came into view as Gillian was thinking about it: high up on the bluff, a gray stone cube with ivy grown nearly to the crenellated battlement. Then, as her eye ranged along the cliff edge, she made out other walls, moss-clad and buried in tropic green, but gaunt enough to stand out once you knew what to look for.

The place didn't look like the photographs she'd seen, but, to judge by tree heights, they must have been taken years ago. Most of it seemed to be back from the cliff edge, hidden from an observer at water level. "Not an easy place to get into if you weren't invited," she said to Jake.

"And twice as hard to get out of," he murmured in her ear.

Now she could see the famous stairway—the Thousand Steps, it was called, though the guidebooks pointed out that there were fewer than two hundred hewn out of the cliff's sheer face. Legend had it that three slaves had died in the process, falling from the rock wall into the sea. But the West Indies were full of stories like that, most of them impossible to prove one way or the other.

The steps stood out clearly in the late-afternoon sun, mounting up and up to a stone balcony onto which opened a pair of massive double doors that were set into the wall of Highland House itself.

The launch turned to head offshore, and Gillian, looking past the silent helmsman, saw that here the reef doubled and redoubled its width, until the barrier of seething, foaming water was a good two hundred yards wide between the electric blue of the Caribbean and the narrow, rocky beach.

Suddenly the launch turned back in, not directly toward the shore, but at a sharp angle to it. The water ahead was breaking, it seemed to her, as fiercely as everywhere else, and she could distinctly see a barricade of sawtooth rocks—Barr had told her the natives called it Top Jaw—that looked for all the world like a shark's triangular teeth.

"There's a way through the reef, but it isn't buoyed, not even with stakes or floats," Barr had said. "The Philipian fishermen say the channel's guarded by jumbies—spirits of the dead—who won't let any boat through except The MacIntyre's."

Ahead of the launch Gillian could now make out a narrow foam-streaked path, no more than fifty feet wide, in which the seas never actually broke. Following it with her eye, she saw on the shore a dead tree and, lined up directly behind it, the edge of a stone wall—the only remaining wall of a ruined hut whose foundation was in the very surf.

The launch's skipper spun the wheel hard, and the launch leaned into a turn to port. As they turned, Gillian saw a huge single rock go by, no more than two feet below the surface and almost within arm's reach. When she looked up, she saw that the channel had switch-backed. The new mark was a low cairn of water-smoothed stones on the shore and a pole behind it.

Twice more the channel changed direction. Gillian's fingers itched for pencil and paper with which to note down the marks. Barr might be able to remember the sequence, but she doubted she could.

And then, like a curtain, the harbor entrance opened up. Ahead of the launch was a tiny enclave, formed and camouflaged by a low breakwater of barnacle-clad stones that looked exactly like the boulder-strewn shore on either side. The jetty was positioned to protect any boat inside it from the normal northerly surge. A seawall on the south side would catch and deflect waves that swung around St. Philip's southern tip, two miles away. Only if the trade wind reversed itself and blew hard from the southwest would even small seas enter the harbor. But then, she reflected, the place would be a deathtrap for any boat caught inside.

Under Gillian's bare feet the timeworn step was hot. The muscles of her calves felt like overstretched rubber bands.

"A hundred and fifty," said Jake from just behind her.

"A hundred and fifty what?"

"I was counting the steps," Jake replied. He wasn't even breathing hard. "Only about three dozen more to go."

"Great." She risked a glance back over her shoulder. They were only a hundred feet above the patch of loose rocks that passed for a beach, but the stairs were especially narrow at this point, with no barrier between a climber and the drop to the spray-washed rocks below. She felt a moment's dizziness and turned her eyes resolutely back to the stairway. Jake was right; they were nearly to the top—and whatever was waiting for them there. She felt a twinge of what could easily become panic, if she let it, and asked herself again what had led her into this piece of foolishness. And if leaping before she looked weren't bad enough, here she was doing it in a long skirt, for God's sake, a high-necked blouse that was sticking to her shoulder blades, and—dumb move of the year—low heels, which she was now carrying.

"Jesus," said Jake, under his breath, "catch the reception committee."

As their heads cleared the top of the stairs, the heavy double doors had swung slowly open, pushed by a pair of tottery West Indians. Standing in a glow of golden light from the doorway was an apparition that made Gillian wonder if the climb might not have been too much for her: an old, old man with faded, nearly colorless eyes, whose loose skin, almost translucent in the sun, was webbed with a thousand wrinkles. But it was not his age that struck her, or his height, though he looked to be nearly seven feet tall, or his extreme leanness, which made him appear almost two-dimensional. What grabbed her attention and held it was the costume.

From head to toe, from eagle-feathered bonnet to silver-buckled shoes, he was wearing what Gillian assumed to be Scottish evening dress. Faded black dinner jacket that looked to be cut from heavy satinlike material, with turned-back cuffs and explosions of lace at the wrists. More lace cascading down his shirtfront, from the high stock that encircled his long, bony throat. He wore a great, hairy sort of bag—didn't they call it a spoor?—on a chain across his flat stomach and a kilt whose red-green-brown pattern was so unattractive that she assumed it had to have some family connection. The desiccated shins were, thank God, covered by ribbed stockings, though what held them up—especially with a knife tucked into the top of one—was a mystery.

The spectacle seemed to have stopped Jake in his tracks, but Gillian stepped slowly forward, thinking: *That rig must weigh twenty pounds, and half of it's wool, and the temperature's nearly eighty.*

The ancient person swept off the hat with the feather in it, making what was clearly a formal gesture. His hair was dead white and so thick that Gillian automatically suspected a wig. She had the feeling that a curtsy would be in order, if only she had some idea how it was done, but instead she heard a breathless version of her own voice simper, "The MacIntyre, I presume?"

Against all probability, it seemed to be the correct beginning. The old man bared a set of ferocious store teeth and said, "Welcome to Highland House, Miss Verdean." His voice, a raspy baritone, was stronger than Gillian expected. He was looking past her, and she heard Jake clear his throat.

"This is—" she began, but the old man, still grinning, cut right across her.

"And you are welcome, too, Colonel Adler."

Uh-oh, thought Gillian. *This is it. Pay dirt or up against the wall.* But The MacIntyre, having bowed to Adler, half turned. From the shadows behind him there emerged another figure, a short, round man in a gray suit and clerical collar. His brown skin gleamed with moisture, and he was blinking rapidly, as if sweat had run into his eyes. "Hello-'ello-'ello," he said, in high, piping tones. And before either Jake or Gillian could respond, added, "Here you are; here you are."

"Reverend Harkness," announced The MacIntyre, looking sideways at the little man, "our spiritual adviser."

Harkness scuttled—it was, thought Gillian, the only word—up to her, his hand extended. She held out her own, realizing too late that it contained a shoe, a rather battered shoe that showed, in the sharply angled sunlight, the scratch marks of the steel wool with which Barr had scraped off nearly all the mold. She snatched it back, feeling the hot blood rush to her cheeks.

Their eyes met. His were brown like her own, amused, intelligent, and compassionate, and she had the instinctive feeling that this was a man you could trust. It was an unusual face, though—quite round, with a short, straight nose almost like a beak, straight black hair parted in the middle, and a cupid's bow mouth that was smiling gently. "I think," he said, "that we would all be the better for a libation—while the sun is still, as you sailors put it, above the yardarm." Not a West Indian, she thought immediately. But the Reverend Harkness had learned his English in England; of that she was positive.

By the time the libation caught up with them, they had moved inside the big old building, down long, empty, echoing hallways, to a high-ceilinged, windowless room lined with bookshelves that were jammed with volumes whose leather backs were in every stage of decay. "My office" The MacIntyre called it, and Gillian, ensconced in a huge overstuffed chair with her throbbing feet off the ground, was not disposed to argue. What might be a typewriter sat shrouded on a desk on one corner, but whatever business took place here must, she thought, be pretty leisurely since the calendar over the desk had expired three years before.

One of the ancient servants wheeled in a cart made of wicker, on which sat three glasses and a bottle covered with dust and cobwebs, through which cold be read only the words "PRIVATE STOCK." For some reason, the old servant seemed unable to take his eyes off Reverend Harkness, and the wicker cart sideswiped Jake's chair. The bottle wobbled, tipped, and seemed about to crash to the floor when Harkness, with a nimbleness she would never have expected, fielded it. The servant, whose skin had paled to an unpleasant gray-brown, was opening and shutting his mouth like a landed fish. Gillian had struggled halfway out of her imprisoning chair when Harkness, having replaced the bottle, took the old man by the elbows and gently eased him out of the room.

The MacIntyre bared his teeth again—it was not, Gillian decided, a smile at all—and poured a healthy slug of something thick and golden brown into each of the glasses. "You'll not want ice with this," he said, and downed his glass in a single swallow. Gillian and Jake looked first at each other and then at Harkness.

"Please," said the reverend, with an upward, encouraging motion of both hands, as if he were tipping up their glasses. "I do not imbibe."

"It was my father's," The MacIntyre announced, glaring at them.

Jake picked up his glass and poised it. "To your father, sir."

Feeling she had no choice but to follow, Gillian murmured, "Father," and took a tentative sip. To her astonishment it was delicious— no, she decided after a second, deeper sip, better than delicious. Hot as liquid sunlight, with an underlying deep, smooth sweetness she couldn't quite place. Groping for something—anything—to construct a conversation, she said, "This is terribly good, sir."

"Sugarcane brandy," The MacIntyre said. "Have another." And, following his prescription, filled his own glass.

Two drinks later the apprehension that had been riding her shoulders had dissipated like fog burned off by the sun. At the same time her perception seemed to have sharpened; from across the room she could feel Jake almost throbbing with frustration as he tossed ever more leaden hints at The MacIntyre, who kept right on ignoring them. Purposely ignoring them, she was sure, though the old man had taken enough alcohol aboard to pickle a small whale.

At her side Reverend Harkness was murmuring an apparently endless series of blameless anecdotes, the kind of small talk that Gillian recognized (having done it herself to *Glory*'s charterers) as allowing the talker to concentrate on something or someone else. Jake and The MacIntyre, in this case.

She became aware that another person had slipped into the room, and for a moment she thought it was the skipper of The MacIntyre's launch. No, she saw, the new arrival was slender and young, like the launch skipper, but shorter and so tightly wound she half expected him to self-destruct before her eyes. He whispered something in Harkness's ear. The reverend, consulting his watch, returned some words that Gillian couldn't catch but that clearly meant "no."

The young man looked furious, but he faded away as silently as he had come. As he did, Gillian suddenly arrived at her decision: Jake's visit was a failure; old MacIntyre was nobody's contact; Gillian's obligation was first to Patrick and then to *Glory*; and the man who could help her was obviously Harkness.

She turned to him, and his anecdote dried up in mid-delivery. "Something troubles you," he said.

"Yes." She felt reassured already. "I have a kind of strange problem."

He beamed at her. "I am at your service."

"It's—maybe we could talk about it in private." To her own irritation, she was unable to keep her eyes from flicking toward Jake.

"Of course," he replied. "May I ask if your . . . problem is of a religious nature?" He smiled. "I see not. Then may I suggest after dinner? The MacIntyre always likes to linger over the port. We could inspect the view from the parapet. Unless, of course—"

"That would be fine," she said quickly. "Just great."

Barr: William Bay, 6:00 P.M.

He was scraping the last residue of cold chili from the can with his knife blade when he heard the sound he'd been waiting for, a gentle splashing from close alongside. "Captain Barr!" The hoarse whisper managed to carry a sense of urgency, but Barr finished his exploration, then licked the result off the blade.

"Barr! Come over here!" He set down the empty tin and wiped the sheath knife's blade on a scrap of wastepaper, got slowly to his feet, and stretched. He pulled himself up out of the cockpit and stood by the mizzen shrouds, as if admiring the sunset that was silently exploding off *Glory*'s port side. The ground swell, pushing down from the island's north end, had got steeper in the last couple of hours, and *Glory* was beginning to pitch just slightly as she put her bow into it.

Careful not to look down at the source of the splashing, he addressed the violent turmoil of scarlet, purple, and gold on the horizon. "Welcome back, Hubert," he said. "Did your boat sink?"

"Shee-*it!*" said the voice from below his feet. "Will you for chrissake drop me a line or something to grab on to?" Hubert's voice—without, Barr noted, Hubert's accent.

"Why?" said Barr. "You want to sell me some more junk?" As he spoke, he unzipped the fly of his khakis.

"You piss on my head," Hubert said, "and I'll come up there and tear your throat out."

"Think of it as cover," Barr said. "For the benefit of whoever's watching *Glory* from shore."

"You sure?" The accent, Barr decided, was California, but California overlaying a basic island lilt. If he was right—Patrick would've been able to dissect the accent in a minute—then he knew who was swimming alongside.

"Someone's on the roof of the old MacIntyre warehouse," Barr said. "The sun's been bouncing off his binocular lenses for the last half hour."

"Damn." The voice sounded tired, and no wonder: Barr had watched him scissor-kick his way from the harbor's north end, pushing an untidy floating heap of vegetation as disguise. He wondered if the unknown watcher ashore had noticed just how fast that pile of dead palm fronds was drifting.

"Wait a minute," Barr said. "I'll get something for you to hang on to." He zipped his pants, stretched again, and went slowly to the companionway. As he slid down the ladder, he grabbed a handful of the extra sail ties that hung from a hook. In the small guest cabin across from the chart table, he undogged the porthole and swung it open. "You still there, Son?" he called. "It is Son Douglas, right?"

"Thought you didn't recognize me," came the voice from the water. "What's it been—eight years?"

"Only seven," Barr replied as he knotted the sail ties together. "And I didn't. You put on a lot of weight up there in Berkeley." He tied a bowline into the end. "Here, grab this."

"About time."

Barr felt the swimmer's weight come on the string of sail ties, and he lashed the last one to the built-in berth. "So what the hell's going on here?"

"I thought *you'd* know." A splash, as the swimmer adjusted his position. "All this spook stuff's not my idea, in case you were wondering."

The hostility was plain, and Barr considered it in silence. Son Douglas had been a teenager the last time he and Barr had seen each other—just before the boy went away to college, the first of the island's sons to go to a university in America. They'd exchanged politenesses (Son's father insisted on that) on Barr's occasional visits to the family's office in William Town, the big, low-ceilinged chamber that served as city room for the *Philippic*, the island's weekly paper.

Had Son realized back then why Barr stopped by every time *Wind-hover* called at St. Philip? Barr had always gone on the presumption that secrets in the islands never lasted long, and certainly not within a family. At the same time he saw nothing to be gained by advertising his employers' errands. Son—the much-beloved only child—had seemed too full of his own affairs to bother with, or care about, what his parents were up to. But maybe not. For the time being, Barr simply recorded the cold dislike in the young man's voice.

He looked out the porthole. The sun was taking a long time dying this evening, and *Glory* would still be silhouetted from the shore. "Assuming you're willing to keep going along with the spook stuff," Barr said, "you're going to have to stay in solution for another fifteen minutes or so, before I can bring you aboard."

"You may not have that much time, man," said Son. "That's what I come out here to tell you."

"What do you mean?" Barr demanded.

"They got your two friends, and they'll be coming back to get you. Soon as it's dark."

So Jake and Gillian had walked into a trap. Barr bit back a frustrated

curse. The MacIntyre's invitation had sounded suspicious, of course—
so much so that Barr had foolishly allowed himself to believe it might
be innocent. Not that he could have kept Gillian from going, once
she'd made up her mind. Reverse was a gear she just didn't have.

It was definitely time to call for help, Barr decided, but not on
something as public as the ship-to-shore. He glanced again out the
porthole. There was still one other thing he had to do, and it was just
about time to do it. "I'll be with you in five minutes," he said.

"You got wax in your ears?" said Son, his voice angry and apprehensive. "You didn't hear what I just told you?"

There was nothing to say and too little time to try to calm the young
man down. Barr went to the chart table. From a drawer he pulled a
cheap portable radio, turned it on, and tuned it to 930, Radio Antilles.

Five minutes later, as the forecast was coming to an end, he heard
Son's voice again. "Barr!" he called. "Jesus, man, where are you?"

"Just about done," Barr called back. "What's the problem?"

"Problem?" Son managed a shaky laugh. "Problem is that old
MacIntyre's boat's coming back, and there's about a hundred guys on
it lusting after your ass."

Barr took a quick look around him, suddenly aware that this might
be the last time he'd see this familiar setting. No time for a good cry,
he told himself. Grabbing the companionway key from a hook, he
scrambled up the ladder. For a moment he saw another boat against
the now-dark sky to the south and then checked out its bow wave,
throwing a shimmer of iridescence to either side. Too damn close,
and coming on fast.

He locked the companionway hatch—probably a pointless gesture—
and, crouched low to keep from showing himself needlessly against
the last light, slid over *Glory*'s gunwale until he was dangling at arm's
length, his legs in the warm water up to the knee. He let go and dropped
the rest of the way without, he hoped, enough of a splash to alert the
crew of the oncoming launch. He came to the surface sputtering; he
could feel through the water the vibration of the launch's propeller.

"C'mon," said Son. Not waiting to see if Barr was following, he
pushed away from *Glory*'s side into the gathering night.

Like a number of deep-water sailors, Barr had a very qualified love
for the water when actually in it, and he was a mediocre swimmer.
Trying not to splash just made swimming harder, and it was all he
could do to track Son's efficient, almost silent progress toward the
shore, which now seemed a dismaying distance off.

Suddenly Son changed direction, making—as Barr observed with relief—for a dark, spherical shape bobbing heavily on the surface. It was St. Philip's only navigational buoy, a gift five years ago from the Canadian government. Since then its flashing light had gone out (bulb and storage battery both stolen by fishermen), and as soon as a Philipian figured out some use for the mooring chain, the remainder would vanish, too.

But even in its diminished condition it made a welcome resting place for at least one gasping swimmer, happy to ignore the heavy incrustation of barnacles sawing at his arms and chest.

"For a sailor," said Son quietly, "you sure are a lousy swimmer."

Barr could only nod his head in acknowledgment. He looked around the side of the buoy and saw The MacIntyre's launch alongside *Glory*—heard it, too, as its bronze guard rail gouged into the yacht's hull. Clatter of metal against wood. The boarding party was now scrambling onto *Glory*'s deck, the weapons they carried hitting cockpit coaming and cabin side.

A couple of flashlights waved erratically. Conversation that Barr didn't understand followed, though he could hear it quite clearly across the water. "What're they saying?" he asked.

"Damn if I know," the younger man replied. "It's some kind of Arab talk they use when they forget we might hear them."

"They?" said Barr. "Who're they?" Before Son could speak, orders volleyed from the launch, followed by the rending crash of metal splitting thin wood. The companionway hatch, Barr guessed. So much for locking it. Another tearing noise as someone ripped the door off its hinges; Barr was surprised how the sound physically sickened him.

"They like that shit," Son remarked. "Busting things. They figure it scares people, and they're right."

"You keep saying 'they'," Barr said. "Who—"

"Well, that's the big question, isn't it?" said Son. "Hey, what's that?"

"Those sons of bitches," Barr heard himself say. "They're stealing *Glory*." Five of them were on the foredeck, heaving more or less together at the anchor rode. Now someone was shouting the time, a high-pitched, rhythmic chant. Slowly, slowly the big ketch crept forward, until at last a voice—a West Indian voice—called out: "Off the bottom, Cap'n!"

Barr felt his heart sink as the launch moved ahead, turning in a wide arc to head back toward the south. Behind it *Glory* began to swing, too, as the unseen towline took up the slack, and whoever was handling her helm brought her around.

"Unless you want to set up house on that buoy," said Son Douglas, "we'd best get out of here. When they bring your boat down to High-land House, somebody with a few more smarts than they got is going to wonder where the hell you're at."

"Where are we going?" Barr asked.

"Going? To Cosy's house, where else?" Son replied. "You ain't forgotten Cosy, have you? Your island sweetie pie and my esteemed mom?" He pushed off from a buoy and headed for shore, not waiting for his companion or even looking back.

Slowly Barr followed him, his mind spinning. If Son believed what he was saying, it was easy to see what had put the acid in his voice. But where on earth had he got such an idea?

Patrick: Highland House, 7:00 P.M.

It wasn't the first time in his life Patrick had known despair—though never before so deep and hopeless. For some time he just lay slumped against the cold, rough stones that formed the wall between him and Isabel.

He had no idea how long he lay or what time it was when, against all hope, he heard a low, dull moan from the cell next to his. The first time he thought the sound came from his own throat; it certainly matched his mood. Then he heard it again. The spurt of hope that flooded him was like coming alive again.

He scrabbled in the floor's accumulated dirt for the bent nail. Find-ing it, he tapped against the wall, lightly at first and then as hard as he could manage. No response—but, he told himself again, the tap-ping probably couldn't be heard on the other side of the thick wall.

He tried calling, his lips close to the wall and cupped by his hands. The noise he made seemed loud enough to bring the guards running, but there was no answer.

He pressed his ear to the stone and heard mostly the throbbing of the blood in his own veins, but behind it what he thought was a dull, uneven sobbing. A woman's voice, though deep. Without hearing words, he couldn't absolutely put a name to it, but he didn't need to. He was convinced, and conviction poured strength into his aching muscles.

He went first to the small window in his cell door, sidling up to it. Was someone standing outside? All he could see, even with his cheek hard against the bars, was maybe twenty-five linear feet of almost featureless stone corridor, lit at ten-foot intervals by bare bulbs strung amateurishly from the ceiling. The wall on the far side was blank, without a single door or window, and the floor was the same fitted stone as the inside of his own cell. The door was solid wood, two inches thick at least, and while he could make out, in the crack between door and frame, the outline of the bolt that held it closed, there was no way he could get at it.

He turned back to his own cell. Starting in one corner, he began to run his fingertips lightly over the wall, trying to assemble a mental picture of its construction. He forced himself to go slowly, to trace each seam. After a time that felt like forever he paused to summarize what he'd learned.

Unlike the carefully squared-off blocks of the outer walls, these partitions were crude work—volcanic rocks bashed into rough oblongs that were laid in courses which didn't fit evenly. The gaps between them were plugged with the same mortar that cemented them together. The long-congealed lava that formed the blocks was far harder than Patrick's bent nail, but the mortar, laid in dampness, seemed loose to even an exploring fingernail.

Working mostly by touch, Patrick located a block near the floor that felt as big across as his shoulders. The stone right above it was even longer and overlapped it at both ends, so there was no danger of starting a noisy landslide.

The first few minutes' work went so well that Patrick felt his spirits shoot up as steeply as they'd fallen. The mortar on one side of the block came out easily, in crumbly chunks. Maybe it had been intended only as filler or bedding. In a short time, the floor at his feet was an inch deep in damp, gritty powder.

Easy as the work was, Patrick's bent nail was already showing signs of wear. The point was long gone, and it felt shorter than when he had started. The question he wouldn't think about was whether it would last the course. His fingertips were mercifully numb, but from their stickiness he knew the skin was mostly abraded away.

The scrape-scrape of his work seemed to echo back and forth off the bare walls, and his ears were tuned for noise from outside. Fortunately the guards who came at last were wearing shoes, not the sneakers that islanders favored. There was no time to hide the debris—only just enough for Patrick to scuttle back to the center of the cell, wrap the cord around his ankles, and lie back, hands behind him.

The guard had enough sense to look through the peephole before unlocking the door. He called something over his shoulder (so there was another guard within hearing) and pushed open the door with his hip. He was holding a pair of shallow bowls, one in each hand, and his wavering flashlight was clamped between his arm and side.

He set the bowls on the floor, and the light panned quickly across them. Some kind of watery stew, Patrick saw. The smell of it was unpleasant and vaguely familiar, but it was definitely food, and Patrick realized he hadn't eaten or drunk anything since before daylight, at least twelve hours ago.

The guard stood watching expectantly; Patrick realized the man was waiting for him to wriggle over and slurp up the food. He would have done it, dignity be damned, if rolling over wouldn't have revealed that his hands were no longer tied. Instead he stared up at the dim ceiling, trying not to think of his dry mouth and swollen tongue.

For what seemed like an eternity to Patrick, the guard waited; once he nudged one of the bowls with his foot and murmured something that sounded like encouragement. At last he lost patience and picked a bowl up, held it over Patrick's face.

"You," he said. "Eat this."

Patrick ignored him, and received a kick in the ribs for his rudeness.

"Eat up," said the guard impatiently. "Now." He set down the bowl he was holding and moved to take his prisoner by the shoulders and roll him over.

Patrick tensed, focusing on the guard's bare throat. Time for a single chop—and what would he do then?

Rescue came from outside the cell, in the form of an impatient shout that obviously asked why Patrick's guard was taking so long. His guard shouted back, straightened up, and delivered a second kick, below the ribs. "Good evening," he said, picking up one of the bowls.

Patrick forced himself to lie still until he heard the door to Isabel's cell slam open. Even as he inhaled the mush—goat water stew, without the goat—he was thinking, *Oh God, don't let him hurt her any more.* His mind rummaged desperately through the forgotten prayers of his Catholic childhood, groping for some vast, overwhelming vow that would save Isabel from any more pain. But that was just dumb. The only way Isabel was going to be saved was if he saved her, and to do that, he had to live, at least until he got her clear of this place.

Her cell door slammed shut again, and he lay still as the guard's feet echoed down the corridor outside, pausing—as he expected they would—for a quick glance at Patrick, again on his back staring upward. Would the man come back? Impossible to say, but there was no time to waste worrying about it.

He hurled himself at the wall—jabbing, scratching, digging with the blunted nail and sometimes with his fingertips, rejoicing fiercely in the pain that came from action.

And then it was done. The nail, a stub now, poked one more time and pushed the last small wedge of mortar free. Patrick found he was gasping from the concentrated effort, yet unwilling to stop so close to his goal. He put his shoulder to the block of stone, braced his feet against the floor, and shoved. Shoved again until his feet slipped under him. He thought there was a hint of movement from the stone, a slight scraping noise, but that was all.

He took a half step back and hurled himself at the block. The stab of pain jarred his shoulder and brought him to his senses. The only thing he'd achieve that way was a sprung collarbone. The smart thing was to use the strongest muscles in his body.

He lay on his back, feet up, and kicked. The impact pushed him a good six inches away from the wall, but he definitely felt the stone shift. He repositioned himself and kicked again. This time the bandage on his shoulder blade tore free, but again the block of stone moved back, with a dull, grating sound.

He checked it with his hand: six inches in and definitely loose. One more kick would do it.

The crash of stone against stone boomed off the bare stone walls, so loud that Patrick's heart missed a beat. He lay in frozen silence while he counted to sixty slowly, but there was not a sound from the corridor outside. At last, when he could tell himself it was safe to move, he got to his knees and pushed his head and shoulders through the gap.

His estimate of the block's size had been generous. Only by hunching and wriggling and leaving what felt like a square foot of skin behind could he force his shoulders through the hole. But that was his widest part. His torso, his hips slid through easily.

At first he didn't see her—or, rather, didn't realize that the blanket-covered heap was Isabel. It was so small and so still. Maybe that guard had finished her off, or maybe she'd just died from what they had done to her.

He pushed his mind away from that thought, away from the memories of things he'd seen done to women in El Salvador and Chad. Slowly, gently he turned the blanket back. She was curled up tightly, her arms pulled into her sides. She was wearing only a man's shirt, and the part of the blanket under her was wet and sticky. But she was breathing, quickly and shallowly. The bowl beside her was empty.

"Isabel!" he whispered. "Isabel—you awake?" She didn't move, didn't answer, and he took her in his arms. Her skin was cold and damp, and he pulled off his own shirt—the shreds of his own shirt—and wrapped them around her. "Please," he said. He could hear the desperation in his voice. "Please, Isabel."

The sound that came out of her was somewhere between a sob and a groan, but at least it was a response. "Patrick?" she said, after a moment. "It *is* you?"

"It's me. Listen, are you—can you walk?"

"I don' know." A gulping sob followed, and her shoulders began to shake silently. He held her, willing heat and life from himself into her. The dry, almost soundless sobbing went on and on, and then she said something he couldn't hear.

"What?" he said.

She sniffed, and he could almost feel her taking a grip on her seared emotions. When she spoke again, her voice was nearly level. "They are going to kill us."

"That's what they think." The determination in his voice surprised even him, and she looked up into his face. In the gloom he could see only her eyes, which seemed twice as large as before, and a trickle of what looked like blood from one puffed lip.

"No, it is true," she insisted. "This—this *loco* is going to kill many people."

"Tell me," he said. "The whole thing."

She hesitated, and he felt her shoulders move in what might have been a shrug. "*Por qué no?*" she said. "What difference now?"

She rattled the information off listlessly: The people here—*here* being Highland House, as Patrick had already guessed—the people who were holding the building and controlling the island were not Philipians at all but some kind of *guerrilleros* from another nation, she thought in the Near East. . . .

Of course. How could I be so dumb? Patrick thought. *You hear what you expect to hear, and I never expected to hear Arabic again, not after I got out of Chad.*

Isabel had come to the United States to infiltrate the Cubans in Miami—yes, of course, she had been assigned; of course, her escape from Cuba was a fake—but when Jake Adler came to South Florida, recruiting exiles for some crazy mission, her superiors put her on to watching him instead.

"It was so easy," she said, her head turned away from Patrick. "He wanted, he *needed* a woman, to make people think he was more of a man. But he doesn 't need women, not that way." When Jake's work among the exiles collapsed, from too much looniness on both sides, she went back with him to his exile at Fort Drum, the upstate New York base where, as Patrick remembered, the First Army tucked away the people it would like to forget but couldn't get rid of.

Then Jake's people had called him about a new scheme. He didn't tell Isabel what it was at first, and her superiors told her to stick with him. But all the while she was drifting away from *la causa*, as the chance opened up for her to live a life of her own.

"I was okay to stay in the U.S.," she said. "Political refugee, not like a Haitian. I began to think, maybe . . ."

And then her past closed in again. Jake's group was on the move, and she had to go with him, keep an eye on him and continue her reports. For a long time Jake wouldn't tell her what was happening. He suspected her, she thought, but wanted to keep her where he could see what she was up to. When at last he told her the target was St. Philip, and she passed the information on, she hoped she could split from him.

"But the word came back: Stay with him. What could I do?" Her small, hard fist beat against Patrick's shoulder. "Tell me, Patrick, what could I do?"

You could've told me, he thought. He heard himself say, "It's all right."

She was sobbing again, but these were not the terrible, racking dry sobs that he thought might tear her apart. Now she was holding him tightly. "What are we going to do?" she said.

"We're going to get out of here," he said, almost believing it. "But tell me what the hell's going on. What are these people up to?"

"I don't know," she said. "All I know is that they plan a big . . ." She tried for the word, shook her head. "In Spanish, *manifestación*—demonstration—but not exactly that either. More like a *venganza*, a revenge." She shook her head again. "I am sorry."

Maybe better not to know more, Patrick thought. *Just concentrate on getting us out of here.* Before he could reassure her, though, he heard the voices in the hall—Arabic for certain, now he knew what to listen for. Not that he could understand it, more than a few words, but the rhythms were impossible to miss.

They were coming for him or for Isabel. His exhausted brain seemed ready to fold up and quit, though the choice was simple: If the guards were coming for him and he was gone, they'd be alerted, and they'd for sure know where to look. But if they could see him, they might get close enough . . .

He was halfway through the hole, scrambling and squirming, as his ears sorted out the sounds in the corridor: voices, two of them, and shod feet to match. But another noise, too, a sort of skidding.

Now he was in the cell, wrapping the string around his ankles, propping himself with his back concealing the hole in the wall, thinking, *Just give me a minute. Just let them get close enough . . .*

He tensed as the door swung open. Ready to spring. Ready to kill, or die trying.

The square-built silhouette in the doorway was familiar. It was Jake Adler. It fell forward on its face.

Gillian: 7:30 P.M.

She propped her elbows on the cold stone of the parapet, leaning out as far as she could.

"I'm afraid you can't see the anchorage from here," said Reverend Harkness, standing just behind her. "That high point—did you know they call it Hangman Hill?—is in the way."

She drew back, shivering slightly in the night breeze. It was blowing strongly up here, at the top of the tower, and seemed to be shifting into the west. She wondered if the wind was doing the same thing at water level, if *Glory* was swinging to it. Well, if the anchor pulled free, Barr could reset it alone; she'd seen him do it before, no fuss, no muss, in that unobtrusive way he had. God, she wished she were back in *Glory*'s aft stateroom and in his arms and away from this place.

"I feel I should apologize for what happened at dinner," said Harkness suddenly. "My manners deserted me. I'm afraid the military have a bad effect on me."

"Oh," she said. "Dinner. It could've been worse." Out here in the evening air, her head was splitting.

Dinner, in the great hall of Highland House, had started disastrously and staggered downhill from there.

All Gillian had wanted—now that she recognized Jake's mission as a failure—was for the meal to end, so she could take Reverend Harkness aside and enlist his help in finding Patrick. That done, *Glory* would be away from St. Philip as quickly as she could make sail. If Barr's former employers in the intelligence racket thought they could blackmail Gillian Verdean any further into playing their fantasy-of-the-month game, she'd be delighted to show them how wrong they were.

It was amazing how much better the resolution made her feel, though she'd known even then that three glasses of The MacIntyre's liquid lightning undoubtedly had something to do with her state of mind. Never mind. There was all the difference in the world between being a little elevated, as she was ready to admit she might be, and soddenly, lurchingly drunk like her host.

The great hall had been designed for dinners of a hundred or so, with a servant behind every chair, under crystal chandeliers that hung from a vaulted ceiling twenty feet overhead. An upper-level gallery that overlooked the diners was probably where the MacIntyres' famous black piper marched back and forth, wreathed in "Scotland the Brave" and "All the Blue Bonnets Are over the Border."

Now all of it was gone except the table, long and wide enough to land a small plane on, and a huddle of unmatched chairs at one end. For light, there was a pair of ordinary reading lamps; for servants, two old men—the same two, Gillian thought, who had opened the gates for them an hour and a half before.

The food was West Indian at its grim worst: the odorous stew with the damning name "goat water," a weak curry whose chicken was represented mostly by gristle; the inevitable tasteless peas and rice; soggy baked breadfruit. The once-noble wine had become vinegar's first cousin, but she managed a glass anyway, just to extinguish the stew.

The Reverend Harkness, across from her, had been drinking what she assumed, in spite of its brownish color, was water, poured from a silver pitcher that carried a decade's tarnish.

Gillian had been placed on the host's right hand, Jake at his left. It was instantly clear that The MacIntyre wanted nothing to do with Jake—indeed, seemed almost afraid to talk to him. He turned instead to Gillian and launched into a largely incomprehensible monologue about "my island" that would have brought the native population to his gates with torches and machetes if they could have heard it.

The MacIntyre, it appeared, had two years before been unseated as the island's ceremonial head of state, and the insult still rankled. "After all I've done for them, the ungrateful buggers," was a phrase that popped up more than once.

Gillian's attempts to deflect him—were there political parties? how was the government constituted?—were ignored. Having hit upon the theme of ingratitude, The MacIntyre was prepared to belabor it for the rest of the evening.

At least she didn't have to do anything but nod agreement, smile, drop in the occasional "of course." No worse than a tedious charter party, and the old man wasn't groping her leg under the tablecloth. She could tune out his loud, firm voice and listen instead, with growing nervousness, to Jake and Reverend Harkness.

Their disagreement had begun in the library, with a remark by Harkness that Gillian had missed. Something about the United States and the Desert Storm war that Jake took issue with. From that it was a small step to American foreign policy generally, with Jake bristling visibly, to the State Department's meddling in the Caribbean, and Jake red-faced, his voice up by several decibels.

The reverend was sweating heavily, his clerical collar had gone limp, but he seemed much less mild. His voice, which seemed to become softer as Jake's picked up volume, had a steely undertone now, and his accent had become very British and superior. The gentle brown eyes glittered, but not with anger; Gillian had the feeling that the man was suppressing a note of triumph.

At that point a deep, ringing boom had brought Jake up off his chair, but it was only the dinner gong, somewhere in the recesses of the house. Down a seemingly endless hallway they went, Gillian on her host's arm (and taking about half his weight), while a servant with a candelabrum walked ahead and Jake and the reverend brought up the rear in sudden smoldering silence.

Pictures had hung on these walls, she saw. The MacIntyre, following her eye, said, "All sold. Years ago. Like everything else."

"And I say"—Reverend Harkness's voice had cut through The MacIntyre's drone like a whiplash—"I say that is a lie. A *Zionist* lie."

Jake was on his feet, his chair over backward, to the sound of splintering wood. "What do you mean, Zionist?" he demanded. His face, red a minute before, had white spots over each cheekbone.

Harkness seemed to have drawn in upon himself, and Gillian felt as if she were in the presence of a snake coiled to strike. But he smiled his former gentle smile and said, "You are Jewish, are you not?"

Jake was standing with his feet slightly apart. "I'm a serving officer in the United States Army," he said this time very quietly. "I don't have political opinions."

"Ah," said Harkness, with the triumph plain in his voice, "you mean only that someone has them on your behalf."

If his words were meant to trigger a larger explosion, they failed.

Jake, Gillian saw, had pulled back within himself and was not to be drawn out. "I think," he said, addressing The MacIntyre, "that we'd better get back to our boat. We've stayed too long."

The old man, whose face had become a mask of bewilderment and fear, turned his bloodshot eyes to Harkness, as if silently asking him what to do. The corners of the minister's mouth pulled up in a parody of a smile. "Of course," he said, but to The MacIntyre, not Jake. "However, Miss Verdean and I will have a private word, if you will excuse us for a few minutes."

Astonishment, dismay, anger twisted Jake's broad face and vanished, leaving a mask behind which his hard eyes watched like sentries.

"Have another drink, man," The MacIntyre said suddenly. "We've not even seen the port. And there're cigars."

"I'll have a port with you, sir," Jake said. "I'm afraid the chair's had it. I apologize."

"Think nothing of it!" the old man boomed, pouncing on a situation he could deal with. "Abraham!" he cried. "Where are you, you old bugger?"

"You wanted to ask me something, I think?" asked Harkness.

She hesitated. There was something different about him, something that made her uneasy. Still, if there was anyone on this goddamned island who could help her find Patrick, it was probably Harkness. "Look," she began, "I've got a problem."

She paused again, unsure where to dive into the mess. Harkness's face was a blur, but she was sure he was smiling. "Please," he said, "feel free to speak. If you've broken one of our little regulations, it cannot be so important."

Encouraged, she pulled herself together. "Well, that's one way of looking at it. The fact is—"

Steps coming fast, up the stone stairway, stopped her. A figure popped out of the hatchway in the floor and pulled up suddenly, his attention seemingly divided between Gillian and Harkness.

"What is it?" the reverend snapped, his voice hard—like Jake's, Gillian found herself thinking. "What has happened?"

The man—not a West Indian, but a thin, intense person who reminded her of the launch's skipper—seemed unable to find the words he needed. Instead he gestured broadly toward the parapet. "There!" he said. "It comes!"

Gillian, following his gesture, saw the lights clearing the point. A passenger ship, a big one, about five miles out to sea. From the way the running lights lined up, she was angling in toward shore. She looked to Harkness, whose silhouetted head was stiffly alert. "A cruise ship?" She asked. And had to repeat herself.

"What? Oh, yes," he replied. "We have been waiting for it."

She could understand the excitement. "Business for the island," she said. "Your people will be pleased."

For once he seemed at a loss for words. At last he said, "It is not a very large vessel. But large enough."

"Looks big to me," she replied. As she glanced back out to sea, a patch of phosphorescence caught her eye. A moving patch that she realized was a boat's bow wave. And another behind it.

Dangerous running in the dark like that, without lights, she thought, but what difference did it make here? Something familiar about the faint, vague outline of the second boat, a sailing vessel, her spars bare against the last race of sunset. "Hey," she said, "what's going on? That's my boat! That's—"

She heard something hissing through the air, just before it hit. An explosion in her head, shower of sparks. Her legs were rubber . . . No, she was lying on the ground, consciousness slipping away, and in the background, exactly in Jake's manner, Harkness was rapping out what had to be orders, in a language she had never heard.

Barr: William Town, 9:00 P.M.

Barr seldom felt at a loss because of his appearance, was seldom even aware of how he looked, but as he sat dripping salt water on Cosima Douglas's highly polished floor, while a coven of St. Philip's leading citizens watched him anxiously, he was distinctly uncomfortable. His sodden shirt and khakis were plastered to his body, and he remembered that he'd forgotten to shave since yesterday. From the dismayed expressions on his audience's faces, Barr had the feeling that his old friend Cosima—Cosy, to everyone who knew her—must have promised a distinguished international yachtsman, and what had turned up was clearly a shipwrecked scarecrow.

"More soup?"

"It's delicious, thanks, but I'm awash." Cosy, her head poked out the kitchen door, flashed him her wonderful smile, and he marveled again at how the years had glided past her. She was, he knew, older than he—on the cusp of forty, he thought, though she could have passed for thirty in the kindly light of the big, low-ceilinged room.

Most Philipian women her age looked more like sixty, wrung dry by too much childbirth and too many years working too hard under a too-harsh sun.

Cosy had escaped all that. The Douglases were rich by St. Philip's standards: a nearly new Daihatsu in the street outside, a VCR on the color TV in the corner of the living room. Her husband's ownership of the *Philippic* hadn't brought in a great deal of cash, but under-the-table payoffs from government and opposition easily made up for the shortage of advertising. More to the point, the paper was *read*. Thursday afternoons, when the LIAT flight brought the still-damp copies from the printer on Antigua, half St. Philip was already salivating to see who Old Sim had stuck his knife into this week. Simeon Douglas might be ignorant of the finer points of journalism, but he had honed to a perfect edge his talent for the kind of sniggering semiaccusation that tiptoed around libel laws while it made its subject a laughingstock.

An unpleasant man, Barr thought, but a damned useful one since he knew absolutely everything that happened on the island—and was willing to tell, for a price. But Sim Douglas had died, Barr had heard, three or four months ago. He'd meant to send Cosy a note, but had never been able to summon the hypocrisy necessary to compose it. Besides, he knew—though she'd never said a word—how she felt about the man she'd stayed married to for thirty years, because he was the father of her only child.

Everybody had come to Cosy's tonight. The usual suspects, Tarleton had always called them: MacLeod, the one-armed police chief; Father Hughes, the Anglican priest, presumably without flock or church now; a pair of other ministers, one of whom ran a sideline in herbal magic that might have shocked his superiors; a huddle of shop owners who were, for Barr, interchangeable; the port captain, who'd come up from Bonaire half a century before and would therefore be an outsider till the day he died.

Van Orden, the elderly, half-Dutch judge who doubled as St. Philip's president and tripled as its Avis rep, was presiding, or trying to. As the others watched Barr mopping up the last of the soup with a piece of bread, Van Orden squeaked away in the background, his thin voice doubly odd coming from so huge and solid a man. Even with no one else talking, Barr found it hard to follow what he was saying, except that it seemed to be an invocation of sorts.

"I shall call on the Organization of Caribbean States," he said, "on the Caribbean Economic Community, on the United Nations . . ."

Barr put down his soup bowl, and as if on signal, all the rest started

to talk at once, drowning out Van Orden's litany. The noise brought
Cosy in from the kitchen; behind her, half hidden, was Son. Cosy
threw Barr a rueful smile; Son's malevolent glare was right on its heels.

"Maybe . . ." Barr began, but the Philipians were already shouting
at one another, the cords in their necks standing out like wire. "Hey,
listen . . ."

Without a word Cosy picked a serving plate from the pine sideboard
and hurled it to the floor. The silence echoed. "Thank you," she said.
The word "majestic" popped unbidden into Barr's head, and he recalled that Tarleton had once used it of her. She had big dark eyes—
not unlike Isabel's—that could melt or blaze on demand, and she was
an inch under six feet and full-bodied. Her perfect mahogany skin
seemed two shades darker than usual, against her bloodred dress.

Every eye was on her, and she let a full ten seconds pass before she
walked to Barr's side. "Most of you remember Cap'n Barr's old boat,
Windhover, used to stop by here pretty often," she said. The soft
murmur of agreement floated back to her, and she went on. "Well,
you know what they say about a friend in need. Here he is again, just
when we're really in need." A rising chorus of assent, but she waved
them silent.

You think you're *in need*, Barr reflected. He said, "Why don't you
tell me what the problem is—one of you at a time?"

"Father Hughes," Cosy said quickly, "you first."

He was an old man and easily confused. Barr sensed that the final
failure of his church had uprooted his spirit. His story, however, was
simple enough.

The year before, Father Hughes began, a self-proclaimed clergyman
named Harkness had come to St. Philip. Come to settle on the island,
a rare event in itself. Father Hughes wasn't clear just which denom-
ination Harkness—Reverend, he called himself—adhered to, but he
had seemed well educated, sincere, a gentleman.

Yes, yes, came the chorus. Definitely a gentleman. From England,
too, which seemed for them to define the term.

St. George's Church had just succumbed to a shortage of parishioners, and Father Hughes had not paid that much attention to the
new arrival or much of anything else. "I was, I must confess, in the
Slough of Despond," he said. "So what happened might almost be a
text on the sin of despair." He looked for a moment as if he were
considering a sermon, but a restless stirring in the other chairs recalled
him to his subject.

One day, passing the closed and shuttered church, Father Hughes saw people in it. He entered and discovered a service in progress. When he protested, the congregation—some of them his former parisioners—had driven him out. Not knowing what else to do, Father Hughes had gone to the police—

"Thank you, Father," Cosy interrupted firmly. "Mr. MacLeod."

The police chief, stocky and gray-haired, made his report standing at near attention, back straight and heels together. Barr remembered that MacLeod had been a warrant officer in the Netherlands Marines before losing an arm in a machinery accident. His job on St. Philip was in the nature of a disability pension.

The chief of police was a direct man. He had called immediately on Reverend Harkness, only to find him in possession of what appeared to be valid documents giving him a long-term lease on the church property. Barr glanced quickly at Cosy, and her face confirmed what he had suspected, that MacLeod, though incorruptible personally, wouldn't know a long-term lease from a phony stock certificate.

In addition, MacLeod continued, St. Philip's only lawyer (who, Barr noted, was not among those present) claimed to have negotiated the deal for Harkness. Faced with this impasse, Father Hughes had backed off. "There was nothing more I could do," said MacLeod unhappily. "Now, was there?"

Harkness, it appeared, was in the saddle. His religious services were soon the center of Philipian social life, drawing not only Father Hughes's former congregation but also those of the island's other three churches.

The attraction was simple enough: money. Instead of asking his parishioners for cash, the Reverend Harkness dispensed it, in what were obviously precisely calculated amounts, to the island's neediest citizens.

"Well, I don't see—" Barr began, and found himself nearly overset by a tempest of objections.

At last one of the other ministers, an ordinary-looking man with a voice of brass, prevailed by sheer volume. "He killed Mr. Jacobus." The man paused, apparently waiting for support, and, finding none, turned to the man next to him. "You know it's true. You, too, MacLeod."

"You cannot say Mr. Jacobus was murdered," MacLeod objected, with the air of having said it many times before. "You can say he jumped or fell or was pushed from Hangman Hill, but that is all."

A storm of jeers from the others in the room, cut through by a woman's voice crying, "Then what about my Derek? What about him, MacLeod?"

"And Old Sim," shouted someone else. "Tell him about Old Sim, Cosy."

Barr turned quickly to Cosy. "Old Sim?" he said. "I heard he was dead, but nobody told me he'd been killed."

Cosy's full mouth was twisted in a half-smile. "That's the problem, Barr. Nobody will say he was killed."

MacLeod jumped as if stung. "I keep telling all of you, you cannot say that kind of thing unless you can prove it." He stared belligerently about him. "And you can't prove it. None of you."

"Would somebody break the code for me?" Barr demanded. "I just got here, remember?"

They all, even MacLeod, looked to Cosy. She surveyed the group silently, nodded. "All right," she said. She held up her forefinger. "Eltie Jacobus, the Seventh-Day Adventist preacher. He talked against Reverend Harkness and his healings. They found him on the beach at the bottom of Hangman Hill with his head broke." She held up another finger. "Derek Bott. He said the reverend was thieving the church from Father Hughes. He went out in his fishing boat, calm day, and he never came back. Three . . ." She looked about the room, found the person she sought. "Three was you, Wandalore. You made complaint about the noise in that chapel of Harkness's and—"

"They burn my store!" said a withered old crone in the back of the room. "I don' care what you say, MacLeod, I seen men go in my store, and then it on fire."

"But you couldn't identify them," MacLeod objected.

"Tell about Old Sim!" cried another voice, joined by three or four more.

"Three months ago," said Cosy. For the first time she looked close to her age and sounded it. "Sim was planning a big exposure in the paper. He told me, and Son, but nobody else."

Barr doubted that. Once Sim was on the track of a juicy scandal, he gloated to everyone he met; it was one of the things that terrified his victims.

"They warned him," she was saying. "Warned him with a note on the door. 'Leave well enough alone,' it said."

"Do you have the note?" Barr asked.

She shook her head, not to be deflected. "He was working downstairs, Sunday morning. Setting stories on the Linotype. Son and I were out. When I came back, the place was on fire, and he was dead." She took a deep breath, her eyes far away. "Machine burst, they said. The reservoir, whatever you call it, with the molten lead. It was all over the floor, and he was lying in it." She looked straight at Barr. "His face was in the lead."

"An' how many times that lino-what's-it broke before?" yelled MacLeod, jumping to his feet. "Three times, right? Three times it sprayed melted lead all over. You can't prove nothing!"

Slowly, painfully Cosy swung to face the police chief. "His face was in it," she said again.

"What about the story?" said Barr. "Sim must've had files, notes, stuff like that."

"Burned up," said Cosy. "Anyway, some papers were burned up, we found the ash. But that was all we found."

"That was—what?—three months ago," said Barr. "Any other . . . accidents since then?"

"Didn' need any," said an anonymous voice. "Nobody dare talk against reverend anymore."

"He run this place," said one of the shop owners. "He got The MacIntyre in his pocket now."

"What they're telling you"—Cosy's voice was acid—"in case you're missing the message, is that people here decided to live with it."

"What else could we do?" said someone. And "You heard Mac-Leod—ain' no proof," called another. Both, as Barr observed, from behind Cosy's back.

"Figured Harkness was maybe a drug lord, something like that," Cosy went on, as if she hadn't heard. "Needed the island as a staging point maybe."

"Is anything coming ashore then?" Barr asked. On an island this size, you couldn't land anything bigger than a dinghy without someone seeing it.

"Yes." It was Son. He pushed his way forward. "Started three weeks ago. Cap'n Vreeland brought in these big crates—like really humongous. The whole cargo deck was full of them."

"And the strangers," said someone. "Tell about the strangers."

"They no strangers," another man put in. "They duppies, for sure. You heard them. That's duppy talk."

Son scowled and Barr realized his anger was at his credulous countrymen. "Duppies, horsepucky," he said. "No such thing as duppies. They're Saudis. Anyway, Arabs. I met a few at the university. You can't miss 'em."

"Slow down," said Barr, who was trying to recall what the two plantain sellers had been saying about Vreeland and the nameless reverend. *Hugeous cases* . . . No, it was gone. "Tell me about the crates. Everything."

"All right," said Son. Barr sensed that the young man didn't mind being the center of attention. Probably didn't mind upstaging his formidable mother either. Barr, an only child who had been reared by a strong-minded woman, could sympathize, even as he stifled his impatience.

Two weeks before, Son began, the *Doris B.* had made an unexpected call. Out of the schedule, but Harkness had evidently expected it. He was down at the beach waiting before Captain Vreeland's bow loader was even on the horizon.

"He hired my trucks, too," Judge Van Orden called out. "Both of 'em—remember, Son?"

"Yeah, I remember," Son said. "I was driving one of them." The judge subsided, muttering.

As Son got further into his account, his hostility toward Barr seemed to fade. There had been three very large packing cases, their marks of origin painted out. "Fresh paint," Son observed. "Still wet." Wood-framed crates, very heavy.

"Man named Monasir was in charge," Son recollected. "He came aboard the *Doris B.*, him and nine others. They all worked for the reverend. And they're all still here."

"What happened to the cargo?" Barr asked.

"Took it first to the church, old St. George's. Left it right on the trucks, with Monasir and the Arabs guarding it."

"They had guns," someone added. "Mista Mongoose brought those, too."

"Rifles, not guns," MacLeod said, perhaps hearing a reproach in the other man's voice. "Rifles not illegal, only handguns."

"Anyway," Son continued, raising his voice, "two days later they move it all up to Highland House. Unloaded it there." He paused, seeming to consider what he had just said. "We were some surprised about that. But it seems like Harkness just moved in on The MacIntyre. Bang, like that."

"They're setting up for something," said Cosy abruptly. "Only we don't know what."

She picked up the story, gleaned from elderly servants in Highland House. One of the mysterious crates had been wrestled to the roof of the tower, the other two moved into The MacIntyre's own apartments, and the regular servants were now forbidden to go into either place. Instead they had been set to clearing out the old storerooms, where the distillery had been.

"Old machinery, hundreds of empty bottles, that kind of thing," said Cosy. "Not cleaning, you understand. Emptying. Making space."

"Space for what?" Son demanded, a second ahead of Barr.

"I don't know," Barr replied. "Point is, whatever's going on here is beyond us. It's time to call for help from outside."

Another dead silence, broken by Son's harsh laugh. "But that's why Mother wanted to see you," he said. "We're cut off."

Barr must have looked his astonishment, because everyone started explaining at once, and this time he was able to pick up the scraps of information from the general torrent. Two days before, the grass runway—the only runway—of Prince Bernhard International Airport, carved out of a cliff on the windward side, had suffered a mysterious slippage. A fifty-foot-wide chunk of it had slid into the sea during a rainstorm, and nothing could land or take off till it was replaced.

The same day the airfield's generator broke down, silencing the transmitter. And yesterday morning the antenna tree that carried the microwave telephone transmissions from the top of Mount Mauvis had fallen down the slope, breaking into a dozen pieces. The old undersea cable running to Antigua was still in place, but only the telephone engineer knew how to hook it up again, and no one had been able to find him—

"What about your transmitter?" Barr interrupted, looking to the port captain.

"VHF," he replied succinctly. "Twenty-mile range, and only to the west, 'cause it's screened by the mountains on the other side."

"And mine's got the same problem," said MacLeod quickly. "Police band, maybe reach ten miles, and Antigua's thirty miles to windward."

In Barr's mind the pieces were at last assuming something like a coherent shape. "Why d'you think somebody wants to cut St. Philip off from the world?"

Before Cosy could reply, MacLeod said, "If it's a revolution you're talkin' about, there's not much I can do to stop it. I got five men with Enfields. Ten more on the retired list, average age sixty." He managed a thin smile. "An' I know about as many others got illegal guns tucked away in their cottages."

"Well, that's it, Captain Barr," said the judge. He was, as Barr recalled, a man in whom pomposity died hard. "That's why we asked Miz Douglas to have you come here. In the circumstances I have declared a national emergency." He glared around him, but the source of the nervous giggle did not reveal itself. "A national emergency," he repeated. "I will use the radio on your vessel to call for assistance." Barr looked quickly to Son, who shrugged helplessly.

"I think," said Barr, "there's something you ought to know . . ."

And just as he was deciding how best to tell them, feet pounded on the stairs, and the Philipian Barr recognized as Joop, the fisherman, burst into the room, his message spilling from him in gasps, completely unintelligible to Barr.

But not to the rest of the group, who hurried to the windows on the seaward side of the building, pulling open the shades. Cosy Douglas's home was back from the water, on the first rise of ground behind the center of town, and it had a superb view of William Bay and the Caribbean beyond. A perfect view of two hundred bright lights, arranged in eight or ten horizontal rows, gliding past about a mile offshore.

"It's a ship," someone gasped. "A liner," said the judge. "We're saved," said one of the ministers, and the other affirmed, "Thank the Lord!"

Cosy had been watching Barr's face. "You know that ship?" she said.

"I've seen her before," Barr replied. "She's called *Euphoric*, but I don't think she's going to make you happy."

THURSDAY

Gillian: Highland House, 2:00 A.M.

Something ran across her ankles. Something small and light and purposeful, with claws on its feet. More than that she didn't want or need to know.

The room's walls and floor were stone, its locked wooden door so thick that pounding on it made hardly any noise; there were no windows. In one corner was the stack of musty old mattresses she was sitting on, and next to them a bucket that had been used as a latrine. Nothing else—or nothing else, at any rate, that she could discover by touch alone.

The headache she'd wakened with was gone; only if she moved her head too quickly did she feel a stab from the lump over her right ear. She could taste aftertraces of The MacIntyre's sugarcane brandy and the awful dinner that had followed.

She forced herself to consider the situation. With the occasional scuttling sound of clawed feet, a worst-case scenario was easy to assemble. She was a prisoner, so Jake must be, too. Harkness and The MacIntyre had stolen *Glory*, and that meant that Barr was taken. Or— her mind shied from the word, but she bore down—taken or dead.

Barr dead. It was an abyss she simply couldn't look into. The thought alone, quickly thrust down below consciousness, left a numb chill around her heart. *Think of something else*, she ordered herself.

Patrick. Even though they'd failed to make contact all day, somehow, Gillian couldn't believe that he'd been captured. Or, more precisely, that Isabel had captured him. Patrick might fall for a pretty face, but when things got serious, no woman was going to deflect him. And thank God for that.

So, Patrick on the loose, with or without Isabel. The possibility alone made her feel better. What would he do? Once he had realized he couldn't raise *Glory* on the hand-held VHF, he'd make his way to William Bay. He'd find the yacht missing, but he'd locate her soon enough, considering the size of St. Philip. And he'd find out what had happened, too; people trusted Patrick on sight. He'd get help. Gillian wasn't sure how, but she knew he could do it. Just as well it wasn't Barr blundering around the island. Much as she loved him—and just the image of that bony, intent face made her heart turn over—he was not a land creature.

But what were they up to, the old man and his slippery little preacher? Why had they taken *Glory*? What on earth would they want with her? And if *Glory* wasn't the target, it must be Jake—and that led right back again to why.

Voices. Coming from outside the thick wooden door. She slid off the piled mattresses and faced the sound, fists clenched. *Damn*, she thought, *I wish I had my knife. I wish I were wearing jeans.*

The clatter sounded like a heavy bolt being drawn. Gillian tensed, her back pressed against the wall. When the door shrieked open, the light from outside, dim as it was, nearly blinded her. Through squinted eyes she had a quick glimpse of a man, an old man, being thrust through the opening. He staggered, and she saw it was The MacIntyre, stripped of his Highland finery and wearing only ratty trousers and a sweat shirt. *He looks like a bum*, she thought as the door slammed behind him.

The darkness seemed even thicker than before. The MacIntyre shouted, "Damn you!" and Gillian jumped. His voice echoed off the bare walls. "Damn you all, you bloody wog bastards!"

He's a prisoner like me, she realized. *And he didn't see me. Or maybe it's an act—some kind of trap. But why, for God's sake? They've already trapped me.* "Hello," she called, her voice unsteady in her own ears.

"Who the devil's that?"

He sounds frightened. "Me," she said, "Gillian Verdean. Your dinner guest."

The throat-clearing sound he made told her the old man was pulling himself together. She waited. "Are you really?" he finally asked. "Why'd they put you in my cell then?"

"How the hell should I know?" she said. "I didn't ask to be tossed in here."

"Maybe not," he allowed. "No more did I when they threw me in."

He sounded sober. That was suspicious in itself, considering the amount she'd seen him put away only a few hours ago. At least she assumed it was a few hours. Maybe he was used to it, though, or maybe he had a head like Barr's; she hadn't yet got over the way Barr could destroy the better part of a fifth of rum at a sitting and then get up—a little wobbly, true—and sail *Glory* out of a crowded harbor.

"They threw you in here?" she said warily.

"Aye." It was the first time he'd sounded Scottish. Did that mean something?

"Reverend Harkness?" Why, she wondered, had the title come so automatically? Even after what he'd done, it somehow seemed to go with him.

"Reverend be damned," snarled The MacIntyre. "He's no more reverend than I am, and that's not at all." A long pause. "I say, Miss Verdean . . ."

"Yes?"

"Could I ask you to turn your back? Just for a minute?"

"What?" Had he gone crazy?

"It's *tempus fugit*, you see," he said. He sounded—there was no other word—embarrassed. "Oh, hell," he continued when she didn't respond, "I need to use the bucket."

Gillian had never considered urination an icebreaker, but it certainly seemed to loosen up The MacIntyre. Almost too much, to begin with. She had had to endure a solid five minutes of invective about Harkness, his associates, the ungrateful citizens of St. Philip, and the world at large, but at last he seemed to be ready to tell her what was going on. Or at least, she reminded herself, his version of it.

"It happened two weeks ago," The MacIntyre said. He was sitting beside Gillian on a pile of mattresses. "That dirty little bugger and his friends drove up to my door, bold as brass, in two of Judge Van Orden's lorries. When my man answered, they forced themselves in. Pushed right past old Joshua"—his voice was rising with recollected outrage—

"without so much as a by-your-leave. When I came downstairs to see what was up, they threw me in here."

"So Harkness has been on the island only two weeks?" asked Gillian.

"No, no," The MacIntyre replied. "He came here months ago, him and his backward collar. Bamboozled that old fool Father Hughes out of his church, if you please. I warned Hughes, but he wouldn't listen. That's what comes"—his voice dropped to a hoarse whisper—"of being a white man these days. Blacks want it all their own way, won't take a little friendly advice."

She was suddenly glad she didn't have to look the old man in the eye when he came out with remarks like that. Though probably nothing would have stopped him, now that he was rolling.

"Had them all in his pocket," the old man was saying. "Mumbo jumbo and the almighty dollar. Can't beat that combination. Especially when you throw in a little violence."

"What's happened since Harkness took over?" Gillian asked. "Has he kept you here all the time?"

"Lets me out for air once in a while," The MacIntyre admitted. "Won't let me talk to anyone, though. Not even my own people." His voice trailed off, and he gave what sounded like a snort, followed by a couple more. When he began again, Gillian realized he was crying. "Killed old Joshua, they did. Right in front of me."

"Killed?" A chill trickled down Gillian's spine.

"No damned reason for it," said The MacIntyre. He was sobbing now. "All he did was say good morning, same as he has for seventy years. That's how long he was with me, seventy years. All my life, since I was a babe. And that red-eyed, skinny bastard shot him down before my eyes."

"Skinny bastard?" Gillian echoed. "Who—"

"Monasir," the old man said venomously. "The blacks call him Mr. Mongoose, and they've got the right of it. Harkness's right-hand man. Came on the *Doris B.*, with the rest of his murdering lot and all their gear."

"But what did they come *for?*" Gillian demanded. "Why are they here?"

The old man's sobs had trailed off into sniffs. Finally he said, "I've asked that, of course. They won't tell me. Tried to eavesdrop a bit, too, but I don't speak whatever flavor of wog it is. Heard Monasir talking about something he called the mission, but I don't know what that means."

"Does it have something to do with us, with my boat, *Glory*, that is? Or with Colonel Adler?"

"Don't know," he said. "Nobody even mentioned you until today— yesterday, it is now. They took me out of here, tarted me up like you saw, told me to behave myself or else. I'm sorry about that."

"Don't mention it," she said, intent on the awful suspicion that had just popped into her head. "Colonel Adler's not part of Harkness's gang, is he?"

"If he is, God help him," The MacIntyre snapped.

"What d'you mean?"

"They took Adler a few minutes after you went off with Harkness," he said. "At the end of dinner. Three of 'em. That colonel of yours can fight, though. One of the wogs'll never be the same."

"You mean Jake—Colonel Adler's—locked up down here, too?"

"He is now," The MacIntyre said. "But they worked him over for a long time before. I was in the next room, you see, they'd forgotten about me. I could hear everything, all the questions Harkness was asking."

"What kind of questions?"

"Why Adler had come to St. Philip," said the MacIntyre. "Why your boat was here, too. Oh, yes"—as if he'd suddenly remembered something—"Did you have someone aboard named"—Gillian held her breath—"Bard, I think it is. No, Barr."

She had barely enough breath for the one syllable. "Yes."

"Well, Harkness was very interested in him, too. Why he was here, what he'd said to Adler."

"What did the colonel tell him?"

"Damn all," The MacIntyre replied, with clear approval. "Scarcely a bloody word. But by God, it cost him. Just listening, I could tell that much."

Could I do as well? she asked herself. *And what could I tell them anyway?*

"Whatever's going on"—The MacIntyre went on, "it's coming to a head."

"How do you know?"

"They've had my servants, my poor old lads, cleaning out these rooms down here, the storage for Father's old distillery. I've heard them, taking out all the casks and machinery. In the last few days Harkness's own black devils have been turning to. Seems they had to get all of it emptied by today. But they never said why."

*   *   *

MacIntyre fell at last into an exhausted sleep, sitting up with his back against the cold stone, and Gillian rearranged him on the mattress, surprised at how light he was. She was barely finished when she realized that she, too, was on the verge of collapse, drained by the night's events. Even the apprehension that had her gut tied in a knot couldn't keep her eyes open, and she felt herself slide away.

A hand, shaking her shoulder, brought her out of unconsciousness. With the first sniff of mildewed mattress, reality rushed back over her, and she had to shake the angry tears from her eyes.

"Come," said the half-seen figure. "Come now." Beside her The MacIntyre was stretched out on his back, eyes closed. From the way his eyelids twitched, Gillian was sure he was awake, but she certainly didn't blame him for pretending to be asleep.

She went down the dimly lit corridor, with a man at each side, grasping her by the biceps. *Notice, Gillian*, she told herself. *Observe. Anything might come in handy.*

The corridor was blank, though. Barrel-vaulted ceiling low overhead, with long loops of wire secured to the roof, and naked light bulbs every few yards. Doors along the left-hand side, like the one on her own cell, except that some of these had small, barred windows And every one of them had a heavy shiny new iron bolt.

Up one flight of stairs, and she sensed, from the height of the ceiling and the scale of her surroundings, that they were on the main floor. Only a few lights, and a pair of men obviously on guard, drinking coffee and staring out a window. The wind was up sharply, and through the window she heard a hard spatter of rain.

Another flight of stairs, she'd seen these the day before, the main stairway to the upper floors. And this time she went up, her guards hustling her along so that her feet barely touched the ground.

Down another corridor, to a big, handsome door. Its size, and the ornateness of the carvings that decorated it, said important. One of her guards knocked, and she heard a muffled "Come!"

At first she felt only disoriented. How could she have moved from a stone-flagged hallway to a ship's cabin? No, she corrected herself, half a ship's cabin—a stage set cabin.

The room was vast, maybe forty feet square. One whole wall was windows, big casements with an upholstered window seat below. The others were hung with faded tapestries that moved eerily in the drafts. A clutter of old-fashioned furniture seemed to have been carpentered for giants: high-backed chairs, a trestle table, a huge highboy standing by itself.

The other half of the chamber, away from the big windows, had been paneled in wood, including the ceiling, some nine feet from the floor. It was fitted with a fancy built-in bar, complete with a row of velvet-covered stools, and a scattering of tables and chairs. Across the back wall were three large portholes—not fakes, as far as Gillian could tell, but the genuine article, complete with polished bronze hardware. In the center of the room, with space all around it, was a peculiar structure that made no sense at all, a sort of painter's scaffold, crudely built from four-by-fours and braced strongly enough so it looked as if you could dance on the crossbeam.

Harkness was sitting at one of the small tables. He had a cup of coffee—she could smell it from across the room—and a stack of papers in front of him, and he looked for all the world like a country parson composing a sermon.

"Ah, Miss Verdean," he said, rising. He indicated the chair across from him. "Please sit down."

Not, she realized, that she had a choice. The two guards simply lifted her into place and pressed her into the seat.

Close to Harkness she saw lines under his slightly bloodshot eyes and patchy stubble on his cheeks. He glanced up and caught her staring at him. "A busy night," he said, and, gesturing toward the cup: "Coffee?"

It would be more defiant to say no, but what would she gain? Besides, she'd never needed a jolt of caffeine more. "Yes," she said. To the tall, slender young man who approached with the pot, she said, "Black, please."

"I think," said Harkness without looking up, "you will find this requires sugar. A great deal of sugar."

She ignored his suggestion and took a swallow, regretting it instantly. The stuff was the consistency of motor oil and bitter as lye. Seeing the ghost of a smile on his round face, she deliberately finished the cup and set it down. "What's all this about?" she said. "Why'd you take *Glory*?"

He looked at her silently, and she glared back, unwilling to drop her eyes. In spite of what had happened, Harkness's face was not, she thought, dangerous or threatening at all. Tired, definitely intelligent—but that was the eyes. In fact, if anyone had asked her—

"Nondescript," he said, and, when she blinked in surprise, added,

"That is how I have been described. Unflattering but, in my line of work, advantageous."

"Yes, and what the hell *is* your line of work?"

"You have not guessed?" He leaned forward and looked at her more closely. "Perhaps not." His smile was slightly skewed, but his eyes seemed alive with self-deprecating amusement. He sat back and seemed to collect himself. When he spoke again, his tone was crisp and authoritative. "Why have you come to St. Philip?"

"None of your business," she snapped back, unthinking.

"Who is Lieutenant Colonel Adler?"

"Ask him yourself."

He sat back, lips pursed, considering her. Nothing about him had changed, but suddenly Gillian had the feeling that this was a man who might kill her like an insect. She was terrified right down to the soles of her feet, and damned if she would let him know it.

She saw he had come to some decision, and she nerved herself for the worst, knowing that the worst was far more terrible than she could imagine. He shrugged. "But all this is so needless," he said mildly. "Miss Machado—our Miss Machado—has told us the essence of Colonel Adler's lunatic scheme. We have your crew." He paused a half beat, and she knew what was coming. "Both of them."

She felt the last shred of hope take wing, but she would play this hand out to the end. "That's what you say." Her voice, she noted, was quite steady. "Let me see them."

Behind her she heard someone enter the room. She looked quickly around. It was another young man, this one more heavyset than the others. "Sir," he began, "the ship is . . ." He seemed to lose his way in the sentence and gestured toward the windows.

Harkness pulled himself to his feet. He took two steps to the window, motioning her to join him. The first gray of dawn had lightened the sky outside; it must, she thought, be a little after five.

A mile or so out was the pale silhouette of an elderly cruise liner, unlit except for an anchor light and rolling slowly in the white-capped seas. "Why, that's . . ." She found the name after a moment. "That's *Euphoric*. What's she doing here?"

But she didn't hear Harkness's answer, if indeed, he answered at all. Her eye had gone to the tiny harbor far below, where men were bustling around The MacIntyre's launch. She barely noticed them because there ahead of it, carelessly made fast to big stone bollards, and with the main hatch open, lay *Glory*.

Barr: Hangman Hill, 9:40 A.M.

Son Douglas was lying right at the edge of the bluff, behind a scrim of gray-green wiry grass. His ancient brassbound telescope was propped on a Turk's-head cactus. "Fifteen," he said. "Yeah, fifteen, not counting the coxswain. How many's that make?"

Barr, who had been inscribing the running total on a cleared swatch of damp ground, did a quick sum. "Ninety-two," he said. From where he was kneeling he had a clear view of *Euphoric*, lying about half a mile off the coral banks that guarded Highland House. She was headed into the wind and seas, which had swung completely around to the north, but every few seconds a leftover swell from the day before took her on the quarter, giving her a slow, corkscrewing lift and roll that must, he thought, be wrenching some digestions on her upper decks.

The liner's tubby motor lifeboat had been running to and from the tiny protected harbor below Highland House for almost an hour; between fifteen and twenty passengers made each trip to land. The old telescope's lens might be fogged and scratched, but the numbers were indisputable.

Son rolled half over and looked at Barr. "I don't get it. Old MacIntyre never lets people come and see that place of his. He could've made a fortune if he did. And all of a sudden he's running tours for cruise line passengers?"

Barr, who had been considering much the same question, grunted and lit another Camel—his last. The Douglas family telescope (used by old Sim to spy on his fellow citizens) showed only the heads and shoulders of the launch's passengers—and heads wearing rain hats, at that. *Euphoric*'s water-level entry port, where the passengers were boarding the shore boat, was on the ship's far side, and the harbor was just out of sight around a ridge, so it was impossible to get a full-length view of the personnel constituting the landing party.

That was the first possibility, Barr thought. Had *Euphoric* somehow ditched its complement of vacationing oldsters, the ones who'd been innocently exploring St. Martin and St.-Bart's? And if so, who were the replacements and where had they boarded?

"One thing I don't understand," said Son. He had the look, Barr thought, of someone who was nerving himself up to do something painful but important.

"What's that?"

"What does she see in you?"

Barr gaped, but Son, deep in his own concern, seemed not to notice.

"I mean, you're just a broken-down sailor who doesn't even own his own boat. Folks say you're all right for a whitey, but as I look at it straight, Barr, you ain't much."

The question was one Barr had asked himself a hundred times since he'd realized the depth of Gillian's love for him, but how the hell had it become any of Son's business? And Son's estimate of Barr's worth was so close to his own that it left him speechless for nearly a minute, until, seeing what the young man was really getting at, he began to laugh helplessly.

"What's so goddamn funny?" said Son. "Just who you laughing at, Barr?" He set the telescope carefully down in a level spot.

"I'm sorry," Barr gasped. "I didn't mean what you think. Honest."

Son was watching him with doubt in his eyes, and Barr hoped he didn't have to explain the unexplainable. With a desperate effort he managed to quell the laughter that kept trying to escape. "You think I'm sleeping with Cosy—with your mother," he said.

Son seemed taken aback by Barr's directness. "Well . . . yes," he said.

"Look," said Barr, trying to see a way through the minefield in front of him, "I haven't been to St. Philip since before I lost *Windhover*. That's four years, anybody on the island'll tell you that."

"Sure," said Son, a jeering note in his voice. "That's probably true, but it don't make no difference."

"What do you mean?" Barr asked, and added, "Here comes the shore boat back out."

"I got it," said Son, rolling back onto his belly. "Same as before. Unless there's people lying on the floorboards, she's empty except for the cox'n."

No, Barr decided, the launch *was* empty—riding six inches higher than when she'd headed in.

"Every two to three months," said Son, his eye still glued to the telescope, "my mother goes off island. Takes the LIAT flight to Antigua, but she don't stay there."

"No?" said Barr, interested but hardly surprised. Cosy Douglas was an intelligent, desirable woman, who'd been tied to a dried-up, malicious older man all her adult life. Of course, she'd want to get away from him once in a while.

"No. She picks up a connecting flight. Usually to St. Martin, but sometimes to St.-Bart's. Once to St. Kitts. Been going on for five years now." And before Barr could ask, he added: "My father was having her watched, he hired some dude over to St. John's. I found the reports after he was killed. Copies of the tickets, immigration slips, every-thing."

"I see," Barr replied slowly. "Did your father's . . . dude say for sure what she did in those places?"

"You mean, did he see you and her doin' it?" The telescope wobbled, and so did Son Douglas's voice. "Not exactly."

"Means what?" Barr demanded.

Son took a long, steadying breath before he answered. "He saw her goin' into hotels. Always alone. Always come out alone, too. But after a while he noticed this white guy—always the same guy—going to the same hotels. Sometimes he comes first, sometimes after her. Some-times he leaves first, sometimes after. But always the same goddamn man. Thin, like you. White, like you."

"But your father didn't get a definite ID. Right?" said Barr. Son's silence was the answer, and Barr continued. "If I'd been the kind of— if I'd been your father, with a newspaper photo file downstairs, I'd have shown my dude pictures of all the men I suspected. All the ones I had pictures of, anyway. Wouldn't you?"

"Maybe." The thought was obviously a new one to Son, and he didn't want to commit himself too quickly.

"Well, I know—and so do you—that the *Philippic* has half a dozen clear shots of me in the file, from when *Windhover* came here with charter parties and the paper would run a story." Barr waited, willing Son to speak.

"Yeah, I s'pose."

"In fact," said Barr, "you could say that I am probably the most photographed whitey on this island, not excepting The MacIntyre himself."

"I guess." He rolled over. "Okay, maybe it's not you."

"Thanks," Barr replied, and saw in Son's eyes that he had misun-derstood again. "Don't get me wrong. A man who has Cosima Douglas love him—well, he's not entitled to any more good luck than that. But I'm not the man. I've got a woman of my own." *And she's trapped in that crazy old fortress, with a bunch of murderers in the middle of God knows what.* "Here comes the shore boat again," he said, glad for the interruption. "Looks like there's more people in it this time."

"Right," said Son, rolling back over and picking up the telescope. "Hold on a second."

Barr's eyes were on the small orange boat, waddling to shore with its silhouetted row of tiny heads, but his mind was spinning with the implications of what Son had told him. Cosy with a white lover was believable enough. But why did it have to be a lover? Barr had long recognized in Cosima Douglas one of those unfortunate people trapped in a world that was far smaller and narrower than they were. What if—just what if—she'd had the same perception and decided to do something about it? She'd been the most powerful woman on St. Philip, and she was smart enough to see how little that amounted to. If something was going to happen on the island, who was more likely to be at the center of it than Cosy?

"I make it eighteen," said Son.

Just to be certain, Barr added up again the pattern of crossed lines on the dirt. "That's it," he affirmed. "A hundred and ninety-two so far."

Son whistled softly. "How many do you think a ship like that *Euphoric* holds?"

"Probably has cabins for three hundred or so," he replied. "but she's an old-timer—hard to fill, with all the competition these days." In fact, he thought, it was surprising to see her working at all, especially in tight times like these. Most vessels of *Euphoric*'s vintage had been broken up for scrap or converted to carrying Muslim pilgrims to and from Jidda, that last employment for nearly dead passenger ships.

"So a hundred and ninety-two's maybe all the passengers she's carrying?" Son asked. "That's still a hell of a—" He broke off as a puff of greasy black smoke belched upward from *Euphoric*'s forward stack A couple of seconds later white water swirled around her stern, and she began to move ahead. "Is she getting under way?" asked Son, disbelief in his tone.

"Sure looks like it," Barr replied. The liner was swinging away from the shore, and as her port side came into view, he saw that the orange shore boat was in its davits, and the entry port closed.

"What the fuck's goin' on?" asked Son, rising to his knees. "This some kind of invasion?"

Again Barr pictured *Euphoric*'s passengers, as he'd seen them in the streets of Gustavia. No possible question of disguise. They were what they'd looked like—a couple of hundred vacationers, nearly all elderly and, from their voices, nearly all American. "No, not an invasion," said Barr, getting to his feet and brushing dead grass and twigs from his still-damp khakis. "And the other possibilities I don't even like to think about."

"That so?" said Son. He was clearly waiting for Barr to explain, and when no explanation came, he shut the telescope with a snap.

Having gone some distance toward winning Son over, Barr didn't want to antagonize him now. "Look," he said "maybe I'm superstitious—hell, I *am* superstitious—and sometimes it's a mistake to put a bad thought into words."

"*Naming calls*," Son said with a wry smile. "That's what the old women say, and maybe they're right." He turned on his heel and started up the ridge, toward the dirt track where the Daihatsu was parked. "Let's see if maybe I can get that transmitter at the airfield going again," he said over his shoulder. "I got a feeling we need some big-time help here."

Son drove the little car like the Jeep he clearly wished it were, slamming up and down through the gears, double-clutching his way through soft patches, and throwing mud in every direction. Barr, holding on with one hand and bracing with both legs, had lost track of where they were headed within the first quarter mile.

They sideslipped down the sandy track to its intersection with the main road—wider, but just as primitive—and Son was already gunning the engine when both of them saw the gaggle of elderly Philipians coming toward them. Four men and two women, Barr noted, and on appearance alone their total age looked to be around five hundred. They were dressed more or less alike, white shirts or blouses, black trousers or skirts, and Barr had a good idea who they were before Son, braking to a skidded halt, told him.

"Inside staff, from Highland House," he said. One of the old people had stepped forward, and Barr, astonished, saw he was carrying a bagpipe slung from his shoulder.

"Hey, Pipey," said Son. "What's shakin', old friend?"

The piper eyed Barr suspiciously, then addressed Son with more indignation than such a dried-up form ought to contain. "He throwed us out! That little fat bugger Harkness"—Barr saw one of the old women cross herself at the name—"he pitched us out the door, right after breakfast!"

"That's right!" cried another man. "We work all night, makin' enough food for an army, and then he tell us to go 'way and not come back."

Son glanced quickly at Barr, who said, "Were you there when the people from the ship landed?"

The man who had spoken looked to Son, who nodded his permission, before answering. "No. We see that old ship lyin' just offshore, but only a couple of crew come in."

"That's right," said Pipey. "And they like Harkness's gang, the ones that's already there. Goddamn Arabs."

"Arabs?" said Barr. "You're sure?"

"Sure I'm sure, man," Pipey snapped. "I seen Arabs in the war, in North Africa—fought with Monty, I did."

It was possible, thought Barr. And unsettling. To Son he said: "Can you really fix a transmitter?"

"Depends on what's been done to it," Son replied. "If it's just the antenna that's down, I can rig up an emergency setup easy. If somebody's smashed up the set, that's a different story."

Only a watchman was at the Prince Bernhard International Airport, and he had camped out in the middle of the arrivals area, a gritty, echoing room with a couple of faded LIAT posters on the wall, a snack bar, and three shuttered shops. The watchman, whose name was Leon, had spread out his blankets on the low counter the customs men used for inspecting luggage and had been cooking his meals on the snack bar's propane hot plate.

While Son let himself into the locked tower, where the airport transmitter was located, Barr kept Leon occupied. "Were you here when the piece of runway slid into the sea?" Barr asked.

"Sure, I was here," Leon said. His eyes kept going to the tower door. "I always here."

"How'd it happen?" From where he stood, by a window that commanded the airport's approaches, Barr had a clear view of both the collapsed antenna tower, a hopeless-looking jungle gym of rusty tubing, and the runway itself, a narrow strip of scrubby grass cut into the hill on one side and falling away sharply into the water on the other. About halfway down its length a steep-sided triangular gap angled clear across it.

"Must of been a fault in the hillside," said Leon. "Waves just chew away and chew away, and all of a sudden it's gone."

"You saw it go?"

"Man, I can't be lookin' everywhere at once. Besides, it happen late at night."

"And besides *that*," said Son, who had come down from the tower without their noticing, "Leon just finished suckin' up a liter of blindy white—isn't that so, Leon?"

" 'Twasn't a liter!" Leon cried. "Wasn't but maybe a pint or little more. Just to keep my old bones warm in the night."

"Uh-huh," said Son. "And where'd you get a pint of blindy white,

Leon? Bill McIver's got his still up in Oldroad Village, and I never heard that he delivers."

"Friend give it to me," Leon said. His back was to Son, his thin shoulders hunched.

"Same friend you let into the tower, Leon?" Son had been leaning easily against the doorjamb. In two great steps he was across the room, his powerful hands grasping Leon by the biceps. "Same friend you let smash the radio to bitty pieces, right? Answer me, Leon, or I'll tear your arms off."

"Never saw him! Never saw nobody!" Leon's anguished voice shot up the register to falsetto. "Bottle was lef' by the door."

"The duppies brung it, right, Leon? So you just pour it down your throat. I bet you slep' real good—didn't you, Leon?" Son's California accent had slipped completely away, and his face was twisted with fury. He shook the unfortunate Leon from side to side, till his head was snapping back and forth.

"Jesus, Son," said Barr, taking a step forward, "take it easy—you'll kill him."

"Stay back, whitey!" Son snarled. "This is my island, my people." But his grip on Leon eased, and the old man sank to the floor, gasping and whimpering. From the torrent of words that poured out, Barr salvaged enough to reconstruct the truth. Leon had discovered, on his nightly round, a half-full bottle of the deadly bootleg rum the islanders called blindy white. A gift from heaven or from the spirits, it didn't matter. Leon slugged it down, and it, in turn, had leveled him.

Barr was not surprised at Leon's collapse—blindy white had the reputation of being a beverage its regular drinkers diluted with paint thinner—but he wondered how Son had known. Not till they were on the road again, and Son seemed to have calmed down, did he ask.

"Oh, that," Son replied. "Leon told everybody about how the spirits brought him a bottle—but not till after he drank it." The Daihatsu jarred across a few more potholes, and Son continued. "You've got to remember something, Barr. On a little island like this, if somebody tells a good story in the morning, everybody else knows it by dinnertime. You being a white man, you're not in the loop. Me being a Douglas, I am the loop."

The little car sobbed pitifully as Son fought it up the steep road from the airport to the island's central ridge. At the top, clear for a moment of the trees and underbrush, they could see the whole center of St. Philip sprawling below them, green and peaceful. The wind had continued backing, Barr saw. The lines of whitecaps were marching down the island's normal leeward side, and they were even starting to angle into William Bay.

Son saw it, too. "Storm coming?" he asked.

"Nothing really big," Barr agreed. "Not a late-season hurricane or anything. But the radio last night said the wind'll back right through to the south."

"What you're saying," Son corrected him, "is that the seas'll be punching right into that harbor below Highland House."

"That's what I'm saying."

"I've seen what happens to boats in there when the wind's in the southwest," Son observed. "Kindling."

If there was one other thing I needed, thought Barr savagely, *it was that.*

Son, however, had his mind on the main problem. "There's still the undersea phone cable," he was saying as the little car began to hurtle down the hill toward William Town. "Cable and Wireless people always kept it for a backup. Soon's we find Caskett, the phone man, we'll get it cranked up."

Fifteen minutes later, just where a side road turned off to Highland House, a man in ragged shorts, waving a machete, emerged from the brush. "Step on it," Barr snapped, though the Daihatsu felt nearly out of control already.

Instead Son stamped on the brakes and brought the car to a slewing, dirt-spitting halt. "He's one of mine," Son said as the man loped up to the car. A young man, Barr noted, one of the few he'd seen on the island. He was clearly upset and nearly dragged Son from behind the wheel. "Over here," he said. "My little girl found him."

The corpse must have been there for a couple of days; it seemed to have sunk into the high grass by the side of the road, and they could smell it from several yards away. Also, the crows had been at the face, which stared up into the thickening clouds. The corpse was wearing a short-sleeved white shirt, with a tie and a tiepin, black pants, and black shoes of some kind of fake leather. *A man of business then,* Barr thought.

Son, on his heels next to the body, was staring down at the torn and bloody holes in the chest. Exit wounds, Barr decided; whoever it was had been shot in the back, by a man who didn't take chances; you could have covered the three holes with a playing card. "D'you know him?" Barr asked.

Slowly Son rose, still staring down. "All my life," he said. "That's Mr. Caskett, of the Cable and Wireless."

Patrick: Highland House, 10:30 A.M.

Something was going on, but Patrick, glued to the cell door, couldn't figure it out. For more than an hour the corridor outside had echoed with shouts and cries—some angry, some frightened, most just confused. The voices were American, and mostly they sounded like older people, thin and quavery. Early on, Patrick had taken the chance of shouting for help, but the only response had been three guards; two of them held him while the third slapped him around half-heartedly.

Their minds were somewhere else, though. They hadn't even noticed he was no longer tied up. Nor did they notice, in the dim half-light from the corridor, the stone block awkwardly wedged back into place in the wall or the lines tied around it that Patrick had used for handles.

"Be silent," said one of them when they'd finished and Patrick lay in a heap, gritting his teeth so as not to groan. "Soon all will be made clear." As they were leaving, the speaker had said something to his two buddies, something that made them laugh.

It was their laughing that brought Adler around, crying out, "No, no, no," before Patrick could pull himself over and cradle the colonel's head in his arms, like a child's.

The sounds outside died down after a while, with an occasional yell or scream, but Patrick just sat on the stone floor in a kind of daze, holding Adler, for he didn't know how long.

At last the colonel opened his eyes. He seemed unsurprised to find Patrick holding him. After a moment he began to speak, clearly and rationally but so faintly that Patrick had to lean well forward to hear what he was saying.

"They always tell you you're going to spill your guts," he said. "They tell you there's no way you can keep a secret from people who really want it. You accept that intellectually, but you don't really believe it." He moved his head, which was in Patrick's lap, very slowly, so that he could look directly upward into the younger man's face.

"Just take it easy, sir," Patrick murmured. "Nothing to worry about." Nothing to worry about except that they'd done something to Adler's feet, and now he couldn't walk.

"When they tell you that, Sergeant," Adler went on, as if he hadn't heard a thing, "when they tell you you're going to say whatever they want to hear, you better believe it, because it's true." His voice caught on the last word, and he slammed his fist weakly against the floor.

We've got to get out of here, Patrick thought. *Got to get out of here soon.* The thought swirled around in his head, going noplace. *How in hell am I going to move the two of them?* A sneaky little voice in the back of his brain piped up then, asking if he really had to take both the colonel and Isabel, one unable to walk and the other not caring if she lived or died.

It didn't occur to him to worry about himself. He had the measure of the men who were guarding them, knew he could handle any two of them if he just had the jump on them. Could, he was pretty sure, have handled the three who'd beaten him up the last time if he'd taken a minute to plan his moves.

"One of us has to get out of here, Sergeant." It was the colonel again, and Patrick bent closer to hear him. "I—I told them every-thing," he said. "Spilled my guts."

"Sir, seems to me they already knew everything. Everything that made any difference." *Wish to Christ I knew everything. I'd even settle for a couple of crumbs at this point.*

"Important thing is to get help. Get word out," Adler whispered. His legs made a couple of scrabbling motions, and he grunted with the pain of it. "I'm not exactly mobile, Sergeant, so it's going to have to be you."

"Whatever you say, sir," Patrick whispered. It was the old, automatic response to rank, but it felt to Patrick as if the words were coming from someone else.

"Get to a telephone," Adler was saying. "I'll give you a number to memorize, a name. They'll come. You can count on it."

No, Patrick thought, *you can count on it, colonel, sir. I can count on me and my friends, and that's all.* "What about Gillian?" he said. "And Barr—d'you know where they are?"

The colonel didn't answer for a few seconds, and Patrick thought that maybe he'd drifted off. Then he said, "Don't worry about them. They're safe, but they can't help us. They took off, in the boat."

Bullshit. Absolutely out of the question. But why was Adler lying? The awful reason came to him: "They're dead, aren't they? These bastards killed them."

"I . . ."

He could feel the cold fury, like an adrenaline rush, only stronger, run through him, right down to his shredded fingertips.

"They could be alive," Adler said slowly. "I'm not a hundred percent sure." But he was still lying; Patrick was sure of it—and right now he didn't want to give in to that kind of hope. What he needed, knew he needed, was the power of raw hate.

"We're getting out of this place," he said. "All three of us."

"Three?" said Adler. "Who—"

"Isabel's in the next cell," he said quickly. "They—" No, that was none of Adler's business. "She's had a rough time."

"Good," said Adler, the venom plain in his voice. "I hope they—"

"Shut up." Patrick was stunned by his own words, but so was Adler, or at least he was silent for the fifteen seconds that Patrick needed to pull his resolve together.

"Look, Sergeant," Adler began, "you don't know about her. She double-crossed both of us. She's been working for the enemy right along, Sergeant, and—"

"I'm not a sergeant," Patrick said. "And I'm for sure not *your* sergeant, Colonel." As the words came out, he knew they were right. "I know how to get out of here, but we're going to do it my way. Understood?"

A long, long silence. "Understood . . . Patrick."

The hardest part of the plan—the plan that had jumped, complete, into his head—was getting Isabel to go along with .it. "Never," she said, her voice at first flat, then: "Never! *Nunca!*"—stronger and angrier. "I don't do it."

"It's the only way," he insisted. "Please. They won't touch you! I swear it."

The pleading wore her down or maybe just brought her back to life. At last she agreed—and then, when she realized that Adler was part of Patrick's plan, he had to go through the whole thing again. But at last it was ready. "Help," she called.

"Louder!" whispered Patrick, from his position behind the cell door.

"Help me! Please help me!" Plenty loud enough now, and the other voices down the hall had died away. Why didn't somebody come? After five minutes Isabel's voice was getting hoarse and weary. Maybe it was more convincing that way, Patrick thought.

Footsteps at last, past Patrick and Adler's cell without pausing. Now they had stopped outside. A beam of light through the little window, and the hiss of breath as the guard saw Isabel, writhing and moaning, her naked body gleaming where the light hit it.

He's excited, all right, Patrick told himself as he heard the guard drop his weapon while trying to work the heavy bolt. *And he's not going to call for help either. Not going to share the magic moment with a buddy.*

The door swung open, pressing Patrick back against the wall. Peering around it, he let it shield him, waiting. First came the flash, wobbling a little but fixed on Isabel; next the gun barrel, pointed at the floor; and last, what he'd been waiting for, the narrow face, eyes intent on the spectacle before him.

Gillian: 11:30 A.M.

Up the Thousand Steps they had come, helped when necessary by uniformed sailors from *Euphoric* or by Harkness's polite young men. From where Gillian was standing, looking down from The MacIntyre's huge upstairs bedroom, the voices of the liner's passengers were a steady murmur punctuated here and there by a shrill complaint or a cry of mock terror at the steepness of the cliff stairway.

At the top of the stairs tottered The MacIntyre himself, dragged from the cell and splendid in his Highland finery. He had greeted his unsuspecting guests, with Harkness at one elbow and a watchful young man at the other. Visibly dazed by the laird's condescension, not to mention the Thousand Steps, the guests were hustled indoors, out of Gillian's line of sight.

"He's kidnapping them, isn't he?" she had demanded of the guard at her side, an unattractively feral young man named Monasir. She knew he could speak at least some English, but he merely bared his beautiful teeth at her by way of reply.

Moments after the last, tottering oldster had been assisted inside, *Euphoric* abruptly got under way, heading straight out to sea. The gray-black cloud that had puffed from her stacks drifted slowly ashore, shredding as it came.

The door behind Gillian opened, and Harkness appeared, wilted but triumphant, his round face gleaming with sweat. He tossed a remark at Monasir that lit up the young man's sallow face and what sounded like an order to another man, who slipped from the room. To Gillian he said, "We have crossed the Rubicon," and threw himself into a chair.

"You're never going to get away with this," she said.

"You think not?" His self-assurance seemed so absolute she was shaken.

"I know not," she snapped, "and so would you, if you gave it a minute's thought."

His expression, which for a moment seemed almost sorrowful, hardened. "A minute's thought?" he echoed. "My dear young woman, what you've just seen is the result of five years' meticulous planning."

A chilling doubt was creeping up her spine, but she refused to acknowledge it. "It won't work," she said. "You'll never see a dime of ransom money. By tonight you'll have cops and Coasties and God knows what crawling all over you."

He eyed her in silence. The door opened, and a young man carrying a tray appeared, wreathed in the smell of fresh coffee. Gillian's achingly hollow stomach contracted at the idea of more caffeine and her dry mouth felt dryer than ever. The young man set the tray down in front of Harkness, who poured thick, steaming black liquid into two cups and handed one to her. She tipped half the bowlful of sugar into her cup, stirred till most of it was dissolved, took what she hoped was a less than greedy mouthful. It still tasted awful, but she could feel the sugar jolt almost instantly.

"As I told you before, sugar helps," he said. "And milk, if there were any. You were right, at least about the ransom money. We shall never receive a dime. And do you know why?"

Her face, she knew, must be betraying her, but the sudden realization was too overwhelming to hide. Her lips moved, but no sound emerged. Still, he seemed to know what she meant to say.

"Correct. We will ask for no ransom."

"Hostages?" she asked unsteadily. "Are you starting that whole thing up again?"

Her answer was in his eyes before he spoke. "No. Not the way you mean."

The final truth was in his tired, unyielding, strangely compassionate face. She knew, and realized that he was aware of her knowledge. "Why, for God's sake?"

"For God's sake exactly. Or so most of my people would say."

Even knowing the answer, she had to ask: "Kill them?" He nodded. "But there must be two hundred passengers. You can't murder two hundred people!"

"One hundred and ninety-two," he said quietly. "Plus, alas, the three of you."

Three. It had slipped out, she was sure. Despite his iron self-control, she saw a tiny flicker of chagrin in his eyes. So one of them—it must be Patrick—was still free. There was still hope. It stiffened her spine at the same time it set her tired brain racing. Even as a prisoner, there had to be some way she could help, something she could contribute. *Stall,* she told herself. *Time has to be Harkness's enemy.*

"A hundred and ninety-two helpless old people," she said. "You must be proud as hell."

From his knowing smile she saw she had laid it on too thick. "I ought to be ashamed of myself? Is that what you mean?" He nodded, pouring himself another cup of coffee. "One of me is, certainly."

She watched him mix in the sugar and empty the cup. The young man who'd brought in the tray swooped forward from his post by the wall. As he collected the utensils, he said something reproachful to Harkness.

"He says I should rest," Harkness explained. "But I am—what's the wonderful American word?—wired. I am wired by the success of my plan. I feel as if my eyes were out on stalks, like a crab's." He glanced down as his wristwatch. "Besides, there is plenty of time before the next act begins. Time to indulge in the great British sport of self-justification." He eyed her sharply. "I am half British, you know."

"You talk like a Brit," she said.

"And I look like a wog. Though only partially. Not as much"—he gestured over his shoulder—"as Ibrahim or Monasir."

"Is your name really Harkness?"

To her surprise, he laughed. "Oh, yes, oddly enough it is. Suleiman bin Daoud Harkness, *à votre service.*" He sketched a bow. "Now you know something a great many people have been trying for ten years to discover."

"Your father was English," she said, "and your mother was— what?"

"Saudi. Beautiful, in the Arab fashion, but not sophisticated." He paused, considering what he had said. "Naïve? Not in her own world. But in a small, cold, damp, narrow-minded, hostile place like—"

He stopped again, and Gillian sensed that talking about himself, while intoxicating, was something he had guarded against for a long time. "Like England?" she offered.

"I was going to say Cambridge," he said. "But England will do."

"She was unhappy there?"

"She never saw it," he said. "My father, who met her while he was an adviser to the court in Riyadh, he understood. That was why he left her behind."

Now she was beginning to see it. "He took you home with him, though."

"He took me to England when he returned there," Harkness corrected her. "I was put in a suitable public school, not unlike the one

Kipling was sent to." His lips twisted with the effort at a superior smile, and she had a picture of a small, fat, desperately lonely child in some grim brick dormitory. On a moor, or maybe a heath.

"The school did what it was supposed to," he continued, master of himself once again. "It confirmed all my prejudices. My Arab prejudices. There are no words—no English words, at any rate—to convey my loathing of the British. When I got to university, however, I found out how to turn impotent hatred into action."

The story, once begun, was unstoppable. Probably he had never told anyone the whole thing, she decided. Even so, a few of Harkness's internal censors were still operating: Names were glided over; details of time and place never arose. But the story, his story, was complete without them.

Recruited as an undergraduate, by an Arabist tutor, the young Harkness had slowly been filtered into the Near East's terrorist system. He was suspect at first, he told Gillian wryly, because to Arabs he looked and sounded so British. Only the staunch backing of his English recruiters carried the day.

"In the 1950s," he said to Gillian, "the university Arabists in England were a brotherhood, rather like the university Communists in the thirties. Some were in touch with foreign governments, some were not, but not one would think of betraying a fellow academic."

Officially dead (of tetanus, in a Beirut hospital), the young Harkness was reincarnated, first under the name Aurens. "I was still a romantic, you see." And seeing that she did not see, he added, "*Aurens*—it was our way of saying the name of another English adherent to the Arab cause, T. E. Lawrence. Another bastard, too."

Unlike many foreign recruits, the young Aurens knew exactly what he wanted to do. Direct, violent action was his forte, and he hurled himself into it so thoroughly that he soon made the name "Aurens" too hot to use, the first burned-out name of many. "For a while—I was still romantic—I employed the names of British generals of the Great War. Gough, Plumer, even the redoubtable Haig. In terms of the damage they had done to England, they were an inspiration to me, but eventually a giveaway."

The international dossier on him grew. "I am now an entire filing cabinet in Langley, and the Mossad has honored me with my own compact disk," he said. There were some narrow escapes, but it never occurred to him to abandon terrorism. "What you call terrorism," he said, "is our only real weapon for the oppressed. But I have never taken pleasure in it. I want you to believe that."

Curiously enough, she did. "It doesn't work, though," she objected. "Not in the long run. I mean, look at hostage taking in the Middle East—all it did was make America angry."

He stared at her, seemingly torn between delight and disbelief. "My dear young woman, it worked like a charm. It brought us attention we could never have attracted another way. It brought us money—far more money than you can know. And it brought us weapons."

"But in the end you let the hostages go."

He shrugged. "No strategy is forever. Some of our leaders felt a new tack was necessary."

"You mean, butchering two hundred old people?" she said. "That's what you call a new tack?"

Her sudden burst of emotion, she saw, only steadied him. "Actually, no. It is an old tack," he said. "A return to first principles. Sacrifice and martyrdom."

"Wait a minute. The people from *Euphoric* are the martyrs."

"*Au contraire*, Miss Verdean. They are the sacrifice, and my young men and I are the martyrs."

"How martyrs?" she demanded.

"Because we are about to die. *Morituri te salutant.* Or is it *salutamus?*"

The little bastard really means it, she thought. *He's totally nuts.* But she didn't believe it for a minute, and the reality was becoming harder and harder to keep at arm's length. "Why don't you stop orating and just explain?" she said.

Again he looked at his watch. "Ten minutes to show time," he said. "Why not?"

The plan was Harkness's own conception, its details researched in bits and pieces over several years; its personnel recruited and tested by him alone, owing allegiance only to him; its financing drained—"a dollar here, a mark there"—from other enterprises.

Two years ago the bankroll was finally large enough. A cover firm in Piraeus had picked up *Euphoric* for next to nothing; destined for the breakers' yards, she was instead given a quick and superficial overhaul and dispatched to the Caribbean, under a flag of convenience and with a crew whose nucleus was of Harkness's choosing. In a couple of seasons she had a reputation as an elderly but reliable vessel, whose owners would bend over backward to accommodate package groups, especially those traveling on tight budgets.

"We didn't have to show a profit," Harkness explained. "It gave a perhaps unfair advantage."

At the same time Harkness's technicians were assembling the electronic equipment necessary. Much of it, to Harkness's satisfaction, was acquired from the American military in the aftermath of Desert Storm. "You people are quite amazing," he said, sounding to Gillian more British than ever. "Everywhere you go, you leave a trail of perfectly good hardware to mark your passage."

Again he glanced at his wrist. "Tonight we shall execute the passengers of the *Euphoric*, one by one, and the world will watch us do it." The door to the room opened, and Gillian held her breath, but Harkness waved off the young man who stood there.

"The executions will take place on television, you see. The broadcast will seem to be originating live from the ship's lounge of *Euphoric*, beamed upward to satellites. In fact, of course, we shall be conducting the affair here, in Highland House. In this very room."

Suddenly she understood: "You'll transmit direct to *Euphoric* from here—"

"Line of sight," he affirmed, nodding. "She will lie just over the visual horizon, but her masthead will be accessible to the microwave transmitter we have installed on the tower roof."

"But why?" she asked. "What's the point?"

"Partly to buy time," he replied. "The scenes we transmit will be terrifying—have you ever seen a person hanged?—and even the laziest Western government will have to spring into action. In short order they will discover *Euphoric*, and when they realize we cannot be swayed from our task, they will attack."

"They'll attack a booby trap," she whispered.

"Just so. A booby trap armed to the teeth. They could sink her, of course, but as long as there is any hope of rescuing the people they see dying on their television screens, they will not dare. By the time they discover the truth, all of you will have died." His quiet smile managed somehow to combine deep satisfaction and equally deep compassion. "We shall, of course, die, too. There is no escape. But it shall be, God willing, an example for all our oppressors. How can they subdue a people who welcome martyrdom?"

Barr: William Town, noon

They all were talking at once, but Son Douglas finally silenced them. When all the faces in the room were turned to him, he went on. "If those people from the ship have been kidnapped, or if it's one of those hostage things," he said, "it'll for sure be on the news. Why don't somebody turn on the Big RA and listen?"

From her post by the kitchen door Cosy Douglas threw Barr a proud, worried, and somehow conspiratorial smile. *I wish she wouldn't do that,* he thought as he saw Son's face suddenly tighten. *Especially right now, when I need all the help I can get.*

The announcers on the big RA—Radio Antilles—were already frothing at the mouth. Cosy's battered old AM set crackled and sputtered, but the announcer's voice fought its way through, and the first words Barr made out were "euphoric" and "executed."

The room erupted—two of the shop owners started to wail, like mourners at an island funeral—and only after several minutes' shouting by Son, Barr and Cosy herself were they able to hear the announcer again. But since the station was simply repeating over and over the text of an emergency broadcast, after a couple of minutes they were back at the beginning: "Authorities in Washington, D.C., announced the hijacking this morning of a cruise liner in the Caribbean with two hundred Americans aboard, most of them elderly—"

"Shut *up!*" shouted Son, as the babel again threatened to rise.

"—Greek-registered vessel *Euphoric* has been hijacked on the high seas, while on a cruise from St. Thomas to Guadeloupe. The hijackers, who call themselves Vengeance of the Oppressed, have been transmitting a live televised statement directly from *Euphoric,* cutting into commercial satellite programming. They have made no ransom or other demands and have said only that they plan to execute all the ship's passengers publicly, one by one."

Now the announcer had their attention completely. The only other sound in the room was someone's asthmatic wheezing. "One moment!" the radio cried, its thin, reedy speaker breaking with second-hand emotion. "One moment, please! We have just received a new bulletin. A man has apparently been killed aboard *Euphoric.* A passenger identified by the hijackers as Walter Cohen, of New York City, has just been executed by hanging in front of a television camera in the ship's lounge—"

Aboard *Euphoric?* Son's puzzled glare said that he had heard the same words, but surely the announcer had made a mistake.

Governments around the world, the announcer was saying, were tumbling over one another in their haste to denounce the terrorists and threaten reprisal. A spokesman aboard the hijacked vessel had just said that any rescue attempt would result in the destruction of *Euphoric* and all aboard her—hostages and crew alike.

The pieces were falling rapidly into place in Barr's mind, but the announcer had more to say: "The terrorist leader, who remains officially unidentified, has said that the next executions will take place at one P.M. eastern standard time—"

"Two, here," somebody murmured.

"Those to be executed next are not passengers from *Euphoric*, but four American spies, two women and two men."

He knew the names before the announcer gave them, assigning Gillian the soft G she hated, and stumbling over "Verdean."

Barr couldn't really blame them for their obvious unwillingness to do anything but talk. Unarmed, bewildered—why should they throw their lives away trying to help a group of strangers? MacLeod, the chief of police, refused to meet Barr's eyes. He sat by himself in a corner, staring silently at the ground.

One of the preachers, a man whose voice seemed to come from high up inside his nose, observed, "If we tried to rescue those poor white people, we would only get them killed sooner. We must let the authorities do it properly."

The port captain eyed the preacher angrily, opened his mouth, and then shut it with a snap.

"We are absolved," intoned St. Philip's president. "There is no way we can call for help, so it would be immoral for us to put our people at risk by starting a fight we cannot win."

At the word "immoral" Father Hughes bristled in his chair, but the judge's ponderous certainty blanketed them all, even Barr. There was nothing they could do, Father Hughes reluctantly agreed, nothing to be done, except pray.

Barr pulled his wallet from his hip pocket and carefully began extracting limp bills. "What's that for?" whispered Cosy.

"I've got a hundred U.S. and another fifty EC," he said, not trying to keep his voice lowered. "Maybe somebody here will sell me a rifle." In the suddenly hushed room his words sounded as crazy as he knew they were. He couldn't hit the side of a house with *Glory's* old U.S. Army M-1, which Patrick had restored to better than new condition. And even if he were the marksman of the world, what could he do alone to help Gillian? But of one thing he was positive: She was what his life was all about, and it would be far better to die trying than to sit by and let anything happen to her. And, of course, to Patrick.

MacLeod looked up. He seemed to have aged ten years. "Selling you a firearm would be illegal, Captain Barr."

Barr ignored him. Poking in the wallet's farthest corner, he discovered another bill, folded down to the size of a fingertip—his emergency ten, which had been out of the light so long that it was quite slippery with mold. He was trying to flatten the bill without tearing it, when Son Douglas got to his feet, drawing everyone's attention.

"I guess we're all agreed about how we can't do anything," he said, and paused as if waiting for agreement. The room was silent, most of its occupants staring at the walls or even the ceiling. Anywhere but at one another.

"I mean, here's these foreign dudes—must be a dozen or fifteen of them—with Uzis and AK-forty-sevens and the Lord knows what, and they're sitting behind those two-foot-thick walls up at Highland House, just waiting for somebody stupid enough to try and dig them out. No, friends, we got every excuse in the world to go home, get in bed, and pull the blanket over our heads till this is over."

From the kitchen the radio was crackling to itself, and rain had begun a metallic patter on the corrugated roof. Barr, who had been waiting impatiently for Son to finish, now found himself waiting for the younger man to continue.

"You all know I been away," Son said, sliding into the soft elisions of island speech. "Been away four long years, so maybe I missed somethin'. All that time, while I was in California, if a man ask' me where I'm from, I look him in the eye, and I say, 'Man, I come from a little island you never heard of, but it's the bes' place in the world. Bes' people, too.' I say, 'Man, my home is the sov'reign nation of St. Philip. What you think of that?' "

Without warning, he slammed a powerful hand down on the table, and everyone in the room jumped at the sound. "Sound like bullshit?" he demanded, his head swinging belligerently. "Maybe it was, a little. Maybe our island's not ever'body's idea of the center of the world. But I tell you one thing I'm sure of"—his voice not only was powerful enough to rattle the windowpanes, Barr thought, but had a sincerity that made doubt simply impossible—"I tell you this, and you remember it: If we here let those poor old people at Highland House get murdered, if we sit here and minge out little excuses or go home and drink ourselves blind so's we don't have to think about it—well, we might's well kiss our country good-bye. 'Cause none of us is ever going to say to that stranger, 'Man, I'm from St. Philip.' That's all I got to say."

There was silence when he had finished, and then Father Hughes got up. "Mr. MacLeod," he said, in his gentle, hesitant voice, "what do we have in the way of guns?"

MacLeod, who had been staring hard-eyed at Son, shook his head as if to clear it. "I have to tell all of you that this is suicide, plain and simple," he said, and after a second added, "Fourteen Enfields in firing condition, six hunting rifles, and one automatic shotgun I'm going to use myself."

Patrick: 1:30 P.M.

Four guards trotted through the dusty vault, weapons at high port. At the far end one of them unlocked the heavy door; as it opened, Patrick heard a wave of human distress—cries and shouts and wailing—which then shut off abruptly as the door slammed shut.

"Maybe they have forgotten us," offered Isabel, slumped on the floor with her head between her knees.

"Don't kid yourself," snapped Adler. "They know they've got us in the can, anytime they want to take this place apart." He was propped against the stone wall, legs extended in front of him. His useless feet were wrapped in bloodstained rags, and Patrick, who had done the wrapping, wondered at the kind of strength it took to absorb that agony and still be coherent.

The chamber they were in seemed to be the nerve center of the old rum distillery. Inspected with the guard's stolen flashlight, it was a maze of rusty pipes that wound back and forth below the ceiling, passing into and out of big kettlelike drums studded with dusty gauges, leading finally into a huge boiler half again as high as a man, behind which Jake, Isabel, and Patrick had found just enough space to conceal themselves.

The breakout from Isabel's cell had gone almost too smoothly: one sweeping overhand chop to lay the incautious guard unconscious on the floor. But the gun he carried was unloaded, and he had no cartridges on him, or any other weapon either. They had left him naked on the floor, savagely bound by Isabel with strips of what had been her clothes. He was a short, slight young man, and his gray-olive fatigues fitted her well enough.

From the far end of the corridor their cells opened onto had come the sounds that Patrick now realized were other prisoners, a lot of them. Jake, who had seen them brought ashore during his second interrogation, explained that these were passengers from *Euphoric*, kidnapped either for ransom or as pawns in some hostage game. They apparently were locked up in other windowless storerooms of the rabbit warren under Highland House.

"Hostage" wasn't a word that meant much to Patrick, who associated it with airliners and Arabs and newspaper headlines. Mostly, as far as he recalled, hostage situations ended in a blaze of gunfire out on an airport runway in Algeria or with some kind of sleazy deal where the kidnappers got away after their prisoners were turned loose. He supposed that was what was going to happen here, and while he could sympathize with the elderly passengers off *Euphoric*, who were probably scared to death, their chances of getting out of this safely looked a lot better than Patrick's own. As for Colonel Jake Adler wanting to stick his oar in, it seemed likely only to make things worse.

At the corridor's near end was a door leading into the chamber they were now hiding in. What Patrick hadn't realized until it was too late, and a search party had locked them in, was that none of the keys he had taken from Isabel's guard fitted the door to the distilling room. So Jake was probably right: Harkness's men considered that the three of them were on ice, safely out of circulation until there was time to search them out. For all they could do to escape, they might as well be back in the cells.

The knowledge was driving Jake almost crazy. "Don't you see?" he said to Patrick. "This was why I was supposed to be here. Somebody knew what was going to happen, or enough so he got in touch with my people, only I fucked up—with a little help from my double-dealing slut here."

The words didn't seem to bother Isabel, who eyed the colonel with weary contempt, but they bothered Patrick a lot. Still, he didn't know what to do; he could hardly hit a man who couldn't even walk.

"Listen!" said Isabel suddenly. "Shooting."

Patrick strained to hear anything but the sound of blood in his own ears, and then it came again. "An MG," he said, "a light one."

"Those others are rifles," said Adler. "Heavy-caliber, not automatic. And only a few."

"Sounds to me like the rifles are outside the walls, and the MG's inside."

"Sí," said Isabel. "I think so, too."

"Think so?" Adler said. "You mean you don't know?"

Jesus, I don't need this, said Patrick to himself. He couldn't even blame the colonel for feeling the way he did. But at least the distraction had allowed a wandering thought to take shape. "Listen," he said, more to himself than the others, "when this place was a distillery, this big tub we're behind was the end of the line, right?"

"I suppose," Jake replied, sounding sullen and uninterested.

"The stuff—the mash or whatever it was—didn't start here, though," Patrick continued, turning the flash onto the pipes above and tracing their paths, one by one. "It came in by pipe, from outside."

"Patrick, those goddamn pipes are maybe six inches in diameter," Adler said. "What good are they to us?"

"Wait one," Patrick replied. The flashlight was beginning to dim, and he wasn't sure of what he had seen. "Isabel, come here."

In the corner, a little higher than a man, was where the pipe entered. And as Patrick had hoped, but dared not hope aloud, the stone block where it came through had been removed and replaced by a sheet of plywood, a crude hole sawed in the wood for the pipe.

"Climb on my shoulders," he said. "See if you can break that wood loose."

She was heavier than he'd thought and badly balanced, sitting on his shoulders with his arms pinning her knees to his sides. Three times she tore with her bare hands at the board, and three times she lost her grip, sending Patrick staggering and reeling backward.

"The wood is tight with the wall," she said, panting. "I can't get my fingers behind."

"What's going on? What're you doing?" Adler's stage whisper seemed to echo off the walls.

"Once more, Isabel," Patrick said. "Give it one more try."

When the plywood sheet tore free, it brought the pipe down with it, and Patrick and Isabel, too. The noise sounded like a landslide in a foundry. Patrick lay for several seconds on his side, sure the next thing he would hear was shouts from the other side. But no shouts came. "Let's get out of here," he said. "Isabel, you go first and tell me what's in the next room."

"If you trust her that far," Adler muttered. Patrick ignored it until Isabel, flashlight in hand, had wriggled her way through and dropped with an audible thud into the next chamber.

"It's empty," she called. A minute later: "There's a door. It's not locked."

"Don't open it," said Patrick quickly. "Wait for us." He turned to Adler. "Sir, I think we'd better get a couple of things straight."

Only a little light came through the opening overhead, but he could see Adler's head tipped to one side, waiting.

"Well?"

"Thing one: I'm in charge," said Patrick. "Thing two: At this point you're just dead weight. Thing three: You keep your mouth off Isabel, or I'll leave you behind." He took a deep breath and realized he was trembling. "I guess that above covers it. Sir."

It took him a second to realize that Adler was shaking with silent laughter. "I'll be damned," he said, after a minute. "I will be damned in four colors."

"Do we have a deal?"

"Patrick, it's an offer I can't refuse," Adler replied. "We have a deal."

Too easy, he thought. *The colonel's holding something back. But that's okay, because so am I. Thing four: The minute we get out of here and find Barr and Gillian, I'm going to get Isabel aboard* Glory, *and the four of us are going to sail away from this grubby little island. If you want to hang around and play hero, colonel, sir, you can fucking well do it on your own time.* "Okay then," he said. "It's settled. Now, I can get you up on my shoulders, but you're going to have to pull yourself through. And the floor on the far side sounds like it's the same distance down as here."

"Let's do it."

"What I'm saying is, this is going to hurt like hell."

"Understood," said Adler impatiently. "But it's going to hurt me a lot more than it does you, so what're we waiting for?"

After more than a year's sailing with Barr, who was hard as old leather but never made a point of it, Patrick found himself only annoyed by Jake Adler's macho talk. Fifteen minutes later, however, he had to admit that the man was as tough as his mouth. Only two or three quick gasps hinted at the pain he endured while Patrick hoisted him up to the wall opening; with a grunt he pulled himself through the hole. A second later Patrick heard the heavy thump of a body hitting the floor on the far side and a single "Oh God!" that cut through the musty air like a knife.

For Patrick himself it was painful enough. He managed the initial leap and grab, but every bruise and ding he'd picked up in the last two days seemed to scrape across the rough stone surface as he pulled himself through the opening headfirst. Below, Adler had dragged himself clear—his trail was marked in the dust, spattered with ugly wet stains—and was waiting, propped on one elbow. Even in the uncertain light of the flickering flash, which Isabel was holding, his face looked very pale.

Without letting himself think about it, Patrick crawled through and jumped, landing with a thump that bruised both heels. "A little out of practice?" said Adler.

"A little." He got to his feet, careful not to wince, and slapped the dust off his clothes.

"Here is the door," Isabel whispered. "There are voices on the other side."

The words were scarcely out of her mouth when the room was jarred by the quick, nervous chatter of a light machine gun from beyond the door and a jeering exclamation that was unmistakably Arabic.

Patrick looked automatically to Adler, saw and read his faintly mocking smile. *You wanted to lead?* it said. *Well, here's your chance.*

Two, maybe three men were on the far side, Patrick thought, *probably shooting out a window. Arms in addition to the MG? Unknown. Our force? Me, and maybe a little help from Isabel. Our only advantage? Surprise.* "Okay," he whispered. "Here's how it goes. I'm going to jump them, bash whoever's holding the gun first. Isabel, you're follow-up. Anybody I hit who's still moving, you swat him. But don't hang around to enjoy it. Soon as he's out of action, move on to the next. Questions?"

She shook her head, set to rolling the too-long sleeves of the fatigue shirt out of the way.

"Fallback?" said Adler. Patrick wasn't sure if the colonel was needling him, and the answer was obvious.

"No fallback. We swing for the bleachers." He paused, half tempted to give Isabel a kiss for luck, then saw she was tightly focused, crouched to go, the flashlight held like a club.

He stepped to the door, making sure it really was unlocked and free to open, took a deep breath, and yanked the handle.

He was through in one leap, hearing himself yell "¡*Arriba!*" just as he'd done it in El Salvador. The three men were at a window, two handling an unfamiliar MG, one holding a rifle.

All three started to turn, but the machine gunner slammed the barrel of his weapon against the stone window frame. It was what Patrick had hoped for, in the instant he'd had to choose a target.

The man holding the rifle weighed, at most, 140. He got off one instinctive shot as he was turning, and the echoing *crack!* deafened Patrick. He heard the bullet's crazed scree as it ricocheted off two walls, but by then his shoulder had slammed the rifleman against the wall. Without hesitating—he'd felt a bone in his victim's chest snap—Patrick recovered himself, grabbed the second man by the throat and crotch, and in a single explosion of energy pitched him out the window.

Isabel, ignoring his orders, had hurled herself at the machine gunner, clawing at his eyes with both hands. At such close quarters his weapon was only in his way, and he shuffled backward, head hunched between his shoulders, trying to make room to shoot.

Patrick's blow took him from the side and slightly behind, so he never saw it coming. His head hit the stone wall with a sound like a pumpkin dropped on the pavement, and he slumped to the floor.

The rifle's second *crack!* sounded to Patrick only half as loud as the first. He heard a "*Huh!*" from Isabel, saw her spin away into the wall and start to sag. By then he was halfway down into a sprinter's crouch. The rifleman, dazed by the noise and spitting blood, was trying to bring his gun to bear when he received Patrick's full weight for the second time in five seconds, this time in the pit of his stomach.

They were on the floor, Patrick on top. He wrenched the rifle out of the man's weakening grasp and brought the butt down into his terrified face, had raised the bloody weapon for a second blow when he heard Adler, in the doorway, yell, "Enough, for Christ's sake!"

Patrick's heart was hammering as if it wanted to burst from his chest. He glanced down at the man he'd struck and then quickly away. *More than enough*, he thought, and dropped the rifle.

Isabel. He was at her side, pulling the loose fatigue shirt up. It was already soaked, and it was hard to see exactly where she'd been hit, but the blood was still pumping out. Working fast, with his mind thrown deliberately out of gear, he ripped the shirt off the unconscious machine gunner, tore a couple of wide strips from it, and wrapped them tightly around her chest.

She was half conscious, gave him an attempt at a smile, but when she tried to talk, the pain obviously swept over her.

"Be quiet," he said. "Leave this to me."

He got up, feeling the rush of energy slackening. In a couple of minutes the reaction would set in. He made himself take deep, even breaths as he assessed the situation. Both of Harkness's men were dead. Adler had dragged himself in and was wiping clean the butt of the rifle. The MG's barrel was bent right out of line where it must have hit the wall.

Out the window there was a meadow almost at eye level, about twenty yards away. So what had happened to the guy he'd tossed out? He stepped to the casement and looked out: Between wall and meadow was a ditch about eight feet deep, choked with scrub and weeds. At the bottom, facedown, lay Harkness's man. Patrick saw, with surprise, that it was raining hard, in slanting sheets. Now that he stopped to notice, he could hear the wind whistling in the treetops. *The wind must be coming off the ocean*, he thought, because even the windowsill was dry.

Patrick's numbed brain was still considering the situation when something hit the window frame beside his head with a sound like an ax on kindling. Instinctively he dropped to the floor. From the other side of the room Adler said, "Somebody's using hollow points out there. Look at that wood."

He was right. The bullet had torn a fist-size chunk of pine from the frame. He rolled over, saw what Adler was doing, and said, "What the hell . . ." before he understood. Adler pulled off the undershirt, still reasonably white, that he was wearing under his torn, stained sport shirt and tossed it to Patrick. "Flag of truce," he said.

"Worth a try." When Patrick waved it out the window, a bullet nearly tore it from his hand. *Now what, peerless leader?* he asked himself.

Barr: Outside Highland House, 1:45 P.M.

The attack's small momentum had mostly dribbled away, and only a scattering of shots now cracked out from the dripping undergrowth that surrounded the walls of Highland House. Barr, lying on his stomach beside Son Douglas, wondered how much longer the ragtag Philipian force would hold on. Already he had seen two men slip silently off, screened by the driving rain.

From the wall came a sudden rattle of gunfire—the jerky, quick burst that Chief MacLeod said was a light machine gun, quite different from the steady, businesslike chug-chug-chug of a heavier gun far off to the right. The gunfire stopped, and Barr heard the splash and smack of feet, someone running toward them, flat-out.

It was a teenager Barr didn't know, and he slid into the shallow gully in a spatter of mud. "Son! Son!" he was calling even as he skidded to a halt. "Somethin' happenin' on the other side."

Son squirmed around to where he could inspect the messenger. He looked worn and angry—and wet and chilled, too. "What's that, Rodney?" he said.

Rodney's eyes were round with excitement. "Man wavin' a white flag," he said. "Maybe they givin' up."

Son's eyes met Barr's. "Not 'less they're laughing themselves to death," he said. "What's this about a white flag?"

"Come see for yo'self," said Rodney. "Better hurry, though. Ol' man Dekker, he nearly shot the man's hand off a couple minutes ago."

Son looked slowly to right and left and then at Barr. He didn't need to say what he was clearly thinking: Once he left this part of the field, the men in the woods around him would melt away. "Why don't I have a look?" Barr said.

"Yeah," said Son. "That's the best idea."

Gasping along behind Rodney, who seemed to be half eel, Barr crashed through the brush, his face flailed with wet branches, his feet grabbed at by trailing vines. Twice he fell full length, and once a marksman in Highland House shredded a bush just where Barr's torso would have been, if he hadn't lost his footing an instant earlier.

He had a stabbing stitch in his side when they finally dived, one behind the other, into a solid clump of shrubbery that turned out to be hollow and nearly dry beneath the tightly interlaced branches. A wizened old man with an even older rifle was lying on his belly, squinting through the leaves. Half a coconut shell filled with cartridges lay at his side, and the spent cases were neatly lined up beside them.

As Barr crawled up beside him, the man lifted the rifle, took aim, then lowered it again. "Almost that time," he observed. "He's gettin' ready to show himself again, and this time I blow his head off." He chuckled happily. "I already killed one of those buggers. First man I shot since 1943."

"That's nice," Barr replied absently. His eyes were fixed on the window. It was almost at ground level, and then he saw the deep ditch between the bushes and the wall. The window frame, which was wood, looked as if some giant beaver had been taking bites out of it.

"Mist' Dekker!" Rodney's whisper was urgent. "Here he come again."

"Ye-es," said Dekker slowly as he snugged the rifle butt into his shoulder. "Now you jes' watch—"

The white cloth—badly shredded—appeared first, and then a smooth, powerfully muscled arm, and then a face . . . For a moment Barr couldn't believe his eyes. As he turned to Dekker, he saw the old man's clawlike finger begin to squeeze the trigger.

Barr slammed the muzzle down just as the rifle went off, and a couple of pounds of mud and chopped vegetable matter geysered into the air in front of them.

"What you doin?" Dekker was clearly outraged. "I had him plain."

"He's a friend of mine," Barr said. "I think they were holding him inside, he must have escaped." He didn't dare say it aloud, but he'd seen a movement in the room behind Patrick, so Gillian must be there, too.

"Oh," said Dekker. He looked disappointed, and then he frowned as another thought occurred to him. "I don' know how your friend going to get out here. Soon's he climb out, they going to shoot him from the wall."

"Can you cover him?" Barr asked. Dekker shook his head. "Why not?" Barr persisted. "Look, I'll pay you for the bullets."

Dekker seemed reluctant to meet his eye. "That ain't it, man. Fact is, I can't exactly see the top of the wall, not without my glasses. Besides, it take more than one rifle to give good coverin' fire."

"Then we'll get more than one," said Barr. "Rodney, come here."

In the end they had five, orchestrated by MacLeod, who'd laid aside his shotgun in favor of old Dekker's rifle.

Barr waited until he was sure he saw the gleam of Patrick's face, a little back from the window, and then stood up. MacLeod grabbed at him, pulling him back down just as two shots rang out from the parapet, and a severed branch dropped next to him.

"Damned fool," muttered MacLeod, then shouted, "Open fire!"

As the scatter—the pitifully thin scatter—of guns blazed away, Patrick appeared once more in the window, with a slight, still form in his arms. Barr was in the open, skidding, slipping, legs pumping, driving toward the wall before he fully realized what he was doing. At the lip of the ditch he saw that it was Isabel, not Gillian, in Patrick's arms, but it was too late for him to stop.

He slithered down the near slope, landed with a splash in six inches of water and cushioning vegetation. He scrambled to his feet, saw that Patrick was holding Isabel by the wrists, lowering her apparently unconscious form toward him. Her loose shirt was dark red all down one side. As Barr held up his arms to receive her body, his anguished gaze locked with Patrick's, and both men spoke at once: "Where's Gillian?"

The question was, after a frozen second or two, its own answer. Suddenly numb, Barr stood holding Isabel, oblivious of the crackle of rifle fire from the bushes behind him. He looked up, saw Adler perched on the sill above him. The soldier's feet were swathed in what seemed to be bloody sacks.

If Adler's feet are that messed up, he thought, *surely he won't jump—* At that moment Adler did, followed a second later by Patrick, carrying a rifle. Old Dekker and young Rodney helped drag them up the slope— it was not so very steep on that side, only slippery—and then they were safely in the bushes, as the gunfire around them died away.

"We need a doctor, quick," said Patrick, taking Isabel's still form from Barr's arms and laying her gently on the ground. On his knees, he began to open her blood-soaked shirt, then noticed that no one had moved. "What the fuck you waiting for?" he snarled. "This woman's hurt bad."

"No doctor on this island," said MacLeod gently. "No real doctor anyhow."

"What d'you mean?" Patrick demanded.

"Only what we call leaf doctor," said MacLeod. He nudged Dekker, who had edged up to Isabel's side. "This old man, he ain't much, but he does know healing."

Patrick regarded Dekker with something close to despair on his face. "Will you—please."

The old Philipian ran his hands over Isabel's torso, under the fatigue shirt. His lined face was thoughtful, almost detached. At last he turned to Rodney. "Boy, you go find me some redwort, a big handful. And some hurryweed. And don't you linger on the way, hear?" To Patrick he said, "You done a good job with the bandage. I don't want to take it off till the boy come back."

"How is she?"

To Barr she seemed as good as dead, her breathing almost imperceptible, her skin already chilled, but Dekker said, "Can't tell yet. She lost a lot of blood—maybe too much." He turned to MacLeod. "Chief, I need your coat to keep her warm."

The one-armed man sighed, and began undoing the gleaming brass buttons.

Gillian: 2:00 P.M.

Windowless, jammed with panic-stricken old people, the damp cellar room had become a festering, echoing hothouse. The woman beside her, Gillian decided, must have drenched herself in duty-free perfume before coming ashore, and the reek of it, tainted by the acrid smell of fear, was coming off her in waves. A man nearby had pulled out a cigar and lit it and for a couple of minutes resisted the outrage of the other two dozen people in the cell, claiming loudly that he had to have it—his doctor had prescribed it—his nerves absolutely required a smoke every two hours, at which point a woman who barely came up to Gillian's shoulder had snatched it from his mouth and ground it to shreds on the floor. But the damage was done. The heavy, burned odor clung to them all.

Still, it was the noise that was hardest for Gillian to take. Not only was everyone talking at once, at various volumes, but over by the door someone was banging loudly on the wood and shouting that he had to go to the bathroom, right *now*. And almost drowning him out was a woman wailing, loudly and on a single note, stopping only long enough to gulp a fresh breath. Faintly, through the human racket, Gillian could hear what sounded like faraway gunfire—a couple of shots and then a sustained burst.

When the door finally burst open, it was a complete surprise, and the man who had been beating on it found that his fist was striking one of Harkness's men in the chest. The young man bared his teeth in a gleaming, humorless grin and, without a word, struck down the elderly passenger with the butt of what looked like a shotgun. Those nearest the door pushed back with thin cries of alarm, revealing the injured man writhing on the stone floor.

The guard with the gun stepped inside, followed by Harkness himself, who had shed both his clerical collar and his avuncular manner. He was now wearing an obviously new set of fatigues, and despite her exhausted apprehension, Gillian could not help thinking how comical they should have looked on his roly-poly shape—should have, but somehow didn't. He barely glanced down at the passenger, whose body was jerking to and fro in what seemed to be convulsions, and turned to the guard at his side. "Shoot him," he said.

The guard's eyes widened in surprise, but a second, sharper order in his own language settled the issue. The gun's hoarse roar sounded like an avalanche in the confined space. The other prisoners' cries and shouts stopped as if someone had turned a switch. They stood frozen, some with their mouths still open, watching in petrified horror.

Harkness ignored them. His gaze—cool, almost clinical—swept the room and settled on Gillian. She felt an icy hollowness below her rib cage as he pointed. "Miss Verdean," he said. "Over here, please."

A path to the door opened as if by magic, and she found herself walking toward him. In the utter silence she heard more gunfire outside, a sustained volley that made the guard half turn. Harkness snapped out a command that brought his attention back into the room; up close, Gillian could see tiny beads of sweat at Harkness's hairline, his left hand, down at his side, clenching and unclenching.

It gave her just enough courage to hold up her head, though when Harkness said, "Outside, please," she didn't trust herself to speak.

What was there to say anyway? Part of her had given up; it would, she knew, obediently follow instructions, even to her death. But there was still the other, rebellious part that was ready to hurl her body at her captors, go down fighting, clawing, screaming. And curiously removed from both was her brain, stunned for a minute by the gratuitous murder but recovering fast. It was the brain she had to listen to; she knew that and clung desperately to her knowledge.

The MacIntyre was standing in the corridor outside the cell, in his ceremonial kilt again, but looking a million years old and utterly defeated. Two more armed men were behind him, and both, she thought, looked edgy and worried.

From the cell behind her came a concerted wail. Gillian turned, to see the first guard dragging out a woman by the arm. She was grayhaired and short, dressed in an ugly but obviously expensive white pantsuit. She came without a struggle, almost as if she were sleepwalking, and Harkness, right behind her, slammed the heavy door closed.

The big upstairs room was even hotter than the room full of prisoners, but the heat was searingly dry, coming not from sweating human bodies but from a row of arc spots hung from a metal frame. Their almost painful light bathed the stage set ship's lounge that took up half a room, sharpening every detail of the bar, with its row of bottles (empty, Gillian could see) and stacked glasses, the tables and chairs pushed to one side, the brassbound portholes. The hard rattling of rain on the metal roof overhead and the muted wail of the wind added a note of realism to the scene. For some reason the crude, dreadfully functional framework of the gallows—in center stage, with the single TV camera pointed at it seemed almost natural. Gillian glanced quickly at the woman beside her, but she appeared to be, mercifully, in deep shock, unaware of her surroundings.

The room seemed full of Harkness's young men, milling about and doing nothing in particular, their slung rifles clattering together and against the furniture. Harkness himself surveyed the setting with a single, bleak stare, and Gillian saw that none of his men seemed eager to meet his eye.

"It is just like everywhere else," he said to her, shaping what might have been a smile. "They all want to be on television." Shifting to what she assumed was Arabic, he rapped out an angry question that sent two thirds of them scurrying out.

The vulpine Monasir, wearing a coverall and looking thoroughly harassed, rushed up, talking a mile a minute. From the way he kept tapping the crystal of his ornate watch, Gillian assumed that something was late or about to be.

Harkness shook his head, just as a sudden burst of gunfire resounded outside, sounding much closer. Everyone in the room spun toward the sound at once, and for one hallucinatory moment Gillian found herself expecting Patrick to come crashing through the big glass doors from the balcony outside. Instead one of the doors opened, and an Arab face, streaming wet, appeared for what sounded like a brief, embarrassed apology.

"Do not expect a rescue, Miss Verdean." Harkness had obviously been reading her expression, and he was wearing his quietly confident demeanor again. But she saw he couldn't keep his left hand from twitching, and once again the sight of even that small nervousness sent a spurt of hope through her.

Patrick was out there somewhere. She was sure of it now. They'd get her out somehow.

Monasir was standing by the camera, and he clapped his hands for silence. Someone produced a length of rope, with a slipknot already tied in its end, and two men hustled the woman passenger forward. As they did, she twisted to look at Gillian, who realized that she was not in shock at all. Her eyes—only one of them framed by grotesquely thick false eyelashes—were wide with fear. She wanted to say something, Gillian could see, but no sound came from her moving lips.

Harkness stepped in front of the camera, and Monasir brought his hand down in a sweeping arc.

Ten minutes later as Harkness was in the midst of his speech to the world (which he coyly referred to as "our apologia"), the woman broke free, dashing blindly in front of him, toward the balcony. Perhaps, Gillian thought afterward, she thought freedom was that way, but two of the guards caught her, dragged her back, as the visibly shaken Harkness wobbled through the rest of his address.

When they put the woman under the crossbeam, held her, struggling feebly now, while one of them fitted the noose over her head, Gillian's self-control deserted her. She made a desperate grab for the slung rifle of a very young guard standing beside her, his own face a mask of fascinated revulsion. What she would have done with the weapon if she'd got hold of it she never knew. Something hard and cold struck the side of her head, exactly over the previous injury, and she slid gratefully into unconsciousness.

*   *   *

She came to with a searing pain in her temple. Someone was holding her, and someone else was slapping her face with a dripping towel. The first thing her eyes lit on was the gallows, and the dreadful, pathetic bundle that swung from the crossbar.

Quickly she turned her face away, but not quickly enough. For the first time she felt absolute terror, like a cold blade, slice through her gut. *That's going to be me,* she thought. Her own wrists had been lashed together behind her back, so tightly the feeling was already leaving her fingers. *So it's going to be soon.* The thought that she was going to die was terrible, but that she would never see Barr again was almost more than she could bear. She closed her eyes tightly, to block out the scene in front of her, seal in the tears.

From the throbbing blackness she became aware of angry, excited voices, accusing and denying. Suddenly she was hauled to her feet, and her eyes opened involuntarily. Harkness was standing in front of her, and fury had splintered his smooth exterior. She watched, baffled, as he struggled to pull himself together.

"We are experiencing," he said, lips twitching with the effort at self-control, "what one might call technical difficulties. These idiots"—his gesture included half a dozen of his followers—"have allowed your friends to elude us. It seems they actually escaped from confinement some time ago, but none of these . . . young people had the courage to tell me." As Harkness spoke, his self-possession gradually returned, but Gillian, fighting to grasp what he was saying through the waves of agony from her right temple, could see that his rage was only banked and could burst out again at any time.

"My young associates had your friends trapped—so they thought—in the old distilling chamber," Harkness went on, speaking so slowly that Gillian knew his words were meant as much for his men as for her. "Somehow they broke out, killing three of my people in the process. But it does not matter," he went on, raising his voice. "It is unimportant. The Cuban woman is dead, and the foolish colonel so badly injured he is no longer a threat to us."

His words were echoed by another burst of gunfire from outside. "No longer a threat!" Harkness said again, even louder. "But we cannot now stage the execution of the four American spies since we have lost three of them." His voice dropped to a whisper, in Gillian's ear. "And frankly, my dear, I have need of you."

Patrick: Outside Highland House, 2:45 P.M.

Isabel had fallen into almost a coma, her breathing so light that Patrick had to put his ear to her lips to feel it. But she seemed a little warmer under the police chief's fancy uniform coat, and Patrick accepted that she might as well be here as anyplace else on the island. What they had to do was get her off or, better still, helicopter some real medics in.

The old witch doctor they called Dekker had produced an unlabeled bottle of syrupy fluid and taken a healthy snort. As the police chief, MacLeod, pointedly looked the other way, the old man passed the bottle to Barr. He looked at it, one eyebrow raised, and tipped it up; a second later he lowered it, coughing and choking, his angular face scarlet under his tan. Patrick wondered what the stuff must be like to produce such a reaction; he'd watched Barr swallow practically anything wet, stuff that smelled like brake fluid, without changing expression.

"I'll take a slug," said Adler. His face was gray, and a fresh, damp redness was soaking through the rust-colored stains on his bandages. *I hope you choke*, Patrick thought.

Both Dekker and MacLeod looked nervously at Barr, but he shrugged and handed the bottle to Adler, who sniffed it, blinked, and then poured what looked like a tumblerful down his throat. " 'Sgood," he pronounced, in a hoarse whisper. "Now, let's hear the reports."

Chief MacLeod was the first to react. Bristling, the one-armed policeman looked Adler up and down before asking, "What reports, Mr. White Man?"

Adler set the bottle down on the ground and heaved himself to a more comfortable position. He was a wreck, Patrick thought, smeared from head to foot with mud (gray-black that had been dust from Highland House, red-brown from out here); his shirt ripped, his trouser legs hacked off at mid-calf, his feet two bundles of damp rust-colored rags. And yet, almost for the first time since Patrick had met him, he seemed completely at home and completely in charge.

"Sitreps, mister," he said. "Situation reports on your siege. I want personnel strengths, ammo returns, the works." He grinned through his two-day beard, and both MacLeod and Dekker returned it.

As far as the situation went, it was a disaster, Patrick decided a couple of minutes later. MacLeod thought there might be thirty Philipians left in the woods, but it might just as easily be twenty. The fourteen of them armed with old British Army Enfield rifles, from the police chief's gun locker still had fifty or so rounds apiece; but the ones who'd brought their own hunting rifles . . . MacLeod threw up his hands in frustrated ignorance. Two machine guns were mounted on the parapet of Highland House, and no attack, however desperate, was going to get past them to the main door.

"What about the entrance on the other side?" asked Adler. "The gate at the top of those steps?"

"That's the problem," MacLeod answered. "The steps. You can't get onto the stairway except at the bottom, and by the time you get to the top, you be pretty dead."

"After sunset," said Adler. "This storm looks like it's going to hold right through the night, so it'll be dark early."

"That's still more than three hours," Barr replied. "Gillian could be dead by then, not to mention a lot of the hostages." Patrick marveled at the coolness in Barr's tone, and then he saw the muscle jumping below his cheekbone.

"She might be dead now," said Adler. "All we know about what's going on in there is what we're hearing from Radio Antilles—and they're getting their information from that goddamn TV studio of Harkness's." The colonel, Patrick saw, was only thinking out loud. He wasn't even looking at Barr, so he didn't see the sudden glitter of murderous rage in the skipper's eyes. Or maybe he did and chose not to see it. Adler was turning out to be a far more complicated character than Patrick had imagined.

"Harkness is no fool," said MacLeod. "His people be waiting."

A little color seemed to have come back into Adler's cheeks. Was it the booze, Patrick thought, or was he sore at not being in command, or what? In the background Son Douglas was arguing in whispers with the boy—Randal or Rodney, his name was. Patrick instinctively liked Son but couldn't figure out what it was between him and Barr that was making the Philipian act like a jealous tomcat whose turf was being threatened.

"The trouble is," Adler was saying, "whoever designed Highland House knew what he was doing. Unless you've got artillery—Christ, what I'd give for even one Stinger!—there're only two approaches. You can make a frontal assault, with a solid barrage beforehand and good covering fire, or you can crawl up those goddamn steps and hope they don't pick you off one by one." He paused—for effect, Patrick was sure—and then tossed the clincher: "In daylight, with that big MG, it'll be hundred percent casualties. Believe it."

Someone was tugging at Patrick's sleeve. He turned his head and saw Old Dekker's wrinkled, unreadable face. "Mister," he said, "I'm sorry."

Patrick felt his heart lock up. Barr's icy voice—"I'm not letting Gillian get hanged"—was clear but a thousand miles away.

"Mister," Dekker whispered, "I think your woman dead."

Gillian: 3:30 P.M.

"I didn't want to do it," The MacIntyre was saying in her ear, softly but earnestly, over and over. "Truly I didn't. I didn't have any choice."

"It doesn't matter," she said, meaning "Shut up." Her head was hurting more, and it was harder to make sense out of what was happening around them.

It seemed as if they'd been standing in the hall outside the big upper room for hours, though Gillian knew it could only be minutes. She had put her back against the wall, locked her knees, but the strength was draining out of her legs, and she knew she was going to fall over soon. For some reason just the idea of collapsing in front of Harkness was still hateful enough so that every time she let the thought form it stiffened her rubbery legs again.

Not that Harkness was paying attention to her. His own people were climbing all over one another to get his ear. One of them came with a report from *Euphoric*. Gillian knew, because Harkness made a point of translating it for her.

"Success!" he crowed. He was beaming, but the way his eyes darted from side to side told her his enthusiasm was meant to rally the troops. And some of them looked to her as if they needed it; the smell of fear in the corridor was not all that different from the smell of fear in the hostages' cell.

"The enemy has taken the bait," Harkness announced, raising his voice. "An American Coast Guard ship is standing by a quarter mile from *Euphoric*, and there are three other large ships—probably destroyers—coming up very fast on the radar screen." He clapped his hands together, as if unable to contain his delight. "And aircraft! My captain says it is as if someone tipped over a bee skep. Circling, swooping down—buzzing, I think the term is. But they are not attacking."

He turned to Monasir, who had materialized at his side, and fired off an order, then gave another to the gun-carrying guard who stood beside The MacIntyre. Gillian and the old man were hustled into a smaller room that seemed to be lined with closets, perhaps some kind of dressing room in the original house. Their guards pushed them to the ground, and Gillian gratefully let her legs fold under her. Being made to sit down wasn't shaming, she decided, and anyway her calf muscles felt like used chewing gum.

On a built-in bureau sat a small TV set with one bent rabbit-ear antenna protruding from its top. The picture was black and white and mostly snow, but after a minute Gillian saw it was the room next door.

Her guard dropped to one knee beside her. "It is a retrans—a broadcast from Antigua," he said. "They are picking up the satellite signal." Clearly the technical achievement impressed him, and, politely, he wanted to share it with her. "It would be much clearer with a proper antenna."

In another incarnation, Gillian thought, he was probably a cheerful, pleasant young man, kind to his mother and respectful to older people. It was surprisingly hard for her to picture him as a killer.

Five minutes later Harkness appeared on the screen, with another installment of his justification. His eloquence seemed to be shredding at the edges as he reminded the watching world that what they were seeing was their fault. He told his audience yet again how he and his fellows on the cruise liner were prepared to die in a greater cause, prepared to demonstrate the true glory of martyrdom, the unshakable determination of the oppressed—but his voice was definitely shriller, and he had forgotten that there was no need to yell at a microphone.

"Attack *Euphoric* if you dare!" Harkness challenged. "It will only hasten the deaths of the unfortunate sacrifices. This ship will defend herself against you, and the passengers' bodies are our shield." *So that's it*, she thought, *the illusionist's misdirection: Keep your eye on my left hand, folks, while I pick your pocket with the other.*

Harkness vanished, and another victim was dragged in front of the camera. A man this time, and Gillian thought it might be the cigar smoker. He seemed almost unconscious as the rope was pulled down over his head, but then, just as the executioner's assistants stepped away, he looked straight into the camera.

"These are murderers," he said. His voice was shaking but clear. "Never forget it." There was no time to say more. Gillian, whose eyes had been frozen to the screen, turned her head from the jerking, struggling spectacle. Beside her the young guard suddenly choked and vomited into his own lap.

They were cleaning it up and scolding the embarrassed guard when Harkness burst into the room, spitting commands. In a matter of seconds it had emptied of all but Harkness, Monasir beside him, and the two prisoners. With the door still open Gillian could hear the renewed sound of gunfire from outside. Heavier, she thought, as if . . .

"It sounds like an attack, does it not?" said Harkness, echoing her thinking. "To tell you the truth, I thought there were fewer of them. But"—his smile was definitely forced, she thought—"but it does not signify. They will not assault the wall."

She wanted to rage at him, defy him, and it must have shown on her face. "Oh, it is not a matter of courage, Miss Verdean. Courage has nothing to do with it. The ancestors of this man"—he patted The MacIntyre's head—"built Highland House to defy a colonial army. The islanders outside are scarcely even that."

Gillian knew it was foolish to let him get to her, but she couldn't restrain herself. "They're going to stop you just the same. Maybe not these people, but somebody else."

She knew instantly that she'd played into his hands. "My dear, that's what people like you have been saying for years, yet *ecce homo,* as Father Hughes might say." The gunfire faded for a moment, then renewed its strength. "The attack will come any minute," he said to himself.

"What attack?" said Gillian. "I thought you said—"

"They will not assault the walls," he cut her off. "Exactly. It is a feint. Their force will be sneaking up the Thousand Steps even now." He looked at his watch. "And our heavy machine gun has just been placed to sweep them into the sea."

Patrick: 4:15 P.M.

Son Douglas was sitting on his heels, scanning the steep, thickly wooded slope in front of them. The rain had molded his sopping clothes to his body, but he didn't seem to notice it. Patrick had begun shivering almost as soon as they'd stopped moving forward through the trees. He ached in every muscle, and only the smoldering rage that seemed to be centered just below his rib cage was sustaining him. Looking down, he saw his knuckles were white where he held the rifle he'd taken from the dead guard. Four rounds in the clip and one up the spout—words he'd been muttering under his breath like a mantra as he slogged head down through the dripping forest.

Son held a police Enfield in one powerful hand; the other was wrapped around young Rodney's skinny bicep like a blood pressure cuff. From Rodney's wide-eyed expression, he wanted very much to be someplace else entirely. "Should be right down there," Son said, "if the boy can find it."

"If he can't, I'm goin' back," said a tall Philipian called Stretch, pulling the collar of his shirt up to his ears. "Maybe go back anyhow. This is craziness, man."

Understatement of the week, Patrick thought. *We are talking inter-galactic madness here—a plan thought up by a raggedy-ass twelve-year old, and when it blows up in our faces, we'll be flushed into the sea like shit.*

It had started behind Patrick's back, while he was kneeling over Isabel's still body, trying to convince himself she wasn't dead; then, when he couldn't do that, trying to bring her back to life. He was on his knees, holding her in his arms, rocking back and forth, when he became aware of Son's urgent voice.

"The old drain for the *bagasse*," he was saying, "the garbage stuff left over after they made the rum. Used to flush it down the bluff through this big old pipe. It runs from the bottom of the main vat an' comes out the side of the bluff, 'bout halfway down."

"It's too small," snapped MacLeod. "You'd have to crawl like a snake, and uphill, too."

"This boy"—Son lifted the unhappy Rodney by his arm—"he says he crawled through it once. A couple of friends were with him, and one of 'em was as big as him."

He'd pointed at Patrick, still on his knees, and Rodney was nodding with desperate intensity. But what Patrick remembered was the desperate appeal on Barr's lean face.

"Down here," called Son. "I see it." That was more than Patrick did. It was hard to ignore the shivering, and the wind-driven rain, and the damn hermit crabs as big as baseballs that all seemed to be out for a stroll. How the hell did they get up here? he wondered. And why did they come?

The men slipped and slid their way down the bluff, grabbing at vines and ramming their heels into the mud. The boy Rodney was first, scuttling as quickly along the ground as a mongoose; Son, right behind him, had his rifle slung diagonally across his back. Barr, carrying the automatic shotgun MacLeod had lent him, was next. The shotgun had no sling, but MacLeod had tied it across Barr's bony chest with string; Patrick wondered how long it would stay there.

Even with his hands free Barr was the clumsiest of them all. Twice Stretch, who was right behind him, carrying a slung Enfield older than he was, had had to grab desperately to keep him from rocketing down the slope. Patrick was behind Stretch, working his way cautiously down a hill that normally wouldn't have given him any pause. *Four in the clip and one up the spout,* he repeated to himself. Bringing up the rear was another Philipian, a transplanted Haitian, actually, with a name that sounded to Patrick like Maguire but probably wasn't.

Every few seconds, when the gusting wind let up, they could hear the firing above and behind them. MacLeod and the colonel had their men spacing their shots, so the crackling was slow but regular, broken every couple of minutes by a quick burst from the light machine gun on the wall.

That was Adler's little contribution. Or maybe blindy white ought to get the credit. The colonel must have drunk nearly a pint of it, but he was standing upright—mostly upright—reeling and lurching through the brush, yelling curses at the men, firing an occasional round at the windows. The gunners on the wall seemed to be firing through the sheeting rain at the noise he made, which was not a whole lot less than you might get from one of the armored fighting vehicles the Army had been bringing in just when Patrick had left the service.

Well, good luck to the old fucker, Patrick thought.

The pipe's mouth, Patrick saw, was plenty large enough for a man. Rodney hadn't bothered to say, though, that it stuck out a good four feet from the hillside. What you had to do, the boy explained, was sit on top of it, pull yourself out to the end, and then just lean forward and dive in. If you missed, it was fifty feet straight down to a patch of ugly-looking rocks, stained with a couple of decades' worth of bagasse that even Hurricane Hugo hadn't been able to wash clean.

Nobody wanted to go first, but at last the Haitian pushed forward, muttering something uncomplimentary about white people and Philipians. He was a big man for a West Indian, as tall and broad as Patrick himself, and his legs were long enough so he could straddle the pipe as he worked his way out to the end.

It went perfectly, in fact, until the moment he swung forward to somersault himself into the opening. Patrick saw the slung Enfield slip, unbalancing its owner. A moment later he was clinging by his fingertips from the lower edge of the pipe's lip, as his rifle hit the rocks below and its stock shattered noisily.

Patrick heard Son say, "Oh, shit." Saw him start reluctantly to get up, but Barr was already out on the pipe, his hair blowing back, eyes half closed against the driving rain. As Patrick watched, his breath sealed in his throat, Barr slid to the farthest edge of the metal tube.

He seemed to be groping at his shirt with his good hand, and Son whispered, "What's he doin'?"

Patrick couldn't make himself answer. Heights had always unnerved him, and though he'd forced himself to the top of *Glory*'s mainmast a dozen times, he was always just as scared the next time. Watching Barr, he found, was even worse than doing it himself. Suddenly Barr pulled the shotgun away from his chest, leaned forward, and tossed it with a clang into the pipe's mouth.

The sound seemed to release an agonized yell from the Haitian, who had been swinging silently, his feet treading the air. Barr said something, braced himself, and dived forward.

"Christ, it worked." The voice was Patrick's own; the words were automatic. Now he saw Barr, doubled over in the opening, reach forward and grab the Haitian's left wrist with his own right hand. Barr extended his left hand, the four fingers taped together, and with a quick grab the Haitian took him by the wrist.

"White man's too light," said Stretch, at Patrick's side. "Can't lift that much weight."

"Shut your mouth," Son said.

It was impossible, but the Haitian seemed to be moving upward and into the opening. Barr must be scrabbling backward, Patrick decided. Scrabbling backward when the Haitian's weight should have pulled him out of the pipe like a cork out of a bottle. After a minute only the Haitian's long legs were visible, and then they were gone.

"Man," said Stretch, shaking his head, "I don' know . . ."

"Tell you what *I* know," said Son. "We can't lose. The island's fighting on our side—the duppies and the jumbies and all."

Not a shadow of doubt in his voice, and Stretch's frown suddenly cleared. "Maybe you right, Son. Let's get 'em."

At the pipe's edge, looking down at the rocks—he could see the wooden rifle stock, in splinters—Patrick froze. *Come on*, he told himself, hearing Son clear his throat behind him. He summoned up Isabel's stony pale face, and the black rage came, too, but it wasn't what he needed.

From the pipe's mouth he heard murmured voices; then the Haitian called up, "Your friend say, jus' pretend you on a mast."

So Barr knew, Patrick thought. *And after all the trouble I took to hide it. ¡Arriba!*

Luckily for the climbers, the pipe was corrugated, and the ridges were a perfect size to brace their feet against. Ten years and a million insects had accounted for most of the bagasse in the corrugations, and the pipe was almost big enough for Patrick to get up on his hands and knees. Almost, however, meant knees and elbows and a whole new set of bloody bruises. Barr was leading the way, and even though he was now holding the shotgun in his good hand, he moved so fast it was hard for the others to keep up.

Four in the clip and one in the spout, Patrick thought. By now young Rodney must be about halfway back to the line of attackers outside the walls. At five o'clock Adler and MacLeod were going to have their men blaze away in one long burst, trying to convince Harkness's men that an attack was coming. The five infiltrators would by then be in position. When they heard the sustained fire, they'd hit the main door from inside, throw it open, and hold the gap until the assault force could relieve them.

That, at least, was the plan—if you could call such an idiot's dream a plan. When Adler had sprung it on them, no one had objected. "Then it's agreed," Adler had said quickly. "Let's go." How many other lost causes had started the same way? Patrick asked himself.

They were falling behind, gasped Son, the only one of them with a wristwatch. No time to sort themselves out at the far end.

That suited Patrick fine. With five against at least fifteen, he wanted no time for second thoughts.

"Ain't got a gun," panted the Haitian Maguire. "What c'n I do with no gun?"

"Here," snapped Barr. "You can have this if you carry it."

Fifteen against five, Patrick thought, and only four of us armed.

The pipe turned vertical, and Patrick knew they must be nearly there, but the blackness was just as thick. Absolutely thick, so thick it seemed to have a feel, like fur. Probably spider webs. The Haitian's bare feet—the soles were as hard as wood, and a lot rougher—were on Patrick's shoulders, and Barr was standing on the Haitian.

"Some kind of hatch," he called down softly. "It's wood. Brace yourself."

Patrick locked his knees and reached out to grab the corrugations at each side. *Thud!* The force, coming down through the Haitian's feet, almost drove Patrick to his knees, but the sound—solid, thick— was disheartening.

"Now the real one," Barr called.

Real one? He had just time to brace himself again, but the thrust was not nearly as great. The wooden cover spun away with a ringing crash, and soft gray light appeared some ten feet above Patrick's head.

The gunfire, a faint whisper inside the pipe, suddenly swelled to a steady roar. "That's the signal," called Son. "Get your asses out of here."

Barr was up and out, and then Son, scrambling up Patrick's back and Maguire's, followed by Stretch. Lowered belts pulled the Haitian and Patrick clear.

The room they were in was lighted by one small barred peephole high up in a wall, but it seemed like noon after the darkness of the drainpipe. "All set?" Patrick gasped. He freed the rifle, checked the safety. "I take the point, Son guides me. Stretch and Maguire watch the flanks."

"Let's go," said Barr. His sheath knife was gleaming in his hand.

Barr: 5:05 P.M.

Outside the room that held the huge vat was a narrow flight of stairs, and Patrick led them up it on the run, with Son at his heels. The hallway at the top was empty, but the big old house was full of sounds—the gusting westerly rattling shutters and whistling in fireplaces, the steady barrage of gunfire from outside, and from somewhere below them a chorus of cries and wails and shouts that drew Barr almost irresistibly. Son grabbed his arm, shouting, "No! The main door—this way!"

Screw the main door, thought Barr, but then followed anyway, realizing that without a guide he'd quickly be lost in the maze of corridors and dusty chambers. They rounded a corner and were suddenly in the high-ceilinged entrance hall, with the broad staircase behind them and the doors in front of them: diagonal-planked oak that must be inches thick, secured with a four-by-eight timber bar in wrought-iron brackets. And two young guards who were standing carefully away from the narrow windows on each side.

They whirled as Patrick came around the corner, but they never had a chance. Without breaking stride or even seeming to aim, he swept his weapon from one side to the other, five shots so close together they sounded like one rolling blast. The guards were jerked from their feet and slammed into the wall behind them, to slide slowly, almost bonelessly, to the stone floor. One of them left a long red streak on the white plaster.

"The door!" yelled Son, dropping his rifle and hurling himself at the four-by-eight. Patrick scooped up one of the dead guard's weapons, checked the clip, and tossed it at Barr all in one motion. He caught it awkwardly, with his free hand, but it got away from him. A round went off as the gun hit the stone floor, and the bullet hit the door with a solid thunk.

As Barr stooped to pick the weapon up, he heard a shout from the top of the staircase and almost instantly another rattling burst of gunfire. Stretch, who with Son had the big bar almost out of its brackets, stumbled and went to one knee. Barr swung his own gun around, groping for the trigger, and had a hazy picture of the Haitian at his side, holding the shotgun at waist level.

The Haitian fired four times in as many seconds, the blasts punctuated by screams from the top of the stairs. A single figure rolled down the faded purple carpeting, his head—or what was left of it—hitting every step.

Barr glanced back at the main door. Stretch was down now but still struggling to rise; Son and Patrick had their shoulders under the four-by-eight and, with a concerted heave, lifted it from its brackets and dropped it to the floor.

From the corner of his eye Barr saw movement at the head of the stairs, but the Haitian had seen it first. This time he fired twice, knocking over a huge brass pot full of dead ivy that sat on a pedestal. From behind the pedestal rose a figure holding a squat gun that was already blazing. Barr's own weapon went off, quite by accident, and the figure toppled over backward, his weapon stitching a line of holes in the ceiling.

"Good shot!" the Haitian said. As he spoke, the front doors swung inward, pushed by a wave of cheering, shouting Philipians. In their midst, carried by two of the biggest men, was Adler, with an automatic pistol in one hand and a bottle in the other.

The charge that had carried the attackers into the hallway faltered. Adler fired twice into the ceiling. "That way! To the cellars!" he roared. His eyes lit on Barr, at the foot of the stairs, and he jerked his head toward the upper floor.

Of course. The cellar was where the hostages were, but upstairs, Adler had said, was Harkness's obscene stage set. Harkness himself might be there, and maybe Gillian.

Somebody else loosed a round into the ceiling, and Barr sprinted up the stairs.

Two men were lying dead at the landing. Barr paused, trying to decide which direction was more promising. A shot that plucked at his sleeve settled it. He pointed his unfamiliar weapon down the hallway and fired several times. The noise was impressive, and one bullet ricocheted off the wall with a fearsome, high-pitched whir.

"Don't shoot! I surrender!" quavered a voice Barr had never heard before. Not an island accent—could it be Harkness?

"Throw your gun out," Barr called. From an open doorway a weapon clattered across the wood floor. He had started down the hall, his weapon trained on the doorway, before a safer course occurred to him. "Put your hands up and come out here!"

"You won't shoot? You promise?"

An old man? Barr wondered. Sure sounded like it. "I won't shoot," he said.

The figure that emerged was fantastic enough for a dream, but the costume told Barr who it had to be. "Mr. MacIntyre?"

"*The* MacIntyre," the tall old man replied, his voice shaking. He craned his head for a better view. "You're not the American Army."

"American, yes. Army, no," said Barr. "I'm looking for a woman. A young woman. Slender, brown hair—"

"Oh, yes," said the old man. "She's with Harkness." He nodded vaguely down the hall.

"She's all right?" *Not like Isabel,* he thought. *Please.*

"She was when they left," the old man replied. Barr gaped at him, his mind suddenly blank. "They went to get the sailboat," MacIntyre continued, staring absently at him. His pupils, Barr saw, were like pinpoints. "Harkness, the girl, and two others. One of them was that scoundrel Monasir. D'you know what the natives call him—"

Barr brushed him aside and ran down the hallway. The room at the end was just as Adler had described it, except for the man swinging from the improvised gallows, turning slowly in the cool, wet breeze from the open balcony door. His eyes were starting from his head, and a thick strip of white cloth gagged his mouth. Barr did his best to hold the body up while his sheath knife sawed through the rope. He knew the whole time that he was too late, that valuable seconds were tearing past, but he laid the corpse gently on the ground and checked for the pulse he knew was not there before climbing to his feet and rushing to the balcony.

Outside, the rain had slackened momentarily, but the westerly was blowing harder—*thirty knots*, he thought, *and more in the puffs*. The wind had backed another ten degrees, and the seas had gone with it. A little more, and it would be blowing right into the little harbor down below. He stepped to the balcony's edge. *Glory* was down there, tugging at the docklines that held her to the stone pier. The tide was up, his mind noted automatically, and the wind was still holding her off. But in another half hour it would bash her to splinters against the stone dock.

Her mainsail was almost completely hoisted—someone had put a sloppy reef in it—and was slatting furiously, the boom all the way out to leeward. There were figures by the base of the mainmast, and as he watched, the mainsail luff slowly drew tight. The small jib was on the foredeck, in its bag. Ready to hoist, though, with its luff snapped to the forestay and its sheets led back to the cockpit. *Still time to stop them*, he thought. *If only it was Patrick instead of me aiming this damn rifle. Maybe if I ran downstairs . . .*

Even as the thought was forming, two figures stepped from behind the mainmast. Both were men, he was sure, though one was nearly slender enough to be a girl. That one went forward, while the other headed aft, and two more appeared in the companionway. This time there was no doubt, and Barr's heart leaped in his chest. She was wearing the rags of the outfit she'd gone to Highland House in—was it only two days ago?—and the short, fat, awkward person beside her could only be Harkness.

Barr dropped to one knee, resting the rifle on the stone railing. He disliked guns and expressed his dislike by staying away from them. Even so, he knew the crude chunk of metal in his hands wasn't a marksman's weapon.

It did have sights, but Harkness was standing right beside Gillian at *Glory's* wheel. Better go for the other two. They were untying the docklines, he realized, and the man on the bow seemed to be having some trouble. He was on his knees, clawing at the cleat. Barr leveled the rifle, trying to remember instructions on a firing range, more than fifteen years before. The hell with it. He lined up between the man's shoulders and squeezed the trigger.

From a good two hundred yards he saw chips fly up out of *Glory's* teak foredeck. He shifted his aim a hair to the left and fired again. this time his target spun halfway around, sprawling on the wood.

Now for the man on the stern. He seemed frozen in place, holding the untied dockline in his hand and staring up toward the parapet Barr was kneeling behind. *An easy shot*, Barr thought, *even for me*. He heard a high-pitched shout, glanced again at Gillian, standing beside the wheel, and saw the glint of metal. Harkness was right behind her, almost completely hidden, and he was holding something—a pistol, a knife, what did it matter?—to her head. Slowly Barr rose and tossed the rifle off the parapet.

Glory's bow was swinging away from the pier, pushed by the wind. The man Barr had shot was on his knees, arm held tightly against his side, but he had finished his job. Now the man with the stern line let it go, climbed into the cockpit, and began to take the mainsheet in, hand over hand. *Glory* steadied on the harbor entrance, gaining speed fast.

She hardened up a hundred feet or so past the breakwater, the mainsail strapped all the way in. Even with the reef in the mainsail, and lacking jib or mizzen, she heeled sharply, and the wounded man on the foredeck lost his balance and slid down to leeward. Barr willed him to fall overboard, but the lifelines stopped him.

Glory tacked, fast and hard, slamming her bow through a hundred degrees. As she heeled the other way, the wounded man on the bow slipped clean across the foredeck, struggling feebly, and once again the lifelines kept him aboard.

Even with the tide high, seas were breaking on the reef. From where Barr was standing, he could see the zigzag of the entrance channel easily. It would be far less obvious down at water level—and now that he thought of it, he was amazed Gillian was threading the maze so well. A second's inattention, a second too soon or too late with a tack, and *Glory* would be on the bricks, her back broken.

And Gillian would be dead an instant later. Of that Barr had no doubts at all. Harkness would go down to hell still striking out at his enemies.

One last tack, and *Glory* would be clear of the reefs. Barr watched as her long bow swung up into the wind, hesitated for a half second—Gillian had tacked too soon but had caught it—then went through the wind's eye. She spun the steering wheel back, steadying up on her close-hauled heading down St. Philip's coast. For a couple of minutes *Glory* was almost broadside to Barr as he stood helpless.

Gillian's slim, tanned arm went up over her head, paused, swung down and forward. It was not a wave of farewell, Barr suddenly realized. It was one of the signals Barr had taught her when *Glory's* inflatable dinghy was leading the larger vessel through dangerous shoals.

It meant "Follow me."

Patrick: 5:30 P.M.

The fight was over too soon; that was the only trouble. Patrick was still boiling with the barely controlled rage of combat. It was something that took you over, that made you faster, stronger, braver, smarter— while it lasted. Something that could make you go bad, too. He remembered, especially from Chad, how some men's fighting madness could slide into depths of atrocity, how he himself had done things, in battle and afterward, that he could never let himself think about, even now.

He was standing in the entrance hallway with his back against the big wooden door, his fingers digging into it, willing himself to come down off his high and not knowing how. Three dead men lay where they had fallen, and a dazed mob of Philipians and passengers from *Euphoric* milled around them. Everybody seemed to be crying or laughing or both.

From the storerooms beneath them came occasional muffled shots. The Philipian cops had the last handful of Harkness's men trapped down there, and were hunting them down one by one like rats in a barn.

The noise and confusion didn't seem to faze Adler, who had commandeered a chair that looked like a throne, from which he was rapping out orders in all directions to anyone who caught his eye. His voice, hoarse but still powerful, cut through the chaos, as he harangued Son Douglas from ten feet away: "Find a transmitter—or Harkness's TV camera: We've got to get word out! Tell the task force they can blow *Euphoric* out of the water . . ."

Son nodded and started up the big staircase, just as Barr came running down it, shoving people aside as he scanned the crowd. *Gillian!* She wasn't with him. The picture of Isabel dead forced itself into Patrick's mind, only she had Gillian's face. If that had happened, Patrick knew he'd kill someone, starting with Adler.

Barr was fighting his way through the crowd, coming straight at Patrick. He'd managed to lose the weapon Patrick had tossed him, which was exactly what you'd expect. In the midst of black fury Patrick was swept by a wave of love stronger than he could believe, and he lifted Barr off his feet into a hug that made his bones creak.

"Jesus!" Barr was gasping. "Christ, Patrick, cut it out." And then the words that cut through the haze like a razor: "Harkness has Gillian."

Patrick dropped the smaller man, and Barr staggered to stay on his feet. "Where?" said Patrick, adding, "Is she . . ." and letting it die, seeing in Barr's face that at least she was alive.

"They're on *Glory*," Barr said. "He made Gillian sail her out of the harbor." Suddenly he was staring into Patrick's eyes, as if he saw something there that scared him. "You all right?"

"No," said Patrick. "But not the way you think. Listen, where's he taking her?"

"I don't know," Barr replied, but it was clear he'd been thinking about it. "They were heading close-hauled down the coast. South, so I'd bet they'll turn east toward Antigua. It's only thirty miles."

Thirty miles downwind, Patrick thought. *And running before this wind, maybe three hours.* "We'd better tell Adler," he said automatically. "He's trying to contact the task force that's got *Euphoric* cornered. . . ." The words dried up by themselves, and he looked into Barr's face. "Maybe not."

"No," said Barr. Each knew what the other meant. Armies and navies and air forces would only fuck this up and get Gillian killed, especially if they knew it was Harkness himself they were chasing.

"How?" said Patrick.

"Only one way; MacIntyre's launch."

"There she goes!" Barr called, pointing. They were standing side by side on a sort of stone porch, at the head of a long, long flight of steps to the tiny harbor. Off to the west the clouds were breaking up, the evening sun trying to fight its way through, and right on the horizon Patrick saw—or thought he saw—black specks on the sea, the fleet that was waiting to close in on *Euphoric*.

Glory was two or three miles away, nearly at St. Philip's southern tip. She was cutting through the big, rolling seas that were coming now from the southwest, throwing spray every time her bow slammed down. As Patrick watched, her foreshortened hull seemed to elongate, and he realized she was turning, changing course—as Barr had predicted—toward the west.

"Still no jib," said Barr. "But Harkness'll have it up as soon as he thinks of it."

"We better hurry," Patrick replied. "That's a big lead."

Trotting down the steps—the steep, narrow, endless stone steps— Patrick took the front, expecting any moment to feel Barr cannon into him.

The rifle he'd grabbed up was jouncing against his bad shoulder, and without breaking stride, he swung it to the other one, adjusting the sling. From behind him he heard Barr say, "Gillian first, right?"

"Of course." A few more steps, and he called back, "You care what happens to Harkness after?"

"No." Two steps' worth of silence. "It won't bring her back, though."

It wouldn't either. He knew that, and didn't care.

They were nearly at the bottom; Patrick's calves felt as if someone had tied constrictor knots in the muscles. Barr said, "What d'you know about steam?"

What the hell did he mean? "Steam like in boiling water?"

"Steam like in steam launch."

Just then the flight of steps switchbacked, and he saw her, saw the high shiny stack and the boiler under it, the rags of what had been an awning streaming off to leeward in the wind. "Oh, shit," he said.

"Right," said Barr. "I guess that means I'm the engineer and you're the pilot."

Now they were on the stone pier, racing side by side toward the old boat, which was bucking and heaving to her docklines. *As long and narrow as a toothpick*, Patrick thought. She'd roll her guts out, and theirs, too, before she got to the end of the island. And then running before those seas . . .

They stood at the edge of the pier, looking down into the narrow boat. Two or three inches of water were sloshing back and forth above the floorboards. "You know steam engines?" Patrick gasped.

"I must've seen *The African Queen* four times," Barr replied. He was grinning, Patrick saw. Squinting anyway.

"Your pair of twos takes the pot," said Patrick. "You get her started, I'll bail her out."

The wheel was tiny, after *Glory*'s, but it felt good: a quick, tight response, and not too many turns lock to lock. The shift was a big bronze rod, and Patrick pushed it forward, felt the stern judder to one side as the propeller turned. It was a big prop with a deep bite; must've got it off a workboat. "Cast off," he said.

A minute later, as they cleared the breakwater, the wind hit like a smack in the face, and even with the awning gone, the launch heeled to it. Patrick narrowed his eyes and spun the wheel, looked up, and said, "Holy Jesus, look at those seas."

Barr, on his knees in front of the boiler, already had coal smoke all over his face. His faded blue eyes and white teeth looked as if they were lit from behind. "Ready for a sharp turn to starboard," he said.

Patrick's flood of relief almost made his knees buckle. "You know the channel, then."

"I've seen it," Barr replied. That was the same thing, with Barr.

The launch put her nose into the first sea. Narrow as she was, she barely rose to it, and solid green water came right over the bow. The second roller was close behind the first, catching the launch with her nose still down.

Barr came up spluttering. "Try taking 'em at an angle," he said.

"Shut up and bail," said Patrick.

It was better, once they were clear of the reef. The seas came at them from the starboard bow, looking as high and steep as house walls, but the launch corkscrewed her way over them, every rib creaking and jets of water spurting between the strained planks. Patrick had the feel of her now, and he could even steer her one-handed between waves, using his free hand for the heavy brass navy pump mounted next to the wheel. Barr, meanwhile, bailed and stoked and twiddled with the boiler's levers and knobs, and gradually the launch seemed to pick up speed.

As they neared South Point, Patrick kept expecting Glory to appear from behind the bluffs, but only when they'd cleared the land completely could they see her, running dead downwind and heartbreakingly far ahead.

"Goes like a witch, doesn't she?" Barr said, reluctant admiration plain in his voice. "Thank God she's running and not reaching; she'd be over the horizon by now."

Now that they were passing the point, the seas were coming more on the beam, not feeling the pull of the land. Patrick glanced down at the binnacle and realized the compass inside had died long ago, its card spinning like a top. But something about Glory's heading tweaked his memory. "Is that the course for Antigua?" he asked.

Barr's coal-blackened face was eager and intent, and he seemed unable to take his eyes off Glory. "You're right," he said. "Gillian's got her about ten degrees to port of the right heading." He saw the question in Patrick's face and added: "She's keeping Glory dead before the wind to slow her down. Give us a chance to catch up."

How could she know they were following? Patrick asked himself. In these seas the launch would be nearly invisible from a deck two miles away—but of course, she didn't have to see them, he realized. She knew Barr.

The launch was clear of South Point, and Patrick let a big sea get under her, then put the wheel hard over. The boat responded like the thoroughbred she once had been, and now they were right in *Glory's* wake.

"Can you get any more out of her?" said Patrick fifteen minutes later. "The light's nearly gone and we're just holding our own."

A big sea from astern picked the launch up, poised her like a spear, and flung her onto the back of the wave ahead. She came up slowly, a good foot of seawater surging back down her cockpit. "That's your answer," said Barr, throwing water over the side. "We're going too fast as it is."

He was right, Patrick knew. The launch had no business out here in seas like these, and sooner or later she'd stick that long, sharp bow too far into one and drive right under. Or pitchpole off the top of an extra-large wave, somersaulting upside down and crushing her crew. Or Patrick would lose control and she'd skid sideways into a broach, and the next wave would roll over her side and sink her. He couldn't let himself think like that, he knew. If he did, what he feared would happen. "What d'you want me to do?" he asked.

"Push as hard as you dare," Barr said. "It's up to Gillian now."

Gillian: Ten Miles WNW of St. Philip, 6:30 P.M.

It's up to me, she thought. *Barr will do his best, and Patrick, too, but I'm the only one who can make it work.* The big steering wheel kicked under her hands, and she amended her thought: Glory *and I. We can do it. We have to.*

Still, Barr's coming; I'm sure of it. Almost sure. She ran through her reasoning, like a ritual, one more time: He'd seen her sail out, seen her signal. Even from that distance, even with Harkness's knife pressing into her neck, she'd recognized Barr, as he must have recognized her.

"*Follow me*," her arm had said, and her heart knew he would do just that. The question was how. Would he do the conservative, sensible thing and call for help? By now it'd be available for sure—destroyers, cutters, choppers. All he had to do was say that Harkness, the chief monster, was getting away, and he'd have whatever he wanted.

Or, rather, the Navy or whoever would grab the ball and run with it. There were plenty of men like Adler on those ships and planes, looking for their star or their eagle or whatever. They'd push Barr out

of their way, but that wouldn't keep him from asking for their help if
he thought it'd save her. But he'd know, as she did, that the military
wouldn't give squat about her once they had Harkness in their sights.

Barr would come by himself then. He'd bring Patrick if he could.

He can do it, she told herself. *Because he loves me and because he's
Barr.* Confidence—not absolute, but surprisingly strong—steadied her
hands on the wheel. *This must be what faith is*, she thought. *Before,
I believed only in me, and sometimes I came up short. Now I believe
in him, and belief buoys me.*

Just the same, her practical side chimed in, *the Lord helps those
and so forth. What can I do to help?* She ransacked her brain for an
answer, then saw it in front of her, low in the eastern sky: Venus,
shining like a beacon.

That's what Barr needs—a mark to steer by. A beacon on Glory.

Monasir, stretched out on the cockpit seat and wrapped in a blanket,
coughed. A wet, spongy cough. She didn't have to see the blood to
know how badly hurt he was. Barr's bullet seemed to have nicked his
lung, and he'd been spitting a pink foam that was gradually getting
thicker. Monasir was still clutching a pistol, the way another man
might clutch a cross, but he wouldn't be a major obstacle to anything
she tried.

Across from Monasir, the square-built young man whose name was
Ibrahim shifted uneasily on the cockpit seat. For all his size and heft
he looked about sixteen, and he was clearly unnerved. Ibrahim had
been on guard duty by the back gate, and when the shooting started
in the entrance hall, and Harkness and Monasir had grabbed Gillian
and fled, Ibrahim had simply drifted along in their wake.

When *Glory* had cleared South Point and headed off on a run,
Gillian thought the yacht's motion—a long, erratic, corkscrewing
roll—might finish Ibrahim off. But the boy was tougher than he looked;
one quick upchuck and he was back on duty, miserable but alert,
fondling his stubby little rifle as if it represented salvation, and maybe
to him it did.

Even so, she'd watched Ibrahim handling the main sheet, saw that
his marine knowledge could be put on the head of a pin, with room
to inscribe the Koran under it. Ibrahim didn't have a clue, as long as
her manner didn't arouse his suspicions.

Best of all, Harkness, the really dangerous one, was belowdecks,
with his ear pasted to *Glory*'s radio. Now or never.

Glory's running lights operated off her main electrical panel, above
the chart table, at the bottom of the companionway. Only two switches

were not on the board—for the red compass light in the binnacle
before her and for the blazing white lights on the main spreaders, used
mostly to illuminate the foredeck in emergencies.

Both switches were on the binnacle itself, where the helmsman
could get at them easily, but they were shielded to prevent the kind
of accident Gillian wanted to stage. Accident it had to be. If Harkness
knew she'd turned the spreader lights on deliberately, he'd guess she
was signaling to another boat, maybe change course. Maybe do something with that knife he'd pressed against her neck before. Thinking
about it again, about the metal edge against her skin, almost drained
off her courage, and she snuffed out the memory.

Go, she told herself. *Go now.* "Ibrahim," she said, "I want a coat."

English was not Ibrahim's strong suit. *"Mem?"*

"Coat," she repeated, louder. She reached forward to pull at his
sleeve, found herself staring down the muzzle of his gun. "Damn it,
I'm freezing my ass off." Now that she said it, she realized she really
was cold.

"What is it?" Harkness called up the companionway. "What is
wrong?"

"I'm cold," she said loudly. "Get me a jacket, will you? In the
locker right by the ladder."

He thought about it; opened the locker and apparently thought
about it some more. But at last she felt his clumsy steps on the companion ladder, and his head appeared. "Here you are," he said, holding it out.

"Pass it over, Ibrahim, would you?" She had rehearsed the phrase
under her breath till it sounded completely natural to her.

Harkness seemed to think so, too. He said something to Ibrahim
and held out the dirty old pea jacket to the boy, who half rose to take
it from him. In the inky cockpit Gillian's foot hooked his ankle, and
he lurched into the binnacle as her hand went to the switch.

The result was even more dramatic than she'd hoped. With the
mainsail all the way out, chafing against the port spreader, the light
from behind lit up the sail like a drive-in movie screen. Barr was sure
to see it.

"What is that? Turn it off!" Harkness was yelling, and Ibrahim,
bless his heart, was howling what sounded like excuses. Best of all,
the sudden glare seemed to send Monasir into a convulsion, and the
pistol he was holding went off with a shattering, flat *bang!*

Harkness dropped out of sight down the companionway, and Ibrahim dived for the gun. Gillian, as startled as anyone, yanked at the wheel, and *Glory* jibed.

The main boom swung past over her head with a noise like a scythe going through grass and fetched up against the starboard shrouds with a twanging, shuddering crash that shook the whole boat and made it stagger. Quickly Gillian snapped off the spreader lights.

Harkness's head popped out of the companionway again. "What happened?"

Ibrahim was holding up Monasir's still-smoking pistol like some kind of prize. He handed it, with a quick, frightened explanation, to Harkness. "What happened with the sail?" he said to Gillian.

She was already struggling into the jacket. It was Barr's, and it carried his smell—tobacco smoke, mostly, which as a rule she disliked. Tonight was different.

"Accidental jibe," she replied. The little man knew a lot about a lot of odd things, and she sensed it was a mistake to lie to him except when it accomplished something.

"Jibe," he repeated, and looked upward. "Ah, of course." He climbed slowly out of the hatch, and she realized from his movements that he was nearly exhausted. Standing beside her, he said, "I trust you are warm now."

She nodded. "Much better."

"And I trust," he continued, "that the jibe was not an attempt to damage the boat." The knife flashed suddenly in his hand. "Such an attempt would be a great mistake." His voice was so soft she only just heard the words. She felt the point against her skin, just below her right eye. The metal was warm, not cold, which somehow made its touch more frightening. Her newfound confidence was leaking out of her like the air from a balloon.

The boy Ibrahim was asleep, and Monasir seemed to be unconscious. Harkness was standing at her side, talking. Gillian, who was concentrating on slowing *Glory*'s pace by using the mainsail to blanket the jib, barely heard him.

"It would be no life for a woman, of course. Always running, always hiding. That is why I have never—"

The flash in the sky was behind them, but so brilliant they both spun around. A moment later, borne on the wind, came a distant rumbling. "*Insh'allah*," said Harkness. "*Euphoric*," he added a moment later. "Our plan failed at Highland House, and I cannot hope for much better results with the ship. All the same, I must know what happened." He stirred Ibrahim with his foot, gave a curt order that had the boy up and blinking, then lowered himself slowly down the ladder.

Ten minutes later he came back up, moving like an old man. "It is finished," he said to Gillian. "They stood off at half a mile and torpedoed her. What we saw was the explosive charges my martyred people had set." Ibrahim was watching Harkness with desperate intentness, but the short, round man ignored him. He seemed not despairing, as Gillian had expected, but newly resolved. "This is a moment when I am glad Ibrahim has no English," he said to Gillian. "He might not understand."

"Understand your total, absolute failure?" she said, unable to restrain herself.

In the binnacle light Harkness seemed to be smiling. "Not exactly," he said. "No, Ibrahim might not understand why I do not seek martyrdom myself. But there is too much yet to do, especially now."

She could feel his excitement, and it scared her. "What do you mean?"

"I have decided," Harkness said. "Since I am the soul of this enterprise, I must live to fight another day."

There ought to be a snappy comeback, she thought. *Why can't I think of one?*

"I have looked at the maps on that table in the cabin," Harkness continued. "I think Antigua is a good place to catch an airplane back to the world, and I think that the quicker we get there, the better. This vessel has an engine. I want you to start it."

Gillian had known this moment might come, but not so soon. "I don't have the key," she said. "You can search me if you want to."

"We have already searched you," Harkness said. "There must be a spare key. Where is it?"

He was not fooling; she remembered the knife point just below her eye. "In the tool chest, behind the companionway steps."

Harkness was back on deck after a few clattering minutes later. "Very good," he said approvingly. "Now start the engine, I shall steer."

Besides the spare keys, Harkness had brought up a flashlight. Ibrahim held it on her while she put the key in the ignition. She turned it, heard the buzz of the engine alarm, and pressed the starter button. The engine turned over but did not catch.

"What's wrong?" Harkness demanded. "Don't play games with me, miss."

"Maybe it needs a little choke," Gillian said. Her heart was in her throat as she spoke. This was the test, and if she failed . . . She shivered.

"Then do that," Harkness ordered. "Use the choke."

With a silent prayer to the spirit of Rudolf Diesel she pulled the T-shaped handle next to the ignition, then turned the key again. The engine groaned but refused to start. Ibrahim said something, and her ear picked out the single word "gas."

"Which is the throttle?" said Harkness. "Ah, I see—it is labeled." He pushed it a quarter of the way forward. "Again, Miss Verdean."

Still nothing. Ibrahim said something else, and Gillian wondered how long she could function with her heart stopping for seconds at a time.

"He says perhaps it is overchoked," said Harkness.

"Can't be," Gillian replied. "You don't smell gas, do you?"

Harkness snarled at Ibrahim, who looked hurt, and they tried again, this time with Ibrahim turning the key. And again, until at last the battery refused to cooperate. Gillian closed her eyes with relief. *Thank you, Dr. Diesel*, she thought. *Thank you for inventing an engine with a fuel shutoff that looks like a choke.* Her eyes opened, and she saw Harkness regarding her with death on his round, soft face. "You have somehow misled me," he said. "But I shall not punish you now."

Gillian shrugged. Inside the pea jacket she was shaking almost uncontrollably.

Ibrahim suddenly cried out, pointing astern. The moon was just up, though still behind the thinning clouds, and behind them—two or three hundred yards, Gillian guessed—was a shape, defined more by the foam V of its bow wave than any outline of its own. Ibrahim's gun was raised, and he fired two or three bursts, till Harkness stopped him with a sharp command.

"We must go faster," he said to Gillian, and, when she didn't respond, snapped something to Ibrahim, who put the muzzle of his gun under her chin. "Stand still," said Harkness. "Stand very still."

She shut her eyes against the rage in his, until the knife was hard against her cheek. "All right," she said. "We can shake the reef out. That'll give us two more knots."

"Shake out the reef. Good," he said.

"You'll let me go when we get to Antigua, won't you?" She meant to sound harmless and afraid, but not as fearful as she did.

"Of course," he replied. He wasn't even trying to sound as if he meant it, she thought. "Now, what must be done?"

"Remember before we started, I said we have to reef?" she said. "And Ibrahim and I rolled up the bottom of the mainsail and tied it off?" She pointed, and Harkness nodded. "Well, now we have to unroll that part, so we can use the whole sail area."

"How is it done?" he said.

"No big deal," she replied. "We pull in the mainsheet till we can get at the sail. Untie the reef points, raise the sail all the way, and that's it."

"All right," he said. "Now explain it again slowly, while I translate for Ibrahim."

About halfway through Ibrahim balked. He gestured over the side, shaking his head emphatically, and Gillian didn't have to understand Arabic to know he didn't want to get out of the cockpit and especially not to stand on *Glory*'s cabin top in the windy night, while the yacht was rolling and swooping down the waves.

Harkness's soft voice had the sudden caress of a whiplash, and Ibrahim recoiled as if it had caught him across the face. The round man was gesturing at Gillian now, his tone dripping contempt. If a mere girl can do it, he seemed to be saying, surely a man cannot draw back.

Whatever his actual words, they did the trick. Ibrahim and Gillian dragged the mainsheet in until the boom was over the leeward edge of *Glory*'s cabin. Gillian could feel the yacht lose speed under her feet, no longer driving down the waves as wildly as before. Harkness might feel the difference, too, but as long as his attention was locked on her, he wouldn't—she hoped he wouldn't—be able to think about what was happening.

With Gillian leading the way, the boy climbed slowly, unhappily up on the low cabin top. Even a few feet of height made a dramatic difference in the feel of the wind and the unsteadiness of the deck, and the darkness, of course, only made it more frightening.

She put Ibrahim's shaking hands on a knotted pair of reef points, and his fingers locked on to them like claws. "Untie!" she shouted in his ear. "Untie them!"

In the cockpit Harkness heard her and shrieked something unflattering at Ibrahim, who only shook his head.

"You must do it alone!" Harkness called to her. She nodded and pulled herself to the forward end of the boom. One by one she undid the paired nylon lines that held the foot of the sail in a loose bundle along the boom. A sloppy reef Barr would call it, and he'd be right, but this was one time when neatness didn't count.

The foot of the sail fell away as the knots came free, flapping wildly as the wind caught it. At last Gillian worked her way back to Ibrahim. His head was buried in the sailcloth, and he seemed to be sobbing. For a moment compassion almost deflected her, but she forced herself to step past him, untying the reef points as she went, until she was standing on the after edge of the cockpit, looking down at the helm. The nearly loosed mainsail was snapping angrily now, held only by the single pair of ties in Ibrahim's death grip.

"I can untie the damn thing," she called to Harkness. "But he's got to let go of it first."

He suspected something, but suspicion was why he was still alive. "When that line is untied, then you raise the sail—correct?"

"That's right," she said, trying to smother her real intent: In the moment when Ibrahim's hands let go of that line, she was going to spill him. The heeling, slippery deck would do the rest. Would have to. It was a lousy plan, but it was all she had.

"I think not, Miss Verdean," said Harkness.

She felt her heart drop like a lead weight. "What d'you mean?"

"I mean that I shall raise the sail, while Ibrahim steers."

"Whatever you say," she replied, her brain madly spinning its wheels. There was still a way—she was sure of it—but the details were just beyond her mind's horizon.

"Get down here, beside me," Harkness said.

It took five minutes' worth of coaxing and threatening to bring Ibrahim back into the cockpit, and he arrived on hands and knees, his nerve completely gone. Harkness placed him behind the wheel, gave him the course to steer, and each time the boy nodded mechanically.

"Now," said Harkness, "you come with me."

So far, so good. She made herself slump with what she hoped looked like despair, as she led him forward to the foot of the mainmast, stopping only to untie the last reef point. The loose foot of the sail was thundering, the luff sagging along the track.

"We ought to head up into the wind," she yelled over the noise. "Make it a lot easier."

"Make it a lot easier for them to catch us, you mean," Harkness shouted back. "Now, what must be done?"

There was a way. She was sure of it, but the answer still hid itself in the crashing of the mainsail. "Now I crank up the sail," she said, taking the handle of the reel winch.

"No," he replied, waving her off. "I do not trust you. I shall raise the sail. You stand down there, by the railing."

Suddenly everything was clear. When the sail was safely up, he was going to shoot her, with Monasir's pistol, and her body would fall over the side. But there was also a hope, the slimmest of hopes, and it depended on his suspicion and her obedience.

She moved down to the leeward lifeline and for a moment thought of hurling herself over the side, swimming for it. As the idea formed, she discarded it. Barr would never even see her in the noisy blackness, and the nearest shore was ten miles to windward.

"Stand where I can see you," Harkness called. "Now, tell me what to do."

"There's nothing to it," she replied. Her mouth was so dry she could scarcely speak. "Just turn the handle. Clockwise."

She saw his hand go to his waist, but he was only checking that the pistol was still in his belt. He pushed ineffectually at the winch handle, then leaned harder. "What is wrong?" he yelled. "It does not turn!"

"You have to release the brake," she called. "The round handle, just below the drum."

He only half believed her, she saw. But he leaned forward to see more clearly. "This?"

"That's it," she said. "Pull down hard."

He did. The winch drum, under the massive load of the huge sail and the wind that filled it, spun wildly, and the winch handle—fifteen inches of stainless steel, with a solid two-handed grip at the end— whizzed backward like a club, slamming down into Harkness's skull. The released mainsail slid halfway down the track, burying him in its folds—and then he shot free from under it, sliding down the cabin top toward her. Gillian leaped aside, but she saw the awful ruin of his face. The one eye that remained was staring straight up.

His body was still struggling faintly as it hit the leeward lifelines. Without a moment's hesitation she grabbed an ankle and pitched him into the sea.

"Now for Ibrahim," she said aloud, as if the words would spur her on.

Glory was heading up into the wind, she realized, mainsail and jib luffing madly. As she raised her head cautiously above the cabin top, she saw the reason why: The wheel was unattended. Ibrahim, his back against the mizzenmast, had jammed the muzzle of his stubby rifle into his mouth. She shut her eyes the instant before he fired, but not before she saw, close astern, The MacIntyre's launch coming up fast and the thin, intent figure standing in the bow.

EPILOGUE: SATURDAY

Barr: William Town, 8:00 A.M.

The public relations lieutenant commander sent down by the Navy insisted that Gillian was to share the platform that afternoon with "the other heroes of St. Philip": Son Douglas, one-armed Chief MacLeod, old MacIntyre, and, of course, Jake Adler.

"You're the little lady who killed the big, bad wolf," the officer explained to her. Barr, standing with her hand in his, felt her stiffen, but the Navy man rattled blithely on. "Anyway, Washington says we've got to have a woman up there for the TV people, and Mrs. Douglas turned us down."

"I see," Gillian replied. "Well, I'm sorry, but Captain Barr and I are busy." She squeezed his hand, and Barr wondered if the delight he was feeling showed on his face.

"Oh, we don't need Captain Barr," the officer replied quickly. "In fact, with Colonel Adler—Brigadier General-designate Adler, I mean—we don't . . . we've got enough American men, if you see what I mean."

"Besides," Gillian continued, as if he hadn't spoken, "I haven't a thing to wear."

The remark was so out of character that Barr turned to stare down at her, but she ignored him, looking innocently out over the crowded harbor to where *Glory* lay placidly at anchor, next to the elderly U.S.

247

Coast Guard eighty-two-footer that was about to change flags and become the Philipian Navy.

"If that's the only problem," the lieutenant commander said with relief, "I'm sure we can fix up something. There must be a dress shop . . ." His optimism faded as he considered the facilities of William Town. "Maybe in the next island," he said.

"Antigua," Gillian supplied. "That'll do."

"All right, Antigua. We'll get on the phone—"

"I'll just fly over in one of your helicopters," she said, and added, "The whole thing's on you, of course."

The lieutenant commander was sweating lightly, Barr saw, and he had the air of a man who was balanced on the edge of a decision.

"I ought to tell you," Barr offered, "that Miss Verdean never negotiates." She squeezed his hand again, twice.

The officer sighed. "One dress."

"My choice—the store *and* the dress."

"You got it." he agreed. After a moment he added, "That Harkness never had a chance, did he?"

"Not for a moment," she said, smiling. But her hand in Barr's was suddenly moist and tense.

The Navy band, flown in that morning from San Juan, was sawing its way gallantly through the Philipian national anthem, which fortunately for the musicians shared its melody with "Ein feste Burg." The Philipians in the crowd were singing lustily. Most of the others—American and token West Indian, Dutch, British and French military—were sweating grimly at attention and salivating to the odors of grilling meat, wafted from the field kitchen set up by the cooks from the American destroyer.

The international press, responding to the godsend of an assignment in the tropics halfway through October, were present in force. They had already interviewed everyone on the island at least once and were now interviewing each other. Six big TV cameras and twice as many portable minicams surveyed the scene from every conceivable angle.

Gillian was seated at the left side of the platform, nearly invisible from Barr's assigned chair, well back in the crowd that nearly filled William Town's main and only square, that morning renamed Douglas Place. After craning his neck fruitlessly for several minutes, Barr got up and edged through the crowd to Cosima Douglas's house, some fifty yards away. A TV crew was arguing fruitlessly with the policeman on duty there, for permission to shoot from the second-story balcony.

The cop winked at Barr, saying, "This man has special pass," and Barr slipped him the pass, which a cynic might have mistaken for a tightly folded American ten-spot.

He climbed the outside stair to the balcony. From there he could see her perfectly, almost in profile, looking about half her real size next to a massive Dutch naval officer in a white uniform. Gillian's new dress was white, too, with a rose of black crepe she had pinned to her shoulder, for Isabel.

Son Douglas was in the same row, trying to look bored but obviously enjoying himself; and MacLeod, in a fresh khaki tunic; and The MacIntyre, a Dorian Gray version of Bonnie Prince Charlie; and an American major general in camouflaged battle dress.

But all of them—even Gillian—were upstaged by Jake Adler. He was on crutches, and his dress blues looked as if they'd been delivered new that morning from the tailor, and the whole left side of his chest was a dazzling, frequently clashing garden of colored ribbons, with the sun winking off his combat infantry badge and his paratrooper's wings.

"He looks very well, doesn't he?" said a low, vibrant voice at Barr's elbow.

He turned and saw Cosy Douglas. The shining pride in her eyes was not for Adler.

"He does indeed," Barr replied. "And they say you'll be St. Philip's next president. Congratulations."

"Thank you," she said, smiling. Her adoring eyes were still on her son, and Barr had the feeling he was watching the birth of yet another Caribbean political dynasty.

In the open door behind Cosy a tall, thin, stooping figure appeared. Without stepping fully into the light of day, he was still able to place his hands on Cosy's surprisingly narrow waist, in an unmistakably proprietary gesture.

"Mr. Tarleton, as I live and breathe," said Barr. "And how long has this been going on?"

"You seem unsurprised," said Tarleton. "I don't mind saying I'm a tad deflated."

"Gillian was the one who figured it out," Barr replied. "Figured it out" might be a little strong for Gillian's raw intuition, but Barr had known instantly that she was right. "It was Cosy who alerted you about Harkness, right?"

Tarleton smiled fondly down at her. "It posed a problem," he admitted. "I was sure her information was reliable, but I had some qualms about revealing the source. My superiors don't approve of Cosima and me."

"So you tipped off Adler's people instead."

"No," said Tarleton. "Cosima did. I merely suggested the wording—knowing the most effective verbal buttons, you might say."

The band ran out of verses at last, and the Philipians applauded furiously. As the scrape of folding chairs on cobblestones slowly died down, Cosy said, "Where is your friend Patrick? There is a medal for him, I know."

"He sends his regrets," Barr said. "He doesn't feel up to celebrations today."

Patrick had dug the grave himself, on the bluff overlooking the sea, and asked Barr to say something. Barr had gone to Father Hughes to borrow a Book of Common Prayer, and the old man had insisted on reading the service. Son and Dekker had appeared, bearing a hand-carved wooden cross with Isabel's name incised on it. And at the last minute Gillian had dropped out of the sky in a Navy helicopter stuffed with what looked like half the flowers of Antigua, as well as two new storage batteries for *Glory*, provenance best unknown.

Patrick was still there, sitting beside the grave and looking out over the Caribbean, when Barr and Gillian and the others left.

The battle-dressed major general, it seemed, was the master of ceremonies, and a good one. In brisk sequence he hailed the men of his international force, the Philipian mob—he called them militia, making MacLeod beam—Son Douglas, "the little lady here on my left" (at which Gillian's face went scarlet), and finally "that fine American fighting man, my old buddy Jake Adler."

"They've hated each other for years," Tarleton confided. "He tried to have Adler court-martialed."

Chief MacLeod, representing the island military, was followed by Son, who spoke for the civilians. His speech was short, with a cryptic reference to "our benefactors."

"He's talking about the Japanese," Cosy said. "They called last night, as soon as the telephone was working. Offered help with the airfield."

"Generous of them," said Barr, but Tarleton, of course, had his own addendum.

"They're buying out The MacIntyre. Going to make Highland House a hotel," he said. "I understand they want to put a marina in, too."

Barr was spared from having to make a comment on that, as the general had just introduced Adler to a tornado of applause. An enlisted man placed the microphone in front of him, tried to shorten it to sitting height. Adler brushed him aside and hauled himself upright, to wild cheering.

"Inside?" said Tarleton.

"I think so," said Barr.

Adler's booming voice made the windows rattle, and they retreated to the kitchen. "I wanted to thank you, too," Tarleton said. "On Cosima's behalf and on my own."

"Yours?" Barr turned from pouring himself a stiff jolt of Cosy's Barbancourt. "How come?"

"My boy, you're looking at a genuine, if sub rosa, Beltway hero— and all thanks to you."

The events of the last week flooded in on Barr, and he found himself not knowing whether to laugh or punch the old man in the mouth, but Tarleton hadn't finished: "You've retrieved my rather battered reputation, and I want to do something in return. A contract, perhaps, like the old days, only with much more generous terms, of course . . ."

On the whole, Barr decided, he would rather listen to Adler. He stepped back out on the balcony, and his eye went automatically to Gillian. She was staring down into her lap, and then he saw she was holding a pencil, scribbling busily on a scrap of paper.

She paused, looking up at Adler but not, Barr was sure, even seeing him. He recognized her calculating stare. She was making a list, and in a sudden flash of empathy he knew it was a repair list for *Glory*.

Her thought complete, Gillian started to write again, then glanced up to the balcony. Her glowing eyes met Barr's in a look of perfect understanding.